THE COWBOY'S NEW HEART

by

SHANNA HATFIELD

D1527768

The Cowboy's New Heart
Copyright 2013
by Shanna Hatfield

ISBN-13: 978-1482699555
ISBN-10: 1482699559

Shanna Hatfield
shanna@shannahatfield.com
shannahatfield.com

Special thanks to Roberta and Julie for providing such fun inspiration for the characters of Denni and Ester!

To those who have survived
a broken heart…

Books by Shanna Hatfield

FICTION

The Christmas Bargain

The Coffee Girl

Learnin' the Ropes

QR Code Killer

Grass Valley Cowboys Series
The Cowboy's Christmas Plan
The Cowboy's Spring Romance
The Cowboy's Summer Love
The Cowboy's Autumn Fall
The Cowboy's New Heart

The Women of Tenacity Series
The Women of Tenacity - A Prelude
Heart of Clay
Country Boy vs. City Girl
Not His Type

NON-FICTION

Savvy Holiday Entertaining
Savvy Spring Entertaining
Savvy Summer Entertaining
Savvy Autumn Entertaining

Prologue

"He won't bite."

Startled by the voice at his side, Drew Thompson looked down into a pair of twinkling ocean-blue eyes and let out the breath he was holding. Removing his hat, he ran tanned fingers through his thick brown hair, trying to calm his nerves.

"Go on in, Drew. He's waiting for you," Ester Nordon said, giving the young man a nudge as he stood outside the home office door of her husband, Graham. "I made him promise to be on his best behavior."

"Yes, ma'am," Drew said, mustering a half-hearted smile for the woman he thought of as a second mother. "Do you think…?"

Putting a small hand to his broad back, Ester opened the door and gave Drew a push. "You'll be fine." The door clicked shut behind him.

Not expecting Ester to shove him into the room, Drew quickly gathered his wits and looked to see Mr. Nordon sitting at his desk, studying a pile of papers. He could hear the neighbor's lawn mower buzzing through the open window and the scent of lilacs drifted on the morning breeze.

"Drew, right on time," Graham said with a grin as the young man stood hesitantly by the door. "Come on in and have a seat."

Drew took a chair across the desk from the man who was either going to make him very happy or cause him to break a young girl's heart.

"So, you said you had something important to discuss with me," Graham said, sitting back in his chair, waiting for Drew to get down to business. He knew exactly why the young cowboy was sitting across from him, nervously twirling his hat around and around in his capable hands.

"Yes, sir," Drew said, feeling like he'd swallowed sawdust as his parched throat refused to work properly and a tight knot tied itself in his stomach.

"And?" Graham asked, frowning to hide his humor in Drew's obvious case of nerves.

Drew began jiggling his foot as he sat back in the chair and took a deep breath. He tried to speak but no words were forthcoming.

"Let's cut to the chase, shall we?" Graham asked, trying to hide his smile. He liked Drew. He'd done business with his father, Tim, for years at the bank he managed in The Dalles, Oregon. From what he knew, the Thompson family was known for their honest, loyal, hard-working approach to life. Graham thought young Drew was doing an admirable job of following in his father's footsteps, learning to manage their ranch, the Triple T, located about an hour away in Grass Valley.

The only fault Graham could find with the kid was that he had taken a shine to his youngest daughter. He couldn't blame the boy for good taste, though.

"Yes, sir," Drew said, running his finger around the inside of his shirt collar, wondering if he'd fastened one too many buttons when he put it on before driving into town.

"You're here to talk about Denni, aren't you?" Graham asked, knowing the answer by the look in Drew's eye, as well as the fact that Ester had informed him the boy was planning to ask for permission to marry his impertinent, head-strong child.

"Yes, sir," Drew said, finally finding his tongue. "I know I have no right to ask and I know she seems so young…"

"Darn right, she's young. She's only seventeen, Drew. Seventeen," Graham said, shaking his head. His independent, stubborn daughter got it in her head when she was only twelve that she was smitten with Drew. She saw him at the movie theater one summer evening when she was there with her sisters and no amount of talking could convince her otherwise.

It was easy to see why the girl was in love with the strapping young man. His wavy brown hair, warm blue eyes, chiseled jaw, and easy smile would turn any girl's head. Not overly tall but well built, he wore an easy confidence some men could go their entire life without developing.

To make matters worse, Drew struck up a friendship with Jack, Graham's only son. He often dropped by the house when he was in town or home from college on break. It was when he graduated and came home to stay a year ago that Drew finally seemed to notice Denni was no longer a gangly child but a beautiful young woman.

Graham and Ester watched the poor young man fight his attraction for their vibrant daughter, but once Denni set her mind on something, it was as good as done.

The fact that Drew was sitting in utter misery across from Graham at this very moment confirmed her determination to have her way.

"I'm well aware of her age, sir," Drew said, straightening in his chair. Acting like a sniveling idiot wasn't going to help his cause so he tamped down his fear and took another deep breath. "You, as well as anyone, know that despite her age she acts older. You also know once she makes up her mind, there isn't any changing it."

"That's for sure," Graham muttered, thinking of all the times he had butted heads with his fractious child.

"What you might not know is how much I love your daughter, sir," Drew said, feeling heat climb up his neck. It was one thing to tell Denni he loved her, but something else entirely to have to share his feelings with her overprotective father. "If you take her age out of the equation, she and I are quite well suited for each other. We love each other deeply, and I'm ready and willing to commit to spending a lifetime making her happy."

"Hmm," Graham said, considering Drew's words. None of it was news to him. He knew Drew would take good care of his daughter, he just thought she should experience more of life before she settled down. He was more concerned about Denni being a fit wife for Drew than him being a good husband.

Glancing outside while Denni's father appeared to be contemplating his decision, Drew noticed movement at the edge of the window. Staring intently, he tried not to grin when he recognized Denni's fingers curled around the edge of the window frame. The little imp was doing her best to eavesdrop.

"On second thought, sir, perhaps I am acting hastily. She is really very young and quite often immature," Drew said, suddenly. When Graham looked at him in surprise, Drew inclined his head toward the window.

Realizing Denni was listening to them, Graham shook his head. He picked up his pen and scratched a note, handing it to Drew.

Drew read it and smiled.

"I'm glad you've come to your senses, son," Graham said, raising the level of his voice to be sure it carried out the open window. "That daughter of mine is too young and flighty to be a wife. I wouldn't even let you hire her to keep house. Why just last week her mother told me she set a pan of grease on fire and nearly torched the kitchen."

Drew heard a noise that sounded like a muffled "humph" and couldn't hold back a chuckle. Graham was laughing out loud as he motioned Drew to the far side of the room where two chairs sat in the corner near a bookcase, away from the open window.

"Honestly, sir, I'm not concerned about her cooking or housekeeping skills. I just want to cherish and love her," Drew said quietly, as he and Graham sat down side by side.

"I know, Drew. I know you'll take good care of her and be a good husband to her. It's not you I'm worried about. I can't get past the fact that she is so young and innocent, with so much life ahead of her yet to be lived," Graham said with a sigh. Leaning back in his chair, he tapped his fingers together and finally looked directly at Drew. "If I don't give you permission to marry her, we both know she's likely to do something crazy like knock you out and drag you to Winnemucca, so I will give you both my blessing on two conditions."

Drew's head snapped up as he realized Denni's father was giving them permission to wed. "Two conditions, sir?"

"Yes. Two," Graham said, studying Drew. The boy appeared calm and ready to listen, so Graham continued. "The first stipulation is that I want her educated. I realize if you two are married, she won't be going off to college. There are, however, any number of schools that would allow her to take courses from home. I expect her to take a minimum of three classes per semester, with summers free of study."

"That sounds fair and reasonable," Drew said, agreeing with Graham that Denni should continue her education.

"I'm glad you agree, because I expect you to help with her classes as needed. You're a college graduate, a bright young man, and she will be your sole responsibility," Graham said, satisfied to see Drew thoughtfully consider his statement. "Now, the other condition you aren't going to want to hear, but I'm going to say it anyway. She's too young to be a mother, yet, Drew. You'll have a hard enough time adjusting to married life, especially with her so young, without throwing a baby in the mix too soon. Let her grow up before you start your family. Give her time to get a degree in something, travel to a few places, live life a little before you take that step. Once you do, there is no going back and life as you know it will never be the same."

When Drew sat looking at him, Graham wondered what the boy was thinking. "Do you have any questions?"

"No, sir," Drew said, realizing Graham had a good point. He hadn't given any consideration to babies but Drew felt his neck warm at the thought of making them with the beautiful girl outside, hanging on the edge of the window.

"One last thing, then," Graham said, plastering a stern look on his face. "You will take good care of my baby girl, mule-headed as she is, or I will hunt you down and shoot you."

Drew grinned. "Yes, sir."

Standing from their chairs, Graham walked Drew to the office door and slapped his back.

"Why don't you go rescue her before she completely destroys the shrubbery," Graham said, smiling at Drew.

"Yes, sir," Drew said, pumping the man's hand in thanks and settling his Stetson back on his head.

Walking out the front door, he crept quietly around the corner of the house and along the porch until he could see Denni balancing on one foot on the porch railing, trying to peek in her father's office window.

"Just what do you think you're doing, Molly?" a deep voice rumbled so near to Denni Nordon, a frightened squeak escaped her lips and her tenuous grasp on the window frame began to slip.

Turning her blond head, she glared into the laughing blue eyes of Drew as he caught her to his chest before she could fall into the lilac bush.

"Great balls of fire! You didn't have to sneak up on me that way," Denni huffed, wrapping her arms around his neck. "And why must you call me Molly? I've told you before I'm not fond of the name."

"Because lots of people refer to a female mule as Molly and you, my charming little miss, are about as mule-headed and stubborn as they come," Drew said, kissing the end of her pert nose.

"Well, what did Dad say?" Denni asked. Although she'd climbed up on the trellis hoping to overhear what was being said between Drew and her father, she hadn't been able to hear anything after her father's comment about the fire in the kitchen. Impatient to know if her dad was going to ruin her life or let her pursue the future she'd dreamed, she wasn't amused when Drew tipped back his head and studied her.

"I'm starting to think your mama's right. If you're going to be sneaking around and pulling childish pranks, maybe you aren't quite grown up enough for this," Drew said with a disapproving look on his handsome face.

Denni knew a moment of panic before Drew broke into another grin.

"He agreed, Molly," Drew said, watching the wonder of his words sink in. Although five years her senior, Drew knew Denni was the one woman he was born to love. It

11

took a while for her to convince him she wasn't too young to be in love, but when she did, he believed her wholeheartedly.

As the tension flowed out of Denni, she relaxed against him and Drew felt heat begin to surge through his veins.

"You're not teasing me, are you?" Denni asked, trying to contain her excitement and act mature when everything in her wanted to run up and down the street calling out the news to everyone within hearing range. "This is not the time to be telling me something that isn't true."

"It's the honest truth," Drew said, kissing Denni's cheek, wanting very much to kiss her ripe lips. "Your daddy gave his permission for you to marry me on two conditions."

"Oh," Denni said, feeling her hopes of soon being Drew Thompson's wife slipping away. Bracing herself for some ridiculous demands in an effort to wait for her to mature, she nodded her head at the cowboy holding her in his strong arms. "Let's hear it."

"Your mama and daddy still think you are too young to get married. Knowing you as well as they do, they also know if they don't give their blessing you're apt to do something crazy like kidnap me, drag me to Nevada, and force me to marry you," Drew said, walking to the porch swing and sitting down with Denni across his lap.

"They didn't say that," Denni said, narrowing her gaze at Drew.

"Are you sure?" Drew asked, raising an eyebrow. "Maybe you could hear better than I thought you could."

"How did you know?" Denni blurted out, thinking she was clever and sly hiding beneath the window.

"I saw you hanging off the window frame when I walked into your dad's office. You, my sweet little Molly, are not James Bond material."

Drew cut off Denni's splutters, by giving her a quick kiss. "Now, do you want to hear the conditions or not?"

"I'm listening," Denni said, trying to sit up straight and regal when she really wanted to stamp her foot with impatience.

"Good. First, your daddy said you can't make any wedding plans until you decide what college you're going to attend. You've put it off all spring and dang it, Denni, you graduate in just a couple weeks. I agree with your folks. You need to continue your education. Most seventeen-year-old girls aren't hanging around old men, trying to convince them to get married. I don't want you to miss out on anything," Drew said, holding Denni's stubborn chin in his hand. He'd accompanied her to every school dance and many functions in an effort for her to experience a normal senior year. He still wasn't sure how normal it was for a young girl to want to be with a man already out of college.

"You aren't an old man by any stretch of the imagination and I won't be missing out on anything. Besides, I'll be eighteen in a few weeks," Denni said, rolling her blue eyes. "We've had this conversation before, Drew. I'm not going away to school. I don't want to be away from you. I can pick a college in Timbuktu, but it doesn't mean I'll go. I thought you agreed I could study at home. You can help me. I don't need a college degree to hang on the wall when all I want is to be your wife."

"Look, Molly, I know you think…" Drew said, but found his thoughts scattering a thousand directions when Denni started rubbing her hand along his jaw and blew in his ear. "You will get a college degree. I don't care how, in what, or from where, but you are getting one. I promised your dad and I won't go back on my word."

"Fine. What's the second condition?" Denni asked with an innocent look on her face as she trailed her fingers down Drew's neck and along the collar of his cotton shirt.

"Second condition?" Drew asked distractedly, trying to remember what they were discussing. For such a young girl, Denni was very good at diverting a man's attention, particularly his. Getting his thoughts back on track, he frowned at her. "That you behave yourself and not distract me when you know I'm right."

When Denni shook her head at him, he gave her a rakish smile.

"Your daddy said no babies until you graduate from college," Drew said, forcing himself not to kiss Denni senseless right there in broad daylight when she leaned into his chest and ran her fingers up and down his arm. He knew her sister Mary was watching them from the living room window and no doubt her mama was keeping an eye on them as well.

"How dare he try to dictate when…" Denni said, her voice loud enough the neighbor across the street watering her flowers looked their direction. Drew put a hand over Denni's mouth and shook his head.

"Either you accept the terms of both conditions or no deal, Molly. I know this is going to irk you, but I agree with your dad. You need to experience life a little before we start a family and I want you to earn a college degree. Someday you might be glad you have it," Drew said, giving her a comforting hug. "No more arguments. The sooner you pick out a college and enroll in a program you can study from home, the sooner you can start planning the wedding."

Denni sat up and glared at him. He knew she felt like he'd turned into a traitor, agreeing with her parents, but Drew was just old enough and smart enough to realize her folks were right.

Putting his hand on the back of her neck, he pulled her close until his breath stirred the blond curls by her ear. "Don't you think it would be a good idea to get married sooner rather than later, Molly girl? I have an idea you're going to enjoy being my wife very much."

Denni felt herself shiver from the warmth of his breath on her neck and nodded her head in agreement. When Drew made her insides turn to mush, she'd do anything he asked. In love with him since she was twelve and saw him standing in line at the movie theater with some tall, pretty brunette, she told herself then and there she was going to marry Drew Thompson if it was the last thing she ever did.

She spent years trying to get Drew to notice her. When he went off to college, it almost broke her heart. He stopped by a few times during summer vacation to visit, but Denni went unnoticed until last summer when Drew graduated from college and returned to the Triple T to help his father run the family ranch.

With an agribusiness degree, Drew was ready to settle down and be a partner with his dad. What he hadn't planned on was Denni growing up while he was gone to college. Drew fought his attraction to the young girl with a rigid determination, but in the end Denni convinced him she was both mature and responsible enough to be in a relationship with him.

It was obvious to everyone the two of them shared a very special love, one most people searched for but never found.

Now that Denni had a future with Drew right in the grasp of her hand, she was holding tight and never letting go.

"Can you be ready for a wedding by the end of June?" Denni asked, jumping off Drew's lap and pulling him to his feet.

Drew laughed and wrapped her in his arms, swinging her around and around on the porch.

"Something tells me ready or not, we're getting married then."

Chapter One

"The heart will break, but broken live on."

Lord Byron

Thirty-Seven Years Later...

Holding sharpened scissors in a skilled hand, Denni Thompson quickly snipped through a piece of bright purple cotton fabric, following the pattern she was cutting with speed and precision.

Glancing up as the bell above her quilt-shop entrance jingled, she sucked in her breath, thinking for a fleeting moment that her Drew was walking in the door.

Blinking hard, she put on a tender smile to greet her oldest son.

"Trey, what are you doing here?" Denni asked, carefully placing the scissors in their holder behind the counter and walking around it to embrace the strapping man who looked like a replica of his deceased father. From the top of his black Stetson to the toes of his well-worn cowboy boots, Trey was the spitting image of Drew Thompson. His eye color was the only thing that distinguished him from the man Denni loved for thirty years before he died way too young.

"Can't I drop by to see my mom without making her think I'm up to something?" Trey asked, his bright turquoise eyes twinkling with life and good humor.

"Of course you can, honey," Denni said, patting his cheek, looking around him expecting his wife and daughter to come in the door any minute. "Where are the girls? What are you doing in town on this bitterly cold day?"

"Since the weather is nasty and Cady was feeling cooped up, I promised we'd come into town just for fun," Trey said, leaning against the counter and pushing up the brim of his hat with his forefinger, a habit that made Denni's heart catch. It was a move Drew executed thousands of times during his lifetime.

"Cass has been jabbering our ears off about some new fairy book that she absolutely must have, so I left her and Cady at the bookstore. I told them I'd see if you could be coerced into having lunch with us and meet them at that place around the corner."

"I'd love to have lunch with you," Denni said, grateful for his unexpected visit. "Spending time with you three will be a treat."

Admitting her thoughts had been as gloomy as the January weather before Trey walked in the door, she was hoping time spent with him would cheer her up. Although everyone thought her youngest son Travis was her favorite, Trey was her first-born and the one most like his father. For that reason alone, she knew he would always hold a very special place in her heart.

"What's eating at you, Mom? You're usually full of pep and sass, but you seem sad today," Trey said, studying his mother.

Although she was nearing her mid-fifties, she looked much younger with her stylish blond hair, trim figure and snapping blue eyes. The laugh lines that fanned from them were the only thing that kept her from looking the same age as her three daughters-in-law.

Today, though, there wasn't a hint of a laugh or even a real smile.

"Nothing," Denni said, gathering her purse and coat from behind the counter where she kept them and locking the cash register drawer. Her afternoon help wouldn't arrive until one, but she didn't mind closing for an hour to have lunch with three of her favorite people.

Thinking about the quilt shop she now owned, Denni reflected on how much her life had changed from her days as a young ranch wife in Grass Valley to a widow running a store in The Dalles.

When her husband first died, Denni fought to keep going. She finally realized she had to get away from the ranch where memories of Drew haunted her every time she turned around. Moving to The Dalles, she went to work managing a friend's quilt shop. With a love of sewing, quilting, and crafts, the store was the therapy she needed to manage her grief and get out of bed each day.

Last fall, her friend announced she wanted to sell the shop, so Denni bought it without hesitation. Making a few changes, she was increasing sales and enjoying the responsibility of being a businesswoman. She was finally putting the degree Drew made her get in business management to good use.

Sighing, Denni slipped her arms into the sleeves of the coat Trey held for her. She started toward the door but his hands settled on her shoulders before she took more than a few steps. Turning her around, he wrapped her in a warm hug and she hugged him back, holding him tightly.

"Thanks, honey. I needed that today," she said, stepping back and plastering on a wobbly smile. Brushing at a wayward tear, she squeezed Trey's hand and started for the door again.

"Mom, what's the matter? You can tell me," Trey said, stopping her a second time. "You look so sad today. Did something happen with the store? Is Nana okay? Is there something I can do to help?"

Patting her son's handsome cheek, she gave him a genuine smile and shook her head. "I'm fine, Trey. Nana's fine. The store is great. I guess the winter blahs have settled in and I'm feeling a little blue."

"You're thinking about dad, aren't you?" Trey asked as he opened the door and turned the sign to closed. Denni checked the lock after Trey closed the door then took her son's arm as they strolled down the street toward a bistro.

"How did you know that?" Denni asked, startled by Trey's perceptiveness. Maybe being married for a year had given him a new insight into how women thought and felt.

"You always get this far away look on your face and you practically wince when you see me," Trey said, matter-of-factly. He was aware just the sight of him sometimes brought his mother as much pain as it did joy. He never doubted for a minute that she loved him, but he knew it was hard to see him when he looked so much like his dad.

"Oh, honey. I don't want you to think I'm ever anything other than happy to see you. I am. Truly I am," Denni said, sorry that she'd been so transparent in her feelings with her oldest son. "Some days are just harder to deal with than others."

"I know, Mom. We all miss Dad. We always will, but don't you think it's time you moved on?" Trey asked as they stood waiting for traffic to pass so they could cross the street.

"I have moved on," Denni said, feeling defensive. "I have my own house, own a nice business, and do things with friends."

"That's not moving on, Mom, that's moving around," Trey said, waving at his wife Cady as she walked down the sidewalk from the direction of the bookstore with their adopted daughter skipping along beside her, red curls bouncing in the frigid air. "Dad wouldn't want you to stop living. I know your heart broke when he died, but don't you think he'd want you to put the pieces back together and get on with your life? He's been gone for almost eight years."

"I'm well aware how long he's been gone," Denni said in a clipped tone as Trey escorted her across the street. "Let's talk about this some other time."

Bending down, Denni held out her arms to Cass and engulfed the energetic little girl in a big hug.

"How's my favorite six-year-old on the planet?" Denni asked, giving Cass a kiss on her cheek.

"I'm great, Grammy. Mama got me a new fairy book. Want to see?" Cass said, pulling a book out of the bag she carried and handing it to Denni. The sparkly cover with splashes of pink and purple would certainly have caught Cass' attention. The child absolutely loved glitter and fairies.

"Maybe we can read this after lunch. Do you think your Mom and Dad would let you come to my store for the afternoon?" Denni asked, taking Cass' hand and walking in the restaurant door Trey held open.

"Well, I... are you sure, Denni?" Cady asked, knowing Cass could be a handful. "You're usually so busy on Saturdays. We're disrupting your day as it is."

"My assistant manager will be there this afternoon and I hardly get to see my only grandchild as it is," Denni said, sliding into a booth and pulling Cass in next to her. "I'd really love to have her for a few hours, if you two don't mind."

"We wouldn't mind at all," Trey said, turning his bright gaze to his wife and giving her a wink as he hung their coats and his hat on the hook at the end of their booth before sitting down beside her. "I'm sure I can think of something to keep us occupied for a few hours, without any responsibilities, or interruptions, or little chatterboxes underfoot."

"I'm not a chatterbox, Daddy," Cass said, giggling as Trey reached under the table and grabbed her jiggling foot.

"Are you sure?" Trey teased, grinning at his daughter.

"Yep. Uncle Trent said I couldn't be a chatterbox because I'm really a goofball," Cass said, looking around the restaurant with wide blue eyes, taking in everything.

"That you are," Denni said, tweaking Cass's little button nose. She loved this child as much as if she'd been born into the family. Raised by an alcoholic mother in poverty, Trey and Cady took Cass in when her mother died. At the time, Cady was Trey's housekeeper and cook, but they worked together to gain custody of the child and then adopt her, squeezing in a wedding between the two events.

Married for only a year, Trey and Cady didn't have many opportunities to spend time alone. Between ranch responsibilities, family obligations, and trying to provide Cass with a sense of security and stability, the couple rarely spent time alone.

Denni wanted Cass to stay with her not only because she loved spending time with the precocious child, but also because she wanted Trey and Cady to have a few carefree hours to enjoy each other.

Although her three sons worked hard to make sure the Triple T Ranch was solid and successful, Trey was the one who seemed to shoulder the bulk of the responsibility. Everyone looked to him for guidance, leadership, and direction. He was much like his father that way.

Cady arrived at the ranch serious and professional in demeanor, but living at the Triple T seemed to bring out a more relaxed, playful side in Denni's beautiful daughter-in-law. Cooking and cleaning for all the family, as well as the ranch hands, kept the young woman hopping from early morning to late at night.

All the more reason Trey and Cady needed some time for fun.

Placing their orders, they chatted about Denni's store, Trey's grandmother, Nana, his cousin's upcoming wedding to one of their very good friends, and life on the ranch.

Moving into town, Denni missed so many things about Grass Valley. She missed the sense of community, she missed friends she'd had for more than thirty years, and she really missed the open spaces and big sky at the ranch.

"Mr. Hammond gave us new swings," Cass said, interrupting Denni's musing as she sucked the last of her milk through a bright pink straw.

"New swings?" Denni asked, trying to follow the child's train of thought. "Oh, at school. Did you get new swings at school?"

"Yep. They're awesome. You can go up, up, up way high in the sky," Cass said shooting her little hand up in the air and zooming it back down, imitating the motion of a swing. "I bet I go up as high as Uncle Trent's head!" Cass said, comparing her swinging abilities to her uncle's six-foot five-inch height.

"My goodness. That sounds like fun. And you say Mr. Hammond gave them to you?" Denni asked, looking at Cady for an explanation.

Hart Hammond moved to Grass Valley before Halloween, buying the run-down gas station and giving it new life. He added a coffee counter, along with a variety of snacks, and made it one of the nicest of the many Renegade gas stations he owned throughout the Northwest. The fact that he bore a striking resemblance to Jon Bon Jovi and always seemed to wear a friendly smile was not lost on Denni. For a man who had to be in his fifties, he was wickedly handsome and obscenely fit.

Apparently, he was also a bit of a philanthropist.

"One evening, when Hart was at the ranch for dinner, the conversation rolled around to the need for new playground equipment at school. We were tossing around ideas on how to raise the money and the next thing we knew, the school received a delivery of all new equipment," Cady said, smiling as she remembered how excited the students were by Hart's gift. "Hart tried to act like he didn't know anything about it, but he finally admitted he ordered the equipment. He's such a nice man. I'm so glad he decided to settle in Grass Valley."

"Me, too," Trey said, finishing his burger and glancing at the uneaten fries on Cady's plate. At her nod, he started munching on them. "He's got good prices on fuel, he's friendly and fair, and he seems willing to get involved in community projects. Did you know he spearheaded the new paint job on the church?"

"I didn't know that," Denni said, irritated with herself for being interested in anything Hart Hammond did. She first met him at the ranch when Travis took it upon himself to invite the man for Thanksgiving dinner. Cady and Travis' wife, Tess, made sure Denni sat right across the table from him. How could she help but notice his blue eyes, easy smile, and that darn cleft in his chin.

"He also said..." Trey stopped mid-sentence at a glare from his mother. Today was evidently not the day to expound on all of Hart Hammond's many fine qualities. He wondered what Hart had done to get on his mother's bad side. She generally liked just about everyone.

Clearing his throat he tipped his head toward Cass. "How long do you want to keep our little flittering fairy?"

"Why don't you pick her up around four? That gives you three hours to do whatever you like," Denni said, helping Cass put on her coat and hat while Trey and Cady continued sitting at the table. Kissing Trey on the cheek, she patted his shoulder. "Better yet, why don't you let her spend the night with me and I can bring her home when I come to church tomorrow."

"That's a lot to ask of you," Cady said, although a hopeful glimmer sparkled in her hazel eyes at the prospect of having her husband all to herself for the rest of the day.

"I'd love to have her company. You two go enjoy yourself. Go to a movie, drive to the city for the afternoon," Denni said, giving Cady a wink. "Go check into one of those fancy boutique hotels in downtown Portland and spend the night. Trey can buy you a new outfit and take you out for a night on the town."

Trey waggled his eyebrows at Cady, making both his wife and mother smile. "Thanks, Mom. We'll see you at church tomorrow."

Cass climbed over Trey to hug Cady and noisily kiss her cheek. "I'll be good, Mama. Grammy and I are going to have loads of fun."

"I'm sure you will, sweetie-pie," Cady said, smiling as Cass hugged Trey then climbed down and wiggled excitedly.

Walking out of the restaurant with a wave at several people she knew, Denni took Cass' mitten-covered hand in hers as they stood waiting to cross the street.

"Can I help cut and sew today, Grammy?" Cass asked, excited at the prospect of spending time in her grandmother's store. Denni always gave her some scraps to play with and Cass had a fine time pretending she was quilting.

"I think that's a great idea, honey," Denni said as they hurried down the sidewalk. Cass hopped from one foot to the other, holding her new fairy book, while Denni unlocked the door.

She turned the sign from closed to open, helped Cass remove her coat and took off her own. Digging in her scrap bin beneath the counter, she looked up when the bell above the door jangled and smiled as her assistant manager breezed in.

"Hi, Amy," Cass said, running around the counter to give her grandmother's employee a hug.

"Hey, Cass," Amy said, removing her outerwear and hanging it in the store room before returning to the counter. "Are you helping Grammy today?"

"Yep. And I get to spend the night, too," Cass said, twirling back and forth while Denni dug through the scraps, picking out pieces for a project she thought would interest Cass.

"It's freezing out there," Amy said, rubbing her hands together to chase away the chill. When her fingers were sufficiently defrosted, she put away fabric, tidied up the already neat store, and sat down at a sewing machine in the corner to continue work she started the previous day on a quilt for a window display. "It looks like everyone is staying home where it's warm today."

"Looks that way," Denni said, watching as Cass explored all the displays in the store. Small for her age, Cass was bright, lively, and extremely active. A head full of red curls and big blue eyes gave her the look of a doll, but Denni knew there was a livewire under the sweet façade.

Since it promised to be a quiet afternoon at the store, she decided to take the little girl home where they both could relax. "Do you mind handling the store alone this afternoon?"

"We're not going to be flooded with customers today. I can handle the store," Amy said nodding her head toward Cass. "Why don't you two go have some fun?"

"Thanks, Amy," Denni said, gathering up the fabric pieces she'd selected and stuffing them in her purse. She put on her coat and then called to Cass. Helping her put on her outerwear and making sure they didn't leave behind the new fairy book, Denni waved at Amy with another word of thanks as she and Cass walked out to her car.

It was a quick five-minute drive to her house where she and Cass decided to have a tea party. Denni made tea while Cass spread peanut butter and jelly on slices of bread.

"We can't have a tea party without hats," Denni said, going to the guest bedroom and digging around on a shelf until she found a couple of hats that belonged to her mother years and years ago.

Setting a white straw hat on Cass's head, Denni placed a navy pillbox hat on her own and sat down at the table with Cass.

Playing along with Cass' pretend game of being fairies having a tea party in their garden, they finished their tea and sandwiches. While Denni washed their cups and rinsed the plates, Cass hopped up and down Denni's short hall, studying the photos on the walls.

"How come my daddy looks funny in this picture, Grammy?" Cass asked as she stared at a large portrait on the wall.

Sticking her head around the corner from the kitchen, Denni sighed and walked over to Cass. She picked up the child so she could get a better look at the picture.

"That's not your daddy, sweetie-pie," Denni said, wondering why today of all days Cass would notice Drew's portrait on the wall. "That's a picture of your Grandpa Drew."

"How come I haven't met him?" Cass asked, looking at the picture with interest.

"Because he died a long time ago," Denni said, feeling tears threaten to spill over her stinging eyes. "He was my husband and I still miss him every single day."

Cass turned in Denni's arms so she was facing her. She put her little hands on Denni's cheeks and patted them softly. "I'm sorry, Grammy. You sound sad. I don't want you to be sad anymore. Let's find you a new husband, one who'll make you happy again."

If only it was that easy.

Denni hugged Cass, knowing with her broken heart she'd never again be as happy as she was all those years she spent with Drew.

Chapter Two

"I would rather have eyes that cannot see;
ears that cannot hear;
lips that cannot speak,
than a heart that cannot love."

Robert Tizon

"Just say you'll do it, Hart. She won't leave either of us alone until you do."

Hart Hammond looked at the man leaning on his counter and realized he was going to be forced to admit defeat. Striking up a friendship with Richard when he happened upon his coffee roastery business in The Dalles, it didn't take long for Hart to become a dedicated customer, offering the coffee exclusively in his convenience store.

Enjoying both Richard's coffee and jovial personality, Hart was not as fond of Chris, Richard's nosy wife. The woman had been hounding him for weeks to go on a date with her friend who was planning a visit from California. Each time Hart told her no it made her even more determined to get him to say yes.

As Hart stood behind the counter in his convenience store and watched his assistant out the window pumping gas, he knew sometimes you had to give in to be able to move on. If Richard didn't roast some of the best coffee he'd ever tasted and deliver it right to his store on a weekly basis, he'd tell him exactly what he thought of Chris' interfering with his love life. Or lack of one.

For the past twenty-six years he'd managed to keep from getting entangled with any woman. It would have been difficult for anyone to win his heart since he was convinced the one he had was incapable of ever loving again.

"You know how I feel about being set up, Richard. Every matchmaking female in a fifty-mile radius has been in here with a list of eligible women and I've already told your wife I'm not interested," Hart said, taking a sip of the new coffee blend Richard brought for him to try. It was good. Really good.

"You know that. I know that. Most of the men and even a few of the women around here know that, but you are never going to convince Chris that you wouldn't be happier with a woman by your side," Richard said, grinning at Hart. He didn't think it would do him any permanent damage to go out on a simple date with his wife's friend when she arrived for a weekend visit. "She just wants you to be happy, man. It's because she thinks all men are happier married."

"She's got a thing or two to learn, then," Hart mumbled to himself, taking another drink of the coffee.

"What's that?" Richard asked, unable to hear what Hart said.

Releasing a sigh and rolling his eyes heavenward, Hart shook his head, looking defeated. "Fine. I'll take her out, but I'm only doing this to make your life easier. Understand?"

"And I'm forever in your debt," Richard said, shaking Hart's hand and grinning broadly. "How can I make it up to you?"

"Keep bringing me coffee like this," Hart said, wearing his trademark friendly smile.

"That I can do," Richard said, gathering up his box of samples and a clipboard with Hart's coffee order. "I'll get in touch toward the end of the week with instructions...um, I mean plans, from the wife."

Hart chuckled and slapped Richard on the back as he walked him outside into the frigid January air. "I can hardly wait."

"You're a terrible liar," Richard said, getting in his truck and waving at Hart as he drove off.

Finishing the coffee, Hart wandered back inside the convenience store. Looking around, he was proud that he had brought something nice, something needed, to the little Grass Valley community.

He liked getting involved and the people who lived in the area were, for the most part, a hard-working, caring bunch. After meeting some of the youngsters, he was more than happy to replace their worn-out playground equipment, even if it didn't happen as anonymously as he'd planned.

Giving up on secretly providing help in the community, he still made sure the church received a new coat of paint and had plans, once spring arrived, to replace the uneven sidewalk and pave the parking lot.

Wandering back to his office, he sank down in his big leather chair and swiveled around, looking at the photos, framed newspaper and magazine articles, and trophies lining his walls.

Spending several years as a professional bull rider, Hart gained a lot of press and notoriety when he placed third in the world champion rankings three years in a row. He took second place the following year and was on track to earn the world champion title when his world fell apart.

After struggling to put his life back together, he could no more get on a bull and ride than he could think about getting into another relationship with a woman.

Although he'd dated more than his share of women in the past two decades, most never made it to a second date.

He thought of the woman who had six kids and was on a mission to find someone who could be a father to her tribe of uncontrollable hellions.

There was the scary female who had so many tattoos he wasn't entirely certain the color of her skin beneath all the ink. The woman with all the body piercings had scared him even more than the tattoo queen.

He'd gone out three times with a seemingly normal girl until she suddenly wanted him to play house as she morphed into some sort of fifties homemaker with an attitude, like a Stepford wife gone bad.

Models, real estate agents, bank tellers, grocery store clerks, spoiled little rich girls, dirt-poor single mothers - Hart had dated them all. He'd been stalked more than once, slapped a few times by women who really needed some classes in anger management, and propositioned and proposed to more times than he could count.

The fact of the matter remained unchanged. Relationships held no interest for him at all. Occasionally, he enjoyed some female companionship, but for the most part, he was content to build a successful business with his eye toward the future instead of lingering in the past.

Now, here he was about to be set up on another crazy blind date with some woman he'd have no interest in seeing again. His one hope was that she'd realize this was just a weekend meeting, a favor for a friend, and nothing more.

Leaning back in his chair and drumming his long fingers on the top of his orderly desk, he had a gut feeling the date would end badly, as so many had in the past. Any friend of Richard's wife would no doubt be a lot like her and she wasn't exactly the type of person who took no for an answer, handled rejection with grace, or knew when to back off.

Hearing his assistant call for him, Hart put aside his musings, pulled on his gloves and a warm coat, and went out to pump gas to his customers.

><><

There wasn't enough good coffee in the world to redeem the blind date Richard and Chris arranged for him with her friend.

Arriving at their house Saturday for lunch, the plan was for Hart to show the woman around The Dalles in the afternoon and then accompany her to a wedding that evening.

Lunch wasn't even over and Hart was more than ready to bolt.

Chris and Richard welcomed him to their home, showing him into the dining room where Chris had a simple but filling meal on the table. Waiting a few minutes, she went to find her friend so they could eat while the food was still hot.

Returning alone, she told the men to go ahead since Mona wasn't yet ready.

Richard shrugged his shoulders and dug in, passing Hart a bowl of thick stew and slices of warm bread. He was enjoying the meal when a middle-aged woman waltzed in on a cloud of cheap perfume, making him choke on the bite he was swallowing. Richard slapped his back and he wiped his watering eyes with a napkin while Chris introduced her friend and seated her across the table from Hart.

Dressed in a skirt that was too short with a blouse that was too tight and unbuttoned too low, she seemed to be under the delusion that she was still in her twenties rather than a woman closer to fifty.

Between too much makeup that caked into her wrinkles and a really bad lip job, Hart could hardly look at the woman without smirking, so he kept his head down and focused on the food.

Trying to sound urbane and sophisticated, her nasally voice grated on his nerves when she spoke. Hart found her to be pretentious and fake, making him swallow back a sigh at the long day ahead followed by what would no doubt be an even longer evening.

"So, Hart," Mona said, batting her fake eyelashes at him. "Chris tells me you own a gas station."

"That's right," Hart said, not looking up from his food. He didn't know what he'd do when his bowl of stew was empty so he began eating very slowly.

"Is that a new enterprise for you? Someone with your physique looks like they'd be used to doing something that called for manual labor," Mona observed, leaning across the table in such a way that even without looking at her, Hart was getting an eyeful of cleavage. The woman must have spent a small fortune in tanning booths without giving a thought to using any sort of lotion or moisturizer because her skin looked as wrinkled and dark as a peach pit.

"I've been in the gas station business for a while and I don't expect my employees to do anything I don't do myself," Hart said, taking another piece of bread.

"You own more than one station?" Mona asked.

"He owns the entire Renegade chain, don't you, Hart?" Chris asked, much to her husband's dismay. The glare he shot her from his end of the table went unnoticed.

"That's correct," Hart said, taking another bite of stew. He could practically hear the jackpot bells ringing in Mona's bleached blond head.

"You've got to be worth millions," Mona said, dropping her spoon in her bowl and splashing stew on her blouse. She didn't seem to notice as she tried to figure out how much money she'd have at her disposal if she could reel in the man across the table.

"Did you see they're having a special winter thing downtown?" Richard asked, trying to change the subject. Chris finally noticed the look he was giving her, warning her to calm down her over-eager friend.

"Oh, yeah, I did see something about that in the paper. You walk around to the different stores and get a stamp from each one. When your card's full you get entered into a chance to win a basket full of prizes. Sounds like fun," Chris said, wondering what she'd done. She hadn't seen Mona in years, but she'd grown up with her and their friend that was getting married later that evening. They'd been great pals as kids, but Chris suddenly acknowledged she didn't really know Mona at all. It certainly wasn't going to make her husband happy to lose one of his best clients if her friend offended him any more than she already had. She made a vow, right then, to mind her own business going forward and not make any more attempts at matchmaking.

"Maybe we could check it out after lunch," Hart suggested, finishing his stew. At least if they were out in public, there was a slim chance Mona might be distracted for a while.

"Are you sure?" Richard asked, giving Hart a speculative eye.

"Yep. It's chilly out, but not terribly so. If you ladies bundle up, you should be warm enough," Hart said, smiling at Chris. "Thank you for the delicious lunch."

"You're very welcome," Chris said, starting to clear the table. Richard jumped up to help her, wanting to escape Mona almost as badly as Hart.

Quickly loading the dishwasher, the couple returned to find Hart holding Mona's coat while she slid her arms in the sleeves. Richard helped Chris with her coat and grabbed his own as they hurried out the door.

Walking around downtown, Mona somehow managed to latch on to Hart's arm with red-painted long-nailed claws and wouldn't let go.

"You are positively yummy, aren't you," Mona said, squeezing Hart's bicep as they strolled down the street behind Chris and Richard. "Do you work out every day?"

Ignoring her question and prying her fingers off his arm, Hart took a step away from her, shoving his hands deep in the pockets of his jeans. Hoping to derail whatever question she planned to ask, he inquired about her work and family. He discovered she was a cocktail waitress and had been married three times. Somehow neither answer surprised him.

Insisting they go to each business listed on the Winter Frolic card, Hart was tired of following Mona from store to store. Opening the door of a quilt and craft shop, Hart looked into a pair of warm blue eyes he'd admired numerous times since moving to Sherman County.

"Hart Hammond, what brings you to my store?" Denni Thompson asked as she cut fabric for a customer waiting at her counter.

Leaning against the counter while Mona and Chris looked around, Hart gave Denni a smile that started at his generous lips and worked its way up to his eyes. He waited until she finished with the customer before speaking quietly, so Chris wouldn't hear what he said. "I somehow got roped into doing a favor for a friend and I'm paying for it big time."

"You what?" Denni asked, confused by Hart's statement until her gaze settled on Mona where she bent over a display of hand-made Valentine's cards and sent Hart what he assumed she meant to be a seductive glance. Instead, it made him want to shiver in revulsion. "Oh, my…"

"You got that right," Hart said, seeing some humor in the situation for the first time since Richard had talked him into this ridiculous fiasco of a date. He could only imagine how the situation appeared to Denni. Hart absently wondered if she'd ever been set up on a miserable blind date then decided she was smart enough not to get herself into such an annoying mess.

Denni studied Hart, from the thick sandy hair on his head, so similar in shade to her youngest son's that they could have been related, to the toes of his polished boots. She wasn't sure how he managed it, but he seemed to get better looking every time she saw him. Fit, tan, and all-man, Hart was ruggedly handsome and always smelled like some expensive cologne meant to make women swoon at his feet.

Not that Denni had ever swooned in her life. She sure wasn't going to start now, especially not for Hart.

"I take it your friend isn't from around here," Denni said, observing the woman's short skirt, cropped coat and made-up face. She looked like someone who was trying desperately to recapture her youth and failing quite spectacularly.

"No, you're correct in your assessment that she isn't from around here," Hart said, watching Denni as she worked tidying up her counter space. As she wrapped fabric back on a bolt, he watched her fingers smooth the material. Her blond head was bent down, but he could see the soft curve of her cheek, the slender column of her neck. If he was ever going to fall for another woman, it would be one like Denni.

Classy, fun and spirited, the lively woman didn't come close to looking her age. Her face was natural and fresh, her hair stylishly trimmed, and she always looked trendy but with a sophisticated flair. It was obvious she was completely devoted to her three sons and their growing families, as well as her friends and aging mother.

Although Hart hadn't spent any time alone with Denni, when he'd spoken with her at community gatherings or across the dinner table at the Triple T Ranch, he found her to be intelligent and witty. She'd made him laugh on numerous occasions.

Lovely, kind, and a little on the sassy side, Denni Thompson was an engaging widow who should have long ago remarried. According to the local gossip, she'd nearly died from a broken heart right after she buried her beloved husband.

Greatly missed in the little community, no one seemed to blame Denni for leaving the ranch and starting over in The Dalles where she could try to get on with her life.

Hart understood that more than most people ever could.

Admiring how beautiful Denni looked with light streaming in the store windows and surrounding her in a special golden aura, he was momentarily transfixed.

Lost in watching her, he failed to notice Mona approach and put a proprietary claw on his arm. "Isn't this store quaint," Mona said in the voice Hart was pretty sure would give him nightmares. "Let's get our card stamped and move on."

Denni smiled and stamped Mona's card, thanking her for coming in.

Hart walked Mona to the door where Chris waited with Richard. Leaving the store, they entered a jewelry store down the block. While Mona fawned over some big, gaudy ring, Hart quietly made his way back to Denni's shop. She was putting away fabric by the door when he entered.

"Forget something?" she asked, surprised to see Hart again so soon.

"Yes, I did," Hart said, glancing around the store, trying to find some excuse for coming back in. He couldn't explain it, but he felt drawn to Denni and decided he wanted to get to know her better. Just as friends. A guy could never have too many friends, unless of course they set him up on dates with man-hunting females interested in bagging him.

Looking at a display on the wall across the store, Hart found his reason for returning. "I want to buy a quilt. Are those for sale?"

Denni looked at the quilts hanging from racks on the wall, not quite sure she heard Hart correctly. The man was worth a fortune, could buy the finest of everything, and he wanted to buy one of her quilts. "You want a quilt?"

"I sure do. I've seen a few of your masterpieces around Grass Valley. I'd like to have one," Hart said, walking to the display and really looking at them. He was correct in calling them masterpieces because it was evident Denni was very talented in her work. He couldn't imagine making such tiny, perfect stitches. He could barely thread a needle to sew on a missing button. "I'm still furnishing my house and I haven't even started on the guest rooms."

Wondering how many bedrooms were in Hart's fancy new house, Denni instead asked him about colors, the size of the bed, what sort of decorating scheme he was going after. He answered her questions, but his gaze kept coming back to a teal and brown quilt.

"I like this one," he said, holding it away from the rest and studying the design. "Is it for sale?"

Yes, of course," Denni said, taking it off the rack and handing it to Hart to examine. "Are you sure you want a quilt?"

"Positive," Hart said, placing the quilt on the counter while he took out his wallet. "I want my house to feel homey, not stuffy. I think quilts are a good way to go about that, don't you?"

"Yes, I do," Denni said, finding it hard to believe Hart would know that a quilt could provide a warm welcome to guests. Unlike fancy comforters or duvets,

Denni thought quilts had the ability to make a guest feel relaxed and at home.

"What's the pattern?" Hart asked, placing his hand on the quilt, enjoying the soft feel of the fabric beneath his fingers.

"Shoo Fly," Denni said, trying to hide her grin when Hart's friend stuck her head in the door and called to him.

"That is particularly appropriate," Hart said, gathering up the quilt Denni placed in a bag, wishing he could tell Mona to shoo. "Thank you, Denni."

"Thank you, Hart. I hope you enjoy the quilt."

"I'm sure I will," Hart managed to say before Mona grabbed his arm and tugged him out the door and down the sidewalk

If Denni didn't know better, she might have thought Hart was showing some interest in her. He obviously just wanted a quilt. Besides, if the woman with him today was any indication of the type of women that interested him, Denni wished him lots of luck.

Chapter Three

*"One of the hardest things in life
is having words in your heart that you can't utter."*
James Earl Jones

Finding a space in the church's graveled parking lot, Denni grabbed her purse and hurried in the door. Heading to the pew where she'd sat with Drew nearly every Sunday during their marriage, she was glad to see an empty spot next to Cass.

Focused on her granddaughter, Denni hurried to take a seat next to the child, oblivious to the man sitting on the end of the pew. Trey gave her an odd look and pointed to his watch from the other side of Cass. Denni mouthed "traffic" just as the pastor stepped up to the pulpit and began the morning service.

Scooting her purse beneath her seat, Denni decided she would roast crammed into their full row if she didn't remove her coat. Quickly unfastening the buttons, she began to work her arm free when Trey reached across Cass and helped her take it off one shoulder. She turned to remove the other side only to look into the warm blue eyes of Hart.

Giving him an appreciative nod as he held her sleeve while she slid out her arm, she couldn't believe her boys had invited him to sit in their pew. They knew how she felt about any matchmaking schemes and when they went to the ranch for lunch, she would make it clear, once again, that she wasn't interested in dating any man. Even if the touch of his hand through her suit jacket was sending warm tendrils of sensation curling down to her fingers and across her shoulders.

When Cass squirmed off the pew and wiggled her way between Denni and Hart, smiling up at the man with her big china blue eyes, Denni decided the little girl had no doubt asked Hart to sit with them.

Looking down the pew, she smiled at Trey and Cady as well as Trent and his wife, Lindsay, who was still suffering from morning sickness. The poor girl seemed to be sick most of the day instead of only in the morning. Due with their first child at the end of May, everyone was excited at the prospect of a new baby to cuddle and love. Denni had already started a baby quilt and her mother, Ester, was busy crocheting any number of things for the newest Thompson.

Denni glanced across the aisle to see Travis and his wife, Tess, sitting with her family. Tess' brother Brice had his arm wrapped around Denni's niece Bailey, as she sat tucked against his side. Engaged since Thanksgiving, the couple had plans for an April wedding at the ranch.

Considering the fact her three boys all wed in the last year and Brice and Bailey would soon marry, she was starting to wonder if there really was something in the water at the Triple T. The community gossip indicated something potent bubbled in the well at the ranch.

Smiling at the direction her thoughts had taken, she turned her focus back to the pastor's sermon. Feeling a small hand slide into hers, Denni gently squeezed Cass's fingers then leaned down and kissed the vibrant child on her button nose.

After the service and a time of fellowship with cookies and cider in the church's hall, Denni walked to her car accompanied by Cass, who was chatting a mile a minute. Since she took any opportunity that arose to spend time with the lively little girl, Denni kept a booster seat in her car for Cass as well as several changes of clothes at her house. She often drove to the ranch house after church with Cass giving her a rundown on what was happening at the Triple T, school, and in her little world.

Following Cass' visit two Sunday's ago, Denni hadn't seen much of her granddaughter and anticipated a lively chat on the way to the ranch. Opening the back door for Cass to climb in, the little girl spun around and ran off with a hasty goodbye. Denni watched Cady hustle Cass into their pickup with a sly grin.

Looking around, Denni saw her youngest daughter-in-law approaching with a reluctant Hart in tow. She didn't know what Tess was up to, but she knew she wasn't going to like it.

"Hart's joining us for lunch. Would you mind giving him a ride?" Tess asked, giving her mother-in-law an innocent smile. "His pickup had a flat this morning and we brought him to church, but Brice and Bailey are riding home with us so it's going to be crowded."

"Sure, climb in," Denni said, ready to throttle the young woman who gave her a smug look and walked away. "It appears my family is quite taken with you."

"The feeling is mutual," Hart said, buckling his seat belt and casting a sideways glance at Denni. Her blond hair gleamed in the midday light, her eyes sparkled with life and she looked lovely with a floral scarf around her neck that softened the tailored cut of her bright pink suit. Quickly buttoning her navy coat, he watched as she slipped on gloves and started the car. "You raised a nice family, Denni."

"Thank you," Denni said, following the pickups her boys were driving onto the highway and south of town toward their ranch. "They're good boys and they married wonderful girls. I'm very fortunate and blessed."

"That you are," Hart commented, realizing Denni Thompson had not only a handsome family; she also had a very kind, loving one. He'd seen the way her sons worked closely together with respect, honesty and integrity. Not all families had that.

All three of the girls who married her boys were sweet, gentle, and smart. There wasn't a lazy one in the whole bunch and Hart liked that they played as hard as they worked.

The Thompsons might know a thing or two about running a successful ranch, but they also knew how to have fun. He'd enjoyed more than one Sunday afternoon with them, which is why he didn't refuse when they invited him to lunch today.

Learning weeks ago that they really didn't mind one more around the table, Hart thought Cady was about the best cook he'd ever met. That girl knew her way around a kitchen and only an idiot would turn down the opportunity to take advantage of her cooking. Hart may be a lot of things, but stupid wasn't one of them.

"Where's your friend?" Denni asked, thinking Hart really had bad taste in women. No wonder he was single.

"What friend?" Hart asked, looking at her quizzically.

"The woman who was with you yesterday," Denni said, wondering about the scantily clad woman she'd seen him escorting around downtown.

Hart's chuckle caught her by surprise and she turned her head his direction. "That…person," Hart finally found a word he could use and not offend Denni "is no friend of mine. Someone who claims to be a friend coerced me into being her date. She and his wife have a mutual friend who was getting married last night. Evidently, they'd been out of touch for several years and had no idea she'd be such a…um, interesting individual. Richard took pity on me and assured his wife and Mona that I was not feeling well and needed to go home after spending all afternoon carrying her bags from store to store yesterday. That was absolutely true by that point, so I was glad to escape her clutches."

Denni was trying not to laugh. Hart could see it bubbling up inside her, ready to spill out.

When he said "go on," Denni erupted into a fit of laughter that sounded like music to Hart's ears. He hadn't realized how much he enjoyed hearing her voice.

Once her laughter subsided, Denni grinned. "So I take it she isn't your typical choice in a date."

"You wound me, Denni," Hart said, looking solemn, although the smile tugging at the corners of his mouth gave him away. "Do you really think I'm interested in what she had to offer?"

"No," Denni said, parking her car near the mudroom door at the Triple T. "I admit I couldn't quite believe you'd willingly be out with a woman like that, but there you were."

"Yeah? The next time a well-meaning friend tries to set me up, I'm sticking to my guns and refusing," Hart said, getting out of the car and waiting for Denni. Her boys were already in the house, having raced down the frozen driveway to see who would get home first.

Going in the mudroom door, Denni and Hart hung their coats on pegs then went into the kitchen where the delicious smells of Cady's meal filled the air.

Cass gave Denni a quick hug around her waist before grabbing Hart's hand and tugging him toward the great room where the guys were hanging out.

Pushing up the sleeves of her suit jacket, Denni opened a drawer and took out an apron, tying it around her trim waist.

"What can I do to help?" she asked Cady who was slicing a roast while Tess made gravy and Bailey made a salad.

"Mash the potatoes?" Cady asked, nodding her head toward a pot sitting on the stove.

Denni took cream and butter out of the fridge and set to work mashing the potatoes. She didn't know how Cady managed to look after Cass, volunteer at school, keep up the house, and cook two big meals a day. When Denni was the woman of the house, she always had a housekeeper and cook to help out. Then again, she had set a pan or two on fire back in her younger days while Cady trained as a chef for a while before she decided to go to business school.

Looking around, she noticed Lindsay was missing from the group of women.

"Where's Lindsay? Is she still not feeling well?"

"No. She's resting in the parlor," Cady said, finishing with the meat and rinsing her hands. "I thought the morning sickness eventually went away. I've never heard of someone who had it all day long this far into their pregnancy. Do you think everything is okay?"

"I'm sure her doctor would let her know if she thought anything was wrong," Denni said, scooping the potatoes into a serving bowl. "Each pregnancy is different and since this is Lindsay's first, it's going to be hard to tell what's normal for her."

"Just think, by the time school is out, we'll have a brand new baby to play with," Tess said, her big chocolate brown eyes taking on a soft glow. Married in October to Travis, they weren't quite ready to start a family, but she loved the thought of having a baby to hold and cuddle until they were.

"If that baby turns out to be a boy, those three cousins of mine won't know what to do with themselves," Bailey observed as she sliced a cucumber for the salad.

"They'll have him out roping and riding before he can walk or talk," Cady observed with a grin. "I think everyone is excited about a new generation of Thompson's entering the world."

Wiping her hands on a towel, Denni put her hand on Cady's arm. "Cass is a Thompson, too, and no one will forget that. She's the first of the next generation."

"I know, Denni," Cady said, appreciating her mother-in-law's concern over their feelings in regard to Cass. "It's just that we'll get to experience this baby from day one instead of coming onto the scene when she's already five. Trey and I are grateful every day for Cass and the way you all include her as a true Thompson."

"How could we not?" Tess asked, looking toward the great room and grinning. "She's definitely a lot like the men in this family."

Cady rolled her eyes to see Cass riding Trey's leg like a bucking bronc while Trent, Travis, Brice and Hart cheered her on. Her frilly dress wasn't exactly meant to be worn for rough-housing, but the guys would make sure she didn't get it too rumpled or dirty playing around.

"That she is," Denni said with a loving smile.

"Shall we get the food on the table and feed these hungry men?" Cady asked, carrying the meat platter to the big dining room table that broke up the space between the kitchen and great room. With the ability to seat more than a dozen people and still leave elbowroom, the table was often filled to capacity.

The house had felt lonely and forsaken when Cady arrived at the ranch a year and a half ago as the cook and housekeeper.

Even with Trey and Trent living in the house, it still seemed shadowed in the past of what had once been a bustling, joy-filled home. With five ranch hands to cook for, it soon began to awake from its slumber. By the time Travis returned from his last tour of duty in Iraq and Cass' adoption was final, the house was lively again. Trent married Lindsay and Travis married Tess, Bailey moved in which meant Brice was there on a regular basis and the house once again became the place everyone gathered.

Denni was glad to walk in the door and feel the welcome from a busy, loving, happy family. Her family. It all started when Cady began working her magic the first day she arrived at the ranch. Looking at the beautiful brunette at the far end of the table, Denni watched her tease Trent, pass Lindsay a dinner roll and give Trey a look filled with love and passion.

Knowing she was very lucky in the daughter-in-law department, Denni loved all three of hers like they were her own daughters.

Loving Tess from the day she was born, Denni considered her part of the family long before she married Travis. Tess had been her honorary daughter throughout her growing up years.

When Lindsay moved to Grass Valley to teach four years earlier, Denni became acquainted with her through school events. It was no wonder Trent had fallen head over heels for the woman, with her blond hair, sky blue eyes and towering height.

Cady entered their lives when Trent and Trey hired her for her culinary talents. Calling to check up on the boys one afternoon soon after their housekeeper retired, Denni was surprised to hear a female voice answer the phone. They ended up visiting for a while and began having weekly calls. In the lovely hazel-eyed girl, Trey not only found the perfect woman for him, but Denni found a friend.

Sharing many of the same interests, Denni felt a connection to Cady she knew was mutual. She felt much more motherly toward Lindsay and Tess than she did Cady, although they were all very close in age.

All three of them, along with Bailey, had joined forces in trying to set her up on dates the past few months. The more she refused to go, the more determined they were to find someone Denni would date.

She couldn't get them to understand she never wanted to risk having her heart shattered so completely again. Losing Drew nearly killed her and there was no way she could face another experience like that. The only way to avoid it was to remain alone. Besides, she was going to love Drew until her dying day and there was no one who could take his place in her broken heart.

Not even the very handsome man across the table who was raptly listening to Cass talk about her dog Buddy. He was so good with the little girl and seemed to have the ability to make her feel extra important and special. With his engaging blue eyes and infectious smile, no wonder her granddaughter was so taken with the good-looking man.

"Isn't that right, Mama?" Travis asked, looking across the table at his mother, waiting for a response.

"I'm sorry, baby. I didn't hear what you said," Denni said, pulling herself out of her musings.

"I asked what day you're leaving for your trip."

"What trip?" Trey asked, trying to remember if his mom mentioned being gone.

"The quilt show in Tucson," Denni said, realizing she neglected to tell the other two boys about her plans. Mulling over the idea of going, she made up her mind last week to attend. Her assistant would take care of the store, a neighbor would watch the house, and Travis promised they would all check on Nana to make sure she was fine.

"You're going to Tucson?" Trent asked, leaning around Brice and Bailey to look at his mother. "Alone?"

"You can't travel alone, Mom. Anything could happen. You're not used to the big city. I think we better discuss this," Trey said, setting down his fork and turning his intense aquamarine gaze Denni's direction.

"I think you boys better just pipe down. I'm not a child. I'm perfectly capable of taking care of myself and I'm going. End of subject," Denni said, slicing into her roast and taking a bite.

"But, Mama, you…" Travis let his words drop off at the look Denni sent him across the table.

Hart hid a smile behind his napkin. For a woman who looked so sweet and easy-going, it was quite entertaining to see Denni put her three strapping sons in their place. He admired her sass and determination, even if he did agree with the boys that she shouldn't travel alone. She seemed excessively innocent and someone would see her as an easy mark.

"Are you taking a quilt to enter in the show?" Cady asked. She shared Denni's love of fabrics although she didn't share her mother-in-law's quilting skills.

"Not this time," Denni said, smiling at Cady. Denni often entered her quilts in shows and competitions around the region. "I'm calling it a research and development trip."

"When is this expedition taking place?" Hart asked, suddenly thinking of a few reasons he could travel to Tucson for a quick trip. He had friends there, business associates, investments he could check on. He ignored the voice in his head telling him he really wanted to go to ensure Denni was safe and spend some time with her away from all the watchful eyes and gossiping tongues of their little community.

That was the one thing he didn't particularly enjoy about living in a tight-knit small community. Everyone seemed to know everyone else's business. He could sneeze at the café and his assistant manager would ask him if he was coming down with a cold when he got back to the gas station.

It did come in handy, though, if he wanted information. A few well-placed questions and he knew all about the Thompson family. People talked about how they'd been in the area for more than a century, how Drew Thompson had been a well-liked, much-respected member of the community until he died of a heart attack almost eight years ago. He heard how Trey looked and acted so much like his dad, people still sometimes did a double take to see him walking down the street. He learned that Denni had been a young bride of only seventeen when Drew brought her to the Triple T Ranch. She was the youngest daughter of a well-to-do banker in The Dalles and spoiled to the point she was nearly impossible to handle. Something about Drew, though, tamed her wild ways and he helped her grow into a woman that everyone seemed to love.

Looking across the table at her sparkling blue eyes and sassy smile, he could imagine her as a high-spirited girl. He liked a woman with gumption and Denni appeared to have it in spades.

"I leave Thursday and will be back Monday," Denni said, pushing potatoes around on her plate, waiting for the fit her boys would throw to erupt. It wasn't long in coming.

"No way, Mom. You aren't going alone. It's just not smart or safe," Trey said, once again setting down his fork and staring at her. "What if someone tries to rob you or talk you into something? Nope. You aren't going."

"Trey's right. Anything could happen. It would be stupid to go alone," Trent said, trying to glare at his mother around Brice and Bailey. "We forbid it."

"Can't you find one of your friends to go with you? Why don't you wait until one of us can take some time off and go?" Travis asked, ignoring the kick he received under the table from his wife.

Denni gave a pointed look to each one of her sons. She wiped her mouth on her napkin and returned it to her lap then folded her hands together to keep from smacking the table in frustration. Taking a deep breath, then another, she willed herself to calm down and remember her boys were just trying to look out for her.

"This should be good," Cady whispered, just loud enough for Lindsay to hear. The two girls grinned and waited for Denni to let her boys have it. Anticipating a showdown, Hart set his fork on the edge of his plate and leaned back in his chair, glad he had a great seat to watch the action.

"If my hearing hasn't completely gone due to my old age, or I'm not misunderstanding what is being said thanks to my senility, what you boys have communicated is that I'm not smart, stupid I believe was the word you used, Trent. I'm incapable of getting myself to Tucson and back again without what? Being kidnapped? Held hostage? Blindly following some sweet-talking scammer and signing over everything I own? And you forbid me from going? Forbid?" Denni felt her temper bubbling and decided to let it go, rather than simmer it back down to a manageable level.

"It would do you boys well to remember a few things, so I'll spell them out for you right now. First, and foremost, I'm not some doddering old fool who's taken leave of my senses. Although you all think I'm ancient, I've still got a few good years left so don't go shoving me into a retirement home just yet. Second, you forget that your father and I traveled every winter. We not only traveled all over this great country of ours, but we also took several trips to Europe and even spent three weeks in Australia. I think I have some idea how to take care of myself while traveling. Last, but not least by a long shot, I will not sit here and let you boys get off with talking to me like a child. Don't you ever, and I mean ever, mention the word forbid to me again. I brought each of you into this world and I can take you right back out! You three keep that in mind and show a little respect."

Trey, Trent and Travis did an admirable job of looking properly scolded while Tess, Cady, and Lindsay tried to hide their smiles, knowing Denni was the one woman who could take on the three stubborn, overbearing Thompson brothers and win. Hart caught Denni's eye and gave her a conspiratorial wink while Cass sat quietly in her chair looking from one adult to the other. Brice and Bailey kept their eyes on their plates, although from Brice's shaking shoulders, he was trying really hard not to laugh.

"Now that's all settled, who wants dessert?" Cady asked, trying to smooth away the tension that lingered around the table.

"I'll help," Tess said, getting to her feet and picking up empty serving bowls as she followed Cady to the kitchen.

"Me too," Bailey said, picking up dirty dishes on her way to the kitchen.

With their backs to the group, their soft giggles could still be heard, causing the three Thompson brothers to scowl their direction. When Denni raised an eyebrow at her boys, they looked back down at their plates and sat quietly waiting for dessert.

Once it was served, Denni patted Bailey's hand where it rested on the table next to her. "Let's hear your wedding plans, honey. You said you wanted to wait until after the holidays to talk about them and here we are half-way through January."

Bailey turned to look at Brice who gave her a heart-stopping smile before she looked around the table. "We'd like to have the wedding here at the ranch, in April, if that's okay with all of you."

"Why wouldn't it be?" Trey asked, eating a piece of coconut cake, his favorite.

"Well, you've had so many weddings and excitement going on here the past year, we weren't sure if you'd be game for another one," Brice said, looking from Trey to Travis, who had been his best friend as long as he could remember.

"We'd love to have your wedding here," Cady said, thrilled at the prospect of another big celebration at the Triple T. People were still talking about Trent and Lindsay's wedding from last summer. "Just tell us what you need us to do."

"We'd like to exchange our vows out by the orchard when the fruit trees are blooming," Bailey said, thinking of her vision for a perfect spring wedding. The most important detail was having Brice there, so everything else was negotiable. "We don't want a huge wedding, just family and friends."

"She doesn't quite get the whole family and friends thing equating to a huge wedding," Brice said, making everyone laugh.

"I do, too," Bailey said, bumping Brice's arm playfully. "But we don't have to invite half the countryside, do we?"

"Of course not, they'll just show up," Travis said, grinning at his cousin. "Plan on a few hundred people being there and you'll be just fine."

Bailey turned eyes, the same color as Trey's, to Brice and he nodded his head in agreement. "I might as well give up now. Invite anyone you like, invite the whole county, just make sure you're there."

"There is nothing that could keep me from showing up, sugar," Brice said, pressing a kiss to Bailey's cheek, making everyone smile. "I'd crawl on two broken knees if I had to."

They continued discussing wedding plans and everyone helped clean up after the meal. Hart watched football with the guys in the great room while the women sat and visited in the parlor.

Cady happened to glance outside and noticed snow beginning to fall so Denni quickly decided to start for home before the roads got bad.

The girls all walked her back to the kitchen where Cady put leftovers she'd set aside for Denni into a bag and placed it on the counter.

So immersed in the game, the guys didn't notice the snow or the fact that Denni was ready to leave. She finally whistled to get their attention. Trent turned the TV to mute and they looked her direction, noticing she was wearing her coat and scarf.

"Leaving so soon, Mom?" Trey asked as they all got to their feet.

"With the snow, I want to head home before the roads get slick," Denni said, pointing toward the patio doors where the ground was already turning white.

"Want one of us to drive you, Mama?" Travis offered, putting his arm around her shoulders. She leaned into him and hugged his waist.

"No, baby, I'm perfectly capable of driving myself home, but I appreciate the offer," Denni said, as he walked with her toward the kitchen door.

Trent and Trey each gave her a hug then Trent took her keys and ran out to start her car and brush off the snow. Brice pecked her cheek and told her drive carefully then Denni hugged each of the girls, ending with Cass, who had been playing in her room with her dolls.

"Are you still mad at the guys, Grammy?" Cass asked as Denni gave the little girl another hug.

"No, sweetie-pie, I'm not mad at them, but sometimes they need put in their place," Denni said, catching Trey's eye and lifting an eyebrow at him in challenge. He looked chastened as he gave her a smile of surrender.

"If we aren't careful, she might give us a whipping and send us to bed without supper," Trey said, hugging his mother again.

"I never sent you to bed hungry," Denni said, knowing all three of her boys received their share of spankings, though.

"No, you didn't. You're a good mom, most of the time."

"Just remember that the next time you decide to get on your high-horse and run rough-shod over me."

"Yes, ma'am," Trey said with a laugh, realizing Hart was putting on his coat and walking out the door behind them.

"One of us can run you home later, Hart, if you want to stay," Trey said, as he held Denni's car door and gave her a hand as she slid into the driver's seat.

"If Denni doesn't mind dropping me off, I've got some things I should take care of at home. Thanks for the offer, though," Hart said, turning to wave at the girls who stood huddled in the door, not wanting to brave the cold or snow. "And for lunch. It was wonderful as always."

"Come anytime," Cady called before disappearing back inside the warmth of the house.

Hart knew she meant it, too. He could show up unannounced at the ranch house, be welcomed inside and fed a good meal, then asked if there was anything else they could do for him. People like the Thompson family were rare.

With a final wave and a promise to call when she arrived home safe and sound, Denni headed down the long driveway and back toward the freeway. Driving through Grass Valley, she asked Hart questions about the gas station and how he liked living in the area.

Purchasing a run-down farm, he was working on turning it into a showplace just a few miles north of Grass Valley, closer to the small town of Moro. Tearing down the old buildings, Hart had a brand-new house and barn constructed along with outbuildings and corrals. As soon as the weather warmed up in the spring, he had plans for landscaping as well as the addition of more fenced pasture for his horses and cattle.

Although Denni hadn't been to his house before, she didn't need to ask directions as she turned off the highway onto a side road then made the turn onto the road that led to his place.

The house looked impressive as it sat on a little hill, overlooking the pastures below. With a façade made of thick logs and river rock, it was both rustic and inviting, especially with porch lights glistening through the white swirls of snow.

"My gracious, Hart, your house is…" Denni was unable to think of an apt description. It was magnificent and imposing, yet something about it that seemed homey.

"Garish, obnoxious, a little too much?" he asked, wearing the broad grin Denni realized she greatly enjoyed seeing.

"No," Denni said, smiling as she stopped in front of the house. "I was thinking more along the lines of inviting and fabulous."

"Oh," Hart said, surprised. "Thank you. I know you're in a rush today, but I'd love to give you a tour sometime. If you're interested, I'd like very much to have you make a custom quilt. Maybe I could show you around another day when you have time and you could see the room I have in mind for the quilt."

"I'd be happy to make you a quilt," Denni said, impulsively squeezing Hart's hand as he started to open his car door. Even through her glove, she could feel the heat from his hand creeping up her arm. She didn't even know words to describe what she was feeling and thought it best to leave well enough alone.

Deciding when Drew died her heart would never again speak of romance, she was convinced, even if she was willing, the words had long ago been forgotten.

Hart gave her a long look that made her want to squirm in her seat before he gently squeezed her fingers in response.

"Next time you're in the area, let me know," Hart said, opening the car door and getting out. "Thanks for the ride, Denni. I appreciate it."

"You're welcome. I'm sorry about you having to witness our little family disagreement at lunch. Once in a while I've got to turn those boys on their ears," Denni said, making Hart laugh.

"Remind me not to get on your bad side," Hart said, smiling at Denni with warmth radiating from his eyes. "And for the record, there is no way anyone would take you for doddering or stupid. Sexy and spirited, definitely, but not old. Not in the least."

Hart shut the car door and walked up the steps to his house, leaving a speechless Denni watching him go.

Hoping she hadn't dropped her chin at his statement, she pulled back out on the road and pondered Hart's words.

Thoughts and feelings she thought she'd buried with Drew began slowly working their way out of the tidy compartment where Denni had locked them. Did he really think was sexy and spirited?

SHANNA HATFIELD

Chapter Four

"Let the rays of your heart shine on all who pass by."
Terri Guillemets

Standing at the baggage carousel waiting for her suitcase to appear, Denni felt excitement wash through her at the prospect of not only attending the quilt show, but also taking in a few of Tucson's attractions. Never visiting Tucson before, she looked forward to exploring a little of the city in the short time she'd be in town.

Seeing her purple suitcase with her initials stitched on the front pocket, Denni stepped close and reached out to grasp it when a hand grabbed the handle and plucked it up.

Turning to see who she was going to have to dress down for stealing her luggage, Denni was left speechless to find Hart Hammond holding her suitcase, wearing a broad grin.

"This yours?" Hart asked, setting down the suitcase and pulling out the handle so it would be easy to roll. He had a large leather bag slung over his shoulder, and wore a black sports jacket with a white cotton shirt, pressed jeans and polished boots. A tan cowboy hat finished off his look of well-to-do rancher.

Dumbly nodding her head, Denni watched as Hart started rolling her bag toward the car rental area.

Gathering her wits, she caught up to him and placed a hand on his arm, stopping him.

"What are you doing here?" she asked, wondering if her boys had somehow talked Hart into watching over her. She hadn't seen him on the plane, though, so she couldn't be sure why he was in Tucson.

"I had some business to take care of and realized I'd be here the same days you were. My plane got in just a few minutes ago, so I thought I'd look for you before I left," Hart said. He was telling the truth, mostly. Deciding the Thompson boys were right and their mother shouldn't travel alone, he quickly found out her schedule from Travis, made his travel plans, and arranged to check on a few investments he had in the area so he could honestly say he was in town on business.

He didn't want Denni to feel like he was keeping an eye on her, so he'd gone to the trouble of finding a hotel near hers, hoping she would think it was a coincidence and nothing more. He also flew on a different airline to keep from raising any suspicion, making sure his flight and hers would land close to the same time.

For someone who was only interested in Denni as a friend, Hart realized he was going to an incredible amount of trouble to spend time with her.

He kept telling himself he was just doing a good deed for people who had become his friends. Although Denni thought she was quite the world traveler, Hart bet she never took a trip alone. If her husband had been anything like her watchful boys, she likely was never out of his sight when they traveled.

Hart planned to give her plenty of space and freedom while still keeping an eye out for her well-being.

When he told Travis he had business in Tucson close to the same dates that his mother would be in town, the young man looked so relieved Hart nearly laughed. Recalling how Travis had asked, if it wasn't any bother, if he could check up on his mom a time or two, Hart readily agreed. He'd do better than check up on her. He'd spend the next several days enjoying her company.

Thoughts of having the beautiful woman with the sparkling blue eyes and teasing smile all to himself for a few days made Hart's blood zing a little faster through his veins. Reminding himself he was just watching out for Denni because he wanted to be her friend, he looped her arm around his and smiled at her.

"I've got a rental car lined up. May I give you a ride to your hotel?" Hart asked, walking to the rental car agency he'd used to reserve an SUV.

"I don't want you to go out of your way," Denni said, stepping back while Hart signed papers and took the keys for the vehicle from the attendant.

"Where are you staying?" Hart asked, knowing full well her hotel was only a block from his. She gave him the name and address and he grinned. "I think my hotel isn't far from there. Let's go find out."

Denni was hard pressed to believe she'd run into Hart at the airport or that he'd be doing business in Tucson the same days she was in town. She still couldn't help but wonder if one of her boys talked him into keeping tabs on her.

"What sort of business brought you to town?" she asked, curious to see if he was telling her the truth. When Hart mentioned the two companies in which he owned stock, Denni looked impressed and nodded her head.

They kept up a lively conversation while Hart drove to Denni's hotel and carried her bag inside. Once she had her room key, he knew offering to escort her to her room would raise a red flag, so instead he invited her to have dinner with him.

"I'd love to Hart, but I've already promised a couple of friends that I'd dine with them this evening. Can I take a rain check?" Denni asked, sounding hopeful.

"Tomorrow night?" Hart asked, hoping she'd say yes. He couldn't remember the last time he'd been on a date when he'd done the asking because he wanted to, not because someone had talked him into it or the woman had asked him.

Seeming to consider his invitation for a moment, Denni finally smiled at him and nodded her head. "Tomorrow would be great. Just tell me where to meet you."

"How about I pick you up here? Around six?" Hart asked, backing a step toward the door.

"Perfect. See you then and enjoy your day tomorrow."

Hart backed up another step, right into a bronze statue of a cactus in the lobby. Glad it wasn't real, he offered Denni a sheepish look before he waved and went out the door.

Shaking her head, she went up to her room, amazed at how much she enjoyed being around Hart. They never seemed to lack for things to discuss and he was so easy for her to talk to. Even if she wasn't open to the idea of romance, she did like the notion of having Hart as a friend.

Sleeping in the next morning, Denni ate a leisurely breakfast then took a taxi to the quilt show where she spent the entire day taking notes and snapping photos with her phone, wanting to remember as many details as possible. Expert quilters provided demonstrations and Denni gleaned some shortcuts and tricks from watching them work.

Staring at a quilt featuring red hearts with jagged edges, pieces of red fabric fell into the intricately stitched black fabric that made up the background. Entitled *Broken Hearts,* the quilt was beautiful in a very sad sort of way. She wondered if the person who made it had moved on past their grief.

Examining the detailed stitching, she felt a warm presence beside her and smelled a familiar masculine scent.

Looking up, she caught Hart's gaze and his friendly smile.

"The quilt show? Seriously? I know for a fact you can't possibly have any business here," Denni said, a smile lighting her face and filling her eyes.

"You're right, I don't," Hart said, looking at the quilt Denni had been studying and finding it too melancholy for his liking. "My meeting finished early so I thought I'd come see what a quilt show entailed. I've never been to one before."

"Prepare to be amazed and dazzled by calico cloth and fancy stitches," Denni said in a voice that could have come from a circus ringleader. Hart thought all she needed was a platform to stand on, a top hat with a red cutaway coat, and a megaphone.

Hart laughed and the deep, friendly sound worked its way right into Denni's chest and nudged at the scattered pieces of her heart.

"I can already tell these quilts are works of art, but I don't particularly care for this one," Hart said, pointing to the broken hearts.

"What's wrong with this one?"

"It's sad and mournful. Who wants that hanging on a wall or gracing a guest room bed? People want happy and cheerful in their bedding selections, don't they? Unless, of course, you're into that whole vampire, Goth stuff. If you start painting your nails black and wearing leather, I'm telling your boys."

Denni laughter spilled out, encouraging Hart's silliness.

"Or maybe you could open The Heartbreak Hotel and each room could offer a desolate theme. You know, like one of the anniversary hotels that have themed rooms, except this would be an evil twin property, walking on the dark side."

Smacking at Hart's arm she shook her head although her smile was big and bright.

"No need to worry," she said, taking one last look at the quilt. "I can relate to the quilter on this project. She is a very talented artist, although I agree it is kind of depressing."

"Someone should make a quilt with hearts on the mend. Couldn't you patch them together somehow?"

Thinking that Hart had a very clever idea for a quilt, Denni jotted down some quick notes before taking his hand and showing him the quilts she liked the best.

An hour later, he was still following her around, asking thoughtful questions and Denni couldn't believe he would really spend his valuable time with her.

"Aren't you bored? Ready to leave?" Denni asked as Hart studied a Bear Paw quilt in shades of blue.

"No, this is fascinating," Hart said, truly interested in how many different quilt patterns there seemed to be. He'd seen dozens of variations on what Denni called "basics" like the Flying Dutchman and Log Cabin. Besides, being at the quilt show meant spending time with Denni and that was his main objective anyway.

"You're kidding me," Denni said, sure Hart was mocking her. Looking at him, she saw only sincerity.

Drew's eyes had glazed over and he only listened half-heartedly anytime she mentioned fabrics, quilting, or crafts. He would have rather done just about anything than go to a quilt show with her, yet here was Hart, walking along asking questions like he really cared.

"No kidding, Denni. This really is like walking through an art gallery only the medium is fabric."

Deciding not to question him further, they made one more tour through the displays before Denni suggested they leave.

"Are you sure?" Hart asked, wanting her to take as long as she liked to see the quilts.

"Positive," Denni said, feeling a growing thrill of anticipation at having dinner with Hart. "I'd like a little time to change before dinner, if you still want to go this evening."

"I haven't changed my mind and I may have even made us a reservation," Hart said with a smile that made Denni's stomach flutter. Ignoring it, she walked with Hart out the door and let him lead the way to his rented vehicle.

Hart dropped her off at the hotel and told her he'd be back at six, just a little more than an hour away.

Hurrying to her room, Denni gave in to her desire to dress up and started by taking a quick shower. Blow-drying her hair with her head tipped upside down to get the most volume, she finished styling her hair, applied makeup, and slipped on a stylish black dress with moderate heels.

Digging in her suitcase for a dressy swing coat in a metallic shade of blue, she put a few essentials into a little handbag and gave herself one more glance. Applying a spritz of perfume, she refused to admit she wanted to look nice for Hart. She also didn't dwell on the fact she packed clothes suitable for a date or an evening out when she didn't have anything of the sort planned.

Snapping her watch in place, she hurried out the door and down to the lobby. She stepped off the elevator to find Hart seated by a big rock fireplace, reading a newspaper. He'd left off the cowboy hat, wearing a dark gray sports coat with a burgundy shirt and dark jeans along with a freshly shined pair of black boots. Denni was certain he looked even more handsome than he had just an hour before when he dropped her off.

Hearing footsteps, he looked up and quickly dropped the paper, coming to his feet.

"Wow, Denni, you look amazing," Hart said, subduing his desire to whistle and drool a little. For a woman who'd given birth to three strapping boys, was in her mid-fifties, and liked to sit quilting, she somehow managed to stay in shape. Really great shape.

The simple black dress she wore was understated, yet highlighted her nice curves. Her skin looked so soft Hart longed to run his fingers up the side of her arm and down her slender neck. If it wasn't for the laugh lines that bracketed her eyes, he would have sworn she was a woman in her thirties. A very attractive, very desirable woman who had captured his interest like none had in a very long time.

Denni was a bright spot of sunshine and Hart felt drawn to both her warmth and her light. He couldn't explain it, didn't want to examine it, and decided to soak up every minute of it he could while it lasted.

He watched her blush under his perusal and took the coat from her hand, holding it so she could slip it on. The dark metallic blue made her eyes glimmer and Hart suddenly wanted to fall right into their depths.

Clearing his throat, he held out his arm and tipped his head toward the door. "Ready to paint the town red?"

"Why not? Let's go," Denni said with a sassy grin, walking out the door.

><><

Tying her shoe as her phone rang, Denni frowned when she saw the caller ID but answered it anyway.

"Mama, exactly what is going on down there?" Travis asked in a tone that Denni didn't particularly like.

"Nothing is going on. What's going on at home?" Denni asked, sounding innocent. Other than brief conversations to let her kids know she'd arrived in one piece, she avoided talking to them on the phone. She sent each of the boys a text message every evening, letting them know she had survived the day and was back in the safety of her room. It had been nice to get away and just be Denni Thompson instead of a mother, grandmother, friend, storeowner, or anything else.

Flying out in the morning, Denni planned to make the most of her last day in town and Hart had invited her to spend the day with him. Again.

After dinner Friday evening at a fun restaurant with the best Mexican food she'd ever had, they strolled through some shops, enjoying both the architecture of the buildings and getting to know one another.

Hart took her to see Mission San Xavier Del Bac south of the city yesterday. They both enjoyed walking through the national historic landmark built in the late 1700s.

Denni had no idea the White Dove of the Desert, as the mission was called, even existed. Constructed from low-fired clay brick, stone, and lime mortar, the white color of the mission stood in stark contrast to the earthy tones of the surrounding desert. Touring through the church's interior filled with statuary and murals, Denni briefly felt like she'd stepped back in time to the eighteenth century.

Leaving the mission, Hart took her on a drive in the desert, pointing out various types of cactus. Denni was thrilled when he stopped at a museum that highlighted both the animal and plant life of the region. She giggled like a schoolgirl in the hummingbird aviary and hid her face against Hart's sleeve as they went past the reptile exhibit. She couldn't remember the last time she'd felt so young and carefree.

After that, they went out for a casual dinner and then rode a trolley car from downtown to the university district and back again.

Today, he was taking her out to the Old Tucson movie studio and, if they had time left, promised to drive her to a mall to pick up a few gifts for her family. She'd had more fun with Hart in the past few days than she'd had for years. Refusing to think about the reasons why, she decided to enjoy exploring the town with a very attractive and amusing companion.

There was no way she was letting Travis dampen her spirits. A whole day of fun was ahead of her and she planned to make the most of it.

"Mama, we've hardly heard from you since you left. Are you okay? Is everything fine? Do you need one of us to come get you?" Travis asked. Trent was generally the one who worried more about her safekeeping, but Travis had definitely matured in the past several months, especially since he married Tess. If he didn't watch it, he'd end up as bossy as his oldest brother.

"Baby, I'm fine. Stop worrying. I'm having a great time and I'll be home tomorrow. Give everyone my love and I'll talk to you when I get home. Thanks for calling. Bye, bye."

Denni disconnected the call before Travis could say anything further. Smiling, she grabbed her purse, put her sunglasses on her head and hurried out of her room to meet Hart for breakfast.

Hours later, as they sat eating lunch, she finally asked him how he became so familiar with the area.

"When I was riding bulls, Tucson was one of the rodeos on my circuit. I loved it the first time I came here. There's just something about the town that still captures the old southwest. Years later, I invested in a few businesses here. It gives me an excuse to come to town once a year or so," Hart said, leaning back in his chair and watching Denni.

She looked so young and happy today, just seeing her made him smile. She wore sneakers with rolled up jeans and a bright pink shirt with a pink and white striped hooded sweatshirt.

"I can't begin to thank you for showing me around. Left on my own, I would probably have gone somewhere like the mall then holed up in my room with a good book," Denni said, grateful to Hart for making her trip so enjoyable. "I'm sure you had better things to do than be stuck with me the last couple of days."

"Nope. I've enjoyed every minute of it," Hart said, studying Denni as an idea popped into his head. "Hey, I just thought of a way to keep the meddling well-meaning people from tormenting us quite so much."

At Denni's quizzical look, he continued. "I've got a proposition for you."

Here was what Denni had been waiting for - some inappropriate suggestion, something that would show Hart's true colors as something less than a gentleman. From what she'd seen so far, he was just too good to be true. Funny, smart, successful, kind, and gorgeous, she knew there had to be something wrong with him that she just hadn't yet discovered.

"A proposition," Denni said, taking a sip of her iced tea. "I don't know that I like the sound of a proposition. It sounds…"

"Sleazy, illicit, full of debauchery," Hart teased. His broad grin was infectious and Denni found herself smiling at him despite her reservations.

"What I had in mind was a way to keep your family and my friends from continually trying to set us up on dates and play matchmaker."

Interested, Denni leaned forward in her chair. "Go on."

"What if you and I agree to escort each other to events and activities, to be seen together just enough that people get the idea we're dating, without actually confirming or denying the fact should the question arise.

That way we aren't saying something that isn't true, but we're also saving ourselves from the misguided attempts at matchmaking that seem to go on in Grass Valley."

Denni grabbed Hart's hand and squeezed it, forgetting how the contact of his skin to hers made her heart pound. Pulling back her hand she grinned and gave him a flirty look.

"I think that is a marvelous idea. Absolutely marvelous," Denni said, picking up her glass of tea and holding it up toward Hart. "To your brilliance and a future without meddling matchmakers."

Chapter Five

"There is no charm equal to tenderness of heart."
Jane Austen

Lost in her thoughts as she worked on a quilt block at the sewing machine in her store, Denni didn't hear the bell above the door jingle. Voices rumbled in the background at the counter and she knew unless there was a problem, Amy would take care of the customer.

Since returning from the quilt show, Denni had been inspired to create. Back at her store on Tuesday, she designed a new wall hanging and finished it Wednesday. Today, she started on a quilt for Brice and Bailey's wedding gift. Carefully piecing together the blocks that would form the top, she sewed them while a deep feeling of satisfaction filled her.

Her quilts and crafts brought her such pleasure. Denni sometimes felt guilty that she made a profit from something she loved so much.

"You're either plotting something wicked or having way too much fun making that."

Denni startled at the sound of Hart's rich voice and looked up into his blue eyes, glad to see his smile.

Although they didn't share a flight home from Tucson, he called to make sure she made it back without any problems. She hadn't heard from him since Monday afternoon and assumed he'd grown tired of her company after spending the weekend escorting her around Tucson.

A part of her heart she didn't even think still functioned tripped slightly at the sight of his handsome face and broad shoulders.

"What brings you by today?" Denni tried to sound nonchalant, but she was too eager to know what he was doing in her quilt shop.

"I had a few errands to run and thought I'd swing by to see you," he said, looking at the block she was sewing. "What are you working on?"

"I'm making a quilt for Brice and Bailey's wedding. I got an idea for a design and wanted to get started on it," Denni said, holding up the partially sewn square.

"Are you making up a pattern?" Hart asked, having learned a few things about quilting from the show.

"I'm using two patterns, Thistle Bloom and Oak Leaf, and combining them," Denni said, showing Hart the blocks she'd already made. "Oak Leaf seemed particularly fitting for Brice since that is one of his favorite woods to work with. Speaking of working wood, how's he coming on your furniture projects?"

"Considering he's barely back on both feet, he's made good progress." Hart had no idea how the young man accomplished as much as he had when he'd been healing from an unfortunate accident involving his leg and a chainsaw right before Thanksgiving. Brice made beautiful hand-crafted furniture and Hart hired him to make several pieces for his house.

"He's a go-getter for sure," Denni said, thinking of the young man, just days apart in age from Travis, who had always been like a son to her. "I'm glad he's feeling well enough to get back to his work full-time. Trent and Lindsay have big plans for him to help with furniture for the nursery and the new rooms they're adding to the house."

"He won't lack for business, that's for sure," Hart said. Clearing his throat, he held out a beautifully wrapped square box to Denni. "I wanted to give you this. It's just a little something to help you remember your trip to Tucson."

"You didn't need to bring me a gift, but I won't refuse it," Denni admitted, removing the ribbon and ripping off the wrapping paper. Unless she lost all function of her memory, she'd never forget the days she spent with Hart in Tucson. They'd been some of the best she'd experienced in a very long time.

Opening the lid of the box, she dug through layers of tissue paper to pull out a small hummingbird figurine that looked so realistic she caught her breath, waiting for it to fly away. Gently running her finger over a delicate wing, she held it up to better see the detail.

"Oh, Hart, this is beautiful. Absolutely beautiful," Denni raved, getting to her feet and throwing her arms around the thoughtful man, the figurine held carefully in her hand. When he wrapped her in his arms and hugged her back, Denni felt light headed. Her boys were good to give hugs but it was something else entirely to be held against Hart's solid chest, his strong arms around her, his heady scent filling her senses. Frightened by the intensity of her feelings, Denni stepped back and studied the figurine.

"I know you enjoyed the hummingbird exhibit at the desert museum and when I saw this it made me think of you," Hart said, shoving his hands in his coat pockets to keep from pulling her to his chest again. It felt so right to have his arms around her, he wanted to hold on and not let go.

"You've got to be the sweetest man ever, as Cass would say," Denni said, placing the hummingbird on the counter and looking around. Amy had mysteriously disappeared into the back room, leaving Denni alone with Hart in the store. She wasn't sure in her current frame of mind that was a good idea. She might give in to her desire to hug him again. Thoughts of kissing his strong jaw or that darn cleft in his chin filled her mind and she wanted to stamp her foot in irritation. She was not, under any circumstance, going to allow herself to get involved with a man. Especially not the tenderhearted cowboy who brought her hummingbird figurines and made her feel young again.

"I don't know about that," Hart said, looking at Denni with such an intense gaze of longing, she began to feel overheated. "Anyway, I wanted you to have it."

"It's perfect, Hart, and I love it."

Tipping his hat, Hart walked toward the door and was about to leave when Denni called out to him. "I'm spending the weekend at the ranch. If you'd like, I could come by your house and talk about the quilt you want me to make, if you're still interested."

"That'd be great, Denni. Give me a call Saturday when you're ready to come over and I'll be waiting to give you a grand tour." He tipped his hat and walked outside, letting in a breeze of frigid air that did nothing to cool Denni's elevated temperature.

Watching Hart saunter down the sidewalk toward his pickup, Denni felt her cheeks heat as she thought about how well he filled out his jeans, how good he looked in his boots, hat and leather coat. He could easily pass for someone several years younger than his fifty-two years. She felt a hot twist of jealousy when she noticed a couple of women walk past Hart then turn around and give him a second glance.

Marching back to her sewing machine, she tried to lose herself in her project, but found her gaze kept returning to the colorful hummingbird on the counter.

Leaving work for the evening, she carefully rewrapped the little bird and took it home with her. Placing it on a shelf where Cass wouldn't be able to reach it, she sat curled up by her fireplace, sipping a cup of tea and listening to soft music playing in the background, helpless to ignore her growing feelings for Hart.

><><

"Trey, may I borrow your truck for a little while?" Denni asked as they finished eating lunch. Arriving at the ranch soon as Cady washed the last of the breakfast dishes, Denni spent the morning playing with Cass, as well as visiting with Cady and Tess. Lindsay was home sick with a cold, and Bailey was at the Morgan ranch with Brice.

Looking up from the cookie he was dunking in his coffee, Trey nodded his head. "Sure, Mom. Is there somewhere I can take you? Do you need help with anything?"

"No. I need to run an errand and I'm afraid with all this mud my car might get bogged down," Denni said. The temperature had warmed a few days ago melting the snow and churning up a big mess on the unpaved roads around Grass Valley. Denni knew the road to Hart's house wasn't paved and she couldn't remember if it had gravel. Trey's big four-wheel drive pickup would get her through the worst of the mud with no problem.

"It's pretty soupy out there for January," Travis said, leaning back from his empty plate and dropping his arm around Tess. "Weather forecast says we're in for another hard freeze and more snow next week, though."

"I'd be perfectly happy if spring arrived early this year," Cady said, thinking about another month or two of being cooped up in the house. She loved time spent outdoors when she wasn't busy cooking or cleaning, but being from Seattle, she wasn't used to temperatures that hovered in the teens for days on end.

"Now why would you want to wish away this perfect weather?" Trey asked, turning his intense blue gaze on his wife.

"What's it perfect for, exactly, boss-man?" Cady asked, trying to think of anything redeeming about freezing temperatures.

"It's perfect for hot chocolate, cuddling by the fire and keeping each other warm," Trey said, giving Cady a heat-filled gaze that it made her face flush.

"You're incorrigible," Cady said, shooting Trey a narrowed glare.

"So you've mentioned before," Trey said, waggling his eyebrow at her. "I must be doing something wrong if I haven't made it to 'completely impossible' with your insults yet."

"Oh, you!" Cady got to her feet and gathered up a stack of dirty dishes to take into the kitchen.

"Where are you going, Mom?" Trey asked, watching his wife busy herself in the kitchen.

"To see a friend," Denni said, studying the snowflake pattern in the tablecloth Cady recently made.

"Mom and Dad are gone today. They went to Portland to see Ben and meet his new girlfriend," Tess said, knowing Denni always liked to visit with her parents. Michele and Mike Morgan had been best friends with Drew and Denni. After Drew's death, Denni was even closer to them. They'd helped her through several really rough times and she treasured their friendship.

"I didn't know Ben broke up with the last one. Wasn't her name Sheena?" Cady said as she refilled coffee cups and sat back down at the table.

"You're two girls behind," Tess said with a smile. "It's hard to keep track of that brother of mine and Brice has been teasing him relentlessly about this new girl. She seems nice and quite normal."

"Well, that's good news," Trey said, turning the conversation back around to Denni. He was like a bloodhound tracking a scent once something piqued his interest. "Was that were you were going? Over to the Running M Ranch?"

"No, honey, it wasn't. If it's an imposition for me to borrow your truck, I'll just take my car," Denni said, irritated at her offspring for being so inquisitive. She was even more irritated when she realized they inherited that particular trait from her.

Stuffing his hand in the pocket of his jeans, Trey fished out a ring of keys and set it on the table next to Denni's plate. "Take the truck. Have fun. Go off-roading in the hills if you want, just don't bring it home empty."

Denni grinned at her son, realizing the phrase "bring it home empty" was one Drew always said to the boys when they wanted to borrow a vehicle. "Thanks, honey."

"Do you want some company?" Tess asked, thinking Denni might like someone to chat with on the way to wherever she was going.

"No!" she said sharply, causing every head at the table to turn her direction. Reaching across the table, she patted Tess' hand. "I meant no thanks, sugarplum. It's a quick errand and I won't be gone long."

"Where was it you said you're going?" Trey asked, trying to get his mother to reveal her plans.

"Yeah, Mama. What's all the secrecy about?" Travis asked then gave his brother a nod before turning to Denni with a teasing grin. "You got a hot date you don't want to tell us about?"

"Just leave your mother alone, you two hooligans," Cady said, looking pointedly at Trey.

"What's a hot date, Grammy? Are you going somewhere warm? I'm tired of the cold. Can I come, too?" Cass asked. She had been sitting so quietly listening to the adults, they forgot she was still at the table.

Denni glowered at her two boys and let out an exasperated sigh.

Before Denni could answer, Cady asked Cass if she'd had a chance to show Denni her latest fairy drawing. Cass ran off to her room to find it, forgetting all about Denni's hot date.

An hour later, after Trey and Travis took Cass out to the barn with them while Tess and Cady discussed plans for a bridal shower for Bailey, Denni quietly took Trey's keys and made her way out the door.

With the coast clear, she started the big pickup and headed down the drive, realizing it had been quite a while since she'd driven a stick-shift. At the end of the long driveway, where it connected with the highway, Denni called Hart to let him know she was on her way.

Pulling up at his house a short while later, Denni was relieved to discover Hart did indeed have a nicely-packed gravel driveway that was free of too much mud.

Carefully getting out of the pickup so she wouldn't get the gumbo on her clothes, Denni walked up the porch steps. The door swung open before she could knock and she looked into the smiling face of Hart. He was so handsome, Denni suddenly felt the urge to run her fingers through his sandy hair and lean into his broad, strong chest.

"Hi, there. I'm glad you could come over today," Hart said, opening the door wider and motioning for her to walk inside.

Wiping her feet on the doormat, Denni stepped inside the foyer and looked around. Hart helped her off with her coat and hung it in a closet then, placing a hand to her back, escorted her inside an impressive room with a huge rock fireplace highlighted by a thick timber mantle. A gas fire cast an inviting glow around the room, furnished simply with comfortable-looking pieces placed in a welcoming configuration.

"This is amazing, Hart," Denni said, running her hand along the back of a brown leather couch. "I love that everything groups around the fire."

"Thanks. I know I probably should have gone with a traditional fireplace, but the thought of chopping wood, hauling ash, and dealing with wood smoke didn't appeal to me, so I went with gas."

"I think it's great," Denni said, stepping near the fire that put out a surprising amount of heat. "It's perfect for a cold afternoon like today."

"I'm glad you like it," Hart said, watching the firelight play off Denni's features and picturing her there when the evening shadows would enhance the fire's glow on her creamy skin. Shutting down those thoughts before they went any further, he held his hand out in the direction of his kitchen. "Want to see the rest of the house?"

"I'd love to."

Denni admired not only the house, but the excellent taste Hart exhibited with his furnishings and décor. Done in a mixture of log walls, wood accents and sheetrock, she thought the house was remarkable. The only thing that could improve it was a few feminine touches, but she wisely kept that thought to herself.

She smiled to see the quilt Hart purchased from her on a guest room bed. The colors in the quilt blended perfectly with the tones of the walls and furniture.

The last room they entered was Hart's master suite. Denni had to keep her jaw from dropping as they walked in the room.

"My gracious, Hart. This is fabulous."

A massive bed made of logs sat at an angle in front of a bank of windows. A rock fireplace filled one wall with a cozy seating arrangement in front of it. Two nightstands and a chest of drawers matched the bed. She walked through an adjoining door into a spa-like bathroom with one of the biggest soaking tubs she'd ever seen. It could easily fit two people with room to spare. A big walk-in closet was attached to the bathroom. Peeking in the door when Hart turned on the light, she noticed his clothes only filled a small portion of the closet.

"You need to go shopping," Denni said, looking at Hart with a jaunty grin.

"Why's that?" he asked, following her back into the bedroom.

"It's just wrong to have all that room in a closet and not take advantage of it. You obviously need more clothes to fill it up. Believe me, I'd have no problem utilizing all that space," Denni said, taking a tape measure and small notepad out of her pocket, ready to get down to the business of planning Hart's custom quilt.

Struck with the thought of seeing Denni's clothes sharing his closet, her golden head on the pillow next to his, her vitality and bright light filling his home, Hart felt his blood surge in his veins. He didn't want to have feelings for the beautiful woman. He didn't plan to become so enraptured with her teasing smile, her sparkling eyes, or her glorious laugh. He had no intention of ever feeling this way about another woman, but the feelings for her were there and they were very real.

How had this happened? He spent twenty-some years successfully avoiding falling for a woman. Hart assumed his heart had been so thoroughly destroyed, he wouldn't ever have to worry about feeling anything again.

Now here he was, wanting to kiss Denni so badly his chest hurt, his lips ached to be pressed to hers, and he could barely keep from reaching out and losing himself in her soft sweetness.

The realization made him catch his breath and, at the same time, feel somewhat woozy.

Yanking his thoughts back together, Hart noticed Denni was studying him, concerned.

"Are you okay?"

"I'm fine," he said, pasting on a smile. "Tell me what you need measured and I can hold one end of your tape."

He helped her record the measurements needed, they discussed colors, and Denni asked him if he had a pattern in mind.

When he said no, she rattled off some ideas, but Hart shook his head.

"Let's go to my office and you can point out some suggestions online if it's all the same to you. I don't remember any of the names or designs from the quilt show, except that ridiculous broken hearted one," Hart said, taking her elbow in his hand as they walked down the stairs and escorting her to his office.

Hart made her sit down in his big leather office chair behind a hulking desk that Brice recently completed for him. Running her hand across the smooth wood, Denni felt a rush of pride at the beautiful furniture the young man crafted.

"Brice did a nice job," Hart said, noticing Denni admiring the desk. "I can't believe such a talented artist lives here in Grass Valley."

"We can't either," Denni said, grinning. "If he ever gets caught up on all his other orders, I've got a few things I'd like him to make for me."

"From the sound of things, you'll have to get in line but I imagine he'd make anything you wanted as quickly as he could if you asked," Hart said, bringing up a search engine on his computer. "Why don't you show me some ideas and I'll pick something I like."

Denni brought up a page filled with images of quilts in a variety of designs. It didn't take Hart long to point to a photo.

"What's that pattern?"

"Lone Star," Denni said, intrigued by the thought that Hart liked the design. It had always been one of her favorites.

"That's the one," Hart said, liking the name as well as the design. The idea of a lone star, something strong yet all alone, hit home with him. He'd been alone far too long.

"Lone Star it is, then. If we incorporate the blue, tan, burgundy and green colors we discussed, I think it would work well in your room and be a nice way to highlight your wonderful bed. You'd be able to use any accent colors you wanted with it."

"Sounds great," Hart said, grinning as Denni pointed to the screen and offered more suggestions. He could care less what covered his bed, but somehow the thought of sleeping under something made by Denni's two lovely hands warmed him more than a quilt likely ever would.

"I've got a few projects I need to finish first, but I should be able to start on your quilt in a few weeks. When do you need to have it done?"

"Whenever you get it finished," Hart said, finding it hard to concentrate when Denni looked up at him with her blue eyes glimmering in the fading afternoon light.

"Oh," Denni said, wondering if Hart knew just exactly how appealing he looked leaning against the edge of the desk, strong arms folded across his solid chest and booted feet crossed at the ankle, highlighting not just the length of his legs, but also the muscles of his thighs. Trying to corral her thoughts, she jotted down a few more notes, got to her feet and tucked the notebook in her pocket. "I better get going or the kids will likely think I've gotten lost. Apparently, I've reached the age of the senile and decrepit."

"We wouldn't want them to send out a search party, especially in their delusional state, thinking their mother is ready for a retirement home," Hart said, chuckling as Denni walked back to the entry foyer. Hart took her coat from the closet and helped her put it on before grabbing a jacket and shoving his arms in the sleeves as he walked her outside and down the steps.

Denni was part-way to the pickup when she stopped and looked out at his pasture. About twenty head of the oddest-looking cattle she'd ever seen made her come to a complete stop and stare in fascination.

"What are those, Hart?" Denni asked, forgetting about hurrying home or the mud as she walked over to the fence to peer at cattle unlike any she'd seen before.

"They're Belgian Blue cattle," Hart said, amused as he always was when people gawked at his herd. "I take it you've never seen one before?"

"No, I haven't," Denni said, studying the animals before her, trying to decide if she could even think of a point of reference in which to compare them. Their hindquarters almost reminded her of a well-fed pig.

"They originated in Belgium and were bred to be double-muscled, which gives them their odd appearance. They have the ability to convert their feed into lean muscle resulting in reduced fat content. Some studies show their meat has less fat, cholesterol, and calories than baked chicken," Hart said, pointing to a thickly muscled cow. "It tastes pretty good, too. If you'd like to try it sometime, I could throw some steaks on the barbecue. You'd be surprised by how tender and tasty the meat is."

"I just might take you up on that," Denni said, looking over the cattle with interest. "How many head do you run?"

"You're looking at it," Hart said, placing a boot on the bottom pole and resting his arms on top of the fence. "I've got just enough to play with and keep me in beef."

"Smart man," Denni said, turning to look at Hart with a smile. He put his foot back on the ground and took a step closer to Denni. Goosebumps rippled up her arms and she felt her knees wobble at the look of blatant desire in Hart's eyes, reflecting what she was sure was in her own. They stood lost in each other for a moment before Denni slammed the door on her emotions and stepped back. "I really better run or the boys will ground me."

"I'd like to see them try," Hart said, holding the pickup door while Denni climbed in.

"Thanks for the tour. You've got such a beautiful home," Denni said, starting the truck and shutting the door. She gave a quick wave then disappeared down Hart's drive, leaving him standing in the cold, wondering how one went about pursuing a woman who obviously didn't want to be caught.

Chapter Six

*"A good head and a good heart
are always a formidable combination."*
Nelson Mandela

Knocking on her mother's apartment door, Denni wondered if she'd caught the elderly woman napping or visiting down the hall with one of her many friends.

Glancing at her watch, she knew her mom should be up and about since it was close to time for dinner.

"Mama?" she said, knocking on the door again. She started to turn the knob when the door opened and Ester Nordon smiled at her youngest daughter with brilliant aquamarine eyes, yet undimmed by age.

"Hello, Denni. What are you up to?" Ester asked, opening the door wider for Denni to enter her apartment at the assisted living facility where she'd resided for the past few years. With a nice sitting area, a small kitchen space and a comfortable bedroom, Ester was happy living at the center where she had friends, someone to cook her meals and do her laundry, as well as nursing care available around the clock, should she need it. Between planned activities, a game room, a library, and the ability for Ester to come and go when she pleased, she was enjoying what she referred to as her twilight years.

"It's been a few days since I stopped by and I wanted to make sure you were fine," Denni said, removing her coat and scarf, draping them over a chair at Ester's small kitchen table.

"I'm pretty good for a crazy old lady," Ester said, grinning at her most headstrong child as she sat in her rocking chair and set it in motion. She studied Denni as she took a seat in an armchair and looked around the apartment to make sure Ester was not in need of anything. "You don't have to check on me, you know. The telephone does work and I am still capable of caring for myself."

"I know, Mama, but I wanted to make sure you're fine and to do that I have to see for myself. You tend to gloss right over any problems."

"Oh, fiddle," Ester said, waving a hand dismissively at Denni. "You worry entirely too much. If you put half as much effort into your personal life you wouldn't have so much time to pester me. You don't see your brother or sisters here checking on me several times a week."

"No, I don't, and we both know they would if they lived in the same state," Denni said, rolling her eyes. "What's got you so sassy today? Someone pour vinegar in your prune juice?"

Ester laughed. "Of course not, you nut. No one would do that in the first place and besides, you know I can't stand prune juice. It's disgusting. Absolutely disgusting."

"Then what's the problem? You twist your pantyhose when you put them on today? Sit on your knitting needle?"

Ester shook her head at her golden-haired daughter. Denni was as silly and fun loving as she'd been as a child. She and Graham didn't know how they'd ever tame the wild, frolicsome girl. Then Drew came along and Denni grew into the person she was meant to be under his tender care and loving guidance.

When Denni lost Drew, Ester wondered if she'd ever hear her laugh again or see her smile. It took a long time for Denni to get to the point where she could tease and laugh without feeling guilty at finding a little happiness.

her mother's lap. Ester brushed Denni's hair back from her face with a cool, soft hand. "Sweetheart, everyone knows you loved Drew. There's a big part of your heart that will always belong just to him, but that doesn't mean you aren't allowed to have feelings for someone else. You've mourned Drew long past the time he would have wanted you to. He wouldn't want you to be alone and sad. Drew would want you to find happiness and love again. You know that's what he'd tell you."

"I know, Mama, but it's so hard to let go. I feel so guilty for even giving a second glance to another man, like I'm cheating on Drew."

Ester chuckled. "Honey, you'd have to be blind, deaf and dumb not to give a second, third, and possibly a fourth glance to someone like Hart Hammond. Why, if I was thirty years younger, I'd give you a run for your money."

Denni sat up and gave her mother a watery smile. Ester grabbed a tissue from the box by her chair and dabbed at Denni's wet cheeks.

"Don't feel guilty. You still have a lot of living ahead of you and Drew wouldn't want you to face it alone. Maybe Hart's the one, maybe there's someone else out there, but don't close the door on love before you even find out if it's knocking."

Although Denni thought she'd moved on with her life, Ester had long thought that her daughter was really just killing time. She went through the motions of life, but from what she could see, Denni had given up on really living. Until now. Some vital spark that had been missing since Drew died was now flickering in Denni for all to see.

"What about you?" Denni asked, taking her mother's aged hand in hers and giving it a gentle squeeze. "Why didn't you remarry after Daddy died?"

"For one thing, your father passed away not that many years ago. We had a long and very happy life together. I'm in my eighties and way past the age to be thinking about love and romance. Some of the gals here would tell you different, but I don't view the facility as a swinging singles joint, full of eligible bachelors. I see it more as a peaceful place to live out the rest of my days. There's still plenty of love in my heart, but I'm short on years to use it up."

"What if you met someone?" Denni asked, looking up at her mother's dear face. "Someone who made your heart pound and your stomach feel full of butterflies, who made you want things you thought you'd never have again - would you give them a chance?"

"I'd grab his hand, plant a big ol' kiss on his lips and drag him down the aisle so fast he wouldn't know what hit him," Ester said, giving her daughter a feisty grin. "Does Hart make you feel like that?"

"Yes, he does," Denni said, getting a dreamy look on her face. "He's so sweet and kind and gentle. I think he could buy and sell the entire community of Grass Valley three-times over yet he acts like a regular guy. According to the kids, he's provided new playground equipment at the school, is making repairs at the church, and is always ready to lend a hand to someone in need."

"Sounds like he might just have that rare combination of a good head and a good heart," Ester observed, patting Denni's hand.

"He does, Mama, although I keep waiting for the 'but.'"

"The butt? As in posterior?" Ester asked, confused. "From what I saw, his is quite remarkable."

"Good gracious, Mama. Not that kind of butt. I mean the 'but' as in he's dangerously handsome, funny, smart, strong, giving, and perfectly wonderful, but…there has to be something wrong with him. Why else would he still be single? Why hasn't someone else snatched him up?"

"Maybe he didn't want to be snatched. Ever think of that?" Ester asked, grabbing Denni's chin in her hand and looking her full in the face. "Drew's been gone almost eight years. In that time, how many proposals of marriage or propositions have you had? How many men would have gladly snatched you up, Denni?"

"Several, but I wasn't interested. I didn't want a relationship. Not when my heart hurt so badly," Denni said, realizing since meeting Hart the huge aching chasm in her heart hurt less and less with each passing day.

"That's my point. Maybe he's got a few hurts of his own he's trying to work through. Has he mentioned a wife or any family in his past?"

"No," Denni said with a sigh, getting up and regaining her seat in the chair. "He doesn't seem to want to talk about his past. He jokes about his days in the rodeo and talks about building his business, but he hasn't ever said why he quit riding bulls, how he came to own all the gas stations and he never, ever mentions any family or past relationships."

"Give him time. When he's ready, he'll share the details you need to know," Ester said, setting her chair back in motion. "Don't be so afraid to try out a new relationship, Denni. It's not like you're making a commitment just by going on a date or two. Spend some time with the man, get to know him, see if you could envision spending the next thirty or so years with him. The answer might surprise you if you'll just keep an open mind and heart. In the meantime, though, I think you should see if he's as good a kisser as he looks like he'd be. Talk to one of your girls if you need some pointers. All newly married, I'm sure they could give you some good ideas."

"Mama, you are impossible," Denni said, starting to feel better as she smiled at her mother. No wonder her boys were so ornery. She was sure they inherited it straight from their grandmother. "I'm not going to walk up to him and plant one on his lips, luscious as they may be."

"See, there you go. I'd just smack him a good one and worry about the rest of the details later," Ester said, getting to her feet. "Now, why don't you come have dinner with me and you can fill me in on what you do know about hunky Hart."

Shaking her head, Denni took her mother's arm and walked with her toward the dining room. If it was up to her mother, she'd be practically engaged to Hart after the first date, if they ever got around to one.

Sitting at home later that evening, cutting out pieces for Hart's quilt, Denni was drawn from her musings about the conversation she had with her mother when the phone rang. Making one more cut then setting aside her scissors, she hurried to grab the phone before the answering machine picked up.

"Hello," she said, sounding out of breath from her sprint across the room.

"Denni?" a deep male voice she was becoming all too familiar with questioned from the other end of the line.

"Oh, hi, Hart. How are you?" she asked, feeling like a giddy school girl as she leaned against the counter and absently twirled a strand of hair around her finger.

"I'm just fine? Are you okay?" Hart liked the slightly breathy way Denni answered the phone. It definitely kicked all his senses into high gear.

"I'm great. Just sitting here working on cutting out pieces for your quilt," Denni said, wondering why Hart was calling. She hadn't spoken with him for a few days, although he had sent her a couple of text messages, just saying hello and asking how things were at the quilt shop.

"I told you I'm not in any hurry," he said, wondering if she wanted to rush to finish the quilt so she wouldn't have to talk to him anymore. If that was the case, he'd order one for every bedroom in his house and when they were finished, he'd move on to wall hangings. She could make quilts for his horses if that's what it took to keep in contact with her.

"I know, but I'm excited to get started on it. I finished the quilt for Brice and Bailey as well as another one for Trent and Lindsay's baby. Your quilt was next on my project list."

"Thanks. I know you'll do an amazing job with it," Hart said, thinking many of Denni's creations were like works of art. "I was calling to talk about something we discussed when we were in Tucson."

"Oh, what's that?" Denni said, wondering which particular thing Hart was referencing. They spent days doing nothing but talking and sight-seeing.

"About pretending to be a couple. With Valentine's Day coming up soon, I've already been asked three times just today if I'd go out on blind dates with friends of some well-meaning matchmakers. I'd really like to be able to tell them I already have plans with someone special. I don't know if anyone is trying to set you up, but I thought if we declared our intention to go out on a date that evening, they might leave us alone." Hart could care less about the matchmakers and had already turned them down, but it gave him a great excuse to try to talk Denni into a date.

"As a matter of fact, a couple of my friends have been hounding me relentlessly. I think your idea is sound. Did you have something specific in mind?"

"If you wouldn't mind coming here, I'd be happy to cook some steaks and make a nice dinner. I don't know about you, but it seems to me restaurants are typically overcrowded, noisy, and not all that fun on Valentine's Day," Hart said, hoping like everything Denni would agree to his plan.

"That sounds nice, actually. Let's call it a date," Denni said, truly pleased at the thought of spending time with Hart. Thinking about what her mother said, especially about his lips, Denni decided to be brave and bold. "You know, I wouldn't want anyone to get the idea we were just going out on a date because it's Valentine's Day. Do you think we should try to get in a couple before then, so people think we're really seeing each other?"

"Absolutely," Hart said, trying to sound serious while pumping his fist in the air and wanting to do a victory dance around his kitchen. That was exactly what he wanted, but thought he'd be pushing his luck to finagle anything beyond a date for Valentine's Day. "Why don't we start by being seen together at Viv's Café. There is no more public place in Grass Valley that I can think of."

"Okay. How about Friday night? I can leave the store early and be there around five-thirty," Denni said, hoping like everything Hart would say yes.

"Perfect. Do you want me to pick you up or just meet you there?"

"Why don't I come to your place? I'll have some fabric swatches and the beginnings of your quilt for you to look at. Since your house is on the way there, it's really no problem to swing by," Denni said, anxious to see Hart's beautiful home again, as well as the undeniably gorgeous man living there.

"You got yourself a date," Hart said, grinning like an idiot and unable to do anything about it. "I'll see you Friday."

"Wonderful. See you then," Denni said and hung up the phone. She sank down on a kitchen chair and stared dreamily into space for a good five minutes, before she pulled herself together and began worrying about what she'd wear, what exactly she'd done. Once the local gossips spied her out on a date, they'd burn up the phone lines with the news.

Taking a deep breath, she decided to stop worrying and allow herself to enjoy whatever came from time spent with Hart.

Chapter Seven

*"A kiss makes the heart young again
and wipes out the years."*

Rupert Brooke

"If you two intended to set all the tongues in Sherman County wagging, I think you nailed it."

Looking up from her bite of salad at the owner of Viv's Café, who also happened to be Cady's aunt and a good friend, Denni set down her fork.

"I'm sure I don't know what you're talking about, Viv," Denni said with a grin Hart thought looked like pure sass.

"Don't you pull that with me, Denni. I know you too well to fall for your innocent act," Viv said with a wink. "What everyone wants to know is what took you two so long? We've had bets down since this one moved to town you two would get together."

"You did not!" Denni said, her face showing every bit of her shock.

Viv laughed and slapped Hart on the shoulder. "Maybe we did, maybe we didn't, but you're here, nonetheless."

Walking back to her kitchen, Hart and Denni watched her go. Denni looked like she'd been caught unawares in the spotlight, while Hart found the entire thing humorous. He was reminded on an almost daily basis that living in a small community could be like living in a fishbowl, with your every move scrutinized. If you got past that one inconvenience, though, he loved it.

Returning his attention to the meatloaf on his plate, he glanced over at Denni who had finally picked up her fork and resumed eating her salad.

He asked her about the quilt shop, her mother, and how Lindsay was feeling since she'd been sick with a bad cold.

In turn, she inquired about how the gas station was doing, what new flavors of coffee he was trying, and if his cows had dropped any calves.

Falling into the comfortable rhythm of the friendship they'd shared in Tucson, they talked and laughed, oblivious to the interested looks cast their direction by patrons of the café.

Finishing their meal, they thanked Viv for a great dinner and Hart paid the bill. Denni tried to talk him into splitting it, but Hart informed her as an old-fashioned kind of guy he would be paying for any meals she ate while they were out together.

His comment made Viv grin as she sent Denni another wink and waved them out the door.

"Thank you, Hart, for dinner. It was fun," Denni said, sliding behind the wheel of her car and pulling out on the highway to take Hart home.

Intending to show him the fabric swatches she brought along as well as the beginnings of the quilt top when she picked him up, he ran out the door before she'd even braked to a stop in front of his house, ready to go to dinner.

Now, parking in his circular drive in front of the wide porch steps, she turned off the car and opened her door.

"Coming in for a while?" Hart asked, his grin so broad it reminded Denni of the Cheshire cat.

"Yes, if you don't mind. I wanted to show you the quilt top and some fabric swatches," Denni said, snagging a bag from the back seat and walking around the car to join Hart where he waited at the base of the steps.

Taking her hand in his, Denni was surprised how natural and right it felt to have his warm, callused palm pressed against hers.

Hart opened the door and pushed it in so Denni could precede him into the house. He flipped a switch and lights glowed softly in the foyer. Helping Denni remove her coat, and then taking his off, he pointed down the hall.

"Let's go sit by the fire," Hart said, leading the way into the main room. Clicking another switch brought the fire roaring to life.

Taking a seat on the couch, Denni looked around, admiring again Hart's beautiful home. She felt the cushion dip as Hart sat beside her. He studied her with a smile, accenting the cleft in his chin that completely enthralled Denni.

Yanking the fabric bag to her lap, she dug around inside, pulling out the swatches and placing them on Hart's leg, since he sat so close it nearly brushed hers.

"What do you think of these colors?" Denni asked, pointing to rich shades of blue, burgundy and green. She took the beginnings of the quilt top from her bag and held it out to Hart. When he stared at it, she pointed out how each individual piece was joined to create the points of the star and how she needed him to decide on the colors before she could precede any farther in the process.

"It's perfect, Denni. I like them all," Hart said, trying to picture how she'd take hundreds of little pieces of fabric and assemble them into something that would no doubt be an amazing work of art.

"Great. I'll cut the rest of the pieces and get down to business," Denni said, stuffing the fabric back in the bag and relaxing against the comfortable couch. She stiffened slightly when she felt Hart's arm go around her shoulders. He began rubbing light circles on her upper arm, where his hand rested, and she found herself enjoying the sensation of his touch, even through the fabric of her blouse.

They sat quietly for a few moments, watching the flames of the fire flicker and dance.

"Can I get you anything? A cup of tea or some coffee?" Hart asked, his voice sounding husky and deep in the quiet of the room. He wished now he'd thought to turn on some music.

"No, I'm fine, but thank you," Denni said, realizing the mistake she made looking into Hart's face as she answered. She felt herself fall into the inviting depths of his eyes and admitted to herself she wanted to linger there a while. Inhaling, she breathed in his amazing, masculine scent.

Her gaze eventually drifted down to his tempting lips. The man had the unsettling ability to look both teasing and seductive at the same time.

"Denni," Hart whispered, his hand moving to the back of her neck. He gently caressed the soft skin beneath his fingers before applying just enough pressure that Denni moved her head closer to his.

He'd dreamed of kissing the entrancing woman since the first time he'd seen her Thanksgiving Day at the Triple T Ranch. Now that the moment had finally arrived, Hart wanted to make sure it was special for Denni, something they'd both remember.

Raising his other hand, he gingerly cupped her cheek, admiring the way the firelight played over her skin. It felt as smooth and velvety beneath his fingers as he imagined it would. Tracing his fingers down her jaw to her chin, he watched the storm brewing in her eyes grow in intensity.

Brushing his thumb across her bottom lip, Hart felt Denni shudder and watched her eyes drift close. Moving slowly, he wrapped both arms around her and pulled her to his chest.

"You're so beautiful," he whispered softly before pressing his lips to hers.

Their kiss was tender and sweet. Hart wasn't in a rush to let it end and lingered just long enough to let her know he thought she was special.

Opening his eyes with their lips still tantalizingly close, he watched a teardrop roll down Denni's cheek.

"I'm sorry," he said, brushing the drop away with the pad of his thumb. "I thought…I'm so sorry, Denni."

Before he could slide away from her, Denni placed her hand on his cheek. "Don't apologize, Hart. Please don't. That was lovely. Thank you. It's just…I…um…"

"What is it? Please tell me," Hart said, staring into her face, wanting to fix whatever was wrong. His lips still tingled from their contact with Denni's, his heart was galloping madly in his chest, and his stomach felt tied in knots. He wanted more than anything to pull her close and kiss her again. "What's wrong?"

Letting out a choppy breath, Denni leaned forward until her forehead rested on Hart's chest. She inhaled his unique scent, absorbed his warmth, and struggled to find the words she wanted to say.

"I'm not crying because I didn't want you to kiss me, Hart. I'm crying because I've wanted you to for a while, even if I wasn't willing to admit it. I haven't been kissed for a long time and I'd forgotten how nice it can be," Denni said, staring at the buttons on Hart's dark blue cotton shirt. "Thank you for that special reminder."

"You're welcome," Hart said, moving so he could wrap his arms around Denni and let her rest fully against his chest. He lightly brushed the hair back from her face, breathed deeply of her pleasing fragrance, and decided all the years of avoided relationships with women was because he'd been waiting to find Denni. She felt so perfect in his arms, like she was the one person meant to be there.

Lifting her chin with his forefinger, he was lowering his head for another kiss when his home phone began to ring. Knowing he shouldn't ignore it since he'd turned off his cell phone, he let out a sigh and hurried to pick it up.

He was somewhat surprised to find Travis Thompson on the other end of the line, asking him if he'd seen Denni.

"As a matter of fact, I have seen her," Hart said, gazing at the woman in question with such a look of longing, Denni felt her insides heat while her limbs were limp and somewhat useless. "She's sitting right here on my couch."

Denni took the phone when Hart handed it to her and assured Travis she was fine. So caught up in her date with Hart, she'd forgotten she planned to spend the night at the Triple T. Disconnecting the call, she had no idea how Travis tracked her down at Hart's but decided she better cut the evening short before her boys got any ideas about giving her a personal escort to the ranch.

Gathering up her bag of fabric, she smiled at Hart as he helped her on with her coat and walked her out to her car.

He held her door while she slid in and started the car, giving it a minute to warm in the cold winter air.

"Thank you for having dinner with me tonight," Hart said, squatting so he was looking at her eye to eye.

"Thank you for buying me dinner," Denni said, reaching out to run her fingers down Hart's firm jaw line. "And thank you for giving me such a special first kiss. I'll remember it always."

"I'm happy to be of service," Hart said with a wicked grin. "Anytime you want to practice, I'm willing to help."

Denni smirked at his teasing and he took her hand in his, kissing her palm, causing heat to sear her skin at the contact.

"Are you going to be around tomorrow?" Hart asked, hoping the answer would be yes.

"I'm planning to spend the weekend at the ranch, but I could sneak away for a while. What did you have in mind?"

"Do you like to ride horses?"

"I love to ride horses. I just don't do it very often now that I'm an old granny," Denni said with a jaunty tilt of her head.

Hart laughed. "Would you go riding with me tomorrow? Here? I'd like to show you my horses and you could get a better look at some of the new calves."

"That sounds marvelous. If I'm here around two, would that work for you?"

"Absolutely," Hart said, giving Denni a quick peck on the cheek before standing up. "I'll see you then. And by the way, you are, without a doubt, the sexiest grandma I've ever seen."

He shut the car door, chuckling at Denni's flabbergasted expression and waved as she headed out of his driveway.

Driving to the Triple T, Denni felt like her cheeks were on fire. The things that man said were positively...fabulous! He made her feel young and beautiful, smart and witty. Things she hadn't felt for a very long time.

Parking her car and taking her small overnight bag off the backseat, Denni hurried inside the kitchen at the Triple T to find all three of her sons sitting around the table scowling while the girls visited at the other end of the table.

"Hello, hello," Denni said, setting her bag on a barstool and taking off her coat. She stepped back in the mudroom to hang it up, made herself a cup of tea on her way through the kitchen, then sat at the table, wondering what had her boys looking so grumpy.

"What do you think you're doing?" Travis asked, leaning back in his chair and drumming his fingers on the table.

"Having a cup of tea. What does it look like?" Denni said, offering her youngest child her sweetest smile.

Tess, Cady and Lindsay all worked to hide their smiles.

"That's not what I meant, Mama, and you know it. Where have you been for the last…" Travis looked at his watch, "hour and forty-nine minutes? You were seen having dinner with that… that…roadside Romeo at Viv's. Everyone's talking about it. The phone practically rang off the hook with play by play descriptions of you two making lovey-dovey faces at each other over the meatloaf special."

"I'm sorry," Denni said, standing, which made all three of her boys give her a strange look. "I think I've arrived at the wrong house. This one is full of cranky men who disrespect their mother, treating her like a child, so I know I can't be at the right place."

"Please, Mom, sit down," Trent said, getting up and placing a hand on her arm. "We'll behave."

Denni sank down in her chair and gave each one of her boys a long, motherly glare until they all three seemed subdued. "Now, how about we start this conversation over?"

"Yes, ma'am," Travis said, releasing a beleaguered sigh.

Before he could say anything, Tess leaned across the table and patted Denni's hand, giving her a big grin with her warm brown eyes all aglow.

"Did you have a good time?"

"Yes, I did," Denni said, winking at Tess and nodding her head.

"Is this the first time you've had dinner with Hart?" Cady asked, glaring at Trey, daring him or his brothers to make any comment. The guys managed to remain silent.

"No. It was our first official date, but we've eaten together several times," Denni said, sipping her tea and acting nonchalant when she really wanted to shout that she'd had a wonderful date with a very special man who made her feel alive for the first time in years. "He asked me to go riding with him tomorrow afternoon, so I said yes."

"Really? That's great," Lindsay added, rubbing her hand absently on her belly. She was just starting to show and Denni took it as a good sign that Lindsay was feeling better since she was at the table with everyone else this evening.

"It appears to me that you must like him a little," Cady said with a knowing grin. "I've never seen your eyes sparkle like that or your cheeks look so rosy. You are positively glowing, Denni."

Denni blushed when Lindsay and Tess offered their own compliments.

The girls turned to look at the sour-faced men on the other end of the table. Tess leveled her gaze at Travis and lifted a shapely brow his direction.

Clearing his throat, he seemed to consider his words then looked to his brothers for support. Finding them with their eyes glued to the table, he knew they were beat. "You do look happy, Mama."

"I am, baby," Denni said, leaning back in her chair as the tension in the room seemed to lighten. "Hart and I are just friends, good friends, at this point in time. We enjoy each other's company, we make each other laugh, and I think I deserve that in my life. Please don't be upset with me because I've decided to date someone again. I don't love your daddy any less, I'm just finally ready to see if there's room left in my heart to find love again."

Trey stood and walked around the table to where Denni sat. He hunkered down next to her chair and took her hands in his. "Mom, we want, more than anything, for you to be happy. Goodness knows you've had more than your share of grief since Daddy died. We know you love him and always will. It isn't that. We just don't want anyone trifling with your feelings or hurting you. I guess we're feeling a little overprotective because, from what we hear, you're considered quite a catch around Sherman County. If word gets out you're back in the dating pool, every eligible bachelor will start chasing you."

"Honey, that's so sweet of you boys," Denni said, kissing Trey on the cheek. "But I'm a big girl perfectly capable of taking care of myself. Just because someone chases me, sure doesn't mean I'll let them catch me. That's part of why I enjoy being with Hart so much. No pressure, no chasing, we just have fun together."

"I'm glad, Mom," Trey said, getting up and returning to his chair at the head of the table. "If he truly makes you happy, we'll refrain from acting like club-dragging cavedwellers and leave this to your judgment. But if anyone gives you any trouble, you'll let us know?"

"I've got you on speed-dial," Denni said, making Cady and Tess laugh. "After all that, I think I could use some dessert if you've got any left, Cady."

"I think we all could use a little something," Trey said, getting up to help his wife bring plates of pie to the table along with a fresh pot of coffee. Between him and his two brothers, they'd keep an eye on Hart. He might be a great guy and someone they called a friend, but all bets were off if he messed with their mom.

><><

"You guys are being ridiculous," Cady said from the bathroom in their master suite where she brushed her long, wavy hair.

Trey leaned against the bathroom door, watching her. All he had to do was look at his beautiful wife and feelings

103

of desire washed over him in great, overpowering waves. Married for a year, he hoped the wonder and magic of their love never dimmed. Crazier in love with her as each day passed, he thought they had a good shot of keeping the wild sparks that flew between them going for a very long time.

"No, we aren't," Trey said, catching Cady's eye in the mirror as she continued to brush her hair. It gleamed and glistened in the light, practically begging him to bury his hands in the rich, dark tresses. He breathed deeply, inhaling her scent that always made him think of the sweet, fresh air after a summer rainstorm.

"Your poor mother has been utterly alone for almost eight years. She hasn't shown any inclination to date until now and you boys are making a difficult situation even more challenging for her," Cady said, setting down her brush and staring at Trey in the mirror. She could tell he was only halfway paying attention to what she was saying by the heat turning his amazing turquoise eyes into liquid blue fire. Those tantalizing eyes, along with the fact that the only thing he had on was a pair of Wranglers that fit him to perfection, were about to distract her from the topic at hand.

"What do you mean a difficult situation?" Trey asked, pushing away from the door with his shoulder and stepping behind Cady. He moved her hair to one side and placed his hands on her shoulders, kneading her tired muscles. She dropped her chin forward to give him better access.

"Your mother was only seventeen when she married your dad. She's now fifty-four. Don't you think she's probably a little overwhelmed with the whole idea of dating again? Things have changed a lot since she had her last date. It can't be easy for her to put herself out there, make herself vulnerable, and it sure isn't going to help her when you boys are acting so overbearing and obnoxious.

Besides, we all like Hart. He's a real gentleman, kind-hearted and caring, not to mention he is one of the most handsome men I've ever seen."

"Is that so? What were you doing checking him out?" Trey asked, switching from rubbing Cady's shoulders to kissing the creamy skin of her neck.

"I wasn't checking him out, boss-man. It's just hard not to notice someone who looks like a celebrity and has such a friendly smile. Besides, I didn't say he was the most handsome man I've ever seen, just one of."

"Who's the most handsome?" Trey asked, sliding the strap of Cady's nightgown off her shoulder and kissing his way down her arm. He watched goose bumps pop out on her soft skin, pleased that he could so easily stir a reaction in her.

"This cowboy I know with the most incredible eyes, broad chest, and chiseled jaw. He makes a pair of Wranglers look pretty good, too." Cady turned around and wrapped her arms around his neck, pressing against his bare chest. "You're just lucky I love you beyond reason, or you could be in big trouble."

"I'm already in big trouble, Cady-girl," Trey said in a husky voice, picking her up in his arms and carrying her to their bed. "I have been since the day I fell in love with you."

Chapter Eight

"The heart has reasons that reason does not understand."
Jacques Bénigne Bossuel

Glancing up from his desk at a knock on his door, Hart took in Travis Thompson standing in the doorway wearing a frown.

Deciding it must be serious business, Hart stood and walked across the room, extending his hand to the young man he'd grown to not only know, but like and admire in the months since he'd moved to Grass Valley.

Hart felt some unexplainable connection to the youngest Thompson brother who seemed to have the same unsettled wild streak he often recognized in himself.

No one would dare say anything directly to him, but he'd heard plenty of people mention how he and Travis seemed so much alike, from their sandy hair and easy grins to their love of adventure.

From what Hart knew, Travis suffered from post-traumatic stress disorder after returning from his last tour of duty in Iraq more than a year ago. An accident that left him bedridden for several weeks at the end of summer seemed to be the turning point in his willingness to seek help and start down the road to recovery.

Marrying his beautiful, vivacious wife in October probably didn't hurt his healing process, either. The girl looked at Travis like he could rope the moon and hand it to her gift-wrapped.

"Travis, what can I do for you today?" Hart asked, slapping the broad-shouldered cowboy on the back and walking him into his office, motioning him to have a seat.

Travis sat in a chair in front of Hart's desk and looked around at the walls covered with memorabilia from Hart's bull riding days. His gaze fell on a photo of Hart riding a bull, wearing a huge grin, looking like he was on top of the world. Knowing that feeling well, Travis refocused his thoughts on his reason for coming to see the gas station owner.

Clearing his throat, he hung his hat from his knee and hoped his mother would forgive him for interfering in her life, but despite Trey and Trent telling him to leave things alone with his mother's budding romance, Travis still felt the need to intervene before she wound up with a broken heart.

"Hart, I won't waste your time or beat around the bush so here it is - we know you've been seeing Mom. She finally fessed up to spending all that time with you in Tucson and everyone in a fifty-mile radius knows you had dinner with her at Viv's, went horseback riding, and took both her and Nana out to dinner last Sunday," Travis said, fastening a cool stare on the man sitting across from him. Hart was leaning back, his hands relaxed on the arm of the chair. "That's all fine and dandy, but what, exactly, are your intentions toward her? We don't want her to get hurt."

"I don't plan on hurting her, Travis. I respect your mother too much to willingly cause her any harm," Hart said, amused that Denni's sons were so protective of her. "We enjoy one another's company and have fun together."

"So she's just a fun diversion until you find someone else who strikes your fancy?" Travis asked accusingly.

"Not at all," Hart said, sitting up in his chair and cracking his knuckles, a bad habit he'd developed as a teenager. "I admit I've dated a lot of women in my time, but your mother is the first woman I've had a fourth date with in the past twenty-five years. That should tell you something right there."

Travis seemed to consider that information.

"Before you want to know my motives, let me assure you I'm not dating her for her money, because I think she's a lonely widow, or to try and work my wiles on her," Hart said, leaning forward with his arms resting on his desk.

"Then why are you dating her?" Travis asked, knowing it wasn't for the money. Hart could buy the Triple T Ranch and all their holdings five times over and still have plenty to spare. He assumed Hart thought his mom would be an easy mark for some meaningless fun.

"Because I care about her very much," Hart said. His face softened as he thought about how much he really did care about Denni. "I didn't set out with the intention of moving here to find female companionship, Travis. I generally try to avoid it because in the past it brought me nothing but…well, that's in the past. I can't give you a detailed or specific reason why your sweet mother wants to spend time with me, but I'm glad she does. She makes me laugh like I haven't in years, she makes me feel on top of the world, and she makes me feel young again. Sometimes the heart has reasons for things we just aren't meant to understand, but I'm not going to ignore it or pretend it isn't there."

When Travis sat quietly, continuing to glare at him, Hart shook his head and let out a sigh. "Look, Travis, I don't know where this is heading, this thing between your mom and me. I can't predict the future, but I can enjoy the present. I promise I will never willingly do anything to hurt Denni. After all her years of grieving, I can't think that you boys would deny her a little fun and happiness. From what I can tell, she seems to enjoy spending time with me."

Leaning forward on his knees, Travis nodded his head. "She is. I haven't seen her this happy since before Dad died. We appreciate that, Hart. Truly we do. Mama has been through so much, we just don't want her to be in a situation that's going to end badly and make her sad again."

"When you first fell in love with Tess, did you worry about how it would end, or did you enjoy the moment?" Hart asked.

Travis grinned. "Since I was only six at the time, I was most concerned about getting girl cooties from her."

Hart laughed and leaned back in his chair again.

"I grew up loving Tess. She was the only girl I ever wanted to be with, the only one I've ever loved," Travis said, temporarily lost in his thoughts of the past. "But I guess to answer your question I didn't worry about how or when it would end. I was convinced she'd never fall in love with me at all. Turns out, she'd loved me as long as I loved her."

"That's a great story, Travis. You Thompsons seem to be quite a romantic bunch."

"Don't go spreading that news around. You know it's a well-guarded secret," Travis said with a teasing gleam in his eye. In the last year, it had become a running joke about the lengths the Thompson brothers would go to in wooing the women they loved. Maybe their mother wasn't much different.

"One that is safe with me," Hart said, grinning broadly. "I have no intention of doing anything but enjoying time spent with your mother. Only she knows why she'd want to spend time with an ol' cowboy like me, but she does. Can you boys step back and let us see where this thing is going to go? It might lead nowhere and we'll continue being friends, or it might lead to something else. Regardless, I'll do everything I can to keep your mother from being hurt. Fair enough?"

"Fair enough," Travis said, getting to his feet and shaking Hart's hand with a genuine smile. Moving toward the office door, Travis started to walk out when he turned back, looking thoughtful. "Do you ever miss it, Hart?"

"Miss it?" Hart asked, realizing Travis was talking about bull riding. "Sometimes. I've never found anything that quite equaled the high from being on the back of a bull. But then, again, I don't have a beautiful wife who can no doubt make you feel ten times better than you ever did even on your best bull ride."

Grinning, Travis put his hat on his head. "True. Tess does that for sure. Thanks again, Hart, I'm…"

Travis was interrupted by the gas station attendant who ran in the door looking for Hart.

"Hart, there's a man out there looking for you with a really ugly bull."

"Thanks, Evan. I'll be right there." Hart placed his hat on his head, pulling on his coat as they walked toward the door. "Want to check out my new bull?"

"You bet," Travis said, stepping up to the stock trailer waiting outside where the sounds of a bull snorting and moving around carried across the parking lot. Peeking inside the slats, Travis shook his head. "That is one ugly bull."

"Beauty is in the eye of the beholder," Hart said, shaking hands with the owner of the bull who was delivering it out to Hart's place. "Ever had a thick Belgian Blue steak?"

"Nope."

"You've got to try one, man. You'll never want to eat your Angus beef again," Hart said with a teasing grin.

"Maybe you'll have to prove it to me."

"Maybe I will. Want to help me get this big guy unloaded?"

"Why not? Mom said you had some alien looking cows out there. I've got to see the spectacle for myself," Travis said, grinning mischievously at Hart who cuffed him on the shoulder.

"Just for that I'll make you chase him out of the trailer."

><><

"Do they really look as weird as Mom said?" Trey asked that evening as the Thompson clan gathered around the Triple T dinner table, along with their hands.

"Yep. I think even more so. I've seen photos of Belgian Blues, but until you see them up close, you have no idea how different they really are," Travis said, grinning as he thought about helping Hart unload his bull and seeing the rest of his small herd. "Their back ends almost remind me of a market hog's hindquarters. Hart claims the meat is unbelievable, though. He promised to cook me a steak one of these days. Have you guys seen his horses?"

"No," Trent said, looking down the table at Travis. "Are they some strange breed, too?"

"Not strange, but they sure do make you look twice," Travis said, relishing the fact that he was the first of his brothers to see Hart's livestock. Although Brice, who helped build Hart's house and barn and was now making several pieces of furniture for him, was quite familiar with his place, Trey and Trent had yet to receive Hart's grand tour. Hart mentioned that his horses and cattle had arrived just a few weeks ago, so that was probably why the community wasn't buzzing about them yet. "He's got a dozen registered Appaloosas out there. They're beautiful."

"I love Appaloosas," Tess said, wondering if Hart would mind if they paid a visit to see the horses.

"I'm sure he'd be happy to show them to you," Travis said as he took another helping of the lasagna Cady made for dinner. "He seemed quite proud of them."

"Maybe we can make it a family field trip," Trey said, hoping Hart wouldn't mind if all the Thompsons descended on his place for a visit. He didn't seem to mind having Denni there, for sure.

"We can ask," Travis said with a grin.

"And just how was it you came to be over there today?" Trey asked, wondering what mischief Travis had been making.

"I was at the gas station when his new bull arrived and he asked if I'd help him get it unloaded. If you think ol' Leroy is a big, bad bull, wait until you see Brutus," Travis said, referring to the prize bull Trent bought the previous spring. Leroy was huge, ornery, and kept all the other bulls on the ranch in their place.

"Brutus? Is that the name of Hart's bull?" Cady asked, shaking her head. "Sounds like a bully."

"He looks like one, too," Travis said, nodding his head.

"Bullies are naughty and we're supposed to tell our teacher if we see one," Cass said, looking at Lindsay, who also happened to be her teacher. "Right, Aunt Lindsay?"

"That's right, sweetie-pie," Lindsay said, smiling at Cass, glad the little girl had been paying attention at the school assembly they recently held to teach the students about how to handle a bully. She started to say something about Trent's bull when the baby kicked and made her catch her breath.

"What's wrong, princess?" Trent asked, leaning over her with a concerned frown creasing his forehead. Lindsay grabbed his hand and placed it on her stomach so he could feel the baby moving.

Everyone watched as Trent's eyes took on a look of wonder and a huge grin spread across his face.

"That one is going to be a mover and a shaker," Trent said with pride. Not one to keep the excitement to themselves, Trent reached across Lindsay and grabbed Travis' hand, placing it on Lindsay's belly. Not sure if Lindsay would appreciate such close contact with a brother-in-law, Travis looked to her for approval. She smiled and nodded her head, so he relaxed his hand and felt little flutters of motion against his palm.

"That is so awesome!" Travis turned to grin at his wife with a soft look in his eyes. Although he and Tess weren't anywhere close to being ready to start a family, he looked forward to the day when they did. "That one's going to be a star quarterback."

"It might be a she, you know," Lindsay said, looking first at Travis, then Trent. The guys were all convinced it would be a boy while the women on the ranch were hoping for a girl.

"Why don't you two just find out what it is and stop with the guessing?" Trey asked.

"Because we want it to be a surprise," Trent said, taking Lindsay's hand in his and kissing the back of it.

"Surprises are good," Cass said, not quite certain what the adults were talking about but smiling when her comment made them all laugh.

Tommy, one of the ranch hands sitting next to her, ruffled her head of wild red curls. "That they are, Cass."

Chapter Nine

*"A merry heart doeth good like a medicine:
but a broken spirit drieth the bones."*
Proverbs 17:22 KJV

Quickly applying one last coat of shimmery lip-gloss, Denni checked her reflection in the rearview mirror before getting out of her car. Balancing a large cake plate in her hands, she carefully walked up the steps of Hart's porch to the door.

Ringing the bell, she waited only a few seconds before the door opened to reveal Hart staring at her with an astonished look on his handsome face.

Smiling at him, she was glad she decided to go all out for their date tonight. Taking Tess with her shopping one evening after work, she found a perfect black dress that made her feel both stylish and attractive. The new heels on her feet were higher than she would normally wear, but Tess insisted they would make Hart drop his jaw and drool. Spending additional time on her hair and makeup, she added an extra spritz of favorite perfume and put on a little red coat that accented her outfit perfectly.

Although he wasn't drooling, from the way he stood in the door speechless Denni decided Tess didn't miss the mark by much.

"May I come in?" she asked, still standing on the porch in the cold.

Hart nodded his head and stepped back. Opening the door and finding Denni looking so beguiling on his front step rendered Hart temporarily incapable of speech or coherent thought.

She always appeared lovely and put together, but tonight she looked so hot, his retinas felt scorched gazing at her. Someone casually glancing at her would automatically assume Denni was a woman in her mid-thirties, a very attractive, alluring woman. It was only when you got close enough to see the laugh lines around her eyes that she looked closer to her true age. Hart thought those lines gave her more character.

Taking the cake plate from her hands, he set it on the entry table then helped her remove her red velvet coat. The fabric felt soft against his rough hands and he carefully hung it in the closet before turning around to ogle Denni again.

The dress she was wearing made his heart tempo triple and his blood warm several degrees. He had no idea about the terms women used to describe fashions. All he knew was that the little black number highlighted Denni's curves and made her look long and sleek, especially with those high heels and the silver hoop earrings dangling from her ears.

"Wow! Denni, you look absolutely…Wow!" Hart finally managed to say, kissing her cheek before picking up the cake plate and placing his hand at the small of her back. He walked her into the kitchen where he was finishing preparations for their dinner.

"You look pretty good yourself," Denni said, thinking Hart could pass for someone much younger, as fit and hunky as he always looked. Tonight his tousled sandy hair practically begged her to run her fingers through it. He wore a deep red shirt, creased jeans, and a pair of boots that appeared to have recently been polished. His scent filled her senses and made her knees feel a little wobbly.

115

The warm hand he placed on her back caused her stomach to flutter and her heart to skip a beat as they walked into the kitchen. She was going to have to be careful or she could find herself way more attracted to the man than she intended. He was supposed to be her introduction back into the dating world, not the man with whom she fell hopelessly in love.

"What can I do to help?" she asked, looking around the large and orderly kitchen. If she could have custom-designed her dream kitchen it would look exactly like Hart's. She loved everything about it from the stone countertops to the warm wood on the floor.

"You've done enough by bringing dessert," Hart said, setting the cake plate on the counter of the kitchen's island.

"A little birdie told me you're partial to red velvet cake, so I hope you like it," Denni said, sitting down at a barstool. The way Hart kept looking at her was making her feel a bit lightheaded. She wasn't sure she could continue to stand in her high heels with her knees threatening to turn rubbery under his heated gaze.

"You really made me red velvet cake?" Hart was pleasantly surprised she'd go to so much effort on his behalf. He assumed the little bird's name was Cady since he'd eaten two pieces the day she served the cake when he was at the ranch for dinner. When she realized he liked it, she'd wrapped up an extra piece to send home with him. "You're not kidding me, are you?"

"Technically, it's red velvet cheesecake, but my family seems to like it. We should probably put it in the fridge for now."

"Then I'm sure I'll love it," Hart said, setting the covered cake plate in his large refrigerator before turning back to the counter where he'd been assembling a green salad. Remembering he had steaks on the grill, he excused himself and hurried out the adjoining door to the deck to check on the meat. Not quite done, he returned to the kitchen to find Denni chopping vegetables for the salad.

He studied the way she leaned against the counter, her shapely calves visible beneath the hem of her knee-length dress. Her hair just touched the top of her dress, making Hart wonder what she'd do if he brushed aside the golden strands and pressed a hot kiss to her slender neck.

Shaking his head to clear his thoughts, he opened a loaf of French bread and cut a few slices, liberally buttering them and running them out to the grill.

"Almost done," he said when he came back in the kitchen and washed his hands. "Are you ready to sample the best beef you're ever going to eat?"

Denni laughed. "This steak had better be really good for all the hype you've given it. You've even got Travis talking about trying it."

"I've been meaning to invite all your family over for a meal," Hart said, pushing a button on the microwave, making Denni wonder what he was making. "I've had more than my share of mouth-watering meals around the Triple T's table and I think it's long past time for me to play host. Maybe we can find a day in the next few weeks that would work for everyone and you could be here as well."

"I'd like that. I'm sure they all would, too. Cass has never seen an Appaloosa and keeps asking about Hart's spotted horses."

"That Cass is something else," Hart said, more than a little fond of the lively child. The feeling seemed to be mutual since she often sought him out after church or when he joined the Thompsons for a meal. If she was along when her mom or dad stopped by the gas station, she always ran over and gave him a big hug.

"She is at that. I'm so glad things worked out for Trey and Cady to adopt her," Denni said, grateful for the joy the little girl brought to the entire family. "I can't even think about what would have happened to her if the judge hadn't ruled in their favor then helped rush along the adoption proceedings."

"Cass is a lucky little girl," Hart said, thinking not every child had so many people to love and spoil them.

"She is, but so are we." Denni didn't want the conversation to turn maudlin, so she sent a bright smile Hart's direction. "As great as you look, I was half expecting to see you in a cupid's costume. It is Valentine's Day, you know."

"I'm fully aware of the day," Hart said, grinning at Denni as he took glasses out of a cupboard and a bottle of sparkling cider from the fridge. "The thought of greeting my gorgeous date wearing a diaper and a carrying a bow and arrow just seemed wrong. You'd think some senile old coot from the geriatric ward escaped and was up to no good with vicious weaponry."

Laughing so hard she wiped tears from her eyes, Denni glanced over her shoulder at Hart. "Even if you had worn the costume, there'd be no confusing all that with someone from the retirement home." Denni waved her knife at Hart for emphasis.

"You think I look good for an old geezer, do you?" Hart teased, stepping behind Denni and kissing the soft skin beneath her ear. He watched a shiver of pleasure ripple through her as she shut her eyes and swallowed twice.

"For an old geezer, you don't look too bad. You smell pretty good, too." The thought of seeing Hart's fine physique exposed in a cupid costume made Denni feel like her knees were about to fold beneath her.

Turning from Hart, she tried to gather her composure under the guise of finishing the salad and stirring in the dressing he left next to the bowl. He ran out and pulled the steaks from the grill along with the bread, carrying them to a cozy table for two he set up in the front room by the fireplace.

Lighting candles and dimming the rest of the lights he returned to the kitchen and carried in the glasses and sparkling cider while Denni brought the salad. One more trip and he retrieved a cheesy potato dish he cooked in the microwave.

Admiring the beautifully set table, Denni was surprised to see a bachelor would have a nice white linen tablecloth with matching napkins and a set of lovely china. Then again, nothing about Hart should surprise her. He was definitely a man of many talents and mysteries.

"This is wonderful, Hart," Denni said, turning soft blue eyes his direction as he held her chair. He momentarily lost his ability to move as he fell into their depths. Finally taking his seat, he asked a blessing on the food then poured Denni a glass of the cider.

"A toast to broken hearts," Hart said, holding his glass up toward hers. "May they all find a way to heal."

Although Denni thought the toast somewhat odd, she did like the sentiment. For the first time since Drew passed away, she held out hope that the pieces of her broken heart might someday find their way back together.

"And love again," she said, giving Hart a look filled with something he was afraid to define.

Hart sat waiting while Denni sliced into her steak and took a bite. She closed her eyes and savored the richness of the meat, grilled to her idea of perfection.

"You win. That is the best beef I've ever tasted and I've eaten a lot of really good steaks over the years," Denni said, grinning at Hart as she sliced off another bite.

"Just make sure you tell that to your boys. They've been razzing me ever since I told Travis my beef is better than your Angus meat."

"I will, although you might as well know they'll have to experience it themselves before you make believers out of them. I don't know where they get that from," Denni said with a hint of self-depreciating humor.

They talked about things happening in the community, neighbors, progress on the church's remodel projects that Hart was overseeing, and business at the gas station.

After dinner, Denni sliced the cake and smiled as Hart devoured his piece and asked for a second slice.

"That is over the top, Denni," Hart said, completely in awe of the dessert she made. It had to be one of the best he'd ever had. "Thank you so much."

"You're welcome. Red velvet cheesecake seemed like a fitting dessert for the day."

"And so it is," Hart agreed. Denni helped him carry the dishes to the kitchen, load the dishwasher, and put the food away.

When they were through, they wandered back out to the front room and sat together on the couch.

Denni told Hart a few funny stories about some of her more quirky customers and he made her laugh so hard she nearly cried, talking about an odd couple passing through who stopped at the gas station the previous day.

The conversation turned to people who lived in the area for a long time and Hart asked how the Thompson family came to be in Grass Valley.

"Drew's great-great-grandparents settled here in the late 1800s. They started with one section of ground then bought another and another. They had three girls and one boy. The son, of course, inherited the place. He continued to add more land and cattle, working hard to make the ranch prosperous and uphold the good name his father established in the community. He had two girls and one boy. Their names were Teresa, Tillie and Thomas. It was during their childhood when the ranch became known as the Triple T. Tom didn't think it was right for him to inherit the ranch when his sisters had worked hard on it, too, so when his parents passed away he bought them out, giving them a good price for their shares. He and his wife had three boys, but Timothy Andrew was the only one who survived to adulthood. His two younger brothers were killed in a freak harvest accident when he was twelve. Tim married a wonderful girl and they had one son, Timothy Andrew Thompson II, my Drew."

Denni seemed to be lost in her thoughts for a moment before she continued. "The Thompson family did business at the bank my father managed in The Dalles. My brother was friends with Drew and he even dated one of my sisters for a while. One summer he came home from college and finally noticed I'd grown up. We wed a few weeks after I graduated from high school. At one point, when Drew and I were first married, we shared the house with his folks and his Grandpa Tom. Those were some interesting times."

"I'm sure they were," Hart commented, looking at her with interest, hoping she'd continue her story."

"Drew wanted to carry on the tradition of his name. He was so excited when Trey was born. I insisted we call him Trey, since he is the third Timothy Andrew. It was my idea to give the boys all names that started with T, although there were plenty of times when they were young and in trouble I'd regret that decision. Sometimes I'd run through all their names before the right one would come out."

Hart chuckled and clasped Denni's hand in his. "I can't imagine those boys of yours being anything but angelic and well-behaved all the time."

Denni almost snorted at his comment, making Hart laugh. "Well behaved and angelic weren't exactly terms anyone would use to describe my boys. The words I most often heard were hooligans, rambunctious rebels, or rowdy troublemakers. But angelic? Never."

"They're good men, though, Denni. You must be proud of them," Hart said, rubbing tantalizing circles with his thumb on Denni's soft wrist.

"I am proud of them. Trey was always solid and dependable, if a little bossy and moody. He got that from his dad, along with his sense of responsibility. Trent is the peacemaker, easy going and laid back, although he worries most about everyone. Travis, my wild child, is the one I'm probably the most proud of because he's had to work the hardest to find his way. We count our blessings every day with that one. Tess has been such a big help in him settling down and moving forward in a good direction. I think there is something in him that will always be a little unsettled, a little wild, but he's got a heart of gold."

Denni studied Hart for a minute and grinned. "He reminds me of someone else I know, who seems a bit rough around the edges for all his tamed façade."

"Really? Do I know this person?" Hart asked, flustered Denni had read him so well. Despite the millions of dollars he'd made over the years, despite his business successes and all he'd accomplished, there was a part of him that was still looking for adventure, still waiting for the next big thrill to come along. He managed to keep the longing subdued most of the time, but once in a while he had the urge to do something wild and reckless.

When Travis asked him the other day if he missed riding bulls, it reminded him just how much he did miss the thrill of the ride, the shot of pure adrenalin. He supposed it was something he'd always miss, but that part of his life was long gone.

"What about you, Hart? How did you come to be here?" Denni asked, curious about Hart's story. In all the conversations they'd shared, he'd never told her why he decided to settle in Grass Valley when he could have chosen to live anywhere. She knew he grew up in Spokane and spent all the time he could with his grandparents on their ranch near Prineville, but other than that, she had no idea about his history.

Releasing her hand, Hart leaned forward on his knees and stared into the fire for a long moment. It was time to tell Denni the truth. Because of her warmth, her laughter, her tender care, he felt the broken pieces of his heart starting to mend. Without her, he'd still be carrying around the cold, shattered shards of what had once been a vessel filled with love. Her positive outlook on life refreshed him, like pouring restorative water on parched ground. He couldn't get enough of her, of the special light she brought to his life.

Leaning back against the cushions of the couch, he put his arm around Denni's shoulders, pulling her over so her back rested against his chest.

"You sure you want to know my story? It isn't the most cheerful one you'll ever hear." Hart wanted to be sure Denni really wanted to know his history before he shared it with her.

"Please, Hart. I want to know," Denni said, twining her fingers with his where they rested on her leg. She wondered if he knew how much she enjoyed sitting with him, just like this.

She felt Hart sigh before he squeezed her hand.

"My parents both grew up in small towns. My mom was raised on a ranch outside of Prineville. She hated country life, almost as much as my dad, who'd never even experienced it. They met at a Bible college and had some grandiose plans of saving the world. They ministered at several churches in Washington and ended up in Spokane when I was old enough to start school. When I was fifteen, they decided their calling was to be missionaries, so they took off on a trip to the wilds of Africa and were killed a few weeks later."

"Oh, Hart, how awful for you," Denni said, feeling compassion for the teen boy who lost both his parents.

"It was hard. I was mad at them, mad at God, mad at the world. I'd been staying with my best friend and his family while my parents were gone, but when they died my grandparents insisted I move in with them," Hart said, remembering how hard it had been for his grandparents to reach through his rebellious shell and work with his wounded heart. "My grandpa ranched and I spent all my free time there, but when I moved in with them I learned all about running a ranch, riding horses, and raising cattle. When I told Gramps I wanted to join the high school rodeo team, he encouraged me, hoping that having some way to focus my energy and anger would help me get over the pain. I don't think he or Grams planned for me to choose bull riding, but it was the one thing I enjoyed the most. And I was good at it."

Denni could picture a young Hart on the back of the bull, looking much like Travis did when he rode. "Did it help you?"

"In some ways, I guess it did," Hart said, holding Denni a little tighter. "I was only eighteen when I entered my first professional rodeo and walked away with second place. After that, it was all I wanted to do. I managed to make it into the top picks every year, competing at finals. Every year I placed higher until I walked away with the number two title in the world when I was twenty-five. I was celebrating my successes one evening when I turned around and saw a dark-haired beauty watching me. She was Cuban, hot-tempered, and extremely jealous. It didn't take long for us to become an item and we were married by a justice of the peace about a month after meeting on the way to my next rodeo."

Hart took a moment to gather his thoughts because this next part of the story was the hardest.

"I had an amazing year that year. Yelina traveled with me most of the time. We fought more often than we got along, but even our disagreements seemed to give me the energy I needed to come out on top in the arena. I knew a few days into the marriage I'd made a huge mistake. We had nothing in common, knew next to nothing about each other, and I had mistaken lust for love. She gave up her job, her friends, everything, so she could travel with me. Some of our worst fights were because she'd see me signing an autograph for a pretty girl and assume I was up to no good. I might have been a lot of things at that point in my life, but I took the vows I made to her seriously. She spent a lot of time pouting and angry, filled with a jealous rage. My plan was to work on our marriage after I won the world champion title and life settled down for us. It was time for me to grow up and do something different, but I wanted to go out on top. I couldn't give up bull riding until I'd taken the world championship."

"What happened, Hart?" Denni asked when Hart paused in the telling of his story.

"When the top picks came for the finals that year, I was number one. Everyone was talking about how I'd already won the title; the finals were just a formality. It made me cocky and smug, and admittedly, hard to live with. Everything was all about me and Yelina wanted it to stop. Although the stories I've heard said I disappeared before the finals, the truth is I was there the first night. Yelina begged me not to go, said she had something we needed to discuss. She told me I needed to make a choice between her and the rodeo. So I went to the finals alone, leaving her crying in our room in some cheesy hotel in Vegas. I rode a bull named Renegade that night for the full eight seconds in the best ride of my career. Dismounting, I waved to the crowd one last time before I ran across the arena toward the gate where one of my good friends waited, white-faced, to tell me the police were looking for me. Yelina ordered room service, left the door open and overdosed on some pain meds I'd been taking for an injury

I received when a bull gored me a few months earlier. The poor kid who brought up the food found her on the floor."

Turning around so she could look at him, Denni wiped at the tears on her cheeks then put her hand on Hart's leg. "I'm so sorry. That is more than any one should have to bear."

"It gets worse," Hart said, looking at Denni, feeling remorse and regret flood through him again, like it did anytime he told the story. "Are you sure you want to hear the rest?"

"Please, Hart. Go on," Denni whispered, leaning against his chest and wrapping her arms around his waist. She felt his arm settle around her shoulders.

"It was bad enough she choose death over trying to work things out with me, but she killed our baby. I had no idea she was pregnant. I often wondered if that's what she wanted to discuss. If I'd stayed with her and talked things through, would she have lived? Would the baby be an adult now, married with a baby of his own?"

"Oh, Hart," Denni choked on her tears and felt them roll down her cheeks. She couldn't even fathom the pain Hart had been through. To lose a spouse was hard enough, but to lose a child, a baby, at the same time was unbearable.

"I walked away from the rodeo that night. I haven't even been to one since. I just couldn't. Still angry at God for all He'd taken away from me, the next year was a true low point in my life. I wandered aimlessly. Drinking. Fighting. I pushed away my friends, ignored pleas from my grandparents to come home, and tried to find the will to end my own sad life. Completely broken, I fell asleep in my pickup one night outside a gas station in a small town in California. The next morning the station owner came out and offered me a cup of coffee and a job pumping gas. I took it and he became not only a friend, but a key in my salvation. He taught me all about running a gas station and managing a small business. More than that, though, he taught me how to believe in myself, in others, and in God again. I worked for him for three years as his station manager. When he died, he left me that station. I renamed it Renegade, as a reminder of the last bull I rode and what that ride cost me. When the opportunity came up to buy a second station, I took it. Then I added a third and a fourth and from there I built my little gas station empire around the Northwest. Seeing the station for sale here in Grass Valley, I decided to finally put down some roots and settle in. I always liked this area when I'd travel through on my way from Spokane to see my grandparents. So there you have my story, Denni."

Denni felt like she'd just gotten off an emotional roller coaster ride and was having a hard time regaining her balance. She'd made plenty of bad choices in her lifetime and the last thing she was going to do was judge Hart, but her heart hurt for all he'd lost. For all he endured alone.

"Why didn't you ever remarry? You were so young to be alone," Denni asked, looking up at Hart from where her head rested on his chest. Although losing Drew had nearly killed her, they'd had thirty years of life together, filled with wonderful memories. And she had her three sons. She'd never been alone although there were plenty of times she was lonely.

"I didn't even love Yelina, not like I should have, and it still ripped my heart out and destroyed it when she died. I promised myself I'd never willingly put myself in a position to experience that kind of torment again and I certainly didn't want to hurt someone so badly they'd rather end their life than spend another day with me."

"Hart, you have to know that isn't normal. She must have had some other problems to do that, especially knowing she'd be taking the life of your baby as well. People who have normal thought processes just don't do that," Denni said, sitting up and giving Hart a look filled with love and compassion. "Just like you, she made choices. No one made her overdose. That was her choice."

"I know, but there's a part of me that will probably always carry some burden of guilt about what happened. I lay it down, but seem to have a problem not picking at least a little part of it back up again," Hart said, sitting forward and leaning his elbows on his knees. He let out a deep breath and ran his hands through his hair before looking at Denni.

She was so beautiful, especially with the firelight playing off her lovely features, her eyes glistening from her tears. Tears she'd cried for him and what he'd lost in his youth. Thanks to her, he was starting to think he'd found something, a part of himself, he hadn't even fully realized was lost.

"It's not that I couldn't have found someone else, Denni. All these years I never wanted to," Hart said, taking her hand in his again. "Until now. Until you."

Chapter Ten

"For it was not into my ear you whispered,
but into my heart.
It was not my lips you kissed,
but my soul."

Judy Garland

Staring at Hart, Denni tried to absorb what he was saying. Perplexed, she looked into his sultry blue eyes and felt herself begin to melt.

"I…I'm not entirely sure what you're saying," Denni said, wanting to be sure of his feelings before she said or did anything she'd later regret. She watched the corners of his lips tip up in the grin she loved and wondered what he'd do if she lavished a few kisses on the incredibly deep dimple that rested above has all too enticing upper lip.

"What I'm saying, Denni Thompson, is that I've spent twenty some years successfully avoiding a relationship of any type and now that I've met you, I can't seem to think of anything other than being with you. You make me laugh, you listen to my crazy stories, and you make me feel young again. Since I met you, the ragged, broken pieces of my heart are starting to feel life-like again. Given enough time and exposure to you, they might even find their way back together."

"Hart," Denni whispered, her eyes speaking what her voice could not as he gathered her in his arms and kissed her with a passion she hadn't dared to dream experiencing again in her lifetime. Shifting so she could wrap her arms around Hart's neck, he moved and soon she found herself pulled tightly to his solid chest as he kissed her so deeply and completely, she felt like he'd somehow touched her soul.

Finally breaking apart, Denni felt heat flood her cheeks as she struggled to capture enough thoughts to be able to speak. Instead, Hart put a hand behind her head and gently pulled her to rest against his chest, kissing her temple. His callused hand gently brushed the hair back from her face then traced tempting circles up and down the length of her arm exposed beneath the cap sleeve of her dress. It felt so good, so right, to rest against him. To absorb his strength. To let her breath mingle with his as they both felt their hearts go from wild racing to a calmer beat.

Hating to admit it, her mother was right. Hart knew exactly how to kiss a woman and leave her wanting more. Although they'd shared a few chaste kisses, this was the first time he'd really kissed her. For someone who claimed to have avoided relationships the past few decades, he had either a natural talent or a lot of practice at the art of kissing.

"Dance with me?" Hart asked, much to Denni's delight. Drew had never been fond of dancing, but did it to humor her. Gazing at the man who looked at her so intently, she knew she was beginning to lose herself to him. With the firelight turning his skin to bronze, highlighting gold streaks in that thick hair, Denni felt engulfed by her feelings for this wounded, yet completely loveable man.

"I'd love to," Denni said, pushing away from Hart's chest and watching as he picked up a remote from a side table and soft music filled the room.

Standing, he executed a bow worthy of royalty then held out his hand to her. Denni giggled, placing her hand in his, letting him pull her to her feet.

Walking around behind the grouping of furniture where the hardwood floor was uncovered by rugs, Hart put one arm around Denni's back and held her hand out in a traditional slow dance pose. She placed her free hand on his shoulder and smiled as he waltzed her around the space.

Like his kissing, Hart was either a natural at dancing or had a lot of practice.

"Before you start wondering about my dancing skills, I should probably fess up that my dad's sister spent some time dancing professionally and ran a studio in Seattle for many years. One summer she stayed with us and insisted I learn how to dance. She also gave me an appreciation for music that was beyond the rock and country I liked to listen to," Hart said.

Denni smiled and studied the cleft in his chin. The one she'd wanted numerous times to kiss. She pressed her lips to the spot, ever so lightly, and pulled back to see a storm of emotions flood through Hart's eyes. He grinned down at her and started to sing, astounding her with his ability to carry a tune, and choice of a song.

"Be careful, it's my heart.
It's not my watch you're holding, it's my heart..."

Recognizing the Irving Berlin song, she grinned, leaning her head against Hart's shoulder as they danced. She felt like they had somehow turned a corner in their relationship. Maybe it was in knowing Hart's past, reliving the pain with him. Maybe it was in knowing he truly had no intention of getting involved in a relationship but admittedly couldn't stop himself from caring about her. Maybe it was due to the holiday and they both needed a little romance. Whatever it was, she was thoroughly and utterly enthralled with the handsome, noble man holding her in his arms, singing her a love song in a rich voice.

"It's yours to take, to keep or break.
But please, before you start,
Be careful, it's my heart."

As Hart finished the last note, he looked down into Denni's face and saw the desire and longing in his own reflected there. Lowering his head, he took her lips captive and tasted deeply of the sweetness that was all her. When her arms found their way around his neck, he wrapped his hands around her waist and pulled her close against him.

Long seconds later when the kiss ended, he rested his forehead against hers, inhaled her light, sweet fragrance and realized he never wanted this evening, this moment, to end. He wanted to spend the rest of his life with Denni in his arms.

Stunned by the realization, he kept his thoughts to himself and danced with her a few more minutes before taking her hand and returning to the couch.

Tugging her onto his lap, her heard her gasp of surprise and grinned. "Don't want you too far away," Hart said in explanation and once again bound their lips together in a kiss that was about to push him beyond the edge of reason.

Denni had the fleeting thought that she was way too old to behave with such abandon, but quickly lost herself in the wild, heady kisses Hart continued to rain upon her lips and down her neck. His hands caressed her arms, her shoulders, her waist. She realized the low groan she heard came from her own throat when he nibbled on her ear.

"Hart," she whispered, pleaded, her own hands running through his thick hair, tracing the contours of his sculpted shoulders. He stopped and looked at her, trying to gauge her reaction.

Not sure if she wanted him to stop or continue, she sat with her chest heaving trying to keep from completely losing all her resistance to the magnificent man holding her so temptingly close in his strong arms.

"What's wrong? Did I hurt you? I'm sorry, Denni. I guess I'm a little out…"

Whatever Hart would have said was cut off by Denni's hand over his mouth. A grin tugged at her lips and her eyes sparkled with humor and vibrancy. "Don't you dare say you're out of practice, Hart Hammond. Mama said you look like someone who would know just how to kiss a woman and darn if the ol' girl just might be right."

"Is that so?" Hart said, grinning at Denni, his eyes still smoldering with desire. "You're not sure, though? You only think she might be right? Maybe we better practice some more until you can make up your mind."

"I don't know if that's such a good idea," Denni said, leaning closer to Hart's lips with each word she said, feeling pulled by some force beyond her ability to resist.

"She's right," Denni whispered later, when Hart had kissed her so thoroughly she thought she might fly into a thousand pieces. "No doubt about it."

A deep chuckle from Hart made Denni open her eyes and smile at him. Putting her hands on either side of his face, she kissed each cheek, the cleft in his all too delectable chin and the dimple above his tantalizing upper lip before pulling back and glancing at the clock. Shocked to see how late it was, she got to her feet.

"I had no idea it was so late. I've got to get home," Denni said, not wanting to leave, but knowing she couldn't stay.

"Are you driving back to The Dalles or staying at the ranch?" Hart asked, walking Denni to the foyer and taking her coat from the closet. Helping her put it on, his hands lingered on her shoulders and he gave in to the desire to kiss her neck.

"The Dalles," Denni finally said, turning around to look at Hart as she yanked on black gloves pulled from her coat pocket. "Cass is spending the night with Viv so Trey and Cady can have a rare evening alone. The hands agreed to fend for themselves for dinner, at least the ones who didn't have other plans. Travis took Tess to Portland for a little getaway, and Trent whisked Lindsay off to Bend. I think those three hooligans of mine all have something of a romantic streak."

"You think?" Hart said, having witnessed the Thompson boys romancing their women on more than one occasion. He thought it was both admirable and sweet that they went to such efforts, especially since they were all married. "I'm sure there are a lot of women around here who'd appreciate it if they'd offer lessons."

Denni laughed and shook her head. "Maybe so, but you'd never get them to sit down and teach a class or the guys around here to attend." Finding her keys in the small clutch she carried, Hart took them from her and ran out to start her car. It was cold and frost had already settled on the windshield.

Hurrying back inside, he brought a blast of cold air along with him.

"It's cold out there," Hart said, wrapping his arms around Denni and pressing a cold nose to her warm cheek.

"You are chilly," Denni agreed, giving him a sassy grin. "I guess I'll have to do my best to warm you up before I go."

Hart didn't have time to give her statement any thought before she pulled his head down and gave him a kiss that had his blood roaring past warm right into boiling within a few seconds.

"Will you do that anytime I get chilled?" Hart whispered near her ear, making her tingle from head to toe. "If so, I'll keep the door open and one foot outside at all times."

"You're impossible," Denni said with a laugh, slapping playfully at Hart's chest before growing serious. Pulling off her glove, she placed her hand on his cheek and looked at him with a tender gaze. "Thank you for sharing your story with me, Hart. And for a lovely, lovely evening. It's one I'll never forget."

"Thank you, Denni, for being here. For being so special," Hart said, folding her in another warm hug. "Before I forget, don't run away."

He disappeared down the hall and came back carrying a huge bouquet of pink and white roses, a box of chocolate truffles, and a gift bag.

"My stars, Hart. What's all this?" Denni asked, taking the gift bag he held out to her. Opening it, she grinned to see a copy of a new romance by one of her favorite authors. She had no idea how he knew who she liked to read, but it was perfect.

"It's not Valentine's Day without flowers, candy, and romance," Hart said, grinning broadly.

"You are too much, Mr. Hammond. Entirely too much and I thank you," Denni said, kissing his cheek.

Opening her clutch, she took out a red envelope and handed it to Hart. Setting the flowers and candy on the foyer table, he opened the envelope, smiling to see it was two tickets to a comedy show coming to The Dalles.

"These are perfect, Denni. Thank you. I'm assuming since there are two tickets, you'll go with me?"

"Of course, although you don't have to feel obligated if you'd rather someone else accompanied you," Denni said, putting her glove back on and picking up the candy and gift bag while Hart took the flowers.

"There is no one else on the planet I'd rather spend time with. Oh, I almost forgot your cake," Hart said, turning back toward the kitchen.

Laughing, Denni put a hand on his arm. "It's yours. Enjoy. Just give me back the cake plate when you're through. You can give it to one of the kids if you want or I'll pick it up sometime."

"If I hold it hostage, you promise to come see me here again?"

"I promise," Denni said, giving Hart one last, lingering kiss before she opened the door and hurried out to her car. Hart helped her buckle the vase of flowers into the passenger seat so they wouldn't tip over and kissed her on the tip of her nose before shutting her door and watching her drive away.

"It's yours to take, to keep or break... Be careful, it's my heart," Hart hummed to himself as he walked back in the house and closed the door. "Don't break it, Denni. Please don't break it."

Chapter Eleven

*"Sometimes the heart sees
what is invisible to the eye."*
H. Jackson Brown, Jr.

"Well, was I right?" Ester asked, holding onto Denni's arm as they walked down the hall at the retirement center to the entry area. Denni was taking her to Sunday morning church services, out to lunch, then to her house for the afternoon.

"Right about what, Mama?" Denni asked, keeping her steps slower to match her mother's pace as they walked outside. Glad Ester was bundled against the frigid temperatures, the chill in the air still took their breath away, making it impossible to talk as they hurried to her car.

When Denni climbed behind the wheel and cranked up the heat, Ester turned her turquoise gaze to her daughter and grinned.

"I was right, wasn't I?"

"About what? Did you take a spoonful of crazy old lady this morning or does this conversation have a point?" Denni asked as she backed up and pulled onto the street.

"Hart, you silly goose! Is he a good kisser?" Ester asked, holding her gloved hands together to keep from clapping them in glee. "I know you spent Valentine's Day with him at his house. Anyone with sense in their head would have laid a good smooch or two on him and I didn't raise you to be stupid."

So distracted by what her mother said, Denni nearly ran through a stop sign. Slamming on the brakes, she threw an arm out across her mother and gasped, rattled by both the question and the fact she could have caused an accident.

"Good grief, Mama! What are you trying to do?" Denni asked, flustered and unsettled as she continued down the street toward the church.

"Find out if he was a good kisser. I thought that was obvious," Ester said, knowing from Denni's reaction she enjoyed his kisses probably more than she intended. "If I took a dose of crazy old lady, what did you eat? A heaping spoon of addlepated ninny? Just answer the question. I'll keep asking until you do."

Releasing a long-suffering sigh, Denni rolled her eyes as she turned a corner and pulled into the church parking lot. "Fine, if it will stop your infernal questioning and inappropriate delving into my private life, then the answer is yes. Happy now?"

"Extremely," Ester said, unfastening her seat belt and waiting for Denni to help her out of the car. "Did it take a while to warm up or was it bing, bang, boom right out of the gate? You know, you are a little out of practice."

"Mother!" Denni said, absolutely exasperated. "That is enough. One more word and I'll pour prune juice in with your grape juice."

"You wouldn't dare!" Ester said, stopping on the church step and glaring at her daughter.

"Just try me, old woman," Denni said with an impish grin, kissing Ester's cheek and taking her arm to help her up the rest of the steps.

After the service, Denni took Ester out to lunch at her favorite restaurant and visited with a few people they knew before returning to Denni's house. Ester read the Sunday paper and even helped Denni work on some piecing for the quilt she was making Hart. It was starting to take shape and look like something besides a flurry of colorful diamond-cut pieces of fabric.

"This might be your best quilt yet when you get it done, Denni." Ester ran her gnarled fingers over one point of the star that was finished. "I love the colors you chose."

"I do, too. It's going to look great on Hart's bed. He's got a big pine, custom-made job and needed a bold quilt to carry it off."

"And how would you know all about Hart's bed?" Ester asked, still feeling like needling her daughter.

"I had to measure it for the quilt," Denni said, agitated with her mother's line of questioning. What had gotten into her today? She wasn't usually this cantankerous. "Besides, I needed to see the color scheme of the room to know what to use in the quilt."

"I see," Ester said, enjoying the look of frustration on Denni's face. It was past time for Denni to meet someone and fall in love again. Glad that Hart was the one who seemed to tickle Denni's fancy, Ester relished the thought of giving her daughter a hard time about the whole thing. It did her good to have her orderly, self-contained world pushed off kilter once in a while.

"Just what do you see, Mama?"

"Nothing, darling," Ester said, smiling sweetly.

Denni rolled her eyes and bit back her comment when the doorbell rang. Setting aside her sewing, she opened the door to find Brice and Bailey standing on the step.

"Well, hello you two," Denni said, welcoming them in and giving Bailey a warm hug. Spending the weekdays a couple of hours southeast of Grass Valley where she worked as a paleontologist at a fossil bed site, Bailey left work early on Fridays so she could drive home to see Brice on the weekends. She generally drove back to Dayville late Sunday afternoons to the little house she rented just a few miles from the research center where she worked.

Brice was still living at the Running M Ranch with his folks until the April wedding then he planned to move into Bailey's rental. Although Bailey recently accepted a permanent position at the center, she and Brice weren't in a hurry to buy a house. Brice could take his wood working equipment anywhere, although his parents offered to let him keep his workshop at the ranch for as long as he liked. He figured he could move some of the smaller pieces of equipment to Bailey's place and when he needed to use the bigger pieces, he could drive to the ranch to do the work.

"What brings you into town today? Aren't you usually on your way back to Dayville by now, Bailey?" Denni asked as she took their coats and ushered them into her living room where Ester sat smiling, holding out a hand to each of them. They both kissed her cheek and Bailey sank down on the floor next to her beloved Nana. Of Ester's many grandchildren, Bailey was the one who looked the most like her, making her a favorite.

"Bailey had something she wanted to ask Nana so we decided to come in person. Trey told us you'd both be here this afternoon," Brice said, nodding encouragingly at Bailey.

"Nana, you know how I love retro fashions and how I haven't been able to find a wedding dress I really like. I was wondering…um, that is, if you wouldn't mind…" Bailey said, trying to get to the point.

"Just spit it out, honey," Ester said, patting her granddaughter's hand, smiling into eyes the same brilliant-blue shade as her own.

"May I borrow your wedding dress? From the photo of your wedding on display at the ranch, it appears to be exactly the style for which I've been searching," Bailey said, glancing from Ester to Denni. None of Ester's girls wanted to wear the dress, calling it outdated and old-fashioned. It was stored in Denni's guest room, along with her own wedding gown.

"Of course. I'd love for you to wear my dress, if it's still fit to be worn," Ester said, thumping Brice on the arm to help her out of the chair. Knowing Ester all his life, he grinned and offered her his arm then walked her down the hall to the bedroom where Denni dug though a cedar chest. Pulling out a tissue wrapped bundle, she placed it on the bed and folded back the yellowed sheets.

"Here it is," she said, carefully lifting out the dress and gently shaking it so the skirt floated down to the floor.

"Oh, Nana, it's absolutely stunning," Bailey said, afraid to touch the vintage fabric. Hurrying into the bathroom, she washed her hands and came back, running her fingers across the smooth pearl-encrusted satin. "You really wouldn't mind if I wore it?"

Ester smiled and wrapped her thin arms around her granddaughter. "Not at all, Bailey. I'd be honored to see you marry this rascal wearing it. Now, Brice, you skedaddle out of here and we'll see if this dress is going to fit our girl."

"Yes, Nana," Brice said, kissing Bailey's cheek. "I'll be in the living room, sugar, if you need me to help with anything."

Bailey was soon standing in front of the mirror in the gown, beaming as Denni and Ester smiled at her reflection.

"It's perfect. Just perfect," Denni said, adjusting a seam here and a tuck there. "We could sew some lace on the bottom if you wanted to take it back to floor length since you're several inches taller than Nana, otherwise you could definitely get away with it as a tea length gown."

"I don't want to alter it at all," Bailey said, running her hands along the full skirt. "Let's leave it like it is. I'm so glad it fits everywhere else."

"Me, too, sweetie," Ester said, turning Bailey around to study the gown from every angle. She was pleased beyond words to know her dress would be worn again. "You're going to make a beautiful bride."

"Thanks, Nana," Bailey said, hugging her grandmother. "I hope my marriage to Brice is as happy as yours was to Papa."

"It will be. You've got that sinfully handsome boy out there who'll be waiting to whisk you off and make you his own," Ester said, patting Bailey's back. "You need any pointers for the honeymoon?"

"Nana!" Bailey said, blushing at her grandmother's question.

"Just ignore her, Bailey. Your grandmother has been on a real toot today," Denni said, digging around in the cedar chest, looking for the veil that went with the dress. Finding it, she placed it on Bailey's head, completing the look.

"You're just spitting sour grapes because I quizzed you about your hot date with hunky Hart," Ester said, sitting down on the bed and admiring the way the veil sat on Bailey's golden head. At a glare from Denni, Ester grinned at Bailey and sent her a wink. She hadn't had this much fun in years.

"Ask her about how good he is at kissing," Ester said, trying not to giggle.

"Mama! Last warning or you are going to be guzzling prune juice, ol' girl," Denni said, making Bailey laugh.

A tap on the door made them all gasp.

"What's going on in there? When do I get a preview?" Brice asked from the other side of the door.

"Brice Morgan, you march that sweet hiney of yours right back to the living room and wait there," Ester yelled. "You should know better than to ask to see the bride in her gown."

"But, Nana, it's not just me…" Brice said.

"Go!" all three women yelled.

"But…"

"March it!" Ester called. They heard his boots clomp back down the hall.

Bailey turned to Denni and shrugged her shoulders, making all three women begin to laugh again. After making a few plans to get the dress cleaned, Denni unbuttoned the back and helped Bailey take it off, wrapping it in the tissue and leaving it on the bed. The next time someone went to Portland, they would take the dress to a cleaner that specialized in vintage attire.

Opening the door, the women heard two male voices and walked into the front room, surprised to find Hart visiting with Brice.

"Brice, you should have told us Hart was here," Denni said, smiling in greeting at the good-looking man.

"I tried but you ladies cut me off," Brice said, studying the way Denni came alive as soon as she noticed Hart in the room. He'd have to ask Travis what was going on between the two of them. For as long as Denni had been alone and as much as he liked Hart, he hoped another Thompson was about to fall in love.

"Well, why didn't you say that before you started asking to see the bride?" Ester asked, sitting down on the couch by Hart and patting his leg.

"A young man has to keep his priorities straight," Hart interjected, nodding at a grinning Brice.

"Do you have photos of your wedding, Nana? I'd really like to see more pictures of you wearing the dress," Bailey said, sitting on the arm of the chair Brice was occupying.

"Denni, don't you have most of my old photos around here somewhere?" Ester asked her daughter as she studied Hart. Ester's scrutinizing stare might have left Hart unsettled if he hadn't already fallen into the depths of Denni's sparkling eyes.

"Hmm? What was that, Mama?" Denni asked, pulling her attention from how nice Hart filled out his gray sports coat and black shirt to focus on her mother.

"Photos, Denni. Where are my photo albums?"

"In the guest room, I'll be right back," Denni said, disappearing down the hall and returning with three photo albums held in her hands. Setting them down on the coffee table, Brice and Bailey slid to the floor so they could see them while Ester flipped the pages. Denni sat on the arm of the couch next to Ester as she opened the first one. "Do you want to sit through this trip down memory lane, Hart, or is there something I can do for you?"

"I'm in no hurry," Hart said, leaning forward so he could see the old black and white photographs.

"That's me, right before the wedding. I thought I'd be nervous, but I was so excited to marry Graham. I couldn't wait to say 'I do' and become his bride."

Hart looked at the photo and then at Bailey. It wouldn't be hard for Brice to see what his bride-to-be was going to look like in her eighties because Bailey and Ester could have been twins.

"Wow, Nana. Bailey looks a lot like you," Brice said, staring at the photographs.

"That she does. Wasn't I quite a dish then?" Ester said, making everyone laugh.

"Yes, Mama," Denni said, reaching over and patting Bailey on the arm. "Just like our girl is now."

"Thanks, Aunt Denni," Bailey said, blushing again.

They looked through the rest of the photos while Denni served hot chocolate and cookies. Finishing with the last album, Brice and Bailey decided they needed to head back to Grass Valley.

"You don't have to drive back to Dayville tonight, do you sweetie?" Ester asked as Brice helped Bailey put on her coat.

"No, Nana. I have tomorrow off. Travis is going to help us design our wedding invitations in the morning then I'll head back in the afternoon," Bailey said, hugging her grandmother one last time. "Thanks again for letting me wear your dress. It's just what I wanted and it makes it even more special that it belonged to you."

"You're welcome, our beautiful bride-to-be," Ester said, patting Bailey's arm as Brice opened the door.

"She is beautiful," Brice agreed, kissing Bailey's cheek. "Come on, sugar, time to hit the road. I promised Mom we'd eat dinner with them tonight so we better hustle it up if you don't want me to get my ears boxed for being late."

"Your mother wouldn't box your ears," Bailey said with a teasing smile as they went out the door. "Even if you do deserve it."

Watching the young couple leave, the door had barely shut behind them when Ester turned her attention to Hart. "What brings you to The Dalles this afternoon?" Ester asked.

"I had a few errands to run and thought I'd bring back Denni's cake plate," Hart said, nodding toward the kitchen where Brice set the plate on the table when Hart arrived.

"You didn't need to return it so soon," Denni said, sitting down in the chair across from the couch, wishing she'd taken her mother home for a nap before Hart arrived. In her current sassy mood, there was no telling what she might say to embarrass them both. "I'm in no hurry for it."

"I know, but it was sitting empty on my counter, so I decided to bring it back," Hart said, wishing Ester would quit watching him so closely. He felt like a mouse about to be devoured by a cat with her studying his every move. "Your daughter made the best red velvet cake I've ever eaten in my entire life."

"Who do you think taught her to cook?" Ester said, slapping Hart on the leg. "She was a slow learner in the kitchen, though. Denni preferred to be outside or doing something that involved speed and motion to following a recipe. Why, once she even set a pan of grease on fire and I thought we might lose the whole kitchen."

"Mother," Denni said, glaring at Ester, hoping she would get the message to be quiet. Unfortunately, it seemed to encourage her.

"You don't say," Hart said, looking at Denni and giving her his broad grin. "What else did she do?"

Ester went on to relay a number of stories all designed to show how incompetent Denni had been in the domestic arts growing up. If Hart believed everything Ester said, he was probably confused as to how she knew what end of a spoon to use.

Leaning back in her chair, Denni watched Hart interact with her mother and couldn't help the smile that tugged the corners of her mouth upward. He was so good with the older woman, who seemed bent on being obnoxious and exasperating today. She loved seeing his tousled sandy head bent near Ester's white one, laughing at the story she was telling.

"Is that okay with you?" Hart asked, waiting for Denni's response.

"I'm sorry, I guess I was wool-gathering," Denni said, not wanting to admit she'd been studying Hart. "What did you ask?"

"She was checking you out," Ester said, laughing as she slapped Hart's leg again. "Try not to be so obvious, darling."

Denni blushed and wanted at that moment to stuff the quilt pieces she'd been working on earlier into her mother's mouth.

"I asked if you'd mind if I took you two lovely ladies out to dinner," Hart said, trying to hide his amusement at the way Denni's mother made her so befuddled. He probably shouldn't find as much entertainment in the situation as he did, but he could tell Ester and Denni shared a special bond, despite their ongoing teasing and fussing at each other.

"Are you sure you want to drag this ol' girl out in public. She'd been on quite a roll today," Denni said, raising an eyebrow her mother's direction. "I can't be held responsible for anything she says or does."

Hart laughed while Ester spluttered. "In that case, absolutely. I must take you both out for dinner."

"You heard the man, let's shake a leg," Ester said, grinning while Hart helped her up and then held her coat while she put it on. Denni suggested they take her car rather than Hart's pickup since it would be easier for Ester to get in and out of the smaller vehicle. Hart took her keys and went to warm it up.

"Mama, you better behave or I'll tell the director at the center you are positively dying to share a room with Lydia Bradshaw," Denni said, pulling on her coat and gathering up her purse and gloves.

"You wouldn't!" Ester said in disbelief. Lydia was a negative, bigmouth gossip and one of the few people Ester actively avoided. Her great-grandsons were unholy terrors and had created their share of trouble at the Triple T when they spiked the punch at Trent and Lindsay's wedding, resulting in poor Bailey getting completely sloshed. The very notion of rooming with that woman was unthinkable.

"I would so if you don't button that loose lip of yours. Honestly, did you get a double dose of fiber this morning? You aren't usually quite this...rambunctious."

"Would you deny a poor old woman with one foot in the grave a little fun?" Ester asked as she pulled on her gloves and picked up her purse.

"Nope, but that doesn't come close to describing you. You're feisty, sassy, and way too ornery for your own good," Denni said, giving Ester a hug around her thin shoulders.

"Yet, you love me anyway," Ester patted Denni's cheek as they opened the door and stepped outside just as Hart backed the car to the end of the sidewalk. Hurrying around it, he offered his arm to Ester and helped get her settled in the back seat. Denni climbed behind the wheel and drove to the restaurant.

Ester insisted they sit in a booth then refused to scoot over when Denni tried to slide in beside her. Grinning to herself, she thought her efforts at forcing Denni and Hart together were going quite well.

When the meal was over, Ester declared it time for her to go back to the center, since it had been a long fun-filled day. Denni was going to take her to her room alone, but Ester asked Hart to come along and leaned on his arm as they strolled down the hall, drawing looks from everyone who saw them walk in.

Ester knew Hart would turn heads and provide plenty of fodder for the gossip mill at the center. She could almost count down to the minute before her friends pounded on her door wanting to know if the handsome man walking her in was really a celebrity.

Practically dancing with anticipation, Ester chatted with Hart all the way to her room, leaving Denni trailing behind shaking her head and rolling her eyes.

At her apartment, she unlocked her door and walked inside. Hart helped her off with her coat and Denni hung it in the closet before looking around to make sure Ester didn't need anything.

"Can I get you anything before we go, Mama?"

"No, Denni. I'm fine," Ester said, sinking down in her rocker and turning her vibrant blue gaze to Hart. "Thank you for a wonderful dinner, Hart. I so appreciate it."

"You're welcome, Mrs. Nordon," Hart said, taking the hand she held out to him and pressing a light kiss to the back of it. She reminded him of his own grandmother and wore the same perfume. He thought Ester was a real kick in the pants, especially the way she seemed to work to throw Denni off her game. "It was a pleasure to spend time with you today."

"I'm pretty sure you'd rather have this girl of mine all to yourself, but thanks for putting up with me anyway. And call me Ester."

"Yes, ma'am," Hart said with a grin.

He would have backed away but Ester tugged on his hand and motioned for him to bend down. When he did, she put her lips near his ear and whispered, "Give her time. Her heart knows, even if her head is a little slow on the uptake."

Confused by Ester's cryptic message, Hart smiled and stepped toward the door.

Denni kissed Ester on the cheek, spread an afghan over her lap, and handed her the TV remote before she took one final look around Ester's apartment. "If you need anything, let me know. I'll check on you in day or two. Maybe by then you'll have worked whatever has gotten into you out of your system. Remember, prune juice and Lydia Bradshaw."

"Your idle threats don't scare me, Denni. Now get out of here," Ester said, grinning broadly.

"Love you, Mama," Denni said, waving as she walked out of the apartment.

"Love you, too, baby," Ester called after her. Hart waved one final time at Ester and shut the door. He took Denni's hand and looped it around his arm, walking her back down the hall and out to her car.

Once they were driving toward Denni's house, he turned and studied her for a long moment. "Do you and your Mom always talk like that to each other?"

"Not always," Denni said, realizing the name calling she and her mother engaged in could sound bad to an outsider. It was a familiar way of teasing they both enjoyed and never took seriously. "Sometimes we might even sound insulting."

Hart laughed and leaned back in the seat. "You are something else and I see exactly where you got it from. Ester is a lot of fun."

"I just hope I'm as 'with it' when I'm her age," Denni said, feeling true admiration for how well her mother did considering her age. "She can keep us all on our toes, that's for sure. Poor Trent has been trying for years to lick her at a game of Scrabble and she keeps beating the socks off him, then promises the next time she'll let him win."

"What's the deal with prune juice and Lydia Bradshaw?" Hart asked as Denni pulled into her carport and parked the car.

"Two things she greatly despises. I use them as threats on occasion to keep her in line."

"You are evil and conniving," Hart said, getting out of the car and rushing around it to give Denni his hand as she got out on the driver's side. "I like it."

Denni asked him in and made them both a cup of decaf coffee before Hart decided he should probably head home. Taking their mugs to the kitchen, Denni turned around to see Hart dangling her silver hoop earring from his finger.

"Did you find my earring? I realized when I got home from your place I was no longer wearing it and wondered where I lost it," Denni said, taking it from Hart. "I looked all over my car, but decided it must have fallen off in your driveway."

"I found it in the couch cushions and didn't really want to try to explain how it came to be in my possession to your kids, so I decided to drop it off, along with your cake plate," Hart said, his eyes twinkling with mischief. "I think you might have lost it when you were trying to have your way with me."

Denni dropped the earring on the table and shot her gaze to Hart's, only to see a devilish smile spread across his attractive face.

"You're nearly as impossible as my mother," Denni said, playfully slapping at his chest. "I did not, under any circumstance, try to have my way with you."

"Maybe not then, but I'd be willing to give you another chance. Just name the time and place."

"Aren't you the cocky one, Hart Hammond," Denni said, enjoying his teasing. "What makes you think I'm even interested?"

"The fact that when I do this," Hart said, grabbing her hand and pulling her against his chest. Trailing kisses along her jaw then nibbling on her neck, he felt her shiver in pleasure as she leaned into him. "You do that."

"Hart," Denni said on a soft whisper, turning her head so their lips connected in a fiery kiss that made her knees feel wobbly and her head spin.

"I think this is where I need to say goodbye," Hart said, losing himself in another passionate kiss before taking a step back then another until he was standing near the door. Putting on his coat, he kissed Denni again and told her to have sweet dreams.

"Don't you need to warm up your truck before you leave?" Denni asked, searching for any excuse to keep Hart with her a little longer.

"I'm pretty sure as hot as you've made my blood run in the last few minutes, it will defrost the truck in no time," Hart said, giving Denni one more taunting grin. "But if you want to continue this out there, we can take off the chill and steam up the windows at the same time."

"Good night, Hart," Denni said, giving him a playful shove out the door, feeling her cheeks flush with heat at his teasing. If he'd kissed her a few more times, she might have taken him up on his offer.

Chapter Twelve

"Only one book is worth reading: the heart."
Ajahn Chah

Sitting at her kitchen table, drinking a cup of coffee, Denni was reading a daily devotional book when she heard her doorbell chime.

Wondering who could possibly be at her house at this early hour of the morning, she was glad she'd already showered, dressed and done her makeup for the day.

Hurrying to the door, she pulled it open, surprised to find Hart on her doorstep, offering a friendly smile.

"Morning, sunshine," Hart said, kissing her cheek and stepping inside, leaving his hat and coat on the chair nearest the door. "I apologize profusely for dropping by so early."

"It's fine, Hart," Denni said, closing the door and wondering why Hart kept looking at her with such a funny grin. Glancing down, her blouse was buttoned straight, the creases in her slacks were precise and she'd even put on shoes this morning instead of her fuzzy slippers. "Can I get you a cup of coffee?"

"Sure," he said, continuing to grin at her.

Denni went to the cupboard and took out a mug, filling it with hot, black coffee, and placed it in front of Hart at her small kitchen table. Turning around to get cream and sugar, she caught her reflection in the kitchen window and noticed three bright pink hot rollers perched on top her head.

Sucking in a gulp of air, she was sure she would die right there on the kitchen floor. No wonder Hart was looking at her like she was half-deranged. She always put a few strategically placed rollers on top of her head to give her hair a little boost of volume. At his arrival, she completely forgot they were even there.

"I'll be right back," she said, racing down the hall, tugging on the curlers as she went. Flinging them down on the bathroom counter, she fluffed her hair and returned to the kitchen to find Hart trying to subdue his chuckles.

"Oh, go ahead and laugh, buster. I can tell you want to," Denni said, sinking down on the chair beside him.

Hart's chuckles turned into a full-fledged laugh and Denni found herself laughing right along with him.

"That'll teach you to show up without warning," she said, holding her coffee mug with both hands. She started to get up from the table, needing to do something to deflect her embarrassment. "Can I make you some breakfast?"

"No, Denni. Thank you, but I'm fine. I didn't come here to bum coffee or a meal off you, or even catch you with curlers in your hair," Hart said, his grin still broad and teasing. "I just received word there was an attempted robbery at one of my stations and the manager was injured. I'll be out of town for a while until I get things settled there. I want to make sure he's going to be okay and help the employees handle the situation."

"Hart, I'm so sorry. Is there anything I can do?" Denni asked, placing a gentle hand on top of his callused one.

He sandwiched her hand between his and shook his head. "There's nothing you can do, except maybe say a prayer or two for my manager. It sounds like he was stabbed in the arm. He should have a full recovery, but it's bound to be traumatic and scary for him."

"Absolutely," Denni said, watching as Hart drained his coffee cup and got to his feet.

Walking back to the front room, he put on his coat and stood looking at Denni. "I only found out this morning and didn't want to call too early. The station is near Eugene, so I'm driving down, but I couldn't leave without telling you goodbye in person. I'll try and call you later tonight, if that's okay."

"More than okay," Denni said, hugging Hart as he stood at her door. "I'd be ticked if you didn't let me know you made it there in one piece."

"Don't suppose I could get a kiss for the road. It might be a while before I see you again," Hart said, wrapping his arms around Denni's trim waist and breathing deeply of her scent. Trying to memorize every nuance, every sensation she stirred in him, he marveled again at how right it felt to hold her in his arms. Maybe she was the woman he'd been waiting his entire life to love. If he was reading her signals correctly, she seemed interested in seeing him on a more regular basis.

"I may be coerced to give you one or two," Denni said, her eyes already turning soft at the thought of Hart's lips on hers.

"Feeling generous this morning, are you?"

"At least to handsome cowboys who pound on my door at an indecent hour, laugh at my choice of hair accessories, and drink my coffee."

"Is that so?" Hart asked, lowering his lips to Denni's and feeling the jolt all the way to his toes. It was like that every time they kissed. He was sure someone walking by could see the sparks lighting up around them as they momentarily lost themselves in each other.

"I'll miss you," Denni whispered, resting her head against Hart's chest, her hands clasping the lapels of his coat to steady the world he'd just rocked off kilter with his kisses.

"I'll miss you, too, my little sunshine," Hart said, kissing the top of her head and running his hands up and down her back, loving the feel of the satiny fabric of her blouse against his rough skin. Other visions of satin and lace flew into his head and he quickly chased the thoughts away. "Be nice to your mama while I'm gone."

"I'm always nice to her," Denni said, looking up at him with a grin. "She'd think something was wrong if I didn't give her any sass."

"Sass and spitfire, that's you for sure," Hart said, as he kissed her one more time, settled his hat on his head and opened the door. Before he could take a step outside, Denni grabbed his hand, squeezing it between hers. "Be careful and stay safe."

"I will, Denni. Be a good girl and I might bring you back something."

Hart winked at her then was out the door and gone.

><><

"Denni, have we lost you again?" Cady asked as she, Tess and Lindsay all turned questioning looks at Denni.

"What, honey?" Denni asked, realizing she hadn't listened to anything the girls had said in the last several minutes. She'd been thinking about Hart. Gone for almost two weeks, she missed the man more than she would ever have thought possible.

"She's long gone, girls," Lindsay said with a laugh, patting Denni on the arm.

"I know where to find her," Tess said, a teasing glint filling her warm chocolate brown eyes. "Somewhere with a cowboy about the same height as Trey, same sandy colored hair as Trav, and a striking resemblance to a handsome rock star. Isn't that right, Denni?"

"Well...I...um..." Denni said, trying to regain her mental footing.

"Nana said he's a great kisser," Cady said, joining the teasing. "Care to elaborate on that statement?"

"No, I don't particularly care to, and you should know better than to listen to what Nana says," Denni said, sitting up primly in her chair and madly thumbing through the magazine in front of her.

"Come on, Denni. You can't kiss someone like Hart and not tell," Tess said with a perfect little pout as she pleaded with Denni to spill the beans. "You never did tell us how your Valentine's date went and that was right before he had to leave town."

"Don't you girls have enough to worry about without taking on the details of my love life?" Denni asked, feeling her cheeks heat.

"Look at that blush," Lindsay said, giggling. "She's got stories to tell."

"Oh, for Pete's sake, you three! You are every bit as ornery as those sons of mine," Denni said, exasperated with her daughters-in-law. "You were all so sweet before you married into the Thompson family. If I didn't know better, I'd say my hooligans have corrupted you."

"They have, so you know we won't be easily dissuaded," Cady said, leaning back in her chair.

Denni was spending the weekend at the ranch, helping Cady, Lindsay and Tess finish up details for Bailey's bridal shower and wedding plans. Brice insisted Bailey go to Portland with him to make a furniture delivery to a store that started carrying some of his work or she would have been right in the middle of the teasing.

As the four women sat around the table, sipping tea and studying bridal magazines, the conversation kept coming back around to Denni's budding romance, much to her dismay. She'd been daydreaming about seeing Hart again when Cady noticed her lack of participation in the conversation going on around her.

Releasing a long-suffering sigh, she eyed each girl, hoping to subdue them a little. Instead, they started giggling and Tess wiggled an eyebrow at her.

"Come on, Denni. We absolutely promise not to tell the boys anything," Tess said, crossing her finger over her heart.

"You three vow to never, ever, breathe a word of it to my boys?" Denni asked, making them all promise. Assured of their ability to not repeat the conversation to the Thompson troublemakers, she studied her cup of tea while a smile tugged at her mouth and lit her eyes. "He is a good kisser."

"I knew it," Tess said, slapping the top of the table. "Nana said he just looks like a man who knows how to treat a lady."

"In this particular instance, Nana is correct," Denni said, leaning back in her chair with a dreamy look on her face. "He's amazing."

"If you were in one of the romances Lindsay loves to read, we'd have to title it something like 'One Hunky Hart.' I've never seen you look so happy, Denni," Cady said, reaching across the table and clasping Denni's hand.

"Thanks, honey," Denni said, smiling back at her first daughter-in-law. "He makes me feel young and beautiful again."

"That's awesome," Tess said, reaching for the plate of cookies on the table and taking one. "So what did you do for your big Valentine's date?"

"He made dinner at his house. Hart's been bragging about how much better his beef is than ours and, truth be told, he's right. Those steaks were the best I ever had," Denni said.

"Maybe the company and atmosphere enhanced the flavor," Lindsay said, rubbing her hand across her growing belly.

"Perhaps," Denni said, smiling at Lindsay. "But he really did put a lot of effort into the evening. We sat at a cozy little table, with linen and china, in front of his big fireplace. He asked me to dance and even sang me a song."

"He sang?" Tess asked, looking at Cady. "I just knew he'd be able to sing. Does he have a good voice?"

"It sounded good to me," Denni said, remembering the special moment.

"Well, what did he sing?" Cady asked, dying for more detail.

"An old Irving Berlin song, '*Be Careful, It's My Heart.*' I have to say, it was pretty romantic," Denni said, sipping her tea.

"Good gracious, Denni, that's huge," Cady said, shaking her head.

"What do you mean?" Denni asked, looking at Cady for an explanation.

"I mean the words from that song. If I remember correctly, it basically says 'here's my heart, it's yours to do with it what you will, but please don't break it.' Isn't that right?"

"Well, something along those lines."

"Oh, my gosh," Tess said, leaning back in her chair. "You're right, that is huge."

"I didn't realize…I don't…" Denni said, wondering if the girls were making more of the song than Hart intended.

"Lindsay, you're the expert on romance. What do you think?" Cady asked, turning to the tall blond smiling from her seat next to Denni.

"I think Cady's right. It is huge," Lindsay said, tipping her head to one side as she looked at Denni. "From what you've said, and not said, I think he's trying very hard to let you know he cares about you. The heart is a hard book to read, but it seems to me he's highlighted some pretty important parts and put them out there in bold print for you to see."

"Oh. I…hmm." Denni sat back in her chair, looking a little shocked and uncertain. "As you well know, I've been out of the dating game for almost forty years. Hart's the first man I've dated since Drew died and I guess, in all honesty, I don't have a clue what I'm doing."

"You must be doing something right," Tess observed, offering Denni a saucy grin. "He keeps coming back, doesn't he?"

The girls all laughed and Denni flapped her hand at Tess.

"Behave, sugarplum," Denni said, getting caught up in the good humor of the three girls.

"We really are happy for you," Lindsay said, putting her arms around Denni and giving her a hug. "I know we all give you a hard time, but it's so nice to see you enjoying life so much."

"Besides, it's not every day our mom gets to date a celebrity look-alike then kiss and tell," Tess teased.

"Now, listen here, I didn't kiss and…" Denni said, interrupted when Trey came in the kitchen door.

"Didn't kiss and what, Mom?" Trey asked, grinning as he went over to Cady's chair and kissed her cheek before sitting down beside her.

"Never mind."

"No, I'd love to hear who you've been kissing and what you've been doing. If that gas station Don Juan isn't behaving in a manner we deem appropriate, we'll be sending a chaperone with you from now on," Trey said, turning so only Cady and Tess could see him wink.

"You'll do no such thing," Denni said, giving Trey a motherly scowl. "I've had about all the discussion regarding my love life that I'm willing to tolerate today, so unless you want to face the wrath of a mother pushed beyond endurance, let's change the topic."

"Fine," Trey said, snatching a handful of cookies off the plate on the table and leaning back in his chair. He was thrilled his mother was opening herself up to the idea of dating and he was so glad to see her look happy again. The idea of anyone kissing her, though, was a hard pill to swallow. "Let's talk about Hart keeping his lips, hands, and anything else to himself."

"Trey," Denni said, getting up from her chair and walking to where her son munched on cookies while balancing his chair on it's back legs. He sat with a big smile creasing his rugged face, his turquoise eyes sparkling with amusement as he watched her. "I warned you not to mess with me, honey."

"I'm just funnin' you…" Trey started to say but his words were abruptly cut off when Denni gave him a push and his chair flipped over, scattering cookies every direction while Cady, Tess and Lindsay broke into gales of laughter.

"Don't mess with your mom," Tess said, pointing at Trey. "Or you'll end up tossing your cookies."

Denni smirked and went to the kitchen to get a fresh cup of tea. Her boys might be grown men, but it didn't hurt for her to take them down a peg or two once in a while.

><><

"You did not," Hart said, in disbelief when he called Denni later that evening and she told him about tipping over Trey's chair.

"I did, too. If all three of them had been here, I'd have nailed them all," Denni said, still riding the high of besting one of her boys. They so often played good-natured jokes on her, she wasn't often the one with the upper hand.

"May I ask what prompted you to humiliate Trey in front of the girls?" Hart asked, unable to keep the humor out of his voice. He wished he could have witnessed the look on Trey's face when his mother marched up to him and tipped him over.

"No, you may not. Let's just say he had fair warning to keep his thoughts to himself and faced the consequences of doing otherwise."

"I see," Hart said, feeling the need to taunt Denni. "He wouldn't have been commenting on you turning into a wild woman and chasing after one of Sherman County's eligible bachelors, would he?

Denni swallowed her laugh. "No, he was not commenting on my chasing anyone, which I'm not. He did, however, make a reference to some local Don Juan cozying up to his mother and the need to send along a chaperone."

"Don Juan, is it? When I get home, I'm going to hunt down whoever it is that's sniffing at your door and give them a piece of my mind," Hart teased. "I don't want anyone getting any ideas about my girl."

Denni perked up to hear Hart refer to her as his. She found the idea entirely appealing. If Hart came home tomorrow, it couldn't be soon enough to suit her. Spending time apart made her realize how much she looked forward to seeing him, talking to him. Then there was that whole kissing thing she particularly enjoyed.

"Your girl?" Denni asked, hoping Hart meant what he'd said. "Is that what I am?"

"I'd sure like to think so, sunshine. Is that okay with you?" Hart asked, sounding a little wary. He wondered if he'd pushed Denni too far, assumed too much.

"That's more than okay. It's perfect," Denni said, her voice going as soft as her insides.

"Good," Hart said, his voice sounding low and husky. "That's good. Look, I've got to run. If you can believe it,

I'm working swing shift at the station tonight, but I'll call you in the morning. I wish I could give you a big ol' hug right now. Maybe even a kiss or two, or twenty."

Denni giggled. "I wish you could, too. Thanks for calling, Hart. I miss you."

"Miss you, too, sunshine. Sweet dreams."

Stuffing her phone in her pocket, she turned around to see Trey shaking his head as he rolled his eyes.

"Don't say anything," he said, holding up his hand in hopes of silencing her. "I heard more than I wanted to as it is. I'm not here to eavesdrop or give you more grief. Cass wanted to know if you'd come read her a bedtime story."

"Sure," Denni said, glad to know her boys drew the line somewhere. She started to follow Trey down the hall and smiled when he dropped an arm around her shoulders, kissing the top of her head.

"For the record, Mom, I'm really, really glad you found Hart. He's a good guy and good for you."

"Thanks, honey," Denni said, giving Trey a squeeze around his waist. "I think he is, too."

Chapter Thirteen

*"A joyful heart is the inevitable result
of a heart burning with love."*
Mother Teresa

Breathing deeply of the fresh spring air, Hart stood on his back deck and looked out at the pasture behind his house where his herd of Belgian Blues grazed.

If he'd known the sky was just a little bluer, the air a little sweeter here in Grass Valley than any other place he'd ever been on earth, he might have moved to the community sooner.

Spring finally chased away the lingering remnants of winter and everything seemed to be bursting with growth and new life. He had a dozen baby calves romping around in his herd of cattle and four Appaloosa colts he couldn't wait to show Cass when she arrived.

After much asking and cajoling, he finally talked the Thompson bunch into letting him play host for a meal. They were all arriving after church today for lunch and Hart was looking forward to showing them his place.

Reluctant to descend upon his home with their rambunctious group, Trey and Cady both thanked him for his offer but told him it wouldn't be fair for him to have to put up with all of them at once.

Assuring the couple he wanted to do it, he'd finally convinced them to agree. If he hadn't hinted to Cady that he wouldn't feel right eating another meal at the Triple T until he provided one in return, he wouldn't have gotten her to go along with his plan.

Watching the sun spread its warmth and light as it began to climb higher in the morning sky, Hart thought of Denni, his own little sunshine.

Acknowledging weeks ago he was completely and utterly in love with the wonderful woman, he was still trying to figure out what that meant for him now and for his future.

He'd never, in his life, felt this way before. At fifty-two, he'd finally fallen head over heels in love and didn't have a clue what to do about it, other than take it one day at a time. Otherwise, thoughts of planning a future together began to flood through him and he had to rein himself in. He knew taking things slow was the best course of action, especially when he wasn't sure Denni felt the same way.

The passionate kisses they shared, the way her eyes lit up when they were together, and the soul-deep laughter that erupted when they teased and joked gave him an excellent idea of how she felt. Before he entertained thoughts of taking things to the next level, he wanted to know she was as loopy in love as he'd been with her since the trip to Tucson.

Feeling a smile stretch his cheeks just thinking about Denni, Hart knew he spent the majority of his time these days with an idiotic grin plastered across his face and no reasonable excuse why it was there except that he had never been so happy in his entire life.

Gone for almost three weeks to Eugene while his station manager recuperated, Hart could have left the assistant in charge but that wasn't how he operated. He offered encouragement to the staff, worked any shift that needed filled and led by example. When the manager was ready to return to work, Hart worked three days with him until he felt comfortable resuming management of the station before returning home.

Driving straight to Denni's house, it was late when he arrived, but she met him at the door with a look of welcome and a hungry kiss that let him know she'd missed him as much as he missed her.

He brought her a book of original quilt patterns from some little old woman who had them for sale in a craft shop across the street from his gas station. When Denni glanced through the patterns, with the woman's notes and tips by each design, she threw her arms around Hart and kissed him until they both were breathless. He took that as a good sign that she liked his gift.

Glad to be back at his house, Hart was grateful Brice agreed to keep an eye on it and his livestock while he was gone. He didn't think Brice and Bailey minded having somewhere to hang out free from prying eyes and teasing relatives, either.

Glancing at his watch, Hart took a final drink of his coffee and went back in the house to finish what preparations he could for the lunch he was making for the Thompsons.

Cady volunteered to bring dessert, so Hart agreed to that much. He was smart enough not to turn down something sweet and delicious when Cady offered it. He had yet to eat anything the lovely girl made that wasn't unbelievably good. According to information Denni shared, Cady planned to pursue a career as a chef until she decided she didn't like the long hours required by such a position. With her no-nonsense attitude, he could see how she did well as an assistant to a well-known attorney in Seattle. A run-away fiancé drove her to Grass Valley to work as a waitress in her aunt's cafe and from there it was a short leap to becoming a housekeeper and cook at the Triple T Ranch.

Hart finished making a salad and put it in the fridge then looked to make sure the big table in the dining room was properly set. He hoped his attention to detail would make his grandmother proud. More than once, as she made him set the table, she told him it didn't matter if he was a bull rider, a bank president, or an astronaut, everyone needed to know proper etiquette and manners. He'd ignored most of what he learned during the years he was a bull rider and his time of grieving Yelina, but once he got his life on track, he began applying what his grandmother taught him.

Good manners, perseverance, hard work, and a friendly smile had taken him far from the broken man who lived in his pickup to the successful owner of a small gas station empire.

Running upstairs to his room, Hart brushed his teeth again, slapped on some cologne, changed into a dress shirt and sports jacket, then hurried back downstairs and out the door.

Arriving at the church right on time, he grinned when Cass barreled out of Trey's pickup and ran over to him for a hug. Picking up the lively child, he tossed her in the air, absorbing her giggles into his heart. During the years of building his business, he never had the opportunity to spend much time around children. It was something he missed and regretted. He knew at this point in his life he'd never have his own, but if a family like the Thompson's was willing to adopt him, he'd gladly lay claim to them.

"I can't wait to see your horses today," Cass said, giving Hart one of her trademark stranglehold hugs around the neck.

"I can't wait for you to see them. Did your grammy tell you I have baby horses?"

"You do?" Cass asked, her big china blue eyes going wide with excitement. Jiggling her feet as he carried her toward the church steps and her family, he grinned thinking it was true that she was in perpetual motion.

"I absolutely do. Maybe you can help me think of a name for one of them," Hart said, setting her down and taking her hand as they reached the steps.

"Mama! Did you hear that? Hart needs my help naming the baby horse. Oh, boy!" Cass said, running inside the church to no doubt relay the information to her best friend Ashley.

"Thanks for making her day," Cady said, smiling at Hart as they walked up the steps. "She'll be talking about this for weeks."

"She's a sweet thing," Hart said, stepping inside the foyer and watching Cass's red curls bounce as she waved her hands and talked to her little friend. "Lively, but sweet. If it wasn't for that red hair, I'd think she was a true-blood Thompson."

"Me, too," Cady whispered, leaning toward Hart conspiratorially. "She's definitely got the personality to be one."

"I can only guess if you two are whispering, it means trouble for the rest of us," Denni said, walking in and taking Hart's hand in hers. Her eyes twinkled with joy and humor as she leaned against his side.

Hart looked down at her and felt his heart quicken. Wearing a spring suit in a shade of pale green hat made her eyes glow and her cheeks rosy, Denni took his breath away.

"You look lovely this morning, sunshine," Hart whispered in Denni's ear, making a warm smile spread across her face. "Absolutely beautiful."

"Thank you, Hart. You look pretty snappy yourself," Denni said, admiring the way Hart filled out his navy jacket and light blue shirt with creased jeans and polished boots. He rarely wore a tie, but always looked so nice and put-together. To say he was handsome was an understatement. Agreeing with her mother's assessment, Hart was definitely hunky.

"Are you sure you want my bunch of hooligans shattering your peaceful Sunday afternoon?" Denni asked as they walked down the aisle and sat in the pew the family usually occupied, although they now needed closer to two.

"I'm looking forward to not only showing Cass the colts, but proving to those boys of yours my beef is the best," Hart said with a sly wink.

"I heard that and can't wait for you to try," Trey said, leaning around Denni to grin at Hart.

A few hours later, Trey was leaning back in his chair, once again grinning at their host. "You win, Hart. Hands-down that is the best beef I've ever eaten."

"But if you tell anyone we said that, we'll deny it to our dying day," Trent said, leaning around Lindsay to look at Hart. "We've got way too many Angus to run anything else, but I think we may need to get a few head of Belgian Blues for our own personal eating."

"I'd be happy to sell you a couple or point you in the direction of the some guys I've done business with in the past," Hart said, pleased the Thompsons enjoyed his beef.

"The whole meal was wonderful, Hart. Thank you so much for having us," Cady said, impressed that a bachelor would have the ability to not only put together a nice meal, but cook for their large, rowdy bunch. In addition to the tender steak Hart grilled, he also had baked potatoes with all the trimmings, a big green salad, dinner rolls that he admitted he bought from Viv, and buttery corn. Cady contributed a lemon bundt cake that everyone was too full at the moment to eat. They decided to save it for later to serve with coffee.

"I appreciate you all coming today. I've wanted to show you the place for a while and pay you back for all the fine meals I've eaten at the Triple T," Hart said, smiling at the friendly faces gathered around the table in his big dining room. He never actually gave much thought to using the room, but was glad he went ahead with the original plans to include it and bring in a big table that could seat a dozen people with ease.

In addition to Denni, all three of her boys and their lovely brides were there, along with Cass, Brice and Bailey.

"Would you like a grand tour of the house?" Hart asked after they sat at the table for a while visiting.

"We'd love one," Tess said, excited to finally see the house Brice had talked so much about. Working for the construction company that built the house, Brice knew every inch of it. It was the detailed work he'd done in Hart's office that had gotten his attention. When the construction company downsized and left Brice unemployed, he decided to pursue his dream of building hand-crafted furniture. Hart recognized his talent and hired Brice to build several pieces for the house.

"Brice, since you know the house as well as I do, why don't you show the guys around while I escort the ladies?"

"Sounds good," Brice said, getting to his feet. They all helped carry dishes into the kitchen and the women insisted on loading the dishwasher and cleaning up, which only took a few minutes.

Starting in the kitchen, Brice led the men off toward Hart's office and the back of the house while Hart took the women on a tour of the downstairs, pointing out pieces of furniture Brice made and special details about the house he particularly liked. Denni, who'd had the full tour before, was thrilled to see the entire house again.

Entering the first guest room upstairs, Cady ran her hand over the quilt on the bed and smiled. "I recognize this one, Denni. You had it in the store window for a while, didn't you?"

"You've got a great eye and memory, Cady," Denni said, knowing Cady loved fabrics even if she rarely found time to sew. "Some of the pieces in this one match those I used in your wedding quilt."

"Do you make quilts for all the weddings around here?" Hart asked, as they walked down the hall and looked at another bedroom.

"Not all, just the special ones," Denni said, smiling at the young women walking behind them. "And these girls are extra special."

"Does that mean Brice and I get one, too?" Bailey asked, hoping the answer would be yes. She loved her aunt's quilts and wanted one for her own.

"If I told you that, it would ruin the surprise," Denni said, winking at Bailey.

"In that case, I'll act completely astounded when we open it," Bailey said with a smile.

Continuing on their tour, Hart pushed open the door to his spacious bedroom. "This is the master suite."

"Oh, my gosh. This is fabulous," Tess said, admiring the hulking pine furniture, the fireplace, and the great view of his pasture out the window.

"I kind of like it," Hart said, grinning at the women. "When Denni finishes the quilt for in here, it will be even better."

The girls noted the plain denim blue comforter on the bed. "What pattern are you making, Denni?" Cady asked.

"Lone Star," Denni said, knowing Cady would visualize it exactly like she had.

"What colors?" Tess asked, continuing to look around the room.

"Blue, green, tan, and burgundy," Denni said, picturing the finished quilt on the bed. Envisioning it somehow brought images to mind of Hart on that quilt minus his shirt, beckoning her to join him. Slamming the door on those thoughts, she turned around to see Tess and Cady watching her.

"It will be perfect, Denni," Cady said, giving her mother-in-law a smile that let her know the flush on her cheeks didn't go unnoticed.

"Shall we go down and join the guys? I'd like to show you around outside, too," Hart said, motioning for the girls to precede him out of the room. He heard them chatting as they descended the stairs. Before Denni could follow, he pulled her back in the room and engulfed her in a hug, pressing a quick kiss to her willing lips.

"I wanted to do that since you walked into church this morning," Hart said, breathing in her alluring scent and holding her close. "You completely obliterated my ability to pay attention to the pastor during the service."

Denni leaned back in his arms and gave him a teasing smile. "Maybe I better make you sit back a row, or over by Trent and Lindsay next time."

"No need to be hasty," Hart said, wrapping one arm around Denni's shoulders as they walked out into the hall and down the stairs. Everyone was waiting for them in the living room, admiring the huge rock fireplace. Hart walked over to Cass and crouched so he was on eye level with the child. "Are you ready to go see my spotted horses and alien bovine, as your Uncle Travis calls them?"

"Yep!" Cass said, taking Hart's hand and tugging him toward the door. Everyone laughed as Hart and the precocious redhead led the way outside and around the side of the house where they had a great view of the pasture.

"I had no idea Belgian Blues would look so..." Lindsay struggled for the right words. Although she grew up in a rural community and lived in Grass Valley for more than four years, she still found herself occasionally baffled by livestock and ranching details.

"Freaky?" Hart asked with a teasing grin. "I never said they were the most beautiful or even normal looking animals on the market. But you all have to admit, they make tasty beef."

"You've got us there," Trey said, walking over to the fence and leaning his arms across the top pole. It was hard to miss the bull since he muscled his way among the cattle. "Is that Brutus?"

"Sure is. Looks like one tough old son-of-a-gun, doesn't he?" Hart asked, stepping up beside Trey.

"Told you he could take on Leroy, Trent. I bet he'd chew up your bull and spit him back out without even blinking," Travis taunted his brother. Trent was exceedingly proud of his prize Angus bull and Travis often teased him about it.

"He might," Trent agreed, taking in the size and bulky muscles evident in Hart's bull.

The men stood and talked about breeding details while the women pointed to the calves, commenting on how adorable they were.

Cass grew anxious to check out the horses and walked over to where the men leaned against the fence. She knew better than to interrupt when adults were talking, so she waited until there was a pause in the conversation then grabbed Hart's hand. "Hart, can we please go see the horses?"

"Absolutely, they're down behind the barn," Hart said, taking Cass's hand and walking her across the driveway to the barn. He gave a brief tour of the impressive structure before leading his company through a back door so they could see the pasture where a group of Appaloosa horses stood grazing.

"Look at the babies, Mama!" Cass said, running over to Cady and grabbing her hand. "They look like those funny spotted puppies."

"Dalmatians," Cady said, smiling as she patted Cass on the back.

Trey leaned over and picked Cass up so she could get a better view of the horses. "Daddy, how do they get spotted like that?"

"It's their color. Like your pony is a blue roan, and our cows are black and your dog Buddy is brown," Trey explained to Cass. She nodded her head, sending her uncontrollable curls flying while she wiggled her feet.

"Would you like to pet one, Cass?" Hart asked, stepping close to the fence and whistling. Several of the horses looked at him, but when he whistled a second time, one broke away from the group and trotted over with a colt running alongside.

"She's a beaut," Travis said, leaning over the fence as the horse came right up to Hart. "Looks like a grulla. Great color."

"What's a grooya?" Cass asked as Hart took her from Trey and leaned over the fence so she could pet his favorite horse.

"Grulla, honcy, is the color the horse. It means she has this pretty light and dark coloring," Hart explained.

Cass tipped her head and continued to rub along the horse's neck. "What's her name?"

"Ainia," Hart said. "It means swiftness."

"Ania was an Amazon warrior and sworn enemy of Achilles, in Greek mythology. She fought in the Trojan War," Trey said, grinning at Hart.

"Don't get the professor started," Trent said, shaking his head. Trey was just beginning a career as a history professor when their dad died. He and Trent, who was studying to be a vet, abandoned their professional aspirations to return home and run the Triple T Ranch.

Glaring at his brother, Trey turned back to Hart. "Nice choice. Is she as fast as her name?"

"She comes pretty darn close," Hart said, looking from the horse, back to Cass. "But most of the time I call her Annie."

"I like that name," Cass said, petting the horse with more enthusiasm once she decided the spots wouldn't rub off on her hands. "Have you named her baby?"

"Nope. I was hoping you might like to help me," Hart said, giving Cass a very serious look. "She needs a strong name like her mom."

Cass studied Annie and her filly. She was quiet for a while, then turned to look at Hart with bright eyes and a beaming smile. "I know! How about Amelia? Aunt Lindsay read us a story at school about Amelia... what's her last name, Aunt Lindsay?"

"Earhart, sweetie-pie," Lindsay said, surprised Cass remembered the story she read to the class a few weeks ago.

"Yeah. She was brave and strong and she flew in an airplane like this," Cass said, waving her hand in the air. "Would that be a good name?"

"That would be a perfect name, Cass. Thank you," Hart said, impressed with Cass' quick little mind. "Amelia it is."

Cady and Trey were both beaming at Cass as only proud parents can and Denni walked over to kiss Cass on the cheek. "Aren't you the clever little miss, today?"

"I try, Grammy," Cass said solemnly, making everyone laugh.

They talked about the horses for a few more minutes and Hart showed them the rest of his out buildings, talking about his plans to add more landscaping once the danger of it freezing at night was past.

As they walked up to the back deck, they stood as a group soaking in the great view and peaceful atmosphere.

"This is just awesome, Hart," Trey said, giving the older man an approving look. "You've built yourself a wonderful home here and we're mighty glad to have you in our community."

"I'm glad to be here myself," Hart said, locking his gaze on Denni's as blue eyes fused to blue.

"Everyone ready for some of Cady's delicious cake?" Denni asked, forcing herself to look away from Hart when she really wanted to get lost in his loving gaze.

"I'm always ready for her cake, or pie, or cookies," Trey said, picking up Cass and tossing her in the air as they filed in the back door.

Eating their fill of cake and drinking what seemed like gallons of coffee, Hart stood on the porch waving goodbye to Denni's family.

Looking down he grinned, glad she decided to stay behind.

"That went well, I think," Hart said, draping his arm around her shoulders when the last pickup disappeared around the bend in the road. "At least the boys didn't threaten me bodily harm if I continued seeing you."

"Now, why would they do that?" Denni asked, walking with Hart into the house and back to the front room. Relaxing on the couch, she let out a contented sigh when Hart turned so she rested with her back against his chest, his arms tight around her and his hands clasped at her waist. "Just so you know, the girls think you're Mr. Wonderful. They've made it perfectly clear you are considered quite a catch and if I was smart, I'd be laying claim to you and chasing everyone else away."

"Is that so?" Hart said, chuckling. He could just picture Denni standing in front of him with a broom, batting at any female getting too close.

"If the girls weren't all goofy in love, I think more than one of them would have a huge crush on you," Denni said, loving the deep, rumbling sound of Hart's chuckle. It reverberated against her back and in her heart.

"Are they nuts? I'm an old man," Hart said, shaking his head. "Besides, with those handsome young bucks you raised, what are the girls doing even noticing there are other men around?"

Denni laughed, rubbing her hand on Hart's solid thigh, making his blood zing through his veins and his heartbeat pick up speed. "In case you weren't aware of the fact, a woman would have to be completely devoid of the ability to see, smell, or hear to not notice you. You look like a dead ringer for Bon Jovi, your voice is the kind that sends shivers down women's spines, and then there's your cologne. I don't know where you get it, what it costs, or what it's called, but it gives a girl all kinds of crazy thoughts when you walk by."

Hart let her words sink in before dropping his head and placing a hot, moist kiss to her neck. "Crazy, huh?"

"I can't believe I just said all that to you out loud," Denni said, wondering how her thoughts suddenly found their way out of her mouth. She seemed to have that problem around Hart.

"I'm glad you did, sunshine," Hart said, nuzzling her ear, wanting to do so much more. "What about your boys? Have I passed muster with them?"

"Of course," Denni said, trying to hang on to her ability to think rationally with Hart trailing tempting kisses along her neck. "They all like and respect you, think you've brought a lot of value to our community. Travis thinks the world of you. It constantly amazes me how much alike the two of you are."

"He's a good kid," Hart said, no longer interested in talking about Denni's family. He was absorbed with savoring the taste of her sweet mouth against his. Turning her in his arms, he captured her lips with a hungry kiss that drove all thoughts from their heads.

Exactly when they moved, Denni didn't know, but when she raised her head to take a breath, she realized she was sprawled on top of Hart as he reclined against the soft cushions of the couch.

"We shouldn't be doing this. I shouldn't be here," Denni said firmly, pushing against his chest to rise. Hart pulled her back and kissed her so thoroughly she forgot about her protests. When he finally broke the seal of their lips, Denni gazed at him with a look of pure wanting that made his insides clench.

"You're right, Denni. I don't have to like it, but you're right," Hart said, helping her sit up as he got to his feet, taking a few steps away from her. He needed a little distance before he did something he'd enjoy but later regret.

"We're both too old to be acting like this," Denni said, checking to make sure both earrings were in place before tugging on her blouse to straighten it. She removed her suit jacket along with her shoes when they first sat down. Now, she stood and slipped her feet into her heels then put the jacket on. "You'd think by the way we can't seem to stay away from each other, we're teens with our first crush. This is beyond ridiculous."

Denni blushed and turned away, plumping the couch cushions so Hart wouldn't see her red face. She was getting as bad as her mother, saying whatever came into her head. Sighing, she felt his arms come around her, his breath on her neck, and leaned back against him, against his solid strength.

"Do you really think it's ridiculous?" Hart asked. She shook her head, making him grin. "Me either. I think it's amazing and wonderful, sometimes bordering on magical and improbable. Seriously, Denni, I'm feeling lucky to find someone who flips my switch the way you do, especially at my age. If you ask me, I'd say we're blessed. Some people go their whole life without the opportunity to experience what you and I have enjoyed these past few months."

"I know," Denni whispered, feeling a twinge of guilt that she'd enjoyed such a blessing not once but twice in her lifetime.

"Old or not, I'm going to enjoy every second of this experience, sunshine, because it's just too awesome to do otherwise. Now are you going to kiss me again, or am I going to have to steal one from you?" Hart asked, noisily kissing her cheek and making her giggle.

"By all means, kiss away," Denni, said, throwing her arms around his neck and pulling him close.

Chapter Fourteen

"When your heart speaks, take good notes."
Judith Campbell

Whistling as he worked on the dwindling pile of paperwork on his desk, Hart kept one eye on the customers at the counter in the gas station.

A couple of punk-looking kids he'd never seen before were flirting with his employee in such a way that a few more comments and he'd consider it harassment and run them off.

Megan seemed to be holding her own, though, and he was impressed. The high school girl worked for him some evenings and weekends, trying to save money for college. She was bright, witty and not easily rattled, making her a great addition to his staff.

When some of the regular customers stepped up to the counter, the boys finally sauntered off, their baggy jeans dragging on the floor. Hart smiled as he heard Megan tell one of her friends what jerks they were as she filled a cup with ice and pop. He knew she was a smart girl.

Saturdays were the busiest day of the week at the gas station so Hart liked to keep an attendant outside pumping gas, one behind the counter, and he filled in as needed. Since Evan and Megan had everything under control, Hart took advantage of an opportunity to catch up on paperwork and straighten his desk.

He was filing the last report when he heard Travis Thompson's voice at the counter, laughing at something Tess said as she teased him. Pushing away from his desk, he stood and walked out of his office to greet them.

Noticing someone knocked over a candy display on his way to the counter, Hart bent over to pick up the scattered bags of Skittles. Pain arced across his lower back, making him suck in his breath.

Trying to straighten his back, he found he couldn't and knew a sudden moment of panic. Not sure what to do, he was debating asking for help or crawling back to his office when he smelled a pleasant, citrusy scent and felt a warm hand on his shoulder.

"Hart, are you okay?" Tess asked, concerned when she saw Hart bend over then look like he was in pain. As a physical therapist, she recognized the signs that someone was hurting and in distress. If she had to guess, she'd say he'd thrown out his back.

"Not exactly. Just give me a minute and I'll be fine," Hart said, clenching his teeth against the assault of pain. He'd been gored by bulls three times, had more bones broken than most people knew they had, and been stabbed twice during gas station robberies, yet the pain ripping across his lower back was about the worst thing he'd ever experienced.

"Does your back hurt here?" Tess asked, running light fingers across his lower back. "An intense, makes you want to hurl kind of pain?"

"Yep," Hart said, sweat breaking out on his forehead and upper lip. He knew Tess was a physical therapist, but had never thought about a need to draw on her medical expertise.

Travis and Megan stood nearby, watching.

THE COWBOY'S NEW HEART

"Anything I can do to help?" Travis asked, gazing at Tess with concern. Hart looked miserable.

"We need to get him home," Tess said, looking around. "Megan, can you and Evan handle things if Hart leaves?"

"Absolutely," Megan said, sounding confident. She'd helped Hart close the station multiple times and knew the routine well. Hart could depend on her and Evan to take care of the busines.

"Good. If you run into a problem, call the Triple T or Viv at the Café," Tess said, putting a hand on Hart's shoulder. "Hart, we're going to take you home. Where are your pickup keys?"

"On my desk," Hart said, trying to turn around, managing to do nothing more than wince in pain.

"I'll get them," Travis said, stepping around Hart, grabbing his keys and Stetson then closing the office door behind him. He knew when Hart wasn't at the station he liked to keep the door shut.

"Trav, drive his truck as close to the door as possible," Tess instructed, shifting her purse to her other shoulder. "Megan, get on his other side. We're going to walk him to the door."

Tess and Megan flanked Hart as he shuffle-stepped his way to the door. Feeling like he was ninety instead of only fifty-two, he was embarrassed to be in such a predicament.

"We'd take my car, but I think it will be easier for you to get in and out of the pickup," Tess said as Travis stopped Hart's truck outside the door and ran in to help. Megan opened the passenger door while Travis half-lifted Hart into the truck.

"I'll follow right behind you," Tess said, giving Travis a quick kiss as he hurried back around to the driver's side. She patted Megan on the shoulder before running over to her car. "Remember to call if you two need anything."

"We will, Tess," Megan said, waving as Tess drove off after Travis. Knowing Hart could use someone to sit with him and that Denni would want the job, Tess called and let her know what happened.

"He just bent over and his back went out? Is that normal?" Denni asked as she scribbled a quick note to Amy who was helping a customer, letting her know she had a family emergency and needed to leave.

"Actually, it's pretty common," Tess said, following close behind Hart's truck as Travis drove it to his house outside of Moro. "Research shows that most adults, at some point in their life, will have their back go out on them. It can happen for what appears to be no reason at all and it is excruciatingly painful."

"Poor, Hart. It's probably killing him to not only appear vulnerable, but also to need to rely on someone else's help," Denni said, hurrying out to her car. "I'm going to run home and grab a few things then I'll head that direction. See you in a little while, sugarplum. Thanks for letting me know."

"You're welcome. I assumed you'd want to come to his rescue," Tess said, smiling at the thought of Denni taking care of Hart. He would deny that he needed help, try to bluff his way through it, and end up in more pain.

Disconnecting the call, Tess parked her car in Hart's driveway and caught the keys Travis tossed to her. Running up the front steps, she found the house key and unlocked the door, then stepped aside as Travis helped Hart inside.

"Put him on the couch," Tess said, pointing into the living room while she went to the kitchen. She found a bag of frozen peas in the freezer that would work for an ice pack and fished around in her purse for some ibuprofen. Filling a glass with cold water, she returned to the front room where Hart was lying on the couch, biting his lip with his eyes squeezed shut. Travis managed to pull off Hart's boots and remove his jacket.

"Hart, I've got something here for the pain," Tess said, slipping a hand behind Hart's shoulders, helping him raise his head while he swallowed the pills. Motioning to Travis, he pushed Hart up far enough Tess could slide the bag of peas against his back, making Hart gasp as they lowered his head back down to the pillows on the couch.

"I know this may not be comfortable, but it will help to get your legs elevated," Tess said, gathering random pillows from the furniture and arranging them beneath Hart's legs so his knees rested slightly bent.

Tess went to the guest bathroom and found a washcloth, rinsing it in warm water and bringing it back to place on Hart's forehead. When she wiped off his face, he opened one eye and looked at her, mumbling his thanks.

Since there wasn't much else they could do to help him at that moment, they sat down and waited for Denni to arrive. After thirty minutes of flipping through magazines Hart had on the coffee table, Travis was jiggling his foot. He wasn't one to sit around aimlessly.

"Tee," Tess said, using her nickname for him. "Would you mind making me a cup of tea? I'm sure Hart wouldn't care."

Hart grunted something unintelligible and Travis wandered off to the kitchen.

Tess leaned toward Hart, noticing he opened both eyes, and whispered, "I don't really need tea, but he needs something to do or he gets antsy."

"I'm fine, you can go," Hart rasped out between his still clenched teeth.

"Right. You're in great shape and can walk us to the door," Tess said, shaking her head. "I don't think so. Is the pain worse? If you want we can take you into the clinic."

"No. It's a little better," Hart said, realizing the pain had lessened.

"Good," Tess said with a smile.

When Travis returned with her cup of tea, she took a sip and winked at Hart then had Travis help her move the bag of soggy peas.

"If your back is still bothering you in a day or two, you should definitely go to the doctor, but I'm guessing with some rest and ice, you'll be as good as new. Some people will tell you to put heat on your back, but ice is actually better for the first few days. You can add heat later if you're still having problems after three days."

Hart certainly hoped he wouldn't be this miserable seventy-two hours from now. He didn't even want to think about being in such pain two hours from now.

Turning his head just enough to look at Tess and Travis, he watched the private smile they shared, the way they looked at each other with love and devotion.

"You're lucky to have her around," Hart said to Travis, trying to work up something that resembled a grin. It must have worked because Travis smiled back at him.

"No argument there, man. After I pulled both hamstrings last July and had to spend what seemed like years in bed, this slave-driving maniac was the reason I recuperated as fast as I did," Travis said, leaning over to kiss Tess on her cheek. "She's the best."

"Someone had to keep him on the straight and narrow," Tess said, although the look she shot Travis was full of adoration.

"Tell me again what happened?" Hart asked, wanting something to divert his attention from his back pain.

Travis told Hart about pulling a little boy off a runaway wind surfing board and popping both hamstrings. He woke up in the hospital in The Dalles with nothing but his wetsuit and no idea how he'd gotten there. Although there was nothing humorous about it at the time, Travis told the story in such a way Hart felt himself smiling at Travis' tale.

Hearing the front door open, Tess and Travis shared a look as Denni breezed into the front room.

"Some people will go to great lengths to get attention, won't they? Why didn't you tell us you needed a little pampering, Hart?" Denni teased, leaning down to kiss his cheek.

Assuming Tess was the guilty party in alerting Denni that he was down and out, he'd have to give her an earful later. It was bad enough having Denni's kids treat him like an invalid, although at the current moment the title seemed to fit. He absolutely didn't want Denni waiting on him, babying him. It was humiliating for her to see him like this. Down in his back, as Tess called it, made him feel ancient, feeble, and worthless.

Not the image a tough cowboy really wanted to project to the woman he was pursuing.

"Is he feeling any better?" Denni asked Tess, acting as though Hart was incapable of a response.

"I think so. His color's better and he quit clenching his jaw and hanging on to the edge of the couch in a death grip," Tess said, tipping her head to study Hart. If she was correct, he was more than a little peeved at her for calling Denni. If he was busy stewing over that, it would give him something to concentrate on other than how badly his back hurt.

"I'm going to check on the livestock, make sure they've got feed and water before we go," Travis said, grabbing his jacket and walking out the door.

Tess took her tea cup to the kitchen and washed it while giving Denni some simple instructions about what to do to help Hart, including getting more ice on his back in another hour and keeping him calm and comfortable.

"If you need help, just call. I can come back and sit with him," Tess said, linking arms with Denni as they walked back into the front room to Hart. "He should feel a lot better tomorrow. If he doesn't, then he really does need to go see a doctor."

"I'll stay with him for a while then spend the night at the ranch. That way I can check on him in the morning and see if he needs more help. He'll be fine to leave alone tonight, won't he?" Denni asked.

"He should be. You could sit up with him and hold his hand if you want, but I get the idea he wouldn't appreciate it very much," Tess said with a saucy grin.

"I think you're probably right," Denni said, as they walked next to the couch and studied Hart. He looked to be sleeping, but Denni had a feeling he was pretending, hoping they'd go away and leave him to his misery.

"The livestock should be fine for the night. One of us will come do the feeding in the morning," Travis said, making a racket as he came in the front door and stood on the doormat. "Honeybee, I've got mud and hay all over me and don't want to track it on the floor. You ready to go?"

"Sure, Trav. Be right there," Tess said, giving Hart one final look and kissing Denni's cheek. "Good luck," she whispered in Denni's ear, then grabbed the light jacket she'd been wearing and went out the door with Travis.

Hearing it click shut, Denni turned to Hart and shook her head.

"Okay, buckaroo. Now that they're gone you can quit pretending to be asleep," Denni said, running cool fingers across Hart's forehead. She gave in to the temptation to run her fingers through his thick, tousled hair. She liked that he wore his hair just a little longer than most of the guys in the area. In her eyes, it made him seem a little wild, a little rebellious. Not stopping to think about why that appealed to her, she just knew she loved the feel of her fingers in his sandy hair, highlighted with a slight sprinkling of gray.

Watching him relax and sink into the cushions, Hart opened his eyes and stared at her. "You don't need to babysit me. I'll be fine," he said, sounding quiet and subdued.

"I know you most likely will be, but what are friends for? Seems to me when you're not quite up to par is when you need them most," Denni said, sinking to the floor next to the couch and taking Hart's hand in hers, kissing the back of it. His hands were tan and rough, just like those of her sons, from time spent outside working.

It was a known fact that if Hart wasn't working at the gas station, at his own place, or at some community service project, he could be found helping area ranchers when they needed an extra hand. People saw him doing everything from working farm ground to helping pull calves.

"So, what acrobatics were you doing that caused your back to go out?" Denni asked with a teasing grin.

"You wouldn't believe me if I told you," Hart said, embarrassed that he didn't have some great story to tell. There was no excitement to be found in bending over and losing the ability to function normally.

"Try me," Denni said, leaning forward so her chin rested on the cushion of the couch.

"I bent over to pick up a spilled candy display and couldn't stand back up. That's it. Pathetic, huh?"

"Not pathetic at all. From what Tess said, it happens all the time. I'm fortunate I've never had it happen to me, but I remember Drew did once. He acted like the world had come to an end. It took several days for him to get back to one hundred percent. We didn't have the medical clinic here in Moro at that time, so Trey and I took him to the emergency room. After they ran a bunch of tests, they couldn't find anything wrong. The doctor gave him some pain pills, an anti-inflammatory drug, and a muscle relaxant then sent us home.

"Tess said there isn't a whole lot to be done to fix it, but to go to the doctor tomorrow if I'm not feeling better."

"She's a smart cookie," Denni said, pride filling her voice at thoughts of her sweet and sassy daughter-in-law.

"I won't argue with you there," Hart said, trying to shift on the cushions, making himself wince. He needed to go to the bathroom and realized he should have had Travis help him up before he left. Now he was going to have to hold it or further shame himself by letting Denni witness exactly what sad shape he was in when he dragged himself down the hall.

Knowing she planned to spend the evening, he finally decided he didn't have much choice in the matter and started to swing his legs off the couch. Pain shot through his back with a brutal force and despite his best efforts he sucked in a gulp of air.

"Hart, what are you doing?" Denni asked, getting to her feet and looking at him like he had lost his mind. "You need to stay down, resting."

"I need to...um..." Hart said, and Denni quickly understood.

"Sure," Denni said, smiling at him, knowing how much having her there to witness his misery was damaging his pride. "Take my hands and I'll help you up."

Reluctantly, Hart let her pull him to his feet then shuffled down the hall to the bathroom, still bent over and holding his lower back.

Upon his return to the couch, he listened to Denni bustling around in the kitchen. Hearing him groan as he lifted his legs onto the pillows, she came back in and watched him get settled.

"Do you feel like eating anything?" Denni asked, not sure if Hart would be hungry.

"I could eat something light, I think. Too many meds on an empty stomach is guaranteed to make me sick," Hart said, realizing he better not take any more ibuprofen until he ate some dinner.

"How about some soup? Maybe a sandwich?" Denni asked, wondering what Hart felt like eating.

"Yeah, that would be fine. I should have some cans of soup in the pantry," Hart said, closing his eyes as he attempted to hold still and ride out the current wave of pain shooting through his lower back.

"Okay, soup and sandwiches coming right up," Denni said, returning to the kitchen. Having been in Hart's kitchen many times in the past several weeks, she knew where to find everything she needed to warm up a can of soup and make grilled cheese sandwiches.

Finding a large baking sheet to serve as a tray, she put bowls of soup, a plate of sandwiches, napkins and glasses of tea on it before carrying it back to the front room.

Considering the best way for Hart to eat, she decided it would be easiest from his recliner. Helping him off the couch, he sank down into his chair and grunted as he tried to find a comfortable spot. Denni finally stuck a few pillows behind his back and he leaned against them in relief. Raising the footrest, she added pillows under his legs then set her dinner and tea on the coffee table, placing the improvised tray across Hart's lap.

"Thanks, sunshine," Hart said, looking at the simple meal. Denni asked a blessing on the food and Hart ate quietly, listening to Denni talk about things going on in The Dalles and at her store. She was nearly finished with his quilt and discussed bringing it out as soon as she had it completed.

"I can't wait to see it on your bed. I think it's really going to finish your room," Denni said, taking a bite of her sandwich.

"I don't think it will." Hart wasn't sure if he was getting delirious from the pain or what exactly made him speak his mind, but words just seemed to pop right out of this mouth.

Denni turned to stare at him, a look of hurt on her face. Up to this point, he seemed to be happy with her work on the quilt. Now he was telling her he wasn't going to like it. She wondered what had changed his mind. Picking up her tea she took a drink, looking at Hart over the top of the glass.

"To really finish the room, I think it needs you in it," Hart said, giving Denni a pain-glazed look laced with a liberal dose of longing.

Choking on the tea, Denni was caught completely off guard by his statement. When she could finally talk, she shook her head at him in disbelief. "Hart, that's...I...you don't really mean that."

"I do. Not the way you're taking it, but I love you, Denni. I'm too old and wasted too many years to play games with you," Hart said, staring at her with a tender look on his face, realizing his timing was completely off and not a bit romantic. Now that the words were out there, he couldn't reel them back or pretend he hadn't said them. "I like the thought of growing old with you in this house."

"But Hart...I...I don't know what to say," Denni said, stunned by Hart's admission. She'd hoped and dreamed he might someday say he loved her, but this was not how she'd envisioned the moment. In her mind there should have been whispered words, loving touches, maybe even another serenade.

Wondering if it was his pain talking, Denni decided now was not the time to have an in-depth discussion of their feelings. Hart might feel like laying his soul bare at the moment, but Denni had an idea he would regret it later when he was thinking clearly. For now, she'd take note of what he said and hold it close to her own heart, waiting for the timing to be right to have a real conversation about their intentions.

Aware enough to know his declaration upset Denni, Hart shook his head. "I'm sorry, sunshine. Just forget I said anything and forgive my lack of finesse. This isn't the time or place for me to say something like that."

Denni scooted over by Hart's chair and took his hand in hers. "I won't forget it, but I agree your timing is off. Let's revisit this topic when you're feeling more like yourself."

"Sure," Hart said, feeling a keen sense of disappointment that Denni hadn't enthusiastically replied she loved him, too.

Despite the loving look in her eyes, maybe she really wasn't all that into him.

Chapter Fifteen

"The heart is forever inexperienced."
Henry David Thoreau

"Sugarplum, are you planning to feed a small army?" Denni asked as she surveyed the loaded table in Tess' dining room.

"No. Just a bunch of hungry bridal shower attendees," Tess said as she carried a big bowl of fruit salad to the table. "Besides, I want everything to be perfect. Although I may not be a culinary whiz like Cady, I didn't want her to have to do the food for the party since she's cooking for all the extra company as it is."

Brice and Bailey's wedding was just two days away. It was decided to wait and hold the bridal shower close to the wedding date so friends and family arriving from out of town would have the opportunity to attend.

Although the out-of-towners weren't all staying at the Triple T, they seemed to wind up there for meals. The wedding rehearsal would take place at the ranch the next day with the wedding planned the following afternoon in the small orchard, currently bursting with beautiful blooms on the fruit trees.

Since Lindsay's house was in the midst of an expansion project before the baby arrived, Tess volunteered to not only hold the shower at her big farmhouse, but also provide rooms for extra guests.

Denni's sister June and a handful of Travis' cousins were upstairs getting ready for the bridal shower, having arrived earlier that afternoon.

Tess and Travis, with the help of family, updated a few things to the old house before their wedding in October. After spending the winter living there, the young couple had settled in and definitely made the farmhouse feel like a cherished home.

"You're a great cook, honey, and everything is so pretty. Bailey will be thrilled," Denni said, hugging Tess around the waist as they walked back to the kitchen to make sure coffee and punch were ready. Driving out early to offer her assistance with party preparations, Denni was pleased to arrive and find Tess organized and ready for her guests. Bringing Ester along, Denni dropped her off at Lindsay's so she could check out the addition of nursery, two bedrooms and a master suite to her little home. They had about seven weeks before the baby arrived, so the project was nearing completion.

At the sound of footsteps on the back stairs, Denni and Tess looked up to see Travis. "I'm getting out of here before your hen party commences," he teased, giving his mom a quick hug then pulling Tess into his arms and planting a sloppy, wet kiss on her cheek, making her giggle.

"It's not a hen party, Tee. I think Bailey would be insulted to hear you refer to her bridal shower as such," Tess said, leaning back in Travis' arms so she could look into his deliciously handsome face.

"Whatever you call it, I'm leaving before you girls think of some other chore for me to do. I'll be at Trent's if you need anything," Travis said, taking a handful of cookies from a plate on the counter. He knew Tess left them there just for him, so he wasn't worried about getting in trouble for snitching. "Have a good time."

"We will," Tess said, standing on tiptoe to kiss his cheek.

He caught her in a one-armed hug and kissed her lips. "Everything looks great, honeybee. You outdid yourself. Now, enjoy and have fun."

"Thanks," Tess said, grinning as Travis smacked her bottom playfully and hurried out the door.

"If I didn't know better, I'd say he kind of likes you," Denni teased, as Tess bustled around the kitchen, making sure everything was clean, tidy, and ready for guests.

"Maybe a little," Tess said with another giggle. "Speaking of liking someone, how are things going with Hart?"

"Okay," Denni said, sounding wistful. Since the day he had the problem with his back, he'd been reserved around her. Oh, they still laughed and had fun. They'd been on several dates. Hart had even taken her to a tulip festival outside of Portland that was spectacular.

Where their friendship had been easygoing and genuine before, Denni now felt like there was a strain to it. She admittedly could have handled the situation with Hart better when he said he loved her instead of shutting him down.

With such big dreams about him saying those wonderful three little words, she didn't want to accept the notion that he'd first utter them when he couldn't even give her a hug. Looking back, though, Denni realized she'd hurt him and for that she was sorry.

Although she'd been happily married for many years, she knew there was still much for her to learn when it came to matters of the heart, particularly her own.

Getting caught up in the preparations for Bailey's wedding, Denni didn't have time to analyze or brood over this bump in her relationship. She promised herself as soon as the wedding was over, she and Hart would talk about what was going on between them, where they both wanted it to go.

Thinking she'd never again fall in love, never feel her heart trip at the sound of a man's voice, or teeter on the brink of reason driven there by kisses filled with an all-consuming passion, Hart had given her a second chance to experience all that and more. She couldn't believe how young and happy he made her feel.

With Hart, she felt free to be herself, to let her light shine. He seemed to love her for exactly who she was, not some ideal of whom he thought she could be.

Acknowledging it was long past time to tell him how she felt, how much his love meant to her, she decided she would definitely set aside time to talk to him as soon as Brice and Bailey were happily wed.

"Can you get the door, Denni?" Tess asked as she carried a punch bowl into the dining room.

So lost in her own thoughts, Denni hadn't even heard the bell.

"Sure, sugarplum," Denni said, hurrying to the front door where family and friends began pouring inside.

Cady arrived with Lindsay and Ester. At nearly eight months pregnant, Lindsay carried it well on her tall, lean frame. Everyone talked about Lindsay's baby shower being the next party. Although Cady, Tess and Bailey had it planned, they'd finalize all the details as soon as Bailey and Brice returned from their honeymoon in Hawaii.

Tess recognized many family members from seeing them at Trent and Lindsay's wedding in August and then again at her wedding in October. Between weddings and babies, people were probably starting to wonder what exactly had started gurgling in the Triple T's well water. There was a lot of teasing about someone dumping in a very active love potion.

Bailey came in the door with her mother, Mary, and perky sister, Sierra. Hugging Tess and Denni, Sierra hurried over to put her hand on Lindsay's rounded tummy and wait for the baby to kick. While Bailey was tall, serious and laser-focused on her goals, Sierra was petite, bubbly and a dreamer who often had her head in the clouds, much like their fun-loving mother.

Denni was excited to see all three of her sisters and her brother's wife as well as many of their offspring.

"Aren't you about out of kids to marry off?" her sister June asked as she walked into the room and gave Denni a hug.

"We've still got Tess' brother Ben. From there we could branch out to some others in the community," Denni said with a smile, knowing her sister was teasing. "Maybe we could open a matchmaking service and include wedding planning as part of the package."

"You could throw in a custom quilt to sweeten the deal," June said, accepting the cup of punch Denni held out to her.

"Now you're talking," Denni said, enjoying being with her family again. It wasn't often all five of the Nordon children got together, although with the recent rash of weddings taking place, it seemed like they were seeing each other with some newfound frequency.

She and June followed the rest of the guests to the living room where Tess had bridal shower games planned.

"Mama said you have a new boyfriend. Are we going to get to meet your hunk of burning love at the wedding?" Denni's sister Donna asked with a taunting smile.

Denni rolled her eyes and shot a glare in the direction of her mother who was on cloud nine with so many of her family gathered around her.

"The old girl just can't keep anything to herself these days," Denni said, shaking her head and making June laugh.

"You can't cast all the blame at her door. Bailey told Mary he looked like a movie star and that Tess and Cady said he came fully loaded." The dumbfounded expression on Denni's face caused June to laugh even more, drawing the attention of several guests their direction.

"Apparently nothing's sacred anymore," Denni muttered, finding a chair by Lindsay and taking a seat. Was everyone talking about her relationship with Hart?

By the time the last guest left from the shower, Denni knew the answer to her question was yes. In fact, more than one neighbor inquired as to how things were progressing with the hunky gas station owner. All three of her sisters cornered her in the kitchen where she was rinsing off dishes and asked her a multitude of questions that made her both flushed and annoyed.

The last straw was when her mother walked into the conversation and suggested that perhaps if Denni paid enough attention to what the younger crowd was doing, it might give her a few ideas on how to attract and keep a man since she seemed to be struggling with Hart.

"Look. I know you all find this amusing and you mean well, but this weekend is not about tormenting me or providing a wealth of useless tips in regard to my love life or lack thereof. This weekend is all about Brice and Bailey. Can we please keep that in mind going forward?" Denni gave a pointed look to each one of her sisters then ended with a long stare directed at Ester. "Please?"

"You're right, Denni," Ester said, putting her arm around Denni's waist and squeezing. "We were just having fun, although it was at your expense. We're all so happy to see you dating again and I'm as pleased as can be that you've set your cap for Hart. He's one of a kind."

"Did you see that one of a kind bowl Mrs. Willoughby gave Bailey?" Mary asked, changing the focus of the conversation. Denni gave her an appreciative smile before turning back to the sink full of dishes. Sierra wandered in and helped Denni finish restoring order in the kitchen while Tess and Cady took down the decorations and folded chairs in the living room.

Denni and Ester were planning to stay through the wedding, sharing a bedroom at Cady and Trey's house.

Deciding it was time to get her mother back to the ranch since it was getting late, Denni congratulated Tess on a wonderful party, helped Ester out to her car, and offered to take Lindsay home.

Stopping for a minute to see the progress on the addition, Denni started back to the ranch. She'd barely pulled onto the highway when Ester gave her a teasing smile.

"Sure you don't need to swing by the gas station? Aren't you running a little low on fuel?"

"I've got plenty of gas in the car, Mama," Denni said, turning onto the road that led to the Triple T. "Why can't you just let things be, you nosy old woman?"

"Because it's so fun to push your buttons," Ester said, patting Denni on the leg. "Our little Tess did a grand job playing hostess, didn't she? Travis chose a good wife, like all your sons. I'm really very proud of you, Denni. You and Drew raised those boys right and they grew into fine, fine men."

Feeling a little teary at her mother's sincere compliment, Denni gave her mother a watery smile. "Thanks, Mama. That means a lot to me. We worked hard to give the boys a good foundation. I worried about Trav for awhile, but I think all three of them turned out well, if I do say so myself."

"You didn't turn out too badly either, for a twitterpated girl," Ester said, teasing her daughter. "Who would have thought as wild and unsettled as you always were that you'd be such a good wife and mother? I know it was hard for you to take a different path when Drew died, but you've done well. It's time for you to take another new direction, though. I hope you give Hart a chance, honey.

He really is a good man and from all appearances, he's more than a little crazy about you."

"I'm just about there, Mama. I think I hurt his feelings, though." Denni parked the car as close to the mudroom door at the ranch as she could get with the multitude of other vehicles parked around the area. Before she could get out of the car, Ester put a restraining hand on her arm.

"What did you do? Please tell me you haven't chased him off already."

"No, I didn't chase him off, but he sort of blurted out that he loved me one day and I don't think I handled it very well. Since then he's been reserved and I miss that easy friendship we shared before he said anything," Denni said, staring out the window at nothing, wondering why she was laying her heart open to her mother. "I wish I'd told him how I really feel instead of being disappointed he didn't wait for a more romantic moment to tell me. Now, I'm afraid he'll think I'm just saying it to save face or make him feel better. Not because I truly mean it."

"So you really love him? Deep in your heart, can't get him out of your thoughts, want to spend all your time with him love?" Ester asked, nearly rubbing her hands together in her excitement over Denni's declaration of her true feelings.

"Yes, Mama, I do," Denni said, letting out a sigh. "I'm just afraid I've waited too long to let him know."

"When did he say he loved you?"

Denni explained about Hart hurting his back and what he said. She admitted she basically brushed off his comments and told him they'd talk about it another day.

"I agree. That was a sad, completely pathetic way to tell you. Let's just pretend it was the pain talking and he didn't really mean to say it. Why don't you ask him for a do-over?" Ester said, studying Denni. "He's coming for the rehearsal dinner tomorrow isn't he?"

"I invited him, but he said he didn't want to intrude."

"He'll be here," Ester said, thinking if she had to get one of the grandkids to go kidnap him from the gas station, she'd do it. "Just find a moment and talk to him honestly. Tell him you're sorry about the other day and explain that you were caught off guard. He'll understand. Then I'd take that handsome face in my hands, if I were you, and kiss him like there's no tomorrow."

"Mama! What am I going to do with you?" Denni asked, laughing at the kissy-faces Ester was making.

"Help me out of this car and into the house, I hope. I'm pooped and it will no doubt be a long weekend by the time we get these two married and on their way to their honeymoon. Bailey assured me she didn't need any tips. I hope Mary told her what she needs to know."

"Mother!" Denni said, shaking her head as she walked around the car and helped Ester up the steps and in the house where they were welcomed home by a lively round of hellos from all the extended family gathered in the dining room. If Denni hoped to have a moment alone with Hart, it sure wasn't going to be anywhere on the Triple T Ranch, at least until the wedding was over and all the guests went home.

><><

"Is Mr. Hammond here?" Hart heard a young female voice ask as he sat at his desk finishing a report online. Saving his work, he arose from his chair and walked into the convenience store.

A young girl, looking to be in high school, stood watching him approach when Evan pointed his direction.

"I'm Mr. Hammond. May I help you?" Hart asked, taking in the curly honey-colored hair of the girl and her intensely blue eyes. She had to be related to the Thompson clan. She resembled Bailey and Ester too much for it to be a coincidence.

"My great-grandma asked me to come give you this," she said, holding out an envelope.

"And who is your great-grandmother, if I may ask?" Hart said, smiling at the girl and watching her eyes go wide. It was a reaction he often received when people started mentally comparing his looks to those of a rock-star celebrity.

"Ester Nordon, sir," the girl said, gazing at him with a bit of awe.

Hart liked her manners and the fact that she looked like a normal kid. He was so used to seeing teens with neon colored hair, multiple body piercings and a trove of tattoos, it was refreshing to see this girl fresh-faced and neat in a pink T-shirt, denim shorts, and flip flops.

"Does Ester want a reply to this?" Hart asked, tapping the envelope on the counter.

"Yes, please. Nana told me to wait until you had a chance to read it."

"Okay. Now how about you tell me your name and how you're related to Denni Thompson."

"My grandma June is a sister to Aunt Denni. My name's Alexandra, but everyone calls me Alex."

"It's nice to meet you, Alex. Just give me a minute and I'll see what Ester's got to say. Would you like something? A pop or an ice cream bar? We've got iced coffees or Italian sodas."

"An Italian soda, please," Alex said, noticing Evan for the first time since she'd come in. Evan seemed to have taken note of the lovely girl with the striking blue eyes as well because Hart had to ask him twice to make her drink.

Walking into his office, he opened the envelope and grinned to see Ester's hand-written invitation to join them for the rehearsal dinner that evening, saying it would be a personal favor to her if he attended.

Opening his desk drawer, Hart took out a blank sheet of paper. He wrote a quick reply, penned another brief note, sealing it in a smaller envelope, and put them both in a larger envelope.

Boldly writing Ester's name across the front, he walked back into the store to see Alex chatting with Evan, telling him all about living in Florida. That would explain her dark tan, although it was only April.

"Thank you for bringing this in for me, Alex. If you could give this to Ester I'd very much appreciate it."

"Thank you, sir. And thanks for the drink. It's awesome," Alex said, taking the envelope from Hart and hurrying out the door. She stopped to give Evan a glance over her shoulder before getting into Cady's car where it was parked outside the gas station door and heading off in the direction of the ranch.

"Evan, my friend, can you hold down the fort this evening. It looks like I'm going to a party."

"Sure," Evan said, still looking at the door, like he could wish Alex back and she'd appear.

"Pretty little thing, isn't she?" Hart asked as he stood next to Evan, looking outside at the bright blue spring sky.

"Totally, dude," Evan said, not realizing what he'd said, until he looked up and saw Hart grinning at him. "I mean, yes, sir."

Hart slapped him on the back and smiled. "Be careful. Spring fever's running rampant in Grass Valley. If you don't watch it, it might be catching."

Evan grinned at Hart as he returned to his office to finish a few details before he went home to shower and change.

Driving back to his place, he was glad Ester was, as Denni so often said, a nosy, interfering old woman. He really owed her one for making sure he knew his presence was expected both at the rehearsal tonight and the wedding tomorrow.

Denni asked him a few weeks ago to attend the dinner tonight, but he knew she'd be busy with family and didn't want to be in the way. Ever since the day he blurted out that he loved her, he'd tried to rein in his feelings and slow down the pace of their advancing relationship.

Fairly certain he'd nearly frightened her off with his idiotic declaration, he didn't know how to set things right between them. Their friendship had lost the easy camaraderie he'd so enjoyed before his mouth got ahead of his brain and he told her he loved her.

Thinking of all the times and places he could have declared his feelings for the lively, engaging woman, he couldn't come up with any scenario worse than the one he chose. Women wanted romance and undying devotion. They wanted passionate kisses and warm embraces. They wanted whispered words of endearment and teasing caresses.

Hart had failed big time. In fact, he was sure his timing could be recorded as an epic failure.

With a little help from Denni's family, he hoped at some point in the near future he could find a way to redeem himself. At least he had Ester cheering him on. Between a conniving octogenarian, three conspiring daughters-in-law, and a little effort on his part, maybe he could find a way to romance his way back into Denni's good graces.

Hurrying to take a shower and shave, Hart knew everyone would be dressed casually for the rehearsal. Slapping on some aftershave and combing his hair, he started to leave the bathroom then, feeling a little bit of the devil dancing in him, turned around and tousled his hair in the way he knew garnered quite a bit of attention from Denni.

Taking a cotton shirt and pair of newer jeans out of his closet, he put them on then sat down on the bed to tug on a pair of boots he recently polished. He took a moment to admire the quilt Denni had finished as it draped across his big bed. Every time he came in the room, he thought of her and right now the thought made him smile.

After one more glance in the mirror, he gave himself a mental pep talk to play it cool and confident before running down the stairs. Grabbing a denim jacket and his Stetson on the way out the door, he stopped by the market in Moro and found what he was looking for before heading south toward Grass Valley and the Triple T Ranch.

Parking out by the barn in a row of other vehicles, Hart took a deep breath and walked toward the house. Still early evening, dusk hadn't yet fallen and the warmth of the day made the temperature pleasant.

"Hart, come meet my cousins," Cass called, breaking away from a group of kids and running up to him, throwing her arms around his knees. He picked her up and tossed her in the air, making her giggle.

"You've got cousins? Did I know this?" Hart teased as he set Cass down and she tugged him toward the group of youngsters. Cass introduced him as her friend Mr. Hammond, using the good manners her parents worked so hard to instill in her. Hart was impressed. For as lively as Cass could be, he'd noticed on numerous occasions she had a sharp mind in her sweet little head.

Visiting with the kids, Hart glanced around and saw Denni talking to a couple of women who had to be her sisters. They were flanking Ester and pointing toward a group of teens standing together, laughing and talking.

Deciding to bide his time, Hart walked up to the group of men where the three Thompson brothers stood talking to Brice and his brother, Ben, along with a few other male relatives.

"Hey, glad you could make it," Brice said, sticking out his hand to Hart. "Have you met Bailey's dad?"

Brice introduced Ross Bishop and some relatives from both sides of the family before Tess breezed by carrying a stack of paper plates.

"If some of you guys could put some muscle in it, we could use help bringing out the food," Tess called over her shoulder, heading toward a grouping of tables set up in the front yard.

"We've been summoned by the queen bee," Ben said of his sister, slapping Travis on the shoulder. "How do you put up with her on a daily basis?"

"It's a real hardship, man. Can't you see how I suffer?" Travis said, clutching a hand to his chest and trying to look browbeaten.

"Not really, bro," Trey said, slapping Travis on the back. "Not when she caters to your every whim."

"And here's mister boss-man telling it like it is when he's got his wife so charmed, she makes him special treats and hides them from the rest of us," Travis said, glaring at Trey accusingly. Cass was the one who spilled the beans that Cady made Trey extra goodies and hid them where no one else could find them. It really rankled Travis, knowing the treats probably involved coconut, a favorite of his as well as Trey's.

"It's my stunning good looks and witty personality," Trey said, grinning broadly as he and Trent picked up a galvanized tub full of ice and bottled beverages, carrying it to the picnic tables.

"Nah. It's that humble, modest mystique you've got going on," Trent teased.

"Mystique? You still learning new words from the school teacher," Trey asked as Lindsay came outside, looking radiant with the special glow only pregnant women seemed to possess. "I think there are a few more words you need to learn. Like…"

Trey was cut off by Cady's hand over his mouth, making those around them laugh. "If you boys are done strutting and blustering, there's a whole lot of food in the house that needs carried out here."

"Sure, darlin'. We were just having some fun," Trey said, kissing Cady's cheek. Before he escaped in the house, Cady pulled his head down and whispered something in his ear, making him grin.

He started to walk off, then turned around and grabbed her, bending her over his arm as he planted a kiss soundly on her lips. Raising his head, he gave his wife a wicked smile then stood her back up before disappearing in the house. Cady's cheeks were a bright shade of red as she busied herself removing plastic wrap from the tops of serving bowls.

Hart was trying not to laugh as he watched the tomfoolery of the Thompson boys. If Lindsay hadn't been so pregnant or Tess so adamant that Travis stay on the opposite side of the table where she was arranging platters of food, he was sure the other two boys would have embarrassed their wives to an equal degree.

"They're just rascals sometimes," Denni said, stepping beside him and placing a hand on his arm. When he looked down at her, she gave him a warm smile. "What's a mother to do?"

"Join in the fun?" Hart suggested, a devilish grin spreading across his face in a way that made Denni's insides heat and her heart trip. Half of her wanted Hart to kiss her like Trey had kissed Cady. The other half of her was terrified he would.

Ignoring his statement, she instead took his hand in hers and squeezed it lightly. "I'm so glad you came, Hart. I was afraid you'd be busy or just... wouldn't be able to make it. Also thank you for your note. Mama somehow restrained herself from ripping it open and reading it. I appreciate you letting me know how pleased you were by her invitation and how impressed you were by our Alex. She's a good girl."

"I really am glad to be here, sunshine," Hart said, wanting to kiss Denni in the worst way, but knowing now was not the time. He'd make sure he had the opportunity before the evening was through, though. The sun was setting her golden hair aglow and he thought she looked beautiful in a soft yellow blouse. She wore jeans and boots, looking every bit as good in them as the younger girls did in theirs. It was hard to think of her as a grandmother when she looked so enticing and carefree. Corralling his thoughts before he got himself in trouble, he smiled down at Denni. "Just tell me what I can do to help."

Later, after everyone had eaten and were sitting around in clusters visiting, Hart found himself next to Denni at a table with Brice. Bailey walked by and Brice reached out, snagging her around the waist and pulling her onto his lap. He pressed a kiss to her neck, making her blush.

"It was right here in this yard, at Trent and Lindsay's wedding, when I looked into the prettiest blue eyes and fell in love. I knew as soon as I saw my sugar that she was the girl for me," Brice said, looking at Bailey with his heart in his eyes. "It took her a little longer, but she finally came around to my way of thinking."

"He wouldn't leave me alone. It was either fall in love or get a restraining order," Bailey said dryly, shrugging her shoulders and making everyone laugh.

"Sugar, you are such a bad liar," Brice said, grinning at his bride-to-be.

"You know I fell in love with you even before I got drunk on the Bradshaw boys' special punch recipe," Bailey said. It wasn't funny when she unknowingly drank spiked punch and woke up with her one and only hangover as well as haunting dreams of a handsome cowboy named Brice, but she could see the humor in it now. Especially since she and Brice would be married the next day.

"However it happened, I'm sure glad it did, sugar," Brice said, giving Bailey a kiss that made his dad clear his throat and the guys whistle and cheer.

"Brice Morgan, if you can't behave yourself better than that, I think we better just send you on home," Michele Morgan said, smacking her son on the arm that wasn't supporting Bailey's back.

Brice lifted his head with a devil-may-care smile and winked at Bailey. Her face flushed a deep shade of red.

"On that note, shall we clean up this mess?" Ester asked, picking up an empty bowl and leading the procession back in the house.

Hart helped clear tables and then somehow found himself talked into coming in the morning to help set up before the wedding, scheduled for one that afternoon.

Everyone seemed to be ready to head home as darkness settled around them, knowing they'd have a long day tomorrow.

"Guess I better get going, too," Hart said as he and Denni surveyed the yard, making sure everything looked orderly. "Walk me to my truck?"

"I'd be happy to," Denni said, wrapping her arm around Hart's and leaning against his side as they strolled toward the barn and his pickup.

They walked along in silence, looking up at the sky and breathing deeply of the fresh spring air. Hart thought it was nights like this that led to thoughts of romance and love, especially when there was a beautiful woman right beside him.

"I'm really glad you came tonight, Hart." Denni looked at him with big blue eyes that made his throat parched. He suddenly felt like he was back in high school trying to work up the nerve to ask for his first date.

"Me, too, sunshine," Hart said, leaning against his truck, in no hurry to leave. He brushed his knuckles gently across the soft skin of Denni's cheek. Looking around, he realized most everyone else had left and he was parked in a spot that was somewhat hidden from full view of the house in the shadow of the barn. The big yard light didn't quite illuminate all the way to where they were standing, so he was hopeful they'd have a minute or two of uninterrupted time together.

When Denni turned her face and kissed his fingers, Hart felt heat flood through him. How did the woman make him feel like an inexperienced teen with the slightest touch of her lips?

"Denni, I…" Her fingers on his lips stopped his words and Hart had all he could do not to nibble the palm of her hand.

"Hart, I've got a few things I need to say to you and I know tonight isn't the time. But soon," Denni said, hoping Hart would understand what was in her heart, even if she was having a difficult time putting it into words. When the smile on his face faded and a look of fear crossed his features, she leaned against his chest, wrapping her arms around his neck and kissing the cleft in his chin. "It's a good talk, I promise."

She felt him relax as he folded her in an embrace and buried his face in her hair. "Whenever you want to talk, sunshine, I'm ready to listen."

"Like I said, soon. I just need to get through the wedding first," Denni said, pulling back so she could look up into Hart's face, finding herself falling into his liquid blue gaze. Feeling the need to lighten the mood, she cocked her head and grinned.

"I don't know how you had time to dazzle my sisters, their girls, and even some of their grandkids, but you've got your own fan club started here tonight."

"Is that so?" Hart asked, kissing Denni's temple and holding her close against his chest again, taking a deep breath laden with her scent.

"It is. My sister Donna said you were the most handsome man she'd ever seen, much to the dismay of her husband, and my sister June's oldest daughter was convinced at any moment you'd break out singing hits of the eighties and offer to sign autographs."

Hart's chuckle filled Denni with a warmth she'd been missing. Feeling like they were heading back toward solid relationship ground, Denni hugged Hart tightly then took a step back.

"I better get back inside before they miss me. With Mama leading the charge, they're probably camped out in front of the window with night goggles, trying to see what we're doing out here."

"It wouldn't surprise me," Hart said, grinning. He opened the pickup door and reached across the seat, pulling something toward him. "Close your eyes, sunshine."

"Why? What are you up to?" Denni asked, trying to see what Hart was hiding.

"Just close them and hold out your hand."

Denni closed her eyes, not sure what to expect. She felt Hart place something in her hand, heard the crinkle of cellophane. Opening her eyes, she was surprised to see she was holding one single, long-stemmed rose.

Placing her nose to the bloom, she sniffed its fragrant petals and looked up at Hart.

"It's beautiful, Hart. Thank you so much."

"You're welcome. Just a little something so you don't forget how much I enjoy being with you," Hart said, deciding he didn't care who was watching as he put his arms around Denni again and gave her a kiss that sent sparks dancing between them. "I'll see you in the morning. Sweet dreams."

"Good night, Hart." Denni took a step away from his truck and waved as he turned around and headed down the long driveway to the highway and his home.

Still fazed by his kisses, she wandered back in the house where Cady and Ester took one look at her and grinned.

"What's that you've got, Denni?" her sister June asked, scrutinizing the bright coral bloom in Denni's hand.

"A rose," Denni said, snapping back to reality as she realized a dozen sets of eyes were watching her.

"And where did you get such a beautiful rose?" Ester asked, knowing exactly where the rose came from.

"Outside," Denni said, finding a vase, filling it with water and putting the rose inside.

"Just growing randomly in the yard?" June asked, looking at Donna who'd just entered the room. "Wrapped in cellophane?"

"Where did you get that, Denni?" Donna asked, hurrying over to examine the flower.

"From Hart," Denni said, releasing a sigh. The inquisition would end sooner if she told them the truth.

"You do know what that color means, don't you?" Donna asked, sitting down on a barstool at the counter and winking at Ester.

"No, but I'm sure you're going to enlighten me," Denni said, trying to act uninterested, although she was filled with curiosity.

"Desire," Donna said, fanning her face. "Handsome, hottie, hunky Hart gave you a single perfect rose that means desire. My goodness, girl. How'd you get so lucky? If I had that gorgeous man giving me roses like that, I'd still be out at his truck with my lips locked on his."

Ignoring their teasing, Denni walked back to the bedroom she was sharing with Ester and set the rose on the dresser. If Hart had any idea what the rose meant, she might need to have that talk with him sooner rather than later.

Chapter Sixteen

"To a young heart everything is fun."
Charles Dickens

A rumble of thunder caused Hart to stare up at the cloudy sky, willing the ominous bank of dark clouds to roll on by.

"It won't rain," Travis said, stepping next to Hart and following his gaze upward.

"How can you be so sure?" Hart asked, looking over at Travis with a raised eyebrow. He knew the young man had many talents but he was sure weather forecasting and predicting the future weren't among them.

"It wouldn't dare. The girls would pitch such a royal fit, it would scare all the rain clouds away for a month of Sundays," Travis said, flashing Hart a grin that brought out little brackets around his mouth, a sure sign he was enjoying himself.

Hart chuckled and thumped Travis on the back. "I do believe you're right in that assessment. I'd hate to see them disappointed after they all worked so hard to pull this off."

Travis and Hart surveyed the small orchard where Bailey requested she and Brice exchange their vows. Located behind the big barn at the Triple T Ranch, the fruit trees were in full bloom providing a beautiful backdrop against the green grass that carpeted the ground.

Choosing apple blossoms and tulips for decorations, baskets of flowers sat around the portable arbor the Thompson men constructed for Trent and Lindsay's wedding. Sporting a fresh coat of white paint, branches from apples trees and pastel pink and yellow ribbons twined over the top and down the sides. Fluffy white bows graced the ends of each row of white chairs, placed in a semi-circle facing the arbor, just waiting for guests to arrive.

Hart had no idea where Bailey found someone to play the harp at her wedding, but since that's what she wanted, it was what she was getting. The musician was setting it up in small open tent off to the side of the arbor, erected just in case the weather didn't cooperate.

The walk to the orchard from the main ranch house was short and easy for all to navigate although Hart wondered if it would be a little much for Ester. After one of the girls festooned a four-wheeler with ribbons and bows, Trent offered to give Nana and Lindsay rides, which they said they'd gladly accept.

Noticing Travis' gray cutaway jacket, Hart gave him an approving nod. "Nice duds."

"Thanks. After all these weddings you'd think we'd just buy our own tuxes, but maybe this will be the last one for a while," Travis said, realizing Hart was no longer listening to him as he observed Denni walking out to take one more look at the area with her sisters. Watching Hart watch his mother, Travis grinned. "Or maybe not."

"What's that?" Hart asked, still only half-listening.

"I said we should probably just buy these tuxes then we'll have them on hand for whenever you and Mama get around to tying the knot."

"Sure," Hart said, then turned to pin Travis with a glare.

Travis shook his head and laughed. "Gotcha."

"Smart aleck kid," Hart said, enjoying the teasing banter. Whether things worked out with him and Denni or not, Hart was definitely a goner for her family. Her three boys, as well as Brice, had come to be like the sons Hart had always wanted. He loved the entire family, but there was something about Travis, a kindred spirit that so closely matched his own they seemed to understand each other without the need to say anything. Denni had mentioned more than once how much Travis admired and looked up to him.

"We're all glad Mama has you, Hart. You're good for her," Travis said, before walking off in the direction of the house. He was standing up as Brice's best man and needed to go check on the groom.

Waiting for Denni to approach, Hart hoped he wasn't drooling. She wore an unadorned dress that was anything but simple. The royal blue color highlighted the beautiful blue of her eyes, the silk of the fabric shimmered as she walked, and the cut outlined her shape like a well-fitting glove. With just enough sway in her step to drive him to the far side of distracted, he took a deep breath and tried to keep from doing something crazy like sweeping her into his arms and kissing her repeatedly.

Feeling a familiar clenching in his gut as her scent floated to him on the breeze, Hart wasn't sure how he'd make it through the rest of the day without stealing a kiss or two, or a dozen.

Although he spent the morning at the ranch helping set up chairs and tables, and providing grunt labor with the rest of the men while the women gave orders, he didn't have the opportunity to spend any time with Denni.

Hurrying home to shower and change before the ceremony, Hart was glad he came back early since it gave him a minute to ogle Denni before the guests began arriving.

"Hello, Hart," her sisters chorused, smiling as they walked up to him.

"You ladies all look ravishing. The guests won't know what to think with so many beautiful women here today," Hart said, trying not to fasten his gaze on Denni's. If he did, he wasn't convinced he possessed the fortitude required to keep from falling into the pools of her eyes and spending the rest of the day lingering there.

"What a charmer you are," June said, patting Hart on the arm as she and Donna kept walking. Mary, the mother of the bride, was at the house fussing over Bailey.

When they were out of earshot, Hart bent down close to Denni's ear, his breath warm on her neck. "Sunshine, you look so good, my mouth is watering. It's going to test my patience to be on my best behavior today when I'd much rather drag you off somewhere so I could get up close and personal with that killer dress you're wearing."

"Hart! What's gotten into you?" Denni asked, shivering in pleasure from his presence and his words.

Stepping into the orchard, she almost tripped when she saw Hart near the arbor dressed in a black suit with a light blue shirt and royal blue tie. She had no idea how he knew what color dress she was wearing but it pleased her immensely that his tie and her dress were the exact same color. "Don't tell me my three hooligans are starting to corrupt you, too."

"No, ma'am. If I'm being corrupted, you'll have to take the blame for that," Hart said, unable to resist the urge to feel the fabric of Denni's dress. Running his hand down her back and around her waist, the smooth material was warm and carried her alluring scent. "There's just something wrong about the aunt of the bride being the sexiest woman here today."

"My stars!" Denni said, blushing a deep shade of red although secretly pleased by Hart's teasing and playfulness.

"I think I ought to…"

"Hush and behave yourself," Denni cut in, noticing June and Donna heading back their direction.

"For now," Hart growled in Denni's ear, making tendrils of heat curl from her toes all the way to her head.

"For now," Denni whispered, feeling nearly undone by Hart's words. It was hard enough for her to concentrate on anything just looking at the unbelievably handsome man. Coupled with his teasing and flirting, she wasn't sure she could remember her name let alone anything else this afternoon.

"Shall I walk you ladies back up to the house?" Hart asked, offering Denni one arm while June took the other. Donna walked beside Denni, giving her sister a look that said she was one lucky woman.

It wasn't long before Hart found himself walking with Denni on his arm back down to the orchard to take their seats for the wedding. Glad that Denni insisted he sit right next to her, he couldn't get enough of seeing her today. She looked so beautiful and full of life.

All of Ester's offspring were attractive but Hart thought Mary and Denni looked the most alike, appeared to have the most fun. Right now, Mary was walking down the aisle on the arm of an usher, taking her seat in the front row as mother of the bride and waiting for the ceremony to begin.

Noticing the clouds had moved on, replaced by blue sky and warm sunshine, Hart glanced toward the archway where Brice and his groomsmen waited. Travis caught his eye and looked upward, raising his eyebrow and grinning. Hart smiled and nodded his head.

"You and my baby know something I don't?" Denni asked noticing Hart and Travis sharing some private joke.

"Nope," Hart said, putting his arm around Denni's shoulders and pulling her a little closer to him. "We were just commenting on the weather."

Denni turned her head and studied him a moment to see if he was serious, but got lost in the heat in his blue eyes and the teasing smile on his face. "I was right. My rowdy boys have completely corrupted you."

"Not completely," Hart said, noting that all three of Denni's sons looked quite striking as they stood up with Brice and his brother Ben.

Brice appeared to be calm as he stood in front of the pastor, leaning over to whisper something to Travis, making him grin. Ben stood next to Travis, followed by Trent and Trey.

Light, beautiful notes filled the air from the harp and the ushers hurried to roll out a white runner for the bridesmaids and bride to walk on as they came down the aisle.

Bailey's attendants looked like a freshly picked spring bouquet, wearing vintage-inspired gowns in soft pastel shades. Walking down the little hill to the orchard, Cady led the procession, followed by one of Bailey's coworkers she'd become friends with in the last several months. She wanted Lindsay to stand up with her, but being close to eight months pregnant, Lindsay turned down the offer so Bailey's coworker came to the rescue. Wearing a smile almost as big as Brice's, Tess was next in line. Sierra, Bailey's sister, served as maid of honor and breezed down the aisle taking her place next to Tess.

The crowd couldn't contain their laughter when Cass came down the aisle alternating between tossing flower petals in her role as flower girl and tugging on the arm of the rather reluctant ring bearer. When the little boy looked ready to cry, Cass grabbed his hand and said, "You can do it, Will. Let's hurry it up."

Nearly running the last few feet down the aisle, Cass took her place beside her mother while Will stopped in front of the tall men in tuxedos and stared at them wide-eyed. Trey leaned down and whispered something to the boy who took his hand and went to stand beside him.

Notes from the wedding march floated from the harp, gently falling upon the crowd as they rose to their feet, watching Bailey's beaming father escort her down the aisle.

Wearing Ester's gown and her mother's pearls, Bailey carried a bouquet filled with pale pink roses, cream tulips, white delphinium and calla lilies. Her honey-colored curls were pinned on top of her head where an antique barrette anchored her veil. Her turquoise eyes shone brightly as she floated down the aisle toward Brice, an unmistakable look of love on her face.

Brice grinned broadly at his bride-to-be, wearing a gray cutaway tux that matched those worn by his groomsmen. A cream rose boutonniere decorated his lapel while the other men of the bridal party wore pastel colored roses.

Root beer brown eyes, sparkling with love and excitement, melded to Bailey's as her father placed her hand on Brice's arm and kissed her cheek.

The ceremony went smoothly and Hart soon heard Brice and Bailey each say "I do." Beside him, Denni sniffed quietly and dabbed with her finger at the tears threatening to spill down her cheeks. Hart took a pristine white handkerchief from his pocket and handed it to Denni with a tender smile. He didn't know what it was about women, but he'd yet to attend a wedding that didn't have half of them teary-eyed.

When Denni looked up at him with a watery smile, he kissed her temple and turned his attention back to the bride and groom as the pastor pronounced them husband and wife, giving Brice permission to kiss Bailey.

The young man did so with such intensity and thoroughness, whistles erupted from the crowd, making

Bailey's face flush a bright pink when Brice finally let her up for air.

Turning slightly, Brice, high-fived Travis then hurried Bailey down the aisle and up to the ranch yard where the reception would soon begin.

When Travis walked by Hart and Denni, he nodded his head toward the pastor and shot Hart a teasing grin. Hart shook his head although the thought had crossed his mind that he'd marry Denni right then if she'd agree. It would certainly save her extended family another trip to Grass Valley if he ever did work up the nerve to propose and she actually said yes.

Escorting Denni back up the hill, they joined the festivities. Hours later, the bride and groom both disappeared into the house and returned a short while later, no longer dressed in their wedding finery. Bailey wore a vintage-style turquoise dress that not only played up her figure, but also accented the ocean-blue color of her eyes. Brice wore a crisp gray cotton shirt, creased jeans and the new black boots he bought for the wedding.

Shooting the garter directly at his brother, Brice grinned at Ben and said something Hart couldn't hear from his spot at the back of the crowd. Bailey looked around before turning her back to the crowd and tossing the bouquet straight at Denni. Trying to step back before she was forced to catch it, Cady and Tess nudged her forward and giggled as Denni blushed, holding the flowers in her hand like she'd caught something she shouldn't have.

"You never know, Auntie," Bailey said with a sassy smile, winking at Denni as she and Brice hurried out to his pickup. Seeing Hart in the crowd, Brice stopped to shake his hand and Bailey gave him big hug.

"Thank you so much, Hart, for everything," Brice said, looking happy and excited to be embarking on the adventure that was marriage.

"I didn't do much, but you're very welcome," Hart said, smiling at the young couple.

"Yes, you did," Bailey said. "We wouldn't be going to Hawaii for our honeymoon if it wasn't for you."

"You two just enjoy and have fun," Hart said, thumping Brice good naturedly on the back as they moved through the crowd toward his truck where their parents stood waiting to hug them one more time and tell them goodbye.

Hart felt a hand squeeze his and looked down to see Denni studying him with admiration in her eyes.

"It was so nice of you to let them stay at your condo," Denni said. Brice and Bailey couldn't decide where to go for their honeymoon. Brice offered to take Bailey somewhere she could check out a new fossil site, but she refused, knowing her tendency to be distracted by her work. She wanted to keep her focus entirely on Brice. Hart happened to be at dinner the night they were discussing it and offered Brice and Bailey use of his condo on the beach in Hawaii. Surprised by his generous offer, the couple gladly accepted then became even more excited when Hart showed them a few photos of his place and the amazing sunsets they could see right from the balcony.

What no one knew yet was that Hart arranged to have the fridge and cupboards stocked with food, ordered a romantic dinner to be delivered when Brice and Bailey arrived, and also paid to upgrade their plane tickets from coach to first class. He wished he could be at the airport to see their faces when they found that out.

"What's that look for?" Denni asked, watching a huge, satisfied grin fill Hart's face.

"Just thinking about Brice and Bailey," Hart said, putting his arm around Denni as they waved to the couple one last time.

"They look so happy, don't they?"

"Happy and young and in love," Hart said, kissing the top of Denni's head.

"Rather like some other people I know," Ester commented as she stopped beside Denni and gave her daughter a pointed look.

"You're right, Mama. All three of those boys of mine look besotted with their beautiful brides," Denni said, tipping her head at her mother and narrowing her eyes, daring her to say anything further.

"Mmm, hmm," Ester said, giving Denni a knowing stare.

"Guess it's time to roll up our sleeves and help clean up," Hart said, looking around as the majority of the guests walked out to their cars and began to depart.

"There are enough hands to make light work of it," Ester said, pointing at all the men already folding chairs and taking down the tents set up in the front and side yard. "Why don't you two go relax for a while?"

"Is your girdle cinched too tight, Mama? Is it cutting off circulation to your brain?" Denni asked, looking at her mother like she'd lost her mind. "There's no way we'd go wander off when there's a monumental mess to clean."

"Oh, fiddle," Ester said, wanting to stamp her foot. She'd tried everything to finagle it so Hart and Denni could be together today and neither one of them had been overly cooperative. "What have you two got against having a little fun?"

"Not a thing," Denni said, putting one hand in Hart's and looping her other around her mother's arm, turning them both toward the yard. "I'm all for playing and fun, but let's get the work taken care of first."

"Party pooper," Ester muttered, walking toward June and Donna where they helped Cady clear the cake table. It didn't take long to have everything set to rights with so many hands to do the work.

"Let me run in and change then maybe you and I can go for a walk," Denni said, grabbing Hart's hand as he walked by her carrying the last of the filled trash bags toward the Thompson's commercial-sized garbage container.

"If I asked real nice, would you leave that dress on?" Hart asked, heat turning his eyes a liquid blue as he looked at Denni.

"Well, I...um...Really?"

"Really," Hart said, looking around and noticing no one was close by to overhear him. "Please, Denni. You just look so beautiful."

Flattered and a little flustered by Hart's intense gaze, Denni nodded her head.

"Great. Just give me a minute." Hart dumped the trash in the container, ran inside the house and washed his hands then met Denni at the side of the house by the mudroom door.

"Where do you want to walk?" Hart asked, taking her hand and strolling out of the yard.

"Have you been down to the pond?" Denni asked, knowing it was a favorite spot for romance with her boys.

"Nope. Lead the way, fair lady," Hart said, executing a gallant bow.

Denni laughed and grabbed his hand again, carefully walking in the direction of the pond. She still wore her high heels and found it a little challenging to walk with any degree of surety or speed in them.

Topping the rise and starting down the gentle incline toward the pond, Denni's breath caught in her throat when Hart swept her off her feet and into his arms, hurrying down the hill.

"My stars, Hart! What are you doing?" Denni asked when she could speak again. Her hands looped around his neck and her lips hovered tantalizingly close to his. She inhaled his wonderful scent and entangled her fingers in the back of his hair.

"Sweeping my girl off her feet," Hart said, giving Denni one of his grins that made her desperately want to kiss the cleft in his chin. "I may not have seen your pond, but I've heard all about your kissing bench. Point the way."

Denni laughed and pointed to a bench placed beneath a weeping willow tree. Years ago, her boys had dubbed it the kissing bench.

Hart sat down with Denni across his lap and leaned back, giving her an intense perusal from the top of her golden head to the tips of her royal blue heels.

"You are, hands down, the hottest grandma I've ever seen," Hart said, running his hand up and down her back, enjoying the feel of her silk dress against his rough fingers. "As a matter of fact, I'd say one of the most enticing women I've ever known, period."

Speechless, Denni sat staring at him, more than a little enraptured with Hart, his words and his warm presence. He looked absolutely gorgeous sitting there with his tan face, his tie and jacket long ago removed and the top two buttons of his shirt undone.

Tipping Denni back in his arms, he ran a hand up one smooth leg, making sparks ignite between the two of them.

Placing her hands on either side of Hart's face, Denni pulled his head down for the kiss she'd waited all day to give him. Long, intense and lingering, Hart finally pulled back, resting his forehead against hers.

"Wow, sunshine. That was…incredible," Hart said, feeling a little overwhelmed by the intensity of his feelings, his longing, for the woman in his arms. "In case I haven't mentioned it today, you look absolutely gorgeous."

"You might have hinted at it, but I don't mind if you tell me another time or two," Denni said with a flirty grin that caused Hart to feel overheated as he kissed her again. "You don't look too bad for someone who pumps gas for a living."

"Is that right?" Hart asked, smiling against her mouth. "I'm a regular grease monkey, huh?"

"Yep," Denni said, fighting the urge to unbutton the rest of Hart's shirt and drink her fill of him.

Knowing things were about to get out of hand, Hart raised Denni and turned her so her back rested against his chest.

"Tell me about this kissing bench," Hart said, tapping the wooden seat with the hand that wasn't wrapped around Denni's waist. Since he began dating Denni, Hart decided women's waists were designed to have the arms of the man they loved wrapped around them. It was the perfect place to rest his hand while they were standing, to pull her closer when they were sitting and... he wouldn't let his thoughts go any further.

"My boys started calling this the kissing bench back in high school," Denni said, smiling as she thought about how the bench came to be beneath the willow tree. "Trey was the one who hauled the bench down here, intent on romancing whichever girl he was dating at the time. It used to sit up in the yard by the big oak tree. Anyway, he brought his girl of the week down here for a little kissing and his two brothers snuck down and spied on him. They were sitting in the tree over there, making faces and carrying on so much, Trey ended up chasing them both up the hill and taking his date home."

"I bet Trent and Travis were in for it," Hart said, picturing the two younger boys wreaking havoc with Trey's teenage love life.

"For sure," Denni said, laughing at the memory. "Trent brought Lindsay down here last May to propose to her. He made everyone help him string thousands of white lights in the bushes and trees and set the whole thing on a timer. It was a sight to see when all those lights kicked on. Brice also proposed to Bailey here Thanksgiving Day but you were here then, so you know all about that."

"I didn't realize this was the spot where the proposal was carried out, but I do remember how in love they both looked. And so happy," Hart said, glad that Brice and Bailey, like Denni's boys, had found their true love. "What about Travis? Did he and Tess do some sparking on the bench?"

"Not that I'm aware of. He proposed to her at the fort."

"The fort? Where's that?" Hart asked. In the past several months, he'd ridden over a lot of ground at the Triple T Ranch and no one had mentioned a fort.

"Down by the creek. Drew built it for the boys when they were little guys. My hooligans, along with the Morgan kids, spent a lot of time playing there," Denni said, laughing as she recalled Tess' initiation ceremony. "When Trav and Brice were six, all of the kids were here and I made the boys take Tess out to play with them. Travis, especially, didn't want to take her along. They got it in their head that if Tess wanted to play in the fort, she had to go through an initiation ceremony, which sounded more like a mock wedding. The older boys made her kiss Travis, who was convinced he was going to get girl cooties. Apparently, he became so infected, he lost his heart to our sugarplum that day."

"I love that story," Hart said, kissing Denni on the back of neck. "Do all the Thompson's need some dramatic, elaborate gesture to declare their love?"

"Not all," Denni said, turning so she could look in Hart's eyes, feeling pulled into their warm depths. "Look, Hart, I want to apologize for the day you said you loved me. Honestly, you took me by surprise and I thought it was the pain talking, not you. I could have handled things better and for that, I'm sorry."

"Denni," Hart said, his voice sounding low and husky as he brushed his thumb across her cheek, then along her lower lip. "I'm the one who needs to apologize. Of all the ways I could have found to say I love you, blurting it out while I could barely move was not how I planned it at all. It didn't make it any less sincere or true, just bungled."

"Oh," Denni said, not knowing what else to say. She really wanted to hear Hart say the words again.

Hart studied her for a long moment, brushing his hand up and down her arm. Cupping the back of her head, Hart captured her lips again and kissed her tenderly. "I love you, Denni Thompson. I think I have since I walked in the room Thanksgiving Day and saw you standing there with your mom. You're such a beautiful, vibrant person. When I'm with you, I forget I'm a man in his fifties with responsibilities and duties. I feel young, ready for adventure, set for fun. You do that, sunshine. You make everything seem lively and exciting."

"I love you, too," Denni said, burying her face against Hart's neck, holding him tight. "I love you so much, Hart. I feel so alive and happy when I'm with you. Thank you for giving me a reason to move on."

"If you're moving on, care if I come along for the ride?"

Chapter Seventeen

*"We can only be said to be alive in those moments
when our hearts are conscious of our treasures."*
Thornton Wilder

"Like this, Grammy?" Cass asked as she sat at the sewing machine, carefully stitching together two pieces of fabric. Denni thought the child was old enough to teach some basic stitching and Cass seemed to enjoy learning.

Cady, Lindsay and Tess were spending the day in Portland, shopping for things for the baby's nursery. Trey and Travis were off to a farm sale and Trent was finishing the final coat of paint in the master suite at his house, so Denni offered to keep Cass for the weekend.

Hart picked Cass up after school the previous afternoon and drove her to The Dalles then took her, along with Denni and Ester, out for dinner. Between Cass asking her if Hart was her boyfriend and Ester making sly comments, Denni was sure her cheeks were as red as the pieces of fabric Cass was now sewing together.

With an idea for a new quilt design, Denni decided to make a wall hanging for Hart. Thinking back to the quilt show and his comments about a broken heart, she was going to call the pattern mended hearts.

Done in red and white fabric, she hoped Hart would understand the underlying meaning of the quilted art when she gave it to him.

She cut out all the quilt pieces earlier in the week and planned to start sewing it today. Since Cass was with her, she thought the little girl could help with the project and get in some sewing lessons at the same time.

"You're doing a great job, sweetie-pie," Denni said, rubbing her hand lovingly on the little girl's back as she carefully watched the pieces being sewn together. "Just remember to always, always keep your fingers away from the needle."

"I member, Grammy. You tolded me that four times already," Cass said, concentrating on her work. So intense on what she was doing, Cass wasn't even jiggling a foot or vibrating with exuberant energy as she usually did.

"So I did," Denni said, hiding her smile, especially when Amy tried not to laugh from where she was folding bolts of fabric at the counter.

"If I do this right, can we make something for Aunt Lindsay's baby? Mama said the baby will be here soon," Cass said, letting out a whoosh of breath when the last stitch was complete. Denni showed her how to snip the thread then turned the pieces over so Cass could see how they looked stitched together. "Look what I did, Grammy!"

"You did a great job, honey. And we can certainly make something for Aunt Lindsay. What did you have in mind?"

"Can we make a blanket? Mama said babies need lots of blankets," Cass said, gazing at Denni with a hopeful look on her sweet little face.

"That's a great idea, sweetie-pie," Denni said, ruffling Cass's mop of wild red curls. "Let's pick out some fabric and we'll make it right now."

"Really, Grammy? I can make the whole thing today?" Cass asked, so excited she was hopping off one foot to the other.

"Absolutely," Denni said, kissing Cass on the nose then ushering her over to where she kept fabrics with prints meant to be used for babies. "We need to find two prints that coordinate. Why don't you pick the first one and we'll see what matches?"

Cass studied all her choices, walking back and forth looking at every option several times before reaching out and pointing to a bolt of fabric that featured a sweet little pink rosebud on a pale green background. "Please, Grammy. I think she'll like this one best."

"She? You think the baby is going to be a girl?" Denni asked, bending down so she could look Cass in the eye. Last she heard, Trent and Lindsay didn't want to know the baby's sex and were keeping it a surprise. Maybe they'd changed their minds and someone forgot to tell her. "Did Aunt Lindsay say it's going to be a girl?"

"No," Cass said, pulling the bolt of fabric off the shelf and rubbing her little hand carefully across the soft material. "I just know. She likes pink."

"Maybe we should use one of the little animal prints. Do you like this one with the monkeys?" Denni asked, knowing Trent and Lindsay chose a neutral pale yellow shade for the nursery, thinking it would work well for either a boy or a girl.

"Please, Grammy. Pretty, pretty please. I want to use this one," Cass said. Denni couldn't say no when Cass looked at her with her big china blue eyes starting to fill with tears and her lip stuck out in an adorable pout.

"Okay, sweetie-pie," Denni said, taking the bolt from Cass and walking over to a rack that held gingham prints. "Do you like the green or pink gingham?"

"Pink," Cass said without hesitation. "Emily is going to love this, Grammy."

Knowing Trent and Lindsay picked the name Emily if the baby was a girl, Denni thought it interesting Cass was calling the baby by her name. Picking up the bolt of pink gingham to go along with the rosebud material, Denni hoped Trent would forgive her if the baby was a boy and he ended up using the quilt to keep Cass from having her feelings hurt. The little girl was so intent on the fact that the baby would be a girl and so excited to make a pink blanket, Denni didn't want to spoil her fun.

"Pink it is."

Denni took the fabric to the counter where she and Amy cut out squares of both fabrics and pinned them together, then Denni helped Cass sew the squares. When the top was finished, Amy helped her stretch it over a piece of pink gingham lined with soft batting and pin the edges. Showing Cass how to run a blunt needle through the fabric with a piece of yarn, they tied a piece in each square anchoring the three layers together before Denni added a binding to the edges of the quilt.

She was finishing the last corner when Hart came in the door and Cass ran over to him, talking a mile a minute.

"Hart, guess what Grammy and I made today," Cass said, so excited she was nearly running circles around him before he swung her up in his arms and gave her a hug.

"Let me think," he said, pretending to consider his answer. "You sewed something."

"Of course, silly," Cass said, patting his cheeks as he carried her over to where Denni snipped the last thread and turned off the sewing machine. "We maded baby Emily a blankie. See?"

"Baby Emily?" Hart asked looking at Denni with a questioning glance as he set Cass down.

"It's for Lindsay and Trent," Denni said, smiling as Cass carried the blanket to the fabric counter where Amy helped her spread it out.

"But I thought they were waiting to find out..." Hart asked, confused.

"They are," Denni whispered as she and Hart walked over to the counter. "Cass has decided the baby is a girl and is already calling her Emily. Hence, the very pink blanket."

"Trent's going to love it," Hart said, grinning broadly as he picked up Cass and admired the blanket.

"It's not for Uncle Trent. It's for baby Emily. She likes pink," Cass said, pointing out all the details about the quilt she thought it was important for him to know. He nodded his head and made appropriate comments while looking over Cass's head and winking at Denni. "When Bailey and Brice get home, Mama said we're going to shower Aunt Lindsay."

"A baby shower for Aunt Lindsay," Denni said, trying not to laugh at Cass' take on the upcoming party.

"Yep," Cass said, wiggling for Hart to set her down on the counter, which he did. Cass picked up a corner of the blanket and rubbed the fabric against her cheek. "Did you know Brice and Bailey are on a honeymoon?"

"I did know that," Hart said, tipping back his hat and leaning an elbow on the counter, entertained by Cass and the way her mind worked. He couldn't wait to see where this conversation would lead.

"Have you been on a honeymoon?" Cass asked, shooting her big blue-eyed gaze to him.

"Can't say that I have, Miss Cass." Hart shook his head and tried to look like he'd missed out on something important. "Have you?"

"No," Cass said, giggling. "You have to be a growned up person to go."

"You do?" Hart asked, scratching his chin, looking thoughtful. "Are you sure?"

"Yep. Uncle Trent said so and he wouldn't tell me something that wasn't true, would he, Grammy?" Cass asked, looking to Denni for confirmation.

"No, Uncle Trent wouldn't tell you something that wasn't true."

"See," Cass said, turning her attention back to Hart. "When Mama and Daddy went on their honeymoon last year, Uncle Trent and Uncle Travis took care of me and I asked Uncle Trent all about what peoples do on a honeymoon. He tolded me they play and have fun."

"They do? What else did Uncle Trent say?" Hart asked, leaning forward on the counter until he was nearly nose-to-nose with Cass, making her giggle when he crossed his eyes and rolled his tongue.

"Uncle Trent said when peoples go on a honeymoon they take someone they like. That's why he took Aunt Lindsay and Uncle Travis took Aunt Tess and now Brice took Bailey," Cass said, growing oddly quiet. She stared first at Denni, then Hart, then back to Denni again.

"Oh, Grammy. I've got the bestest idea, ever!" Cass said, her entire body wiggling in excitement.

"You do?" Denni asked, picking Cass up off the counter and setting her down beside her where the little girl bounced off one foot to the other. "Let's hear this bestest idea."

Cass took Denni's hand and began swinging it back and forth. "It's a dandy," Cass said, making Hart swallow back a laugh and Amy roll her eyes from the other side of the counter. Hart had no doubt whatever came out of Cass' mouth would be dandy, indeed.

"And what is your dandy idea?" Denni asked, smiling at Cass indulgently.

"You and Hart can go on a honeymoon, just like everybody else," Cass said in a singsong voice. "You like him and he likes you, so you two can go. That way Hart gets to go on one and won't be sad anymore. Isn't that a great idea?"

"Well...Cass...I...my stars..." Denni spluttered, so shocked by the little girl's statement, she felt lightheaded.

Hart picked up Cass and kissed her cheek. "You're right, Cass. That is one dandy idea. However, for people to go on a honeymoon they have to be married first."

"Then you can marry Grammy and everyone will be happy," Cass said, looking at him like he should have figured out that detail without her help.

"Cass, honey, it…we…" Denni was still trying to find her mental footing when Cass turned to look at her with tears filling her eyes.

"Don't you like Hart, Grammy? I thought you liked him. He's such a nice man and he takes us to dinner and lets us pet his horses and gives me lollipops when Daddy stops at the gas station." Cass' rosebud mouth puckered in a pout that made Hart want to promise to give her unicorns and rainbows if it would keep the tears gathering in her eyes from spilling over.

"Oh, sweetie-pie, I like Hart. I like him very much, but you don't just decide to marry someone so you can go on a honeymoon," Denni said, putting a hand on Cass' leg and giving her a reassuring pat. "I'm sure someday Hart will take a honeymoon and he won't be sad anymore."

"Don't you want to go with him, Grammy? I bet Hart would play and have fun with you. He knows all kinds of games and he always makes me laugh. Don't you, Hart?"

"Thanks, Cass. I appreciate your endorsement, but I don't think your Grammy likes me quite as much as I like her," Hart said, playing right into Cass' efforts to garner sympathy for his lack of experiencing a honeymoon.

"Now, Hart, don't you get started," Denni said, giving him a cool glare.

"But, Grammy, Hart likes you heaps. He said so," Cass said, looking at her grandmother like she was not quite understanding what she was saying. "Whole bunches and heaps."

"I like him whole bunches and heaps myself, but that doesn't mean we'll be going on a honeymoon, Cass. Now, before you decide to continue this conversation, I think we should take Hart to get some ice cream. Isn't that a much better idea than talking about honeymoons?"

"Okay," Cass said, although her response was lacking the enthusiasm Denni was hoping the mention of ice cream would muster.

Hart set Cass down and she ran behind the counter, picking up her little backpack and Denni's purse.

Denni took her purse and put it over her shoulder, accepting the baby quilt Amy had folded and placed inside a bag, then took Cass' hand in hers. Hart took Cass' other hand and the threesome went outside into the warm afternoon sunshine. Hart looked at Denni and had to bite the inside of his cheek to keep from erupting into laughter.

If he had his way, Cass would be dead on the money about him and Denni going on a honeymoon. He had it in mind to show Denni as much fun and play with him as she could take.

><><

Joining Cass and Denni for dinner, Hart hung around for the evening, watching a Disney movie with his girls before Cass requested he read her a bedtime story and tuck her in. Denni supervised, since Hart was sadly inexperienced in putting children to bed. Apparently, he did everything to Cass' expectations because just before her droopy eyes closed in slumber, she reached up and gave him a hug.

"Love you, Hart," she whispered, letting her eyes flutter close while her rosebud lips rested in a little upturned smile as she fell asleep.

"Love you, too, Cass." Hart felt a new kind of tingling in the region of his heart. He'd never had the opportunity to be around children, although he liked them. Cass, who was such a friendly child, introduced him to the wonders of sticky kisses, stranglehold hugs, and the unique little girl scent of strawberries, bubble gum, and sunshine.

Looking at the sweet little thing as she slept, Hart reached out a hand and gently brushed her wild curls away from her face before getting up from the bed and setting her storybook on the nightstand. Denni turned off the light and walked out of the room, followed by Hart. Leaving the door cracked open, they returned to the living room and sat together on the couch.

Usually full of fun and nonsense, Denni was surprised when Hart sat quietly on the end of the couch, lost in his thoughts.

Reaching out to him, she put a hand on his arm. "Everything okay?"

"Hmm?" Hart asked, bringing his focus back to the present. Offering Denni a half-smile, he picked up her hand and kissed it before grasping it tightly in his. "I'm fine, sunshine."

"You don't seem fine," Denni said, wondering what made Hart so pensive. It wasn't like him at all.

"Just thinking deep thoughts," Hart said, not quite sure how to put what was on his mind into words. Denni was so blessed to have her family. Yes, she experienced her share of pain and loss, but she also had three fine sons, three wonderful daughters-in-law, and now grandchildren to gather around her and love. He wondered if she fully appreciated the treasures of her family. Rich monetarily, Hart knew he was a pauper where family was concerned.

"Want to share?" Denni asked, leaning against his chest. She sighed contentedly when Hart wrapped his arm around her and pulled her closer.

"I was just thinking how blessed you are to have your family. You've got your boys and their girls and now your grandkids," Hart said, resting his chin on the top of

Denni's head. "You're so lucky to have them, Denni. It's no fun to be alone."

"I am lucky to have them and count my blessings every single day," Denni said, sitting up so she could look into Hart's eyes. Smiling tenderly, she placed a hand on his cheek. "You're right. Being alone is hard, challenging, and not particularly fun, but you aren't alone. Not anymore. You've got me. You've got my hooligan boys and their teasing wives, and Cass, and even my sassy mother, if you want us."

Hart looked down at her and grinned. "You mean it? You'd share all that with me?"

"Like I have any choice in the matter," Denni said with a laugh that made Hart feel warm from the inside out. "My boys respect and admire you, my girls adore you and Cass thinks you visit just to play with her. My mother... good grief, I won't even get started on her but suffice it to say, she thinks you're something special. Besides, according to Cass, you and I really should plan a honeymoon together."

Hart snapped to attention at Denni's mention of a honeymoon. Not sure if she was teasing or serious, he wasn't taking any chances on bungling a spur of the moment proposal and decided not to make further comment on it. Instead, he decided the two of them could use a little distraction and went about creating one the best way he knew how.

Offering Denni a tantalizing smile, making her knees weak, he ran his thumb along her lower lip then leaned in close to her ear. "She's a smart kid," he said, kissing Denni with all the wanting and love that was currently filling his heart.

Chapter Eighteen

*"There are many things in life that will catch your eye,
but only a few will catch your heart...
pursue those."*
Michael Nolan

Closing her eyes for a moment, Denni breathed in the smell of new paint and carpet, listened to the soft hum of the women she referred to as her girls, laughing as they worked together in Lindsay's small kitchen, and felt her heart catch at how incredibly rich and blessed her life had become.

Today was Lindsay's baby shower. Tess and Cady decided it would be easiest on Lindsay if they held it at her house so she wouldn't have to worry about transferring the gifts from one of their homes to hers. Cady prepared the food, Tess took charge of the decorations, and Bailey made sure Lindsay's house was clean and ready for the guests to arrive. All Lindsay had to do was get dressed and smile when the guests knocked on the door. At least that's what the other girls tried to tell her. Instead, all four girls were in the kitchen giggling and teasing each other as they put the final touches on the food and party games.

Begging and pleading to attend the shower and give Lindsay her gift, Cass flopped down next to Denni and let out a giggle. Opening her eyes, Denni leaned over and kissed the little girl on her forehead.

"My goodness, don't you look nice today, sweetie-pie. That's a pretty dress," Denni said, thinking Cass looked like a big doll as ribbon barrettes on each side of her head helped tame her wild red curls into some sense of order. The blue dress Cass wore set off her china blue eyes and made the child look angelic and sweet, especially with her white stockings and black patent leather shoes.

"Thanks, Grammy," Cass said, wrapping her little hands around Denni's arm and leaning her head against Denni's shoulder. "Daddy said I'm growing like a weed and Mama said it's a good thing school's almost out cause my clothes are getting too small. Mama boughted me this dress to wear today cause she said it's a special occasion. I had to promise to stay in the house and not run around outside and I couldn't even hug Buddy when we left the ranch so I wouldn't get it dirty."

"I see," Denni said, wrapping an arm around Cass and giving her a hug. Cass loved her dog Buddy about as much as anything, so it was a big concession on her part to leave the dog alone when asked. "I'm sure Buddy won't mind."

"Daddy patted him extra times and threw a stick for him to chase, so I spose he's fine," Cass said, picking at the edge of the satin ribbon around her waist. Denni caught her fingers and kissed her little hand, making Cass giggle again.

When Cass first came to live with Trey and Cady she was malnourished and notably small for her age. Now, after a year and a half in their care, she was really starting to fill out and grow. Small-boned and tiny, Cass would never be the tallest or biggest child in her class, but she was starting to look more her age. "Are you excited to give Aunt Lindsay your gift?"

"Oh, yes. I can't wait. She and Emily are going to love it," Cass said, bouncing a little as she spoke. "Grammy?"

"Hmm?"

"Tell me again when Emily's going to get here. I've been waiting for her to come for a long, long time."

Denni picked up Cass and cuddled her on her lap, breathing in the wonderful scent of little girl. She used to volunteer to watch the Morgan kids just so she could get a few minutes of cuddling Tess, who never seemed to mind spending time with Denni while the boys rough-housed outside. With no daughters of her own, Denni sometimes wanted a little-girl fix. She needed to listen to soft chatter and sweet giggles and talk about fairies and princesses instead of the rowdy laughter and non-stop games of war and one-upping her boys engaged in.

"Emily, or Tyson if the baby ends up being a boy, will be here around the time school ends for the summer. The baby might come a little sooner or later, but it will be right around that time. Isn't that exciting?"

"Yep. Mama said the baby will be teeny-tiny and I'll have to wait until she grows up bigger to play with her, but I know Emily will love me," Cass said confidently.

"I know she will, too," Denni said, setting Cass on her feet and taking her hand. "Did you see the baby's bedroom?"

"Not since Uncle Trent painted it," Cass said, pulling Denni down the hall toward the newly finished rooms. Since they planned to add a master suite and a nursery anyway, Trent thought it best if they added two more bedrooms and another bathroom while they were at it. Now the addition was finished, just waiting for the arrival of the baby.

The two new bedrooms were yet unfurnished. Lindsay had Brice making a set of furniture for one room and she'd ordered the pieces for the second room, but they hadn't yet arrived.

She and Trent had a new set of furniture, made by Brice, for the large master suite that looked inviting and relaxing.

"It's pretty blue, just like my dress," Cass said, pointing to the soothing, pale color of the walls. "Aunt Lindsay likes blue."

"Yes, she does," Denni said, surprised Cass would notice colors her aunt liked. The little girl pointed out the quilt Denni made on the bed, the cedar chest Brice carved against one wall, and the new bedroom set made of dark walnut wood.

"I like this room," Cass said, sitting down in a rocking chair placed in front of a big window that looked out over the side yard.

"I do, too," Lindsay said from the doorway where she rested a hand on her mounded tummy.

"Aunt Lindsay," Cass said, running over to the woman who was both teacher and aunt to her. From past lectures, Cass knew to give Lindsay a gentle hug instead of her enthusiastic embrace. "Your room matches my dress."

"It sure does. You look very nice today, sweetie-pie. I appreciate you coming to my shower," Lindsay said, carefully rubbing a hand over Cass' hair, not wanting to disturb what had been tamed into some form of submission.

"I can't wait for Emily to get here," Cass said, staring at her aunt's tummy. She still didn't understand why the baby was in Lindsay's tummy or how it was going to get out, but she learned to stop asking questions about it. Everyone told her to ask her mother and all Cady would tell her is that God put the baby there for safekeeping until it was time for her to come meet everyone.

"Me, either," Lindsay said, grinning at Denni who walked out of the room and stood in the hall, smiling at her daughter-in-law.

Lindsay was six-feet tall, blond and athletic. She ran in marathons, worked out daily, and was long and lean. Now, softened by the months of being sick and pregnant, Denni didn't think she'd ever seen the girl look lovelier.

She had a wonderful glow that filled her being, shining from her face and eyes, illuminating her skin.

Although the couple didn't plan to have a baby so soon, it would be treasured and loved. Everyone thought it was hilarious when Trent and Lindsay realized she'd gotten pregnant on their honeymoon.

Not finding it quite as funny as the rest of the bunch, Denni knew how hard adjusting to marriage could be without throwing a baby into the mix. It took time to get used to the nuances of having someone share every aspect of your life, learning the give and take that made a marriage successful.

Although it made her mad at the time, she was glad her parents and Drew insisted she wait to start a family until she finished college. She and Drew had six years of wedded bliss before they welcomed the arrival of Trey and everything shifted from being a honeymooning couple to being parents.

Knowing Lindsay and Trent were completely devoted to each other, Denni thought they'd be just fine. There was no doubt the baby would be surrounded by love, just like Cass had been since the day Cady brought her home to the Triple T.

"Let's see this nursery I've heard so much about," Denni said, following Lindsay and Cass down the hall. "Tess couldn't stop raving about how cute everything looks."

"It did turn out pretty well," Lindsay said, opening the door.

Denni stepped inside and caught her breath. The room was wonderful. Positively wonderful.

The walls were painted the palest shade of yellow, looking like whipped butter. White furniture matched the white curtains at the windows. Choosing an owl theme, cute little birds added accents of whimsy and color throughout the room. A tree mural highlighted the wall behind the crib with three sweet-faced owls sitting on the branches.

Wandering around the room, Denni smiled to see a plaque on the wall that said, "Grow wise, little owl." It was the perfect thing for the child of a schoolteacher.

"Lindsay, this is adorable. Absolutely perfect," Denni said, giving her daughter-in-law a hug. "I love it."

"Did you see the owl, Grammy?" Cass asked, pointing to a softly feathered stuffed owl where it sat watch over the room from its spot on the dresser. Lindsay handed it to Cass who reverently stroked the feathers before setting it back in place. "Emily will like that."

Lindsay smiled at Denni and raised an eyebrow. Everyone took note that Cass had decided the baby would be a girl.

"Shall we go see if this party is ready to start?" Lindsay asked, taking Cass' hand.

"Yep. I love parties," Cass said, skipping beside Lindsay as she waddled down the hall toward the living room. Denni could hear the chatter of more voices and knew guests had arrived.

Giving the nursery one more glance, Denni felt a burst of love for the grandchild who would soon occupy the room and their hearts.

><><

"You should have seen Trent's face when Cass showed him the blanket," Denni said later that evening as she sat snuggled against Hart outside on his deck.

After the shower, she told her kids she'd be gone for a while and not to worry if she arrived home a little late. Travis walked her to her car and said to tell Hart to behave himself or he'd have three angry Thompson men to deal with. Denni smacked his arm, kissed his cheek and left.

She didn't know whether to be pleased that her boys cared so much or exasperated at their overprotective tendencies. As hard as they tried to keep her in a safe little shell, Denni couldn't wait to see what would happen when Cass, and any daughters they might have, were old enough to date. It might be worth moving back to Grass Valley just to have a front row seat to watch that unfold.

Sitting with her back against Hart's solid chest on a big outdoor chaise lounge, drinking iced tea and cozied up by the outdoor heater he turned on to chase way the evening chill, Denni was so content she felt like purring. She could stay right there, happy with life, thrilled to be wrapped up in Hart's arms, for a very long time.

"Not excited over all the pink?" Hart asked, taking a drink of his tea before setting the glass on a side table and trailing his fingers along Denni's neck. His lips followed his fingers and he felt Denni shiver with pleasure as she relaxed against him.

"Not in the least," Denni said, trying to keep her thoughts on their conversation instead of the heat exploding inside her at Hart's touch. "He's really hoping for a boy. Trent told Trey he went along with the yellow scheme for the nursery because it would be easy to add some John Deere green for a boy and oust the owl decor."

Hart chuckled. "Now that makes sense."

"Oh, you men all stick together," Denni said, shaking her head disapprovingly. "Cass is one hundred percent sure the baby is going to be a girl. She was so sweet at the shower today, talking about how Emily would like this or love that. I sure hope she isn't disappointed if the baby is a boy."

"She'll be fine. Kids adjust so much easier to changes in their plans than adults. Besides, she's got a fifty-fifty chance of being right."

"That she does. Don't tell my kids, but I'm with Cass. I really hope it's a girl," Denni said, turning her head to place a kiss on Hart's cheek.

"Girl, boy, doesn't really matter because I know for a fact that baby will be loved beyond reason," Hart said, nuzzling Denni's ear.

"Lindsay was thrilled with the gift you sent, by the way. You really didn't have to do anything."

"I know, but I wanted to. In case you haven't noticed, I'm more than a little fond of your family, too," Hart said, turning his gaze to Denni's. Their eyes met and he smiled at her with such love she felt her heart catch.

"How did you know books would be the perfect gift?" Everyone was surprised when Lindsay opened Hart's beautifully wrapped package to see a large wicker basket filled with children's books. An entire collection of Dr. Seuss books, several Little Golden books, and classics like *The Velveteen Rabbit* were a huge hit with the mother-to-be as well as Denni. She thought Hart had to be one of the most thoughtful, sweet men she'd ever had the pleasure of meeting.

"Lindsay's a school teacher. Books seemed like a good idea," Hart said, rubbing his hand up and down Denni's arms in a lazy, slow pattern that was making her toes tingle. "I saw an idea for books as a shower gift on Pinterest."

Denni laughed and turned to stare at Hart. "You do not have an account on Pinterest."

"Who says?"

"I do, you crazy man. No matter how hard I try, I don't see you pinning recipes, party theme ideas, or fitness tips," Denni said with a sassy grin. She had spent many hours enjoying all the fun things the social media site had to offer, from quilt ideas to boards created by her favorite romance author, and knew no matter what he said Hart would not be browsing through the offerings and sharing them with friends.

"Okay, fine. Have it your way," Hart said, pulling her back against him again. "Megan was playing around on her phone between customers at the station and showed me a photo someone pinned of me riding a bull back in the day. We searched through some stuff for fun, then I asked her if she could find baby shower gift ideas. When I saw one that suggested books, I had her send me the link and I ordered all the books it listed."

"See, I was right. You aren't a seasoned pinner," Denni said smugly.

"I could be," Hart said, teasing Denni. "Maybe I'll abandon all else in my life to sit and pin photos of celebrities, cleaning tips, and inspirational quotes."

"Somehow, I can't quite picture it. You wouldn't be able to sit still for five minutes, let alone all day," Denni said, patting Hart on his hard thigh, making his temperature begin to climb. "I would, however, like to see the photos of you. I'll have to check those out."

"Why do you want photos from my wasted youth? You've got the real deal right here, in living flesh," Hart said, placing a hot kiss on her neck.

"And such nicely shaped flesh it is, too," Denni said, turning her head and kissing Hart with a feeling of need and longing that frightened her. She was beginning to need, not just want Hart, with an intensity she'd never experienced before. Part of her felt guilty that she'd never felt that way with Drew. Maybe it had something to do with her age, the years of loneliness. Whatever it was, she could easily become consumed with Hart, if she'd give herself permission for it to happen.

When the kiss ended, Denni felt herself picked up and turned so she was facing Hart. He caressed her cheek, brushed his fingers along her jaw, stared for a long moment into her eyes, melting her resolve to keep from giving herself over to him completely.

Hart wasn't the kind of man you could love at arm's length. He was the kind of man who required a woman's whole love, whole heart, whole being become entangled with his because that is how he loved - with everything he had.

"I love you so much, sunshine," Hart said, holding her close and kissing her temple. "You are the best thing that's ever happened to me."

"You are one of the most wonderful things that has ever happened to me. I love you, Hart," Denni said, feeling her emotions bubbling close to the surface. It was still a wonder, a miracle to her, that she had not only found love again, but found someone who could love her so completely and make her feel so alive.

Denni had no idea the hot, wild feelings of her youth had been lying dormant inside her waiting for Hart to stir them to life. She assumed she'd never feel that way again and here she was acting like a woman thirty years younger, infatuated with a handsome, hunky, dreamy man.

"Denni, I..."

"How about we stop talking and you just kiss me some more?" Denni asked, feeling Hart's smile as his lips connected with hers.

After a series of kisses that seemed to steadily increase with passion and heat, Hart finally pulled back and took a ragged breath.

"Look, Denni, there's something I've been meaning to ask you," Hart said, taking her face in his hands and looking into the depths of her eyes. Denni felt like he was staring down into her soul.

"Okay," she said, noting the serious look on his face, the way he grew tense. This wasn't a good sign. Afraid of what the question would be, Denni steeled herself for whatever was to come. "Go ahead."

"This might seem sudden and I know you might not be ready, so I'm not pressuring you for an answer right now, but here's the thing of it, Denni - I love you. So utterly and completely, I spend half my day and most of my nights dreaming of you. I never hoped to find a love like I've found with you and the truth is I want you. I want to wake up in the morning and see your sassy smile on the pillow next to mine. I want to trip over your shoes in my closet and find your curlers on the bathroom counter. I want to cuddle with you in front of the fire on cold nights and sit out here with you during the summer gazing at the stars. I want to love you, Denni, like I've never loved another woman before, with my entire heart and soul. I want to grow old with you, to cherish your family the way you do. I want, more than anything, Denni DeNae Nordon Thompson, for you to be my wife. Would you please consider marrying me?"

Rising, Denni stared at Hart in disbelief. Had he really just asked her to marry him? A flood of thoughts and emotions rushed through her with such force, she had to fight to take a breath. Quickly wading through it all, she realized what she wanted was right there before her.

Looking at Hart, she took his hand in hers and held it to her cheek, then placed a light kiss to his palm. Tears she could no longer contain rolled down her face and she offered a wobbly smile.

Hart watched emotions fly across Denni's face, saw her stiffen as she absorbed his words, felt his chest tighten as tears rolled down her cheeks and she gave him a sad little smile. This was going to be goodbye. He just knew it. She'd tell him...

"Yes," Denni's soft whisper cut through his internal litany of despair and his mouth worked its way into a smile that soon beamed from his eyes and his heart. "Absolutely, yes."

"Oh, Denni, you had me worried for a minute," Hart said before he kissed her again then held her tight to his chest. He suddenly lunged to his feet, Denni in his arms, and swung her around and around until they were both laughing.

"When, sunshine?" Hart asked, certain he had never felt this happy, this loved, in his entire life.

"Let's wait until after the baby arrives. But soon," Denni said, so looking forward to spending her life loving the gentle, blood-stirring man who held her so tenderly in his strong arms.

"Soon," Hart repeated, kissing her again.

Chapter Nineteen

"You change your life by changing your heart."
Max Lucado

Fighting an aching back when she got out of bed that morning, Lindsay wished she'd called in sick. Only partway through the morning lessons with her room full of kindergarten and first-grade students, she felt lethargic and weak. And tired. So tired.

Finding it nearly impossible to sit still because of the increasing pain in her back, her concentration had been lost an hour ago. She still had almost a month to go before her due date, so she hoped this wasn't some new phase of her pregnancy she'd have to endure for several more weeks. Being sick for months had been bad enough, but this feeling that her head was swimming along with the backache was awful.

Rising from her desk chair, she paced back and forth in front of her chalkboard while her little students worked on their assigned tasks. Considering how she could possibly go home, she decided to ask one of the aides to take over for the afternoon since the kindergartners were only there during the mornings.

Lindsay took a step toward the door to let the principal know her plan when pain like she'd never before experienced ripped through her abdomen making her clutch her stomach and gasp in pain.

"Aunt Lindsay, are you okay?" Cass asked from beside her. Cass was always very good about calling her Mrs. Thompson at school like the rest of the children. To hear Cass refer to her as aunt meant the little girl knew something was wrong.

"I'm okay, sweetie-pie," Lindsay said, turning to give Cass a reassuring smile only to be hit by another wave of pain that made her grasp the edge of her desk so tightly her knuckles turned white.

"Cass, I need you to go get Mrs. Andrews, please. Hurry, right now, honey," Lindsay said, managing to sink down in her chair. Blinking several times and taking a series of deep breaths, she looked out over the sea of frightened faces and forced herself to smile. "It's okay, kids. I'm fine. Go on back to your assignments. You're doing so well this morning."

Looking up, Lindsay watched the principal run in the door followed by Cass. After a quick glance at Lindsay, Mrs. Andrews ran back out in the hall and could be heard yelling for someone to call the Triple T Ranch.

Cass came and put her little hand on Lindsay's arm, rubbing it much like she patted her dog Buddy's head.

"It'll be okay, Aunt Lindsay. Daddy and Uncle Trent and Uncle Travis won't let anything happen to you. You'll be fine," Cass said, trying to soothe her aunt. To the little girl's way of thinking, there wasn't anything the three Thompson men couldn't fix.

Trying to breathe through another wave of pain, Lindsay closed her eyes and grasped the arm of her chair tightly. When she opened her eyes, Mrs. Andrews was beside her, along with the school janitor.

"Lindsay? Are you going into labor?" Mrs. Andrews asked, putting a cool hand on Lindsay's hot cheek.

"I'm not sure. My back hurt this morning and I keep having the most awful pain. It's too early. I'm not due for

250

almost another month," Lindsay said, bracing herself as she felt another pain strike.

"Trent's on his way. If you can walk, we'll get you out in the hall," Mrs. Andrews said, placing her hand on Lindsay's shoulder.

"I don't think I can get back on my feet," Lindsay said, knowing her weak knees were not going to hold her.

"I can roll her chair out," the janitor said and put words into action, carefully rolling Lindsay's desk chair through the rows of desks and out the door. Cass trailed along behind, not willing to leave her beloved aunt. No one thought to send her back to the classroom where an aide hurried in to sit with the kids.

Closing her eyes and willing Trent to hurry, Lindsay felt him beside her before she smelled his outdoorsy scent.

"Well, princess, what's all the hubbub about?" Trent asked, trying to sound teasing although fear creased his forehead and bracketed his mouth. "This would be a good time for you not to get all excited and jump ahead of the game plan."

"I know that, but this baby of yours seems to have different ideas," Lindsay said from between clenched teeth.

As soon as the pain passed, Trent swept her into his arms and carried her out to his pickup. Cady and Trey arrived, along with Travis, and Cass ran to her parents, crying against Cady's shoulder.

"Is Aunt Lindsay going to die? Is Emily going to be okay? Please, Mama, make them okay," Cass said, sobbing at the solemn looks on everyone's faces. The only time the adults in her life looked like that was when there was something bad or sad happening.

"It's going to be fine, sweetie-pie. Just fine. I'm going to take you to stay with Aunt Viv and Uncle Joe for the rest of the day. How does that sound?"

"No, I want to go with you and Daddy. Please, I want to be with you," Cass cried. Trey took her in his arms and cuddled her close, kissing her cheek as he carried her out to the pickup.

"Cass, we need to help take care of Aunt Lindsay and it will take all our attention to do that today, so we need you to be a big girl and stay with Aunt Viv. Can you do that for us, honey?"

Cass nodded her head and sniffed. Trey took out his handkerchief and mopped her face, made her blow her nose and then set her in her car seat. Cady climbed in the back seat beside her while Trey and Travis sat in the front. Trent was already on the road to The Dalles. Travis called Tess, who happened to be working at the hospital instead of doing home care, and let her know to give the emergency room staff a heads up as well as Lindsay's doctor.

Dropping off Cass with Viv, Cady waited until they were back in the truck to call Denni. When Amy answered at the store, Cady remembered Hart took Denni to Portland to pick out an engagement ring that morning.

When Denni came back from Hart's the other night, they had never seen her look so happy. Cady thought the woman seemed to be floating on air as she walked in the kitchen and sank down on a barstool, looking dreamy eyed. When the boys continued asking her what was going on, she finally told them Hart proposed and she accepted.

Amid their whoops of excitement and round of hugs and backslapping, Denni mentioned that Hart gave her the option of choosing her own ring or letting him surprise her. She decided she wanted to pick it out together, so he suggested they make a day of it in Portland.

Calling Denni's cell phone, it went straight to voice mail. Trying not to leave an alarming message, Cady thought carefully about what to say. "Denni, this is Cady. When you get this message please give me a call, or call one of the boys. We have a little situation and want to let you know about it. Thanks."

Hoping that the message wouldn't frighten her mother-in-law, Cady closed her phone and returned to her prayers for the safekeeping of Lindsay and her baby.

By the time they arrived at the hospital, the three of them hurried in the emergency room entry to find Tess waiting at the door. By her pale face, they knew things weren't good.

"Honeybee, what happened?" Travis asked, folding her in his arms. The tears she'd kept at bay suddenly spilled down her cheeks.

"Trent said they were almost here when Lindsay suddenly screamed and her water broke. He said there was a lot of blood and she was as white as a sheet when he brought her in. The doctor's with them now, but I'm scared, Trav. What if something has gone terribly wrong?"

"Shh, Tessa, it'll be fine," Travis said, comforting his wife. At her news, he saw Trey put a protective arm around Cady and pull her against his side. Tess wiped her tears and the four of them sat down to wait. A few minutes later a nurse hurried up to Tess.

"Sandy, did you hear anything?" Tess asked, getting to her feet and talking to her friend who worked in the hospital's emergency room.

"They're prepping Lindsay for an emergency C-section and that's all I can tell you at this point. If you want to move to a waiting room near surgery, I'll tell the doctor to look for you there.

"Thank you," Tess said, giving Sandy a hug. "If Denni comes in, please let her know where to find us."

While Trey and Travis paced the waiting room, Tess and Cady alternated between praying and offering encouraging words. Travis tried calling Hart but went straight to his voice mail and calls to Denni's phone resulted in the same. No one could blame them for wanting to spend some time alone without interruptions on the day when they were choosing an engagement ring.

Lindsay's brother, Lonnie, and his fiancé, Maren, arrived, letting everyone know Lindsay's parents were on their way.

Tess was just rising from her seat to go get coffee for everyone when the doctor came in. Recognizing Tess, she walked up to her and the rest of the family gathered around them.

"How is she? How's the baby?" Tess asked.

"Although they gave us quite a scare, I think it's safe to say they'll both be fine," Dr. Rugen said, studying the family waiting for the news. It was easy to tell two of the men were Trent's brothers from their similar features and the tall blond man had to be related to Lindsay.

The doctor smiled when a collective sigh of relief came from the group.

"Can you tell us what happened?" Tess asked as the doctor motioned for them all to sit and took a seat next to Tess.

"Lindsay had a condition called placenta previa," Dr. Rugen said, looking at the confused faces around her. "What that means is the placenta migrated to a place that would have made it impossible for Lindsay to deliver the baby. Due to that, and the bleeding the condition causes, we had to do the emergency C-section, but both mother and daughter will be fine."

"Daughter? It's a girl?" Cady asked.

"She's a beautiful little girl, who, I'm told, is going to be called Emily Ester. Since the baby isn't quite at thirty-six weeks, we want to keep an eye on her to make sure her lungs are developed and she's getting everything she needs on her own before we send her home. When you see her, she'll look like a full-term baby. She's at full birth-height, but it's the last few weeks when the babies put on their weight and finish developing their lungs. Little

Emily seems to be doing really well so far, but she will look thin," the doctor said, smiling at the family and getting to her feet. "Trent will be out soon and then you can take a peek at the baby. If my guess is correct, she's going to be a tall girl."

Trey and Travis shared a high five and Maren hugged Lonnie, while Tess and Cady dabbed at their tears.

Trent soon walked into the waiting room, looking exhausted but happy, sinking down beside Trey.

"Congratulations, bro," Travis said, leaning around Tess to slap Trent on the leg. "Guess you don't get to go with the John Deere green in the nursery after all."

"Guess not," Trent said, wearing a tired yet relieved look on his face. "I'm so glad that's over. I will never, ever put Lindsay through that again."

Trey chuckled and thumped Trent on the shoulder. "Right. This one will barely be walking before you'll announce Emily's about to become a big sister."

"I don't think so," Trent said, leaning back in his chair and allowing himself to absorb everything that had happened in the last few hours. He was working on an equipment repair in the shop when the call came to get Lindsay. He didn't even take time to wash his hands, just jumped in his truck and hurried to the school. Driving as fast as he could to the hospital without being reckless, he almost ran off the road when Lindsay screamed. Thinking about the blood pooled on the floor of his pickup made him never want to get it in again, but he'd worry about that later.

Now, he was trying to wrap his head around the fact that he and Lindsay were parents to a sweet baby girl.

"So, how much does our little Emily weigh? What's she look like? Did you count all her fingers and toes?" Cady asked, moving from her seat and kneeling by Trent.

Smiling with a look of wonder on his face, he let out a sigh. "She's beautiful. Just beautiful. The doctor said babies born C-section usually come out looking a little better than the other route."

The guys laughed and Tess rolled her eyes.

"She has ten very long fingers and toes with soft curly brown hair and the sweetest little lips. The nurse said she weighed five pounds, four ounces. She's twenty-two and a quarter inches long," Trent said, his voice filling with fatherly pride. "She's already tall for her age."

"Maybe she'll be another basketball star like her mother," Lonnie said with a grin.

"But Lindsay is going to be fine, isn't she?" Cady asked, still concerned for her dear friend and sister-in-law.

"Absolutely. The doctor said she's going to be really sore and have a little recovery time, which means she's going to need a lot of help with the baby until she's back on her feet."

"We'll all be glad to help," Cady said, looking around to see everyone nodding in agreement. "You can stay at the ranch house with us or we can take turns staying at your house, whatever works best for you and Lindsay."

"I appreciate that," Trent said. He looked at Lonnie meaningfully. "I mean no offense, Lonnie, but I sure hope your mom isn't planning on staying long. I know she and Lindsay are mending their broken fences, but I don't think it's a good idea for them to have too much quality time together."

"I agree," Lonnie said with a teasing grin. "Let me work on something that will require mother's full attention so she'll only drive you nuts for a day or two."

"Thanks, man," Trent said with relief. Although Christine was trying very hard to be a better mother to Lindsay, the woman still made them all crazy.

"Speaking of mothers, where's Mom?" Trent asked, looking around and noticing for the first time that Denni and Hart weren't among those gathered in the waiting room.

"She and Hart went to pick out her engagement ring today and we haven't been able to get in touch with either of them," Cady said, getting up from her spot by Trent and heading back to her seat. Before she got there, Trey snaked out his arm and pulled her down to sit on his lap.

"That's right, I forgot," Trent said. "Let's keep this a surprise. I think we should tell Hart and have him bring her here to meet Emily."

"I don't know, Trent. Don't you think she might get a little upset when Hart pulls up at the hospital?" Tess asked.

"Not if he tells her it's a surprise. Besides, she comes here occasionally to have lunch with you, so it wouldn't be unheard of to show up when there isn't an emergency," Trent said. "Let's just wait and see which one of them gets back to us first. I don't know about the rest of you, but Lindsay and I are both so glad Mom met Hart. I don't remember the last time she's been this happy."

"Me either," Trey said, looking at Trent, then Travis. "I think we should encourage her to stop wasting time and marry the man. I like the idea of her living closer to us again instead of an hour away."

"Her being married to Hart is going to be awesome," Travis said. "Do you suppose he gives family members free pop at the gas station?"

Tess slapped his leg while everyone else laughed.

"Do you like that one, sunshine?" Hart asked as Denni tried on another ring.

"It's nice," she said, her voice lacking the enthusiasm one would expect from someone choosing an engagement ring.

At the fourth jewelry store of the day, they were both tired of looking. Denni took off the ring and sighed.

"Let's go have some lunch and worry about rings later," Hart suggested.

"I like the way you think," Denni said, taking the arm Hart held out to her as they left the store.

Getting in his truck, Hart drove them to a restaurant Tess recommended that sat on a man-made lake. It was a perfect day for dining outdoors and Hart soon found himself seated next to Denni at a cozy little table, watching ducks preen on the water in the mid-day sunshine.

"This is lovely, Hart," Denni said, looking around after the waiter took their orders. "Tess mentioned eating here, but I've never been before."

"I haven't either, but I'm glad I'm here now, with you," Hart said, feeling his heart trip in his chest as he looked at Denni. She was so beautiful and made him deliriously happy. He'd do his best to give her the world on a silver platter if that's what she wanted, but amazingly, she seemed to be content just spending time with him. He appreciated the fact the amount of money in his bank account had never been of interest to her. She had her own money, could take care of herself, and didn't seem to care if he had two plug nickels to rub together. Denni truly loved him for him. "Have I mentioned today how lovely you look?"

"Only half a dozen times, but knock yourself out," Denni said with a flirty grin.

"You are lovelier than my new bull Brutus, more fragrant than anything in my barn, more enchanting than one of the fairies Cass is always chattering about, more…"

Denni's laughter made him stop and waggle his eyebrows at her.

"You're ridiculous," Denni said, leaning over and squeezing his arm.

"Yes, ma'am, I am," Hart said, feeling particularly punchy as he sat with Denni, looking forward to spending the rest of his life on earth with the teasing, tempting, fun woman who made him realize when he changed his thoughts, changed his heart, he could truly change his life for the better.

"And you're all mine," Denni said, still grinning at Hart.

"That's a fact. You are stuck with me, sunshine," Hart said, leaning over and kissing Denni softly on the lips. He breathed in her scent, wrapped himself in the warmth of her very essence.

"There is no one else I'd rather be stuck with, buckaroo," Denni said, grateful again for Hart working his way into her heart.

Finishing their leisurely lunch, Hart asked Denni if she'd like to take a stroll around the lake and she agreed. They were about half way around it when Hart spied a bench set off the path by a grouping of trees.

"Let's set down a minute," he said and led Denni to the bench. When they sat down, he put his arm around her and she leaned against his side, enjoying the time spent together. Hart picked up her left hand and studied her ring finger for a while. "I'm getting the idea you haven't seen any rings you really like."

"No, I haven't," Denni admitted, not wanting to continue the ring shopping because it stopped being fun after the second store. "They are all nice, Hart, but I truly don't want some big, gaudy diamond. That's just not me."

"What do you want?" Hart asked, thinking he might know the answer.

"Something simple, something that looks like it was meant to stand the test of time, not some big rock made to mimic one received by whichever celebrity got engaged this week."

"I see," Hart said, releasing Denni's hand then digging in his pocket and pulling out a ring box. He handed it to Denni who gave him a puzzled look before opening the lid and sucking in a gasp.

The ring in the box was old, lovely, and perfect. If Denni could have described the ring she truly wanted, it was sitting in the box in her hand.

"Oh, Hart, it's wonderful," she said, running her finger over the white gold band. "I love it."

"I'm glad to hear that, sunshine," Hart said, taking the ring from the box and sliding it down Denni's ring finger where it rested as though it was made just for her. "Look at that, a perfect fit."

Holding out her hand, Denni admired the beautiful band with just enough filigree around the tasteful, yet beautiful princess-cut diamond to make it unique and gorgeous. "It's amazing. Where did you find it? Why were you holding out on me?"

Hart laughed, pulling Denni back against his chest. "I wasn't holding out on you, I wanted to make sure there wasn't a ring out there you liked better. I brought this one along, just in case. I had an idea of what you'd like, but wanted to be sure. This ring belonged to my grandmother. She gave it to me and told me someday I'd find a woman who'd make me forget my past and look forward to my future. Grams was right because I found you."

Denni didn't say anything, just brushed the tears from her eyes and threw her arms around Hart's neck, giving him a sweet kiss.

Someone riding by on a bike yelled "get a room," making them both break out in laughter. Standing, Hart took Denni's hand in his while she got to her feet and they continued their stroll around the pond. Denni kept holding out her hand, admiring the vintage ring, wondering how Hart could possibly make her any happier than she was right at that moment.

While Denni visited the restroom at the restaurant before they left, Hart decided he should probably check his messages in case anything truly important needed his attention. Finding three from Travis, he gave him a call and felt his emotions range from terrified to jubilant. He agreed to try to keep the secret and bring Denni to the hospital right away.

"Shall we hit the road?" he asked as Denni hurried toward him, smiling like she was completely pleased with life. "I need to get back to take care of something that came up."

"Sure, Hart," Denni said, looking concerned as they walked to his truck. "Is everything okay?"

"Everything's fine. There's just something I need to handle. Nothing to worry about, though."

"If you say so," Denni said, still euphoric over her beautiful ring. Hart could have put it on her finger the night he proposed and they would have saved a trip to Portland. Then again, having him spend the morning with her, enjoying a delicious lunch, and walking around the lake was pretty great, so she decided that he'd done everything just right after all.

Arriving at The Dalles an hour later, Hart turned and headed toward the hospital rather than Denni's house.

"That thing I need to take care of is here in town," Hart said, trying not to grin as they neared the hospital.

"Really? Nearby?" Denni asked, noting they were nearly to the hospital and wondering what business Hart could possibly have there.

"Really. You can come in with me if you like," Hart said, parking in the visitor's area at the hospital and hurrying around to open Denni's door.

"In the hospital?" she asked as she took his hand and walked inside with him, still trying to figure out what he was up to.

"We're here aren't we?" he asked, directing Denni to the elevator and pushing a button. Arriving at the floor where Travis said the family was waiting, they took just a few steps down a hallway when Hart noticed Tess and

Travis in the doorway of a waiting room and broke into a broad grin.

Turning Denni their direction, she came to an abrupt halt when she spied her kids gathered in the room, along with Lindsay's family.

"What in the world is going on?" she finally asked, looking from Trey to Travis, and back at Hart.

"Congratulations, Grammy. It's a girl," Tess said, wrapping Denni in a big hug.

"A girl? Lindsay had her baby?" Denni asked, trying to process what Tess was saying. Lindsay wasn't due for another month. "Are they okay? Where's Trent?"

"They're doing fine, Mama," Travis said, giving Denni a hug. From the shocked look on her face, maybe surprising her wasn't their best collective idea. "Trent's with Lindsay. Tess can take you to see Emily, if you like."

"I'd like that very much then I want to hear all about what happened," Denni said, experiencing a surreal feeling. Her first blood-relation grandchild arrived and no one bothered to let her know about it? "Why didn't someone call and tell me?"

"We tried, but your phone kept going to voice mail. Didn't you get our messages?" Tess asked, taking Denni and Hart to go peek in the nursery window at the baby. The doctor declared Emily healthy and fine, without any need for specialized care.

"Oh," Denni said, feeling like the worst mother in the world. Wanting to spend an uninterrupted day with Hart, she'd turned off her phone and promptly forgot about checking it. She didn't think Hart had checked his either, but he must have at some point or they wouldn't be looking in the nursery glass at the most beautiful baby girl Denni thought she'd ever seen.

"Oh, Tess, she's just precious," Denni said, wanting to run right in and scoop the baby into her arms. "Look at her, Hart. Isn't she something?"

"She sure is," Hart said, feeling his heartstrings tug at the sight of the baby. He'd never seen one so tiny and new. "Guess you all have to admit Cass was right."

Tess laughed. "Cady called to tell her Emily arrived and I could hear her shouting into the phone from where I was sitting. She was more than a little excited."

Hart chuckled, placing his hands on Denni's shoulders as she admired the baby.

Returning to the waiting room where the family was gathered, they talked about the baby and how glad they all were Lindsay was going to be fine. Denni was chatting with Cady when Tess noticed the ring on her finger and let out a squeal.

"Denni, that ring is gorgeous," Tess said, grabbing Denni's hand and holding it up for everyone to admire.

"Nice job, man," Travis said, thumping Hart on the back. "That's awesome."

"How beautiful, Denni," Cady said holding Denni's hand up so she could study the ring. "It looks like an antique."

"It is," Denni said, not feeling quite as excited about the ring and her engagement as she did earlier in the day. Thoughts of how she abandoned her kids when they needed her keep racing through her head. "It belonged to Hart's grandmother."

"That makes it ten times more special," Tess said, hugging both Hart and Denni.

Lindsay's parents were congratulating Denni and Hart on their engagement when Trent joined them and said Lindsay could have limited visitors.

The women took quick turns going in to see her then they all decided it was time for everyone to go home.

"I'm so sorry I wasn't here when you needed me, Trent. I'm so, so sorry," Denni said, giving Trent a hug, trying to keep tears from spilling over along with her overwhelming sense of guilt.

"No need to apologize, Mom. There wasn't a thing you could have done if you were here and we all thought it was great you and Hart took some time to spend together. Don't give it another thought," Trent said, bending down to kiss Denni's cheek.

Despite Trent's assurance, Denni knew she'd let him down, let her whole family down by making herself unavailable to them.

Trent wanted to stay with Lindsay for the night, so Travis decided to take his truck and get it cleaned, giving the new parents one less thing to worry about it. Tess said she'd give Travis a ride home when they finished with Trent's truck and promised to stop by Trent and Lindsay's house to pick up the packed hospital bag sitting by the door and drop it off the next morning.

Lonnie and Maren headed back to Portland, making plans to visit on the weekend, while Lindsay's parents went home to Prineville.

As Denni and Hart walked out with Trey and Cady, Trey could tell something was bothering his mother, but he didn't know what exactly.

"So have you two settled on a wedding date?" Trey asked, giving his mother one of his most charming smiles.

"No, not yet. I wanted to wait until after the baby arrived," Denni said, sounding distracted.

"And here she is. You should have let the pastor marry you at the end of Bailey and Brice's shindig," Trey teased, looking at Hart who gave the slightest nod of his head.

"That was their special day, honey," Denni said, looking at the ring on her finger and frowning. "They shouldn't have to share, especially with an old woman."

"Something wrong, Denni?" Cady asked, noticing her mother-in-law seemed to have lost all the excitement she arrived with just an hour or so earlier.

"Nothing's wrong. I'm fine," Denni said, plastering a smile on her face that didn't fool the three people watching her.

"We're sure happy about you two getting engaged," Trey said, shaking Hart's hand again and giving him a look that said he had no idea what was going on with his mother. Hart shrugged his shoulders and watched Denni drawing in on herself. It was so unlike her, he didn't know what to make of it.

"Thanks. I'm looking forward to being part of the ever-expanding Thompson family," Hart said, waggling an eyebrow at Trey. "It seems to me it should be your turn to add to the grandkid pool next."

"We've got Cass," Trey said, shaking his head while Cady blushed. "Trav and Tess need to contribute before it's our turn again. Why don't you offer them that suggestion and see how it goes?"

Hart laughed as he opened Denni's door. "I don't think so."

Before she could climb in the truck, Trey gave his mother a hug and whispered in her ear. "Whatever's bothering you, either talk to Hart or call one of us. Please."

Denni shook her head and scrambled inside the truck, staring out the windshield.

Hart shut her door and gave Trey and Cady a bewildered look.

Driving back to Denni's house, she didn't speak. When Hart walked her to the door, she gave him a kiss on the cheek, thanked him for the ring and a lovely day then closed the door. Hart felt like she was closing more than her front door on him. He got the feeling she was trying to shut him out of her life.

Completely baffled, Hart decided to let her have the space she obviously wanted and drove home pondering what happened to make her act so odd. Everything was great until they got to the hospital. No, that wasn't true. It wasn't until Tess said something about Denni not answering her phone. Maybe Denni was feeling guilty for not being there when Emily arrived.

He'd leave her to her thoughts tonight, but he was checking in with her first thing in the morning and getting to the bottom of the problem, if there still was one.

Chapter Twenty

"The heart is forever making the head its fool."
François de La Rochefoucauld

Sinking down on the couch, Denni stared into space until the evening shadows revealed the lateness of the hour.

The day started out with such promise. Thrilled beyond words when Hart gave her his grandmother's ring and declared his intentions to not only love her, but her family, she thought her heart would burst from sheer happiness.

Now, she was beyond the point of tears by what she knew she had to do.

It wasn't the news of Emily's early arrival that upset her. It was the fact that she had chosen to block out her family and their needs to spend a day fulfilling her own.

She'd never done that before, never been so selfish or careless, and Denni vowed it would never happen again. When Drew died, she accepted the fact that sole responsibility for her family and their well being rested on her shoulders. Her kids came first. They always had and they always would. Yet today she'd forgotten that and missed the birth of her grandchild.

Although it was going to break her heart and quite likely shatter Hart's, she was calling off their engagement and telling him goodbye. When she was around him, she forgot about the rest of the world. Wrapped up in his arms, she didn't want there to be anything else beyond them and their love. Giving in to the desire to have Hart all to herself with no interruptions wasn't something she could do. She had too many responsibilities to her family to do that.

What if Lindsay or the baby had died? Would she have been merrily traipsing around the city while her family was completely devastated? If it wasn't for Hart saying he needed to get back, Denni was going to suggest they go to the mall and do a little shopping. She'd envisioned going out to dinner, maybe catching a movie, before they drove back to The Dalles.

At least Hart was responsible enough to check his phone on occasion instead of acting like a carefree child.

Reflecting over the last several months, some of the most wonderful she could remember experiencing, Denni realized the absence of Hart in her life was going to leave as big a hole as the one left when Drew died. Only this would be worse because she'd see Hart from time to time and be reminded of what she almost had. What could never be hers.

Going to bed, Denni finally let the tears flow in the middle of the night. By early morning, she was dressed and drove her car to Hart's home.

Knowing it was entirely too early to be knocking on anyone's door, Denni rang Hart's bell and waited for him to answer. It took just a moment for Denni to hear footsteps and find herself greeted by Hart's welcoming smile.

"Sunshine! What a great way to start the day," Hart said, missing the look of determination on Denni's face as he pulled her into the house and his arms.

Although he was dressed, he hadn't yet buttoned his shirt and what Denni could see made her swallow twice and take a deep breath. Letting Hart go was going to be even harder than she thought. She could have taken the coward's approach and sent him an email or left him a message, but she needed to tell him goodbye in person. She hadn't counted on him looking so tantalizing and smelling so enticing this early in the day.

Remembering what brought her to his house in the first place, she pushed away from him and took a step back.

"What's wrong, Denni? Did something happen with Lindsay or the baby?" Hart asked, beginning to feel an encroaching sense of panic. Trying to think of any reason Denni would be on his doorstep at half-past six on a weekday morning, some family tragedy was the only thing that came to mind.

"It's nothing like that, Hart," Denni said, putting a hand on his cheek and staring into his eyes one last time. She would remember everything about this kind, passionate man who, one by one, put the pieces of her broken heart back together. She knew there would be no way to reassemble them after today, after she walked away from all that Hart offered her.

"What is it, sunshine?" Hart asked, folding her in a hug once again. For the life of him, he couldn't think what could possibly be making Denni act so strange. When she stiffened in his arms and jerked away, he felt a shaft of dread embed itself in his chest. Dropping his arms to his sides, he tried to keep a relaxed pose, knowing when working with something skittish, like Denni was this morning, it was best to remain calm.

"I need to give you this back," Denni said, taking his grandmother's ring off her finger and holding it out to Hart. She watched the look of disbelief in his eyes give way to confusion.

"No. It's yours. I gave it to you."

"I know, but you gave it to me as our engagement ring. I can't," Denni said, her voice breaking. Yanking her gaze from his troubled blue eyes, she let her eyes rest on that darn cleft in Hart's chin, the one she'd dreamed of so many times, the one she'd kissed so tenderly just yesterday morning. Taking a deep breath, she knew she had to say what she came to say and be quick about it or she'd never leave. "I can't marry you, Hart. I can't, so please take your ring."

"No," Hart said, moving closer to Denni. She stared at him with such a look of pain in her eyes he could feel it. "No, Denni. I won't take it and you can marry me. What's this about? Did I do something yesterday to upset you?"

"It's not something you've done, Hart. You're a wonderful, amazing man. Surrounded by your love, even for a short time, was one of the most incredible experiences of my life. I'll always, always remember you and be grateful to you for showing me that you can find love again, if you open your heart to it."

Reaching out, Denni took Hart's hand in hers, feeling the rough calluses against her soft skin. She'd dreamed of having the rest of her life to hold that hand, to watch it grow old while it held hers. Dreams like that were for people with the luxury of choices and Denni didn't think she had any left.

"I love you, Hart. I love you so, so much and a part of me always will," Denni said, feeling tears begin to trickle down her cheeks while they stung her eyes. "I just can't be with you. Yesterday made me realize I can't be a mother and your wife. I've got a responsibility to my kids and if I'm with you, I'll forsake it."

"Denni, be reasonable," Hart said, putting his hands on her arms, willing her to listen to what he was saying. Where had she gotten such a crazy notion? "There's no reason you can't be both. I would never, ever come between you and your family. They're important to me, too. I'll support you in whatever you need to do in regard to your kids."

"I know you would, but you make me want to block out the world, forget there's anything but you, Hart. Can't you understand? My son could have lost his wife and baby yesterday and instead of being there for him, I was off enjoying myself. I owe it to my sons to always be there for them, no matter what. I don't have a choice. I made a promise when Drew died to take care of our boys and I've got to stand by that."

"That's all well and good, Denni, but your boys are grown men starting their own families. It was one thing when all you had was each other, but they're married with their own lives now. You can't expect them to need you like they used to," Hart said, running his hand through his hair, trying to make sense of anything Denni said. "Denni, this is crazy. You heard Trent yesterday. He wasn't upset you weren't there when Emily was born. Life happens. They all understand that. More than anything, I think they want you to be happy."

"It's not about what they think they want, Hart. It's about what's best for them. Me being selfish and wrapped up in my own life isn't what's best for my family. I can't do this, Hart. As much as I want to grow old with you, I can't."

"Denni, please," Hart said, ready to get on his knees and beg if he had to.

Denni shook her head, squeezing her eyes shut as she took another step back away from him.

"Give it some time, think about this before you do something we're both going to regret," Hart said, wanting to drive his fist through the wall in frustration. Denni wasn't listening to a word he said. There was one thing that had always gotten her attention in the past. Grabbing her, he pulled her to him and kissed her with every ounce of passion and love he possessed. "Please, Denni, don't leave. Don't walk away from me, from what we can have together."

"I have to," she whispered, looking as devastated as he felt. "I can't put my happiness above my kids, Hart. I love you, but this is goodbye." Denni placed the ring on the table in his foyer, turned and ran out to her car.

Stunned by Denni's words, Hart started after her only to see her car speeding out of his driveway.

Shutting the door, Hart leaned against it and sank to the floor. If he'd learned one thing in the past several months of courting Denni, once she made up her mind no one else was going to change it.

The pain ripping through him at the realization the happily ever after he planned with the first woman he'd truly ever loved was not going to happen made it impossible to catch his breath. Expecting to see the shattered pieces of his heart lying around him on the floor, Hart held his hand to his chest and sighed. "Denni, what have you done?"

><><

So distraught over breaking up with Hart, Denni didn't even notice she turned toward Grass Valley and the ranch instead of heading north toward the freeway and The Dalles when she left Hart's place.

Driving through Grass Valley, she was crying so hard she could barely see where she was going. When a horn honked, she realized she was swerving back and forth into the other lane.

Wiping her eyes, she sped up, not knowing where she was going, having already passed the turn-off to the Triple T as well as the old Drexel Ranch where Trent and Travis both lived.

She hadn't traveled much further down the road when she heard honking behind her and noticed a pickup flashing its lights.

Realizing in her current state of distress there was no way she could outrun Travis, she pulled over to the side of the road and stopped her car. Bracing herself for whatever Travis was going to say, she rolled down the window and frantically mopped at her tears.

"What's gotten into you? Are you trying to get yourself killed?" Travis yelled as he approached her car, slipping his cell phone in his pocket. Stepping up to the door, he jerked it open. One glance at his mother's face and he felt his anger dissipate, replaced by bone-deep fear. He'd only seen that look on his mother's face one other time and that was the day his father died. Something awful must have happened.

"Mama?" Travis whispered, crouching next to her in the open car door. He yanked off his glove and wiped his fingers across her wet cheek. "What's wrong? What happened?"

"I told Hart... I broke things off with him," Denni said, feeling more forsaken and desolate than she had in her entire life. Even losing Drew hadn't made her feel so completely alone.

"Why?" Travis thought everything was fine between Hart and his mother. He'd never seen her look as happy as she had since they announced their engagement. Although he knew no one could ever take his dad's place, Hart came pretty close to filling the boots that had been empty far too long. Hart was an all-around good guy and Travis loved him like a father.

"I should have been there for Trent yesterday. I should never have turned off my phone and run off with Hart. I've got to put you kids first," Denni said breaking into sobs.

"Are you crazy?" Travis asked. "That's the looniest thing I've ever heard you say. In case you missed it, we're all grown up now, married, with lives of our own and able to take care of ourselves. You need to move on, Mama. Have your own life."

While Travis was talking he sent a text to Tess asking her to wait a few minutes before leaving for work. He looked up to see Trey pulling in behind his pickup. Glad his brother received the voice message he left when he almost ran into Denni as she wove over both sides of the road, Travis thought he could use some reinforcements in trying to talk some sense into her.

"What's up? What are you doing out here, Mom?" Trey asked, bending down to look in the car, taking in his mother's wracking sobs and Travis' irritation.

"From what I can gather, she thinks she abandoned the family yesterday by spending the day with Hart, and proceeded to drive to his house this morning and dump him," Travis said, his words sounding more annoyed and angry as he spoke. "I've never known Mama to do something stupid, but evidently she's decided to skip past wading and jump right into the deep end of the idiot pool."

Trey glared at Travis, thinking insulting Denni wasn't going to help the situation any. When she began crying harder, he knew he was correct.

"For Pete's sakes, call one of the girls. This is more than we can handle," Trey whispered to Travis as he reached down and unbuckled Denni's seat belt. Wrapping a hand around his mom's arm, he pulled her out of the car. Holding her to his chest, he rubbed her back soothingly, and told her to calm down, that everything would be fine.

"Please stop crying, Mama. We'll take you to talk to Hart and get this straightened out," Travis said, putting a hand on Denni's head.

"No!" Denni said between sobs. "Absolutely, not!"

"But we thought you loved him," Trey said, confused.

"I…do…" Denni said, taking the handkerchief Travis forced into her hand. Mopping at her face, she tried to take a deep breath and found she couldn't.

"What did you two do?" Tess asked in a clipped tone, getting out of the car she parked in front of Denni's. If they didn't all get off the side of the road, they'd have a bunch of people pulling over to see what was going on and that was the last thing any of them needed. Marching over to them, she took one look at Denni and shook her head. Putting her arm around the woman, she led Denni to her car, helping her in the passenger side.

Coming back to Denni's car, Tess grabbed her mother-in-law's purse, then looked at Travis and Trey, waiting for an explanation.

"She broke things off with Hart because of some insane idea about her family needing her and not being there for them. Maybe you can get her to make some sense," Trey said, clamping down his jaw to keep from saying more. Denni was normally laid back and fun, but when she made up her mind about something, you might as well cast it in stone because it wasn't going to change. He wanted to drag her back to Hart's and tell him it was all a mistake, but there was no way Denni would stand for it.

"I'll take her home before I go to work. Can one of you bring her car into town later? I assume everyone will be at the hospital at some point today. Maybe we can eat lunch together and figure this thing out," Tess said, giving Travis a kiss before running back to her car, turning it around and heading toward Grass Valley.

"Oh, man, this is bad," Travis said, slapping his hat against his leg. "What made her think...? Oh, who knows with a woman. If I live to be a hundred, I'll never understand how their minds work."

"At least you've taken the first step of having a successful marriage by acknowledging the futility of trying," Trey said giving his brother a wry smile. "Come on. Let's run your truck home then you can drive Mom's car into town."

Trent joined the other four people who made up his immediate family in the cafeteria at the hospital for lunch and they tried to figure out what had driven Denni to tell Hart goodbye.

Travis stopped by the gas station to fill Denni's car before driving to The Dalles and Evan said Hart called early that morning to say he wasn't feeling well and was staying home.

"She really thinks she let us down because she wasn't here yesterday during all the excitement?" Trent asked, finding it impossible to understand what Denni was thinking. "That's just crazy. No one expected her to be here."

"We all know that, but trying to convince Mom of that is something else entirely," Trey said, leaning back in his chair and releasing a frustrated sigh.

Tess spent the entire hour's drive to The Dalles trying to get Denni to see the only problem was the one she'd concocted in her mind and got nowhere. Calling to tell Travis what his mother said, Travis relayed the details to Trey who promptly called Denni and tried to talk to her. She finally hung up on him.

"What can we do?" Cady asked, unable to believe Denni could walk away from Hart so easily. She loved him too much.

"Leave her alone at this point, I guess," Trey said, looking at Travis who nodded his head in agreement. "I don't think this is about Hart or Trent or missing out on Emily's arrival. I think this is about her feeling guilty for falling in love again."

"She's had a lot of trouble trying to embrace the fact it's long past time to move on," Tess said. Knowing Denni better than Lindsay or Cady because of spending so many of her growing up years in her mother-in-law's presence, the woman had confided a few things to Tess. "I agree with Trey. I think Hart putting the ring on her finger yesterday made her engagement seem real and she panicked, grasping at the first available excuse to call it off."

"We can't let her do this," Travis said, leaning forward in his chair. He took Tess' hand in his and looked at her like she should have some idea on how to fix it.

"It's not like we can force her to marry Hart. He might not want her now, anyway. Who knows what she said to him this morning," Trent said.

"Whatever it was, it made him call in sick to the station," Travis said, shaking his head.

"I think the best course of action is to leave them both alone, for now. Give her a day or two to think things through," Cady said, trying to see the situation from all perspectives. When Trey scowled at her she grinned. "If that doesn't work, you three hooligans can always tie her up and drag her down the aisle."

"Great idea," Trey said, kissing his wife on the cheek. "I'll make sure I've got plenty of rope in the truck."

><><

Startled by a knock on his office door, Hart glanced up to see Travis Thompson standing with his hat in his hand, looking about as down-in-the-mouth as he felt.

It had been almost two weeks since Denni left him so broken, he had no hope of ever feeling whole again. He'd taken a chance, put his heart out there for her to take or leave, and he was devastated when she'd left it without a single glance back.

"Hey, Trav. What's up?" Hart asked, not even trying to muster a smile. He not only felt cheated out of the love of his life, but also the family he'd always dreamed of having. He loved the whole rowdy Thompson clan like they were his own.

"Just wanted to see how you're holding up," Travis said, sitting down in a chair across from Hart's desk.

"I'm taking one day at a time," Hart said honestly. He briefly considered selling his house, finding a full-time manager for the gas station or selling it and never setting foot in Grass Valley again. Knowing he had to maintain whatever ties to Denni he had, at least for the time being, he just couldn't bring himself to walk away.

Travis didn't know what to say to that, so he asked Hart about business and told him a story that seemed a lot funnier when he heard it than it did now.

"How's your mom?" Hart finally asked, unable to stop himself.

"Not good," Travis said, sighing before he leaned forward with his elbows on his knees. "She's sad and depressed and totally not like herself. She's barely speaking to any of us because she doesn't particularly like what we've got to say. Nana read her the riot act, so she's not even going to see her either."

Knowing how much it had to hurt Denni to be cut off from her family, even if she was the one who'd wielded the knife that severed the ties, Hart worried about her.

"I didn't mean to come between her and all of you," Hart said, leaning back in his chair and feeling the ever-present bands around his chest squeeze a little tighter.

"You didn't, Hart. None of this is your doing. None of it is your fault. Mama brought this all on herself and she's going to have to be the one to dig herself out of it," Travis said, sounding angry and betrayed. They were all looking forward to Hart becoming a part of their family, excited to see Denni glowing with joy. Out of some twisted sense of duty or guilt or whatever it was, she'd suddenly decided she wouldn't allow herself to be happy.

"Don't be hard on her, son. Your mother is doing the best she can," Hart said, sitting forward so his hands rested on the top of his overly clean desk. If he didn't find something to do, something to burn off some of his excess energy and emotions, he thought he might explode. He'd cleaned his office, caught up all his paper work, and scrubbed every square inch of the gas station including the restrooms. His house was spotless, the barn was nearly as clean, and yet he still felt wound up and agitated.

"Yeah? Her best doesn't seem to quite cut it," Travis said, frowning. Looking at Hart, Travis got to his feet and pulled a folded piece of paper from his back pocket. Unfolding it, he tossed it on Hart's desk. "I don't know if this would be of interest to you, but all the proceeds are a fundraiser for an area rancher's son who was recently diagnosed with leukemia."

Hart picked up the flyer advertising a bull riding event in Redmond the following Saturday. According to the details listed there, twenty-five bull riders would compete for a sizeable purse with the proceeds from the event going to benefit a six-year-old battling cancer.

Looking up at Travis, Hart wasn't sure what Travis wanted him to do with it.

"I thought you might like to be one of those select twenty-five bull riders," Travis said, raising an eyebrow at Hart. He had a good idea about some of what Hart was experiencing. Having something big, something exciting, to do would help him cope with his feelings. "I called this morning and they are trying to fill the last four slots."

"Travis, you know I haven't ridden a bull in twenty-six years. Do you really think I could just waltz out there and get on one?"

"Actually, I do. You were one of the best, Hart. One of the very best, ever," Travis said, admiration thick in his voice. "I know this thing with Mama is tearing you apart. I thought this might be as good a time as any to get back on a bull and conquer something you've set aside for a very long time."

"It's crazy, Travis. Pure craziness," Hart said, liking the idea more as he thought about it. Travis was right. He needed to ride a bull again to be able to put his past at rest, but he wasn't sure riding one in front of an arena full of fans was a good idea. If he was going to be killed doing it, he'd much rather it be somewhere private. "I might as well go stand in the road and wait for a truck to run over me."

"Maybe, but this would be a heck of a lot more fun way to die," Travis said, grinning. "What do you say?"

"Before I say anything, you better fess up. Are you going to be one of the riders?"

"Yep," Travis said, smiling broadly. "I promised my family I would cut back on my reckless activities and I have. I even promised my sweet little honeybee no more riding in rodeos, but she gave her stamp of approval on this event."

"Okay. Let's do this," Hart said, sticking out his hand and shaking Travis' enthusiastically. "But you better help me get in a few practice rides before this shakes down. As much as I might say otherwise, I really would like to live to a ripe old age."

"You got it," Travis said, slapping Hart on the back as they walked together out to Travis' pickup.

Chapter Twenty-One

"Nothing is impossible to a willing heart."
John Heywood

"He's what?" Denni screeched into the phone, causing the two customers browsing through fabric in her store to jerk their heads her direction with curious stares.

"You heard me loud and clear, Mom. Don't act as if you didn't. Travis is riding a bull tomorrow in Redmond. We'd all like for you to be there to support him," Trey said from the other end of the line.

Successfully ignoring calls from her family, Denni refused to speak to them after they ganged up on her and insisted she talk about what was going on between her and Hart. They had the gall to tell her she was being childish and acting like an idiot. The only way they could get her to talk to them was to call her store when she had no idea who'd be on the other end of the line.

Trey found an undeniable irony in Denni's entire reason for breaking up with Hart hinging on the fact she hadn't answered her phone and missed being at the hospital when Emily was born. Now she refused to speak to any of them unless there was some emergency. It just proved his theory that her decision was based in fear of moving on with her life and not anything to do with taking care of her family.

"What does Tess say about all this?" Denni asked. She thought after Travis' hamstring injury last summer, he'd given up his dangerous activities. She considered bull riding at the top of the list.

"She said it's for a good cause, and she'll be sitting in the front row cheering Travis and Hart on," Trey said, throwing out a little bait for his mother to nibble.

"Wait, did you say Hart?" Denni felt like her head was reeling.

"Yes, I did. Travis asked him to ride, too," Trey said, pleased his mother was circling his hook. "The press is having a field day with Hart coming out of retirement to help raise funds for the little Moore boy."

"But, Trey, he can't ride. He just can't."

"Who? Hart or Travis?" Trey asked, pleased that his mother sounded more upset with the news that Hart was riding than Travis.

"Hart. He gave it up because…never mind. It will kill him to do it," Denni said, knowing Hart was doing this because of her. Because she'd broken his heart and he felt like he had nothing left to lose.

"Like all of your sons, Hart is a big boy who can make his own decisions, even if they get him injured or killed," Trey said, grinning to himself. It was time to reel in his mother. "Although we're all worried about someone his age, so out of practice, jumping onto the back of a bull."

"He'll get himself killed, Trey. You boys can't let him ride. Do something!" Denni wanted to stamp her foot and throw something. Crying herself to sleep at night, short-tempered and depressed during the day, she felt as if she left a huge part of herself at Hart's the day she told him goodbye. It was as if a light had gone off inside her and she had no idea if it would ever come back on. At this point, she didn't really care.

Refusing to admit to any of the kids they were right, she continued retreating further into herself and what she found wasn't someone she particularly liked.

Trey confronted her a few days after she broke up with Hart, saying she did it because she was too stubborn and scared to move on with her life. He called her a coward for using her children as an excuse when everyone knew what she'd done had nothing to do with them.

Fuming from both his words and the fact that her son was correct, she refused to speak to any of them since. When her mother hit her with a tirade about her stupidity after church last Sunday, Denni took Ester home to the center and hadn't returned to see her either.

Feeling completely isolated from the people she professed to care about the most, Denni knew she brought the whole thing on with her stubbornness.

Trey was right. She was a coward. She thought she was ready to move on with her life, but the past was where she'd grown up, grown comfortable. Facing the unknown, reaching out to her future, suddenly scared her witless. That's why she walked away from Hart. Realizing why and what she'd done, she was convinced Hart would never take her back.

Conversations with well-meaning family pointing out how badly she behaved didn't do anything to help her fears.

"We can't do a thing, Mom, except be there to cheer him on. It starts at one. Hope you can be there. Travis would be really disappointed if you weren't." Trey hung up before his mother could say anything else. He could almost feel her flopping around on the other end of the line.

Sitting back in his office chair with a big grin on his face, he could envision her scowling at the phone before slamming the receiver down then stomping around her store, mad at him for telling her something she didn't want to hear.

Trey was mostly right.

Denni did scowl at the phone when he hung up and slammed it down not once but three times, just for good measure. By this time, the two women who'd been browsing around the store gave her a frightened look and hurried out the door.

Now her ornery boys were costing her business. Livid, she slammed things around, knocking over a display. Amy arrived to find her sitting in a corner sobbing hysterically over a pile of spilled bobbins.

"My word, Denni, what's wrong?" the woman asked, sinking down on the floor beside her and putting an arm around her shoulders. "Is something wrong with one of the kids? Is the baby fine?"

"They're fine," Denni said, sniffling as she dug in a pocket for a tissue. As many boxes as she'd cried her way through in the past few weeks, she learned to keep at least one tissue on hand at all times.

"What's the matter?" Amy asked, rubbing Denni's back, making her break into another round of sobs. She couldn't take someone being kind to her. It was going to snap the last thread tying her to her sanity.

"Everything is the matter," Denni said, getting up and grabbing her purse. "I hate to do this Amy, but can you please watch the store tomorrow. I can't come in."

"Sure," Amy said, walking with Denni to the door. Her employer had been quiet, sad, and given to fits of tears or anger the past few weeks, completely out of character. Amy hoped Denni taking the day off would help her find her way back to her old sunny self. "I was going to come in for the afternoon, anyway. Don't worry about a thing, Denni. Are you sure there isn't something I can do to help you?"

"I think I'm beyond anyone helping," Denni said, swiping at her face with the tissue Amy handed her then walked out into the beautiful spring afternoon. Rather than getting in her car, Denni kept walking. She strolled through downtown, looked at the murals that drew tourists, sat on a bench and watched a young mother playing with her children in the park, and finally walked back toward her shop.

Getting in her car, she realized it was long past time for dinner, but decided she wasn't hungry. Driving to the care home, Denni felt such a need for her mother's comforting touch, she couldn't get to Ester's room fast enough.

Knocking on the door, Ester didn't answer. Pressing her ear against it, the room sounded quiet and Denni wondered if her mother was well. Trying to remember the last time she talked to her, she realized she hadn't had a thing to do with Ester since she dumped her off after church the previous Sunday.

Turning the knob, the door opened so she stepped inside, calling for her mother but finding the room empty. Exiting Ester's apartment, she walked to the recreation area where the residents liked to play card games and visit. Ester wasn't there either so Denni ventured on to the library. Ready to find a staff member and start an all-out hunt for her mother, Denni walked past the music room and spied a familiar white head listening to one of the other residents play the piano. Standing at the door, attentive to the soothing music, Denni glanced over and caught Ester's eye. Getting to her feet, Ester hurried toward Denni and took her arm, pulling her down the hall toward her room.

"Baby, you look like death warmed over. What in the world is the matter?" Ester asked, walking in her room and taking a seat on her little loveseat, patting the spot beside her.

Denni sank down and put her head on Ester's lap, letting the tears fall again. "Everything's wrong, Mama. I don't think it will ever be right again."

Wisely, Ester didn't ask more questions, just let Denni cry until she had no tears left. When Denni sat up, Ester handed her a box of tissues and waited while Denni blew her nose and wiped her eyes.

"Now, let's talk," Ester said, crossing her hands primly on her lap, waiting for Denni to say something. She had a good idea this was all about her being a nitwit and dumping Hart, but she'd try to keep quiet until Denni said whatever she came to say.

"I'm such an idiot, Mama. A loser, a coward, and a bad mother on top of everything else," Denni said, feeling like the most despicable person on the planet. Because of her, a good man was most likely going to be hurt, if not killed, tomorrow.

"Tell me something I don't know," Ester said, giving Denni a teasing grin. When Denni's lip started to quiver, Ester kissed her cheek and patted her leg. "Come on. Start at the beginning and tell me everything."

Denni told her mother every detail, from the moment of panic she felt at the hospital to the conversation she had early that afternoon with Trey and her realization that she pushed Hart away because she was still afraid to let go of Drew.

"I've told you this before, but Drew would be so angry with you for holding on to him like you have. You aren't living, Denni, you're just taking up space and treading water. Drew would want you to be happy. Your kids want you to be happy. I want you to be happy, and you were. Hart made you beam. I don't know that even Drew made you light up the way Hart does. You need to get past the guilt you're feeling. I know there is a part of you that feels like you've betrayed Drew for loving Hart as much as you do."

Denni looked at her mother in surprise, not knowing how her mother could see into the very depths of her being where she knew her feelings for Hart were more intense, more passionate, more… everything, than she felt for Drew. She'd loved Drew with all her heart when they were married and they spent three decades happy and in love. Part of her kept up a niggling whisper that if she truly loved Drew as much as she claimed, she wouldn't feel such a powerful, all-consuming love for Hart.

"Baby, I'm only going to say this to you once, so pay attention. Everyone who ever saw you and Drew together knew the two of you were in love. It was a beautiful, wonderful thing you two shared. He was the husband of your youth and the only boy you ever loved. Most girls fall in love many times before they find the man they want to marry. You didn't experience that. You fell for Drew and that was that. We all know you loved him. We also know you love Hart. His love is, in my opinion, even more precious than the love Drew gave you. Loving Drew was easy because you had no history, no hurts, getting in the way. Hart managed to get past all those walls you built around your heart after Drew died and brought out the best in you."

"I know, Mama, but even if I worked up the courage to beg his forgiveness, there's no way he'd want me back now," Denni said, feeling tears trickle down her cheeks again.

"You won't know unless you ask him," Ester said, rubbing Denni's shoulder soothingly.

"I can't just march right up to him and say 'Please forgive me for being stupid. Will you take me back?' It doesn't work that way."

"Why not? It can work any way you want it to if you're willing to give it a try," Ester said, thinking Denni needed to get over her guilt and get on with her life. Smacking Denni on the leg, she watched her daughter turn a startled expression her direction. "Quit whining and crying about what can't work and figure out what will. You go home and find some way tonight to put your guilt to rest, to tell Drew good-bye once and for all, and get on with your life. I expect you to have your backside planted on a hard ol' bleacher seat at that bull-riding event tomorrow cheering for Hart. Sure as anything, you better be prepared to get down on your knees and beg him to take you back if that's what needs to happen. If you don't think you can handle it, I'll come with you just to make sure you get the job done."

"But, Mama," Denni said, wishing her mother wasn't quite so forceful or right. "I can't..."

"Oh, fiddle, you can too," Ester said, getting to her feet, thinking someone needed to put some starch in Denni's backbone. "Stand up."

Denni stared at her mother like she was losing her mind.

"I said stand up," Ester said, shaking a finger at Denni.

Getting to her feet, Denni once again wiped at her tears then turned her attention to Ester.

"Stand up tall, none of this hunched over depressed thing you've been doing the last two weeks. Stand up straight, take a deep breath," Ester said, demonstrating what she expected from Denni. "Good. Now I want to hear what you're going to say to Hart when you see him tomorrow."

"Mama, I don't...I can't...no, absolutely not," Denni said, giving her mother a frightened stare. She had no idea what she'd say if she actually mustered up the courage to say anything at all. After the way she left him with some excuse about her kids needing her, he'd never want her back. Why should he give her a second chance when she wasn't willing to let herself take the first one?

"You can and you will. Go."

"Fine, you batty old woman," Denni muttered, making Ester smile. Taking a deep breath, she took Ester's hands in hers and pretended she was looking into Hart's handsome face instead of her mother's wrinkled, albeit beloved one. "Hart, I'm a first-class dolt and a coward. I panicked the day you put your grandmother's ring on my finger and grasped at any excuse to call things off with you. As my family keeps telling me, I've forgotten how to live, to truly live, and the thought of finally releasing the past and moving into the future scared me so badly I pushed you away. If you can ever find it in your heart to forgive me, to give me a second chance, I'd like very much to start over with you. I've had plenty of time to think during the past few weeks and I know for a fact that the love I feel for you is genuine and special, and not something I want to give up. I love you, Hart, and I always will."

"That's a good start," Ester said, grinning at her daughter. "Just make sure you plant a good smooch or two on him. Maybe squeeze that fine hiney of his. That ought to help."

"Mama!" Denni said, feeling a smile tipping up the corners of her mouth. "You shouldn't say such things."

"Maybe not, but who's going to argue with an old woman like me. Now you scoot on home and do whatever you need to do to be ready to win Hart back tomorrow. Get your beauty rest, put some teabags on those puffy eyes, and pick out something to wear that'll make Hart's eyes pop right out of his head."

"My stars, Mama, you watch too many soap operas," Denni said, hugging her mother and kissing her cheek. "Thank you."

"You're welcome, baby. Now get going," Ester said, walking Denni to the door. "I really will go with you if you want."

"I don't need you to go along to make sure I do what I need to, but I'm happy to take you along if you'd like to go," Denni said, realizing Ester might enjoy watching Travis and Hart ride. She never even thought to ask if Brice was riding, since he and Travis both used to participate in area rodeos.

"Call me in the morning to see if I feel like going before you leave town. And make sure you give yourself plenty of time to get there. You don't want to be rushed, you know."

"Okay, Mama," Denni said, patting Ester on the cheek. "Thank you, again. I'm sorry I've been so awful lately."

"Everyone gets a turn at being stupid. You've used yours up, though, so I expect better behavior from here on out."

"Yes, Mama," Denni said, smiling as she left her mother and drove herself home.

Exhausted, Denni went straight to bed. Tossing and turning, she finally fell into a restless sleep. She dreamed Drew was there beside her, holding her again. She could smell his scent, feel the calluses on his big hands, taste his kiss on her lips.

"Molly, I want you to listen to me," Drew said in the deep voice that she had missed so much, as much as she missed him calling her Molly. "It's time to let go, darlin'. Let me go and move on with your life. I know you love me, that you'll always love me, but it's time to move on. There's room in that great big heart of yours to love another, to let someone else love you."

"But, Drew…"

"I mean it, Molly girl. You've mourned me long enough. There's a whole lot of life ahead of you and you shouldn't go it alone. Live, Molly. Really live and let yourself fall in love again. Hart's a fine man and he cares about our boys. Let yourself be happy with him. You've got my blessing."

With that, Drew was gone and Denni was left holding her pillow and sobbing from the very depths of her heart for the man who had loved her so well for so many years and the man she wanted to love for the rest of her life.

Finally drifting off to sleep, Denni awoke early with a plan in mind. Pulling on whatever clothes she could grab, she didn't bother with makeup or combing her hair, settling a ball cap one of the boys had left behind on her head as she hurried out to her car and raced to her store.

Unlocking the door and flipping on the lights, she dug around until she found the basket with the heart wall hanging she'd been working on. Only half finished, she wanted to give it to Hart today. She would give the quilt to him and explain what it meant. Then if she had to fall at his feet and plead for his forgiveness, she was ready to do that, too.

Working at a frantic pace, pushing both herself and her machine, she was finishing the last corner when Amy arrived and stared at Denni in disbelief. In all the years she'd known the woman, she'd never seen her look anything but fashionable and chic. This morning, Denni sat at the sewing machine wearing a baseball cap bearing the logo of a local seed company, the silk blouse she had on yesterday, and a pair of yoga pants partially stuffed into cowboy boots. The ring of smudged mascara around her eyes complemented the demented look of her boss.

"Denni? Everything okay?" Amy asked, cautiously approaching the machine where Denni was madly clipping threads.

"Never better," Denni said, turning to grin at Amy. "I needed to finish this before I head to Redmond this morning. What time is it?"

"Almost nine," Amy said, still not quite sure what to make of Denni.

"Great balls of fire! I've got to hurry," Denni said, jumping up and grabbing the quilt she'd been working on along with her purse. "Thanks for taking care of the store today. Have a good weekend."

"I will," Amy called as Denni ran out of the store and to her car. Watching Denni speed down the street, Amy hoped she didn't get pulled over. Dressed like she was, there was no telling what the police would do.

Denni raced home, jumped in the shower then dressed in a shirt Cady helped her pick out on one of their shopping trips to Portland. A pale shade of blue with tiny pink and white flowers, it was a perfect fit to her curves and looked great with the jeans she planned to wear. Pulling on her boots, she put hot rollers in her hair, did her makeup and realized she hadn't checked her phone or email messages.

Hurrying to the computer she turned it on, checked her phone messages and was glad to find she hadn't missed any, then opened her email account. A message from Hart caught her attention and she clicked on it.

In the time since she walked away from him, he'd never once called, sent her a message or made any effort to contact her. She appreciated him not making the situation more difficult by trying to change her mind. It was odd that he'd send her an email today, of all days. She wondered if he somehow sensed she was back to herself instead of a certifiable nut case.

Reading the message, Denni wasn't sure what to make of it:

"I know this is a little dated, but no matter what happens, I want you to know..."

Denni clicked on the link beneath his words and found herself watching a video of Clay Walker's song, *"If You Ever Feel Like Loving Me Again."*

Unable to stop from smiling at the words, Denni thought the song was perfect. If Hart truly meant it, maybe she wouldn't have to grovel and beg for him to take her back today. Maybe, just maybe, he'd accept her with open arms.

Grabbing her phone, she called Ester and told her about the video. "Are you gonna ride shotgun with me, old girl?" Denni asked.

"You bet. I'll be ready when you get here. I want to see how this all plays out. This is way better than the soaps I usually watch," Ester said, laughing.

Denni ran to the bathroom and finished her hair, spritzed on some perfume, and took one more glance in the mirror, hoping Hart would like her cowgirl look.

Taking a minute to stuff the quilt she'd frantically finished into a large gift bag, she sent a quick text to Tess, telling her to save two seats for her and Nana and headed to pick up Ester.

Two hours later, they were pulling into the fairgrounds in Redmond where the event would take place. Denni and Ester listened to several ads on the radio for the event during their drive. One of the radio personalities talked about Hart coming out of retirement and speculated that someone out of the circuit that long wouldn't be able to stay on for an eight-second ride.

Denni didn't care how long he stayed on the bull, she just prayed he wouldn't get hurt. Or Travis either.

Hustling Ester as fast as she could into the stands, Denni soon found the Thompson and Morgan clan taking up a block of space close to the chutes.

Settling Ester on a padded seat Cady brought along, Denni apologized to all of them for behaving so reprehensibly and asked their forgiveness. They gave it freely, teasing her about some of the things she'd said and done. While she held baby Emily, relishing the feel of her tiny granddaughter in her arms, the family dared her to go find Hart and let him know she was there for him.

"I'll walk you back to where the riders are waiting, Mom," Trey said, leaning over her shoulder from his seat behind her. He wanted to help his Mom make things right with Hart and was willing to do anything he could to make it happen.

"I think I should wait until after his ride. I don't want to distract him," Denni said, feeling some of her new-found courage slide away.

"At least send him a text," Tess said, bumping Denni with her elbow from her spot beside her. "Just make it short and sweet. You don't have to go into details that way, but at least he'll know you're thinking of him."

"Good idea," Denni said, handing the baby to Trent before fishing her phone out of her purse.

She typed and deleted a dozen messages before Tess rolled her eyes and sighed. "Denni, you're making this way too complicated." Tess snatched her phone and quickly typed a message then handed it back to Denni. It was certainly short and to the point. Before she could talk herself out of it, Denni hit send.

"Way to go, Mom," Trey said, squeezing her shoulder. "Maybe there's hope for you yet."

><><

Hart stood with twenty-four other bull riders thinking he had completely lost his mind. The fact he was old enough to be a father to almost all of them was not lost on him. Being the old man of the group was definitely not helping his outlook.

When word got out he was going to ride today, it was like the floodgates of press inquiries opened and he'd been inundated with questions from local papers to big sports networks. He mostly got by with a short line about doing it for a good cause, but still the questions poured in asking where he'd been for the last twenty-odd years, if he was planning to resurrect his bull riding career, how he thought he'd compete with men half his age.

A few of his friends from his rodeo days had somehow tracked him down online and sent him messages alternating between calling him crazy and wishing him luck. A few of them had threatened to come watch him today. He hoped they were only joking.

Travis did help him get in some practice, taking him to a ranch not far from Grass Valley where the owners raised rodeo stock to supplement their farm income. For the past three days, he'd done nothing but ride bulls and ice his sore muscles. He'd taken a few impressive spills, but he'd also made several good rides. Travis seemed to think Hart could hold his own.

"How're you holding up, old man?" Travis asked, slapping Hart on the back as they hung out behind the chutes, listening to the announcer as the first of the guys prepared to ride. The camera crew that was determined to interview Hart accepted his short statement and asked to speak with him later. Reluctantly, he agreed. Now he was waiting for his turn to get on a bull and give it his best.

"Fine, Trav. Just fine. And if you don't want me to show you up, right here and now, you better knock off that old man business, you smart aleck punk," Hart said, with a teasing grin.

"You two at it again?" Brice asked as he walked up beside them. Although he had never been as intent on bull riding as Travis, he didn't mind doing it for a charity. Bailey was about to come unglued at the idea of him being on the back of a bull, but agreed to let him do it. "If a person didn't know better, they'd think you two were related, the way you go at each other."

Hart smiled at Brice and tried not to think about how close he came to being Travis' stepfather. Deciding he needed a distraction, Hart pulled out his cell phone, ready to call Evan to remind him to restock the candy displays at the gas station. Before he could make the call, he noticed a new text message. He thought his eyes must be deceiving him because he was sure it said it was from Denni. Reading it, he broke into a huge grin.

"What's that look for?" Travis asked, seeing Hart wear the first genuine smile on his face since Denni dumped him.

"Your mother just sent me a message," Hart said, handing Travis his phone. Brice leaned over his shoulder to read the text:

I'm so sorry. Good luck. Love you!

"No way," Travis said, handing the phone back to Hart as Brice popped him on the shoulder. "Mama finally came to her senses. That is awesome."

"I need to go talk to her," Hart said, starting to walk toward the stands, only to have Travis tug on his arm.

"Not now, you don't," Travis said, pointing toward the chutes. "You're number eight and number three just went out. You need to get set for your ride."

"But I... man, how did I let you talk me into this?" Hart asked, stuffing his phone in his equipment bag, adjusting the buckles on his chaps, and pulling on his riding glove. "I hope your mother will forgive you if I get killed today."

"I'm her favorite, she'll always forgive me," Travis said as he and Brice climbed up on the chute with Hart and watched him ease down on the back of the bull.

"See what love will do to you? It can take a sensible, responsible man and turn him into a fool faster than you can blink. It's a good thing you boys are already married," Hart said, tightening the rope around his hand and settling himself deeper onto the back of the bull. "I'm way too old to be doing this. If I manage to ride out there and not make a complete idiot of myself, we'll call it a good day. Then remind me to never, ever do this again."

Travis laughed and slapped Hart on the back. "You'll do great. For an old geezer, you're in pretty good shape. Be safe, Hart. You can do this."

Knowing Hart needed time to find his mental center, Travis moved back, although he stayed on the fence with Brice, where Hart could talk to them if he wanted to.

Although he hadn't ridden in front of a crowd for twenty-six years, the thrill of it rushed back over Hart as he sat on the bull. Despite the fact that he had no business being there, he was excited to ride again.

Just like he used to do so many years ago, he mentally blocked out the noise of the crowd, the riders teasing each other, the sounds of the bulls snorting and banging around in the chutes. He ignored the smells of popcorn and hotdogs, manure, and sweaty animals. He cleared his mind of everything except the bull beneath him, the rope in his hand, and the sound of his heart beating.

Slow and steady.

Taking in a deep breath then letting it out, he tugged on the rope one more time, pulled his hat down low on his head and closed his eyes.

Opening them when he felt a hand touch his arm, he saw Travis nod at him and knew it was his turn to go. Tightening his fingers around the rope in his hand, sticky with rosin, Hart drew one more deep breath then he smiled at Travis. "Let's do this."

The gate swung open and the bull lunged into the arena. Fortunately, riding a bull seemed to be a lot like riding a bike for Hart. The skills he once had fine-tuned to an art rushed back to him.

Feeling the pounding of the bull beneath him, the bunching and twisting of a ton of muscle and bone and wild beast, Hart grinned as he gave the crowd a good performance during his eight-second ride.

As the cheers of the crowd filled the arena after the buzzer sounded, he looked in the stands where he knew the Thompson clan was sitting and saw not only Denni cheering, but Ester as well.

Going off the side of the bull, Hart scrambled to stay out of the way of the animal's horns and raced over to the fence. Climbing on top, he waved his hat to the crowd, then jumped down and ran around to the gate to the stands so he could find Denni. He'd only gone a few feet when he looked up to see her hurrying toward him.

They met in a fiery embrace with such an intense kiss, it made the cowboys around them whistle and a few mothers cover their children's eyes.

"Hart, I've been a fool, a dork, completely stupid. I'm so, so sorry. Can you ever forgive me?" Denni asked as he held her close and breathed in her delectable scent.

"Forgiven, forgotten," Hart said, bending his head to hers again, drinking of the lips he'd missed more than he'd ever imagined possible.

"Did you mean it, that video you sent this morning?" Denni asked as she hugged Hart again. She couldn't get close enough to him, couldn't touch him enough.

"Every word of it," Hart said, stepping back so he could look in her face, fall into the warmth of her eyes. "My door's wide open, baby, walk right in."

"I might just do that," Denni said with a sassy grin, as Hart put his arm around her and walked with her back to the stands.

Giving Ester a kiss on her cheek and hugging a very excited Cass, Hart sat down and watched a few of the riders before excusing himself to check on Brice and Travis before their rides. Trey went along, leaving Trent to cheer with the women. Holding baby Emily, he didn't seem to mind missing out on the action behind the chute.

Tess and Bailey sat nervously waiting for their husbands to ride, praying they'd walk out of the arena in one piece.

"Brice is next," Tess said, squeezing both Bailey's and Denni's hands. Her mother, who sat next to Cady, held onto her husband's arm, not sure she could watch.

"Mom, Brice will be fine," Ben said, trying to sound unconcerned about his brother riding.

Brice was, in fact, fine and gave a good ride although his score tied with Hart's and neither of them had the top score.

The women breathed a sigh of relief and then the tension washed over them again when Travis came out of the chutes. He rode the full eight seconds in a bone-jarring, blood-pounding ride, but as he was dismounting, the bull turned and hooked Travis with his horn, knocking him flat on his stomach in the arena dirt. Brice and Trey were beside him before he could even lift his head. He got to his knees, then his feet and waved his hat as he walked out of the arena.

Tess, who had turned white as soon as the bull flattened Travis, ran down the bleacher steps and to the chutes. Travis met her at the gate and Denni watched as they kissed, then Tess smacked Travis on the arm. She could imagine the feisty girl calling him an idiot and telling him this was the last time he was going to ride a bull. Tess lifted Travis' shirt to make sure he had nothing more than a nasty looking scratch from the bull's horn, much to everyone's relief.

The men soon returned, along with Tess, to the seats. Anxious to speak with Denni, Hart asked if she'd go with him to his truck to put away his gear. She smiled and nodded, taking his hand as he went down the steps and out of the stands.

Walking beside Hart, Denni was struck once again at what a fine man he was, not to mention fine-looking.

She'd never seen him in full cowboy gear before and the effect it was having on her system was making her feel rubbery-kneed and light headed. A dusty Stetson covered his sandy-hair while a royal blue shirt made his eyes even bluer. He wore a pair of perfect-fitting Wranglers with red and silver chaps left over from his rodeo days, boots and spurs. As devastatingly handsome as she found him now, she couldn't help but think he must have been a true heartbreaker when he rode bulls for a living in his younger days.

Lost in her thoughts of how much she loved him, how much she wanted him, Denni didn't realize she'd stopped walking until Hart kissed her cheek.

"Why are you looking at me like that?" Hart asked, grinning broadly. He hoped Denni had missed him even half as much as he missed her.

"You just look so...hot," Denni said, feeling her cheeks heat with a blush.

"Hot, huh? What happened to hunky? I have it from a reliable source you and Ester call me Hunky Hart," Hart teased, dropping his arm around her shoulder, as they walked out to the parking lot.

"Oh, well...I..." Denni said flustered, wondering which one of her boys she'd need to lecture for tattling on her and Ester. Her mother was the one who started calling him hunky, even if Denni agreed it was an apt description. Noticing they were close to her car, she headed that direction. "I've got something in my car for you."

"Okay," Hart said, following Denni. She opened the back door and took out a large gift bag, handing it to him. He set his equipment bag on the ground and took the bag from her, carefully pulling out the wall hanging.

"What's this, sunshine?" Hart asked, unfolding a small quilt done in red and white featuring hearts that appeared to be mended with fancy stitches.

"It's a new design I came up with called mended hearts because that's what you did for me. You took what was broken and put it back together again, maybe even better than new. It isn't perfect, but it is something lovely and interesting and stronger than it ever could have been before. I love you with all I have in me to give, Hart."

"This is perfect, Denni," Hart said, folding her in a tight hug, not caring who saw them. "I love you, too."

Folding the quilt, Hart stuffed it back in the bag, grabbed the duffle he dropped on the ground and took Denni's hand, hurrying her to his truck.

She was a little hurt that was all he had to say, but realized he might be cautious around her after what she'd done to him just a few short weeks ago.

Unlocking his truck, Hart set the bags inside then took something from his jockey box, holding it out to Denni.

Tears pricked the back of her eyes when she realized it was a jewelry box, the exact same one he'd handed to her the day they went to Portland.

"I can't believe you brought this with you," Denni said, opening the box and holding it while Hart took out the ring and slid it on her finger.

"I've been carrying it around with me since you left it on my table," Hart said, kissing the ring and Denni's finger. "I appreciate that little quilt, more than you can know. You didn't just mend the pieces of my shattered heart back together, I feel like you gave me a new one, a much better one. I love you with a depth and intensity I never imagined existing in this heart of mine and if you don't agree to marry me as soon as humanly possible, I think I might just die. You are one tempting grammy, Denni. Please, please put me out of my misery."

"Then by all means, let's not waste any more time," Denni said, guiding Hart's head down to hers. "According to Cady and Trey, you can pull together a wedding in a week. Want to see if they're right? We could always catch a flight to Vegas."

Hart laughed as he swung her around, feeling like his heart had finally found a place to call home.

Chapter Twenty-Two

"Be careful what you set your heart upon –
for it will surely be yours."
James A. Baldwin

"Are you done kissing Grammy?" Cass asked, tugging on the hem of Hart's jacket as he kissed his bride of just a few minutes.

Raising his head from Denni's lips, Hart grinned down at the impish child. "Hate to tell you this, Cass, but I'm just getting started."

"Eww," Cass said with a giggle, pulled away from the couple as Trey picked her up and offered an apologetic look to Hart and his mother.

"Someday, miss nosy, you won't think kissing is so awful," Trey said, tickling Cass' sides as he set her down by Ester's chair while the rest of the family stood around, grinning and laughing.

When Denni agreed to marry Hart he offered to take her anywhere in the world she wanted to exchange vows. She chose to be wed the following Friday on the back deck of his house, overlooking the green pastures with a magnificent view of the surrounding hills.

Wanting a simple ceremony, they invited her boys and their spouses, all the Morgan family, and Cady's Aunt Viv and Uncle Joe, along with Ester.

Gathering on the deck just as the sun began its descent, the sky made a breathtaking backdrop of gold, pink and red for the happy couple.

Michele and Mike Morgan, Denni's oldest and closest friends, served as attendants while everyone watched the two united in marriage by their broadly grinning pastor.

Choosing to keep things casual, Denni wore a dress the same shade of blue as her eyes while Hart wore jeans and a white shirt with a dark gray sport coat. The rest of the men wore jeans with matching blue shirts while the girls wore dresses in bright spring colors, including Cass and baby Emily. Even Ester wore a dress in a vibrant shade of pink.

Denni failed to notice the roses she held or those sitting in baskets around the deck filling the evening air with a sweet, spicy fragrance. Hart didn't hear the sound of crickets chirping or the cows in the pasture adding a gentle lowing to the evening serenade. They were far too lost in each other.

Although brief, the ceremony was filled with such heartfelt sentiment, Cady and Tess sniffled while Viv and Michele both dabbed at their teary eyes. The pastor, who was as happy as anyone to see Denni fall in love again, enthusiastically declared them husband and wife. Hart was more than willing to comply when the pastor said he could kiss the bride, until they were interrupted by Cass' question.

Insisting none of them be put to any extra work or effort for the event, Hart hired a caterer to prepare dinner, serving it on the lawn below the deck.

As the family sat visiting and laughing, Denni didn't know when her heart had felt so full. Leaning over, she kissed Hart's cheek, giving him a smile filled with love and secret promises.

"I love you, Hart Hammond," she said, squeezing his hand in hers.

"I love you, Mrs. Hammond," Hart said, inordinately pleased that she would now be known as his. His wife. His friend. His partner. His love.

"I like the sound of that," Denni said, leaning her head against his shoulder as they watched her family laugh and tease one another. "I like a few other things, too."

"Such as?" Hart asked, settling his arm around her shoulders and pulling her closer to him as they sat side by side.

"The way your eyes spark with humor, the way your smile puts everyone at ease, the way your laugh sinks into my soul, the way that cleft in your chin drives me to distraction. It was one of the first things I noticed about you."

"It distracts you?" Hart asked, interested in knowing what else distracted Denni. He looked forward to finding out each and every detail as soon as her family cleared out for the evening. They decided to wait to take an extended honeymoon until the fall. For now, they planned to spend the next several days hiding away from the world at his, now their, house.

"It certainly does. Almost as much as that little dimple right above your lip," Denni said, giving Hart a flirtatious smile that made him want to chase everyone away right then.

Instead, he grinned and pulled Denni onto his lap, kissing her neck. "Have I told you how blessed I am to know you, to be loved by you?"

"Not in the last ten minutes," Denni said, offering a sassy grin as she trailed her fingers along his jaw, falling into the warmth of his eyes.

"I had no idea when I set my heart on winning you, that I'd get so much more than I planned," Hart said, waving a hand at Denni's beautiful family. "I always wanted a family of my own and look what you've given me - a wonderful, loving, fun bunch of kids with two amazing grandkids, caring friends, and a place to belong. Thank you, Denni. More than you can ever know, I thank you."

"Thank you for not only loving me, but them, too. I'm glad you took us on as a package deal, including Mama."

"How could anyone not love Ester? It's her indomitable spirit I see in all of you," Hart said, giving Denni a long, loving look.

"Be that as it may, not everyone would offer to have their mother-in-law move in with them," Denni said, pleased beyond anything when Hart suggested Ester live with them.

Ester politely but firmly refused, saying the last thing she needed was to be stuck watching Denni and Hart make calf-eyes at each other over the dinner table. Hart told her the offer stood if she ever changed her mind.

"As much as I love the ol' girl, I wasn't really eager to share you. At least not yet," Denni said, sliding her hand inside the neck of Hart's shirt, absorbing the warmth of his skin. "When you come home at night, I plan to be completely selfish with your attention."

"You do?" Hart asked, grinning at Denni. He wondered what would happen if he kissed her as soundly as he wanted to even if her family was there. At that moment, the last of the sun's rays was creating a golden halo around her head, completing the stunning picture he thought she made in her silky blue dress. Stunning, lovely, and so precious to him. "Any ideas on how you're going to capture my attention?"

"One or two," Denni said, turning Hart's head so she could whisper in his ear. Her words started a fire burning at his toes that quickly flamed its way up to his head. Travis told him whenever the family wore out their welcome for the evening to give him a signal and he'd round up the troops. Catching the eye of his new stepson,

Travis winked then loudly suggested the family pack up and leave.

Trey and Cady gathered up Cass while Tess and Travis helped Ester walk out to Tess' car. She decided to spend the weekend at their house since she hadn't yet stayed there. Tess promised they'd spend a good part of the following day visiting Lindsay and baby Emily, who had fallen asleep shortly after everyone sat down for dinner.

Denni held the baby for a minute while Trent helped Lindsay in his pickup and then took Emily, fastening her in her car seat.

Waving to her family and good friends, Denni leaned into Hart, feeling a deep sense of satisfaction at the thought of having him to lean on and love for the rest of her life.

"Did you have some secret code worked out with Travis?" Denni asked, wondering why it was taking everyone so long to leave. She was ready to be alone with her husband.

"Something like that," Hart said, wrapping his arms around Denni and kissing her neck again as they watched the family climb in their vehicles. "Although I think I should have told him there needed to be some hustle in it. How long does it take them to get loaded and out of here?"

"Way too long if you ask me. If they don't get a move on, they might just see me have my way with you right here on the front lawn," Denni teased, giving one last enthusiastic wave to her departing family before turning and racing toward the house.

"Oh, sunshine, being married to you is going to be my best adventure yet," Hart said, chasing her up the steps and into their home.

###

Here's the recipe for the cake Denni made Hart for Valentine's Day. Delicious and moist, the time and effort required to make it is totally worth it!

Red Velvet Cheesecake

1 box German Chocolate Cake mix
1 cup sour cream
1/2 cup water
1/2 cup vegetable oil
1 (1 ounce) bottle red food color
3 large eggs
1 box white chocolate instant pudding (3.3 ounce)
1 tsp. vanilla extract
1 frozen cheesecake
Cream Cheese Frosting
White chocolate curls (optional)

Preheat oven to 350 degrees and grease two 9-inch round cake pans.

Combine all ingredients (except for cheesecake, frosting and chocolate curls) and mix on low speed for a minute. Scrape down edges of bowl then beat an additional two minutes on medium/high speed. Pour into cake pans and bake about 25 minutes or until cake begins to pull away from sides of the pan or bounces back to your touch.

Let cake cool completely before assembling.

You can use a cheesecake mix, buy a ready-made one, or make your own. I highly recommend making your own (recipe following). You'll want to freeze the cheesecake layer before you try to work with it.

Once the red velvet cake has cooled, take the cheesecake out of the freezer and trim off any excess if it is going to be bigger than your cake layers.

Turn one cake layer top side down on a cake plate or platter. Slather on a layer of frosting (see easy recipe below) then gently place the cheesecake on top. Frost the inside of the other cake layer before putting it on the cheesecake, creating a cake and frosting sandwich around the cheesecake. Frost the entire cake with a thin layer of the frosting. If it is getting "crumby", stick it in the freezer until the frosting is set then give it a nice thick coat of the frosting.

If you want to get all fancy-pants, shave some white chocolate curls on top.

Freeze the cake until about an hour before you are ready to serve.

Cream Cheese Frosting

1 box powdered sugar
8 ounces cream cheese, softened
1/2 cup butter, softened
1 tsp. vanilla

Combine all ingredients in a mixing bowl and beat on medium speed until smooth and creamy. If not using immediately refrigerate or freeze.

Cheesecake

2 (8-ounce) packages of cream cheese, room temperature
2/3 cup sugar
1/4 tsp. salt
2 large eggs
1/2 cup sour cream
1/3 cup whipping cream
1 tsp. vanilla extract

Preheat oven to 325 degrees. Place a pan large enough to hold a springform pan in the oven to warm. Put a kettle of water on the stove to boil. Spray a 9-inch springform pan with non-stick spray and line the bottom with a round of parchment paper. Spray it with the non-stick spray as well.

Wrap a double layer (or a layer of heavy-duty foil) around the outside of the springform pan, making sure it comes up the sides of the pan. You want to make sure no water can sneak in a crack and get into the springform pan.

In a large bowl, beat cream cheese until smooth and creamy. Add sugar and salt, mix on medium speed for about two minutes, scraping down the sides of the bowl as needed. Add the eggs, one at a time, mixing after each addition. Mix in sour cream, whipping cream, and vanilla until mixture is smooth.

Remove the large pan from the oven where it has been warming. Place your springform pan into the pan then pour the cheesecake batter into the springform pan. Carefully pour boiling hot water into the large pan so that it comes about an inch or so up the sides of the springform pan. Place in the oven and bake for about 50-60 minutes.

Remove from the oven when the cheesecake is set and no longer jiggly. Remove the springform pan for the larger pan and let cool on a rack for at least an hour. When it has cooled, serve immediately or freeze.

Author's Note:

This is the last book in the Grass Valley Cowboys series. I'm finding it challenging to say goodbye to these characters, having worked their way into my heart as they have.

I will confess, of all the characters in this series, Travis Thompson spoke the loudest to my heart. There was just something about him that kept me awake at night and haunted many of my waking hours while writing his story, wondering what I could do to help this wounded, yet good man. I'm so glad he finally opened his heart to Tess and accepted the help he needed.

As for the girls of Grass Valley, I know I shouldn't have a favorite, but I so admire Cady. She's strong and resilient, not to mention organized and a great cook. She can sing, sew, and decorate a house like nobody's business. Cady puts people above things and loves unconditionally, without reserve. I so want to be like her when I grow up!

Thank you for coming along on the adventures of the Thompson and Morgan families, for sharing your thoughts, and experiencing their triumphs and tribulations.

At times, the Triple T bunch may seem too good to be true, and maybe they are, but for me that is the point of getting lost in a book. It's a means of escape from reality for an hour or two. These characters aren't without their faults and failings. Through it all, though, they stick together, support each other, and keep in mind at the end of the day it's all about lifting up the people they love.

I am forever grateful to my readers who constantly inspire me to continue in this wonderful journey of writing.

Thank you!

Shanna

Grass Valley Cowboys Series

Meet the Thompson family of the Triple T Ranch in Grass Valley, Oregon!

Three handsome brothers, their rowdy friends, and the women who fall for them are at the heart of this contemporary western romance series.

The Women of Tenacity Series

Welcome to Tenacity!

Tenacious, sassy women tangle with the wild, rugged men who love them in this contemporary romance series.

The short story introduction, *A Prelude*, is followed by three full-length novels set in the fictional town of Tenacity, Oregon.

<u>Savvy Entertaining Series</u>

Discover seasonal ideas for decorating, entertaining, party themes, home décor, recipes and more from Savvy Entertaining's blogger!

The QR Code Killer - Murder. Mayhem. Suspense. Romance.

Zeus is a crazed killer who uses QR Codes to taunt the cop hot on his trail.

Mad Dog Weber, a tough-as-nails member of the Seattle police force, is willing to do whatever it takes to bring Zeus down. Despite her best intentions, Maddie (Mad Dog) falls in love with her dad's hired hand, putting them both in danger.

Erik Moore is running from his past and trying to avoid the future when he finds himself falling in love with his boss' daughter. Unknowingly, he puts himself right in the path of the QR Code Killer as he struggles to keep Maddie safe.

From the waterfront of Seattle to the rolling hills of wheat and vineyards of the Walla Walla Valley, suspense and romance fly around every twist and turn.

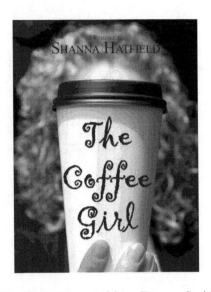

<u>The Coffee Girl</u> - Almost thirty, Brenna Smith isn't sure how much more off-track her life could be. She certainly never pictured herself living at home with her parents, working in a job she dislikes for a loathsome boss. The only bright spot in her mundane existence is the cute guy she runs into every morning as she stops for coffee.

Brock McCrae has worked hard to be able to manage his own construction company. Handsome, successful and full of life, he finds his world turned upside down as he falls for a woman he knows only as The Coffee Girl.

Is there something more than a shared love of coffee brewing between these two?

**Learnin' The Ropes** - Out of work mechanic Ty Lewis is homeless and desperate to find work. Answering a classified ad for a job in Harney County, Oregon, Ty accepts when he is offered the position. Saying goodbye to his sister and his life in Portland, he heads off to the tiny community of Riley to begin a new adventure, unsure about his boss, Lex Ryan, a man he has yet to speak with or meet.

Lexi Ryan, known to her ranch hands and neighbors as Lex Jr., leaves a successful career in Portland to keep the Rockin' R Ranch running smoothly after the untimely death of her father. It doesn't take long to discover her father did a lot of crazy things during the last few months before he died, like hiding half a million dollars that Lexi can't find.

Ty and Lexi are both in for a few surprises as he arrives at the ranch and begins learnin' the ropes.

The Christmas Bargain - As owner and manager of the Hardman bank, Luke Granger is a man of responsibility and integrity in the small 1890s Eastern Oregon town. Calling in a long overdue loan, Luke finds himself reluctantly accepting a bargain in lieu of payment from the shiftless farmer who barters his daughter to settle his debt.

Philamena Booth is both mortified and relieved when her father sends her off with the banker as payment of his debt. Held captive on the farm by her father since the death of her mother more than a decade earlier, Philamena is grateful to leave. If only it had been someone other than the handsome and charismatic Luke Granger riding in to rescue her. Ready to hold up her end of the bargain as Luke's cook and housekeeper, Philamena is prepared for the hard work ahead.

What she isn't prepared for is being forced to marry Luke as part of this crazy Christmas bargain.

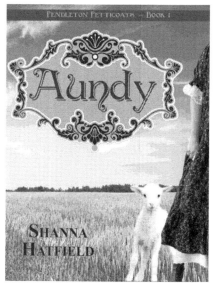

Coming Summer 2013!

Aundy - Desperate to better her situation, Aundy Thorsen agrees to leave behind her life in Chicago to fulfill a farmer's request for a mail-order bride in Pendleton, Oregon. When a tragic accident leaves her a widow soon after becoming a wife, Aundy takes on the challenge of learning how to manage a farm, even if it means her stubborn determination to succeed upsets a few of the neighbors.

Born and raised on the family ranch, Garrett Nash loves life in the bustling community of Pendleton in 1899. When his neighbor passes away and leaves behind a plucky widow, Garrett takes on the role of her protector and guardian. His admiration for her tenacious spirit soon turns to something more. Can he convince the strong-willed Aundy to give love another try?

Turn the page for an exciting excerpt from *Aundy*...

Chapter One

1899 - Eastern Oregon

Clickety-clak. Clickety-clak. Clickety-clak.

The sound of the train kept perfect time with the runaway thumping of Aundy Thorsen's heart. Each beat took her closer to an unknown future and she wondered, again, what madness possessed her to make such a rash decision.

"Miss?" a gentle touch on her arm brought Aundy's head around to look into the friendly face of the porter. "We'll be in Pendleton in about half an hour. Just wanted to let you know."

"Thank you," Aundy said with a smile, nodding her head. The porter had been helpful and kind, answering her many questions and making two rowdy salesmen intent on bothering her relocate to a different car.

Aware that she was asking for trouble traveling alone, Aundy figured since she was taller than most men and far from pretty, she wouldn't have any problems. So far, the persistent salesmen had been the only nuisance in an otherwise uneventful, yet exciting, adventure.

Growing up in Chicago and never traveling any farther than her aunt's stuffy home across town, Aundy was trying to commit to memory each detail of her trip that would soon end in Pendleton, Oregon. Once there, she would marry Erik Erikson, a farmer who wanted a Norwegian bride.

Her betrothed, a man she had yet to meet, offered to travel to Chicago so they could wed there then make the trip back to Pendleton as a married couple. Aundy assured him she would be safe traveling alone, although she was grateful for the train ticket and generous sum of money Erik provided to cover her expenses. So far, Aundy had saved most of it, used to living frugally and making each penny count.

Wishing she'd purchased something at their last stop to eat, Aundy willed her empty stomach to stop fussing.

Suddenly overcome with the thought that she would soon be meeting Erik and become his bride, nerves replaced her hunger.

Although Erik wasn't the first man to whom Aundy had been engaged, he would be the first she married. Not willing to think about the loving gazes and gentle smile of the playful boy who had stolen her heart, she instead focused her thoughts on the man awaiting her.

Six months ago, desperate to make a change in her life, Aundy happened upon a discarded newspaper and her gaze fastened on an advertisement for a mail-order bride.

Normally one to ignore such nonsense, Aundy was drawn to the words written by a farmer named Erik Erikson.

Wanted: loving wife. Seeking woman with a kind heart and gentle spirit. Must be willing to move to Pendleton, Oregon. Hard worker, good cook, and Norwegian ancestry preferred. Farm experience helpful, but not essential. Outward beauty irrelevant. Please reply to…

Ripping the advertisement out of the paper, Aundy carried it around in her pocket with her for two weeks, debating if she should send a reply. Finally, she sat down and composed a letter to Erik Erikson of Pendleton, Oregon, a place she'd never heard of and certainly never dreamed of seeing.

She wrote about her life, how she worked as a seamstress at a factory during the day and helped cook and clean mornings and evenings at a boardinghouse in exchange for her room and board. Explaining she was not beautiful by any sense of the word, Aundy assured him she had a strong constitution, a tender heart, and a willingness to work hard. She described how her parents, both from good Norwegian families, made certain their three children knew their heritage.

Not expecting to receive a reply, Aundy was surprised when a letter arrived from Erik. He invited her to correspond with him so they could get to know one another better before making any decisions or commitments.

Writing back and forth, sharing bits of information about themselves, their families, their hopes and dreams, Aundy came to like the man in the letters, penned with a confident hand.

Erik wrote he wasn't much to look at, had never been married, and owned a farm that was on its way to being prosperous. He shared about how lonely his life seemed and how much he wanted to have a family of his own.

When he wrote saying he was in love with her letters and asked if she'd agree to marry him, she quickly replied with her consent, setting the wheels in motion for changing the course of her future. Bespoken for the second time in her young life, Aundy had no delusions about being in love with Erik. Love had died along with her beloved Gunther two years earlier.

Admiration and respect, though, she had plenty to share with Erik along with her devotion, care, and loyalty.

Bringing her thoughts back to the present, Aundy took a shallow breath in the train car filled with the mingling odors of stale food, unwashed bodies, and smells from the washroom.

Longing to press her warm cheek against the cool glass of the window, she instead turned her head so she could see over the sleeping woman who sat beside her to admire the brilliant blue sky, pine-dotted mountains, and snow-covered ground outside.

As the train chugged through the rugged Blue Mountains of Oregon, Aundy realized she was farther away from her familiar world than she ever thought she would be.

Tamping down her fears of what waited ahead, she pulled a handkerchief out of her reticule, carefully rubbing at her cheeks, hoping to remove the worst of the soot. Convinced grime covered every inch of her being from the long trip, she couldn't wait to soak in a hot tub, wash her hair, and dress in clean clothes.

She sincerely hoped Erik wouldn't mind if she did that before she put on her wedding dress and exchanged nuptials with him. He didn't mention his plans for when they would wed, but Aundy assumed Erik would want to do so as soon as possible. If that was true, she supposed she would most likely be Mrs. Erik Erikson before the end of the day.

That thought made her grip the reticule so tightly in her hands, she felt her fingers cramp through her soft leather gloves.

Feeling a light touch on her arm, Aundy turned her gaze to the woman who sat beside her for much of the trip.

"You'll be fine, dearie," Mrs. Jordan said, her kind brown eyes twinkling. "Nothing to worry about at all."

"Thank you, ma'am," Aundy said, patting the hand resting on her arm and offering the woman a small smile. With mile upon mile of nothing to do but stare out the window and watch the incredible changing scenery, Aundy and Mrs. Jordan discussed their individual reasons for being on the train. The elderly woman was going to Portland to live with her only daughter.

"You're a smart, brave girl," Mrs. Jordan said, sitting up straighter in her seat. "I have no doubt that everything will work out for the best. If it doesn't, you know how to get in touch with me."

"I'm sure all will be well," Aundy said, grateful she did have a slip of paper in her possession with Mrs. Jordan's new address. If she ever needed somewhere to go, at least she had one friend on this side of the Rocky Mountains.

Shaking herself mentally, Aundy adjusted her hat, brushed at her skirt and the sleeves of her jacket then moistened her lips. Although Erik said looks didn't matter to him, she certainly hoped he wouldn't be terribly disappointed when he met her. Perhaps she shouldn't have refused when he asked for her photograph.

Afraid he would break off their commitment once he realized she was no beauty, she figured he would take her as she was or she'd be in an even bigger mess than the one she was leaving behind in Chicago.

If she looked anything like her younger sister, Ilsa, men would be falling all over themselves to do her bidding. Although both blond with blue eyes, that was where the similarities ended.

Gathering her belongings along with her courage, Aundy glanced out the window to see the snow seemed to disappear with only random patches covering the ground as the train made its way out of the mountains. The sky was so blue and wide open, she wondered, briefly, if she could see up to heaven. Would her father and mother be looking down and giving their approval to what she was about to do? She prayed if Gunther could see her, he wasn't chastising her for marrying someone she would never love.

Trapping a sigh behind rolled lips, she brushed at her skirt one last time and sat back to wait as the train rumbled to a stop, willing her heart to slow down as well.

The porter finally announced their arrival and stood outside the car, helping the women disembark.

Giving Mrs. Jordan a quick hug, Aundy slipped on her coat, grabbed the Gladstone bag that had been her mother's, and stepped off the train into the bright sunshine and brisk air.

"Best wishes, Ms. Thorsen," the porter said as he helped her down the steps.

"Thank you, sir," Aundy said, tipping her head at him before turning her attention to the platform where a sea of people churned back and forth. How was she ever going to find Erik?

Cowboys and farmers, businessmen and miners, Indians covered with colorful blankets, Chinese men wearing long braids and strange hats, and women dressed in everything from plain calico to ornately stitched dresses milled together, all blending into a mass of varied colors.

Taking as deep a breath as her corset allowed, Aundy wished, again, she had exchanged photographs with Erik when he asked. His description said he was tall, blond and plain. She'd basically written him the same portrayal of her own appearance.

Looking around, she counted four men who were a good six inches taller than the majority of the crowd. One had dark hair that fell down to his shoulders, one was an extremely handsome cowboy, one wore a nice suit, and the last one appeared to be a farmer in mud-splattered overalls who was not only dirty, but had a mean look about him. She certainly hoped that wasn't her intended.

When the man in the suit removed his hat, his white blond hair glistened in the mid-day sun. Although his boots and the hem of his pants were flecked with mud, he wore a crisp shirt with a vest and tie.

Studying him a moment, Aundy hoped he was Erik. Although the man looked nervous, he had a kind face, even if it was older than she anticipated. Erik never stated his age, never asked hers. While considered an old maid at twenty-one, she would have to guess Erik closer to forty from the lines time and life had etched on his face.

Although not handsome, he had a gentleness about him that held Aundy's interest. If this was, in fact, her betrothed maybe she hadn't lost her mind after all.

Squaring her shoulders and straightening her spine, she marched up to the man as he continued to search the sea of faces around him.

"Mr. Erikson?" Aundy asked, stepping beside him. The surprised look on the man's face when he turned his attention her direction made her smile. "Erik Erikson?"

"Yes, I'm Erik Erikson," he said, studying Aundy cautiously. "May I assist you?"

"I certainly hope so," Aundy said, with a teasing smile. "You did say you needed a bride and asked me to marry you."

"Oh! Ms. Thorsen? Is it really you?" Erik asked, sandwiching Aundy's gloved fingers between his two big hands.

"It is, indeed."

"I had no idea... I didn't think..." Erik stuttered, trying to chase his thoughts back together. "You said you weren't comely and when I saw you get off the train, I thought you were way too lovely to be my bride. You look like one of the Viking queens in the stories my mother used to read me at bedtime - tall, strong, and beautiful."

Erik's comments made her blush. No one had ever called her lovely or compared her to a Viking queen, although her father used to tell her she had the tenacity of her ancestors running through her veins.

Looping her hand around his arm, Erik took her bag and escorted her off the platform over to a wagon hitched to a hulking team of horses.

"Meet Hans and Henry," Erik said, setting her bag in the wagon then giving her a hand as she climbed over the wheel and up to the seat. "If you wait here a moment, I'll retrieve your trunks."

"Thank you," Aundy said, warily eyeing the horses. Growing up in the city in an apartment, she had no experience with animals. She told Erik from the beginning of their correspondence he'd have to teach her about his farm and livestock. Writing about his day-to-day activities, she gleaned information about his horses and Shorthorn cattle, as well as the pigs and chickens he raised.

Wanting to crane her neck and stare at everything she could see, Aundy instead glanced around inconspicuously, taking in a variety of interesting faces and places. Erik wrote the town was growing and was one of the largest cities in Oregon. Hoping she'd have time to explore her new home another day, she smiled to see Erik walking head and shoulders above much of the crowd.

Erik soon returned easily carrying one of her trunks on his broad shoulder while two younger men struggled to carry her other two trunks. Erik set the trunks in the back of the wagon, tossed each man a coin with a nod of his head and climbed up beside Aundy.

"I let the pastor know to expect us as soon as the train arrived," Erik said, turning the horses so they began lumbering down the street.

"The pastor?" Aundy asked, trying to keep from swiveling her head back and forth as Erik drove past stores and business establishments. There were so many interesting buildings and fascinating people.

"Pastor Whitting," Erik said, trying not to stare at Aundy. She was young, tall, and so much prettier than he'd been expecting. Not that her looks mattered, but her smooth skin, dusted by a few freckles across her nose, golden hair, and striking blue eyes made him glad he'd placed an advertisement for a bride.

Although most of his friends thought he had lost use of his mental faculties, Erik was tired of being alone, and didn't have time to find a wife or court a woman properly. He vowed to make it up to Aundy by spending the rest of his life showing her she was special to him. "I thought we could get married, have lunch, and then head out to the farm. By the time we get home, it'll be almost dark."

"Oh," Aundy said, absorbing this information. It looked like her mother's wedding dress would stay firmly packed in the trunk and a bath would have to wait. Resigning herself to exchanging vows with Erik in her current state of disrepair, she smiled at him and put a hand on his arm. "That sounds fine."

"Good," Erik said, grinning at her, making his face appear much younger as he turned the horses down a side street. Aundy could see the church ahead and tried to calm her nerves. The warmth of the sun beating down, despite it being February, forced her to remove her coat. Erik tucked it behind the seat, placing it on top of one of her trunks.

Stopping the horses close to the church steps, Erik walked around the wagon and reached up to Aundy. When she started to put her hand in his, he gently placed his hands to her waist and swung her around, setting her down on the bottom step.

The breath she was holding whooshed out of her and she looked at Erik with wide eyes. She'd never been handled so by a man and wasn't sure if she liked it or not. Part of her thought a repeat of the experience might be in order for her to fully make up her mind.

"Shall we?" Erik asked, offering her his arm as they went up the church steps.

Before she could fully grasp what was happening, she and Erik exchanged vows, he slid a plain gold band on her finger, and the pastor and his wife offered congratulations on their marriage. Walking back out into the bright afternoon sunshine, Aundy had to blink back her disbelief that she was finally a married woman.

"We can eat just around the corner, if you don't mind the walk," Erik said, gesturing toward the sidewalk that would take them back toward the heart of town.

Aundy nodded her head and felt Erik place a hand to the small of her back, urging her forward.

Taking a seat in a well-lit restaurant, they were soon enjoying a filling, savory meal. Several people approached their table, offering words of congratulations. Aundy smiled when a few of the women invited her to stop by for a visit sometime soon. It appeared that Erik was a well-liked member of the community and for that Aundy was grateful. She'd never lived in a rural town before, but assumed getting along with your neighbors spoke well of a man's character.

Watching Erik finish his piece of pie, Aundy hoped this marriage would be a blessing to them both. She didn't know what had prompted her to act so boldly, writing to a stranger, but right at this moment she was glad she sent Erik that first letter.

"Well, Mrs. Erickson, are you ready to go home?" Erik asked as she took her last bite of cherry pie and wiped her lips on a linen napkin.

"I suppose so," Aundy said, realizing she was no longer Aundy Thorsen, but Erik's wife.

Leaving money for their lunch along with a tip on the table, Erik stood and put on his hat, offered Aundy his arm, and escorted her back to the wagon.

Expecting him to help her into the wagon, Aundy was surprised when Erik pulled her into his arms, right there in front of the church for any and all to see as they passed by.

"Thank you for coming, Aundy. For marrying me," Erik said, kissing her quickly on the lips. He seemed unable to stop himself from giving her a warm hug. "I promise to be a good husband to you."

Looking into his eyes and seeing the questions there, Aundy tamped down her unease at having a man who was still a stranger kiss her. She placed a hand to his cheek and patted it with a growing fondness. "I know you will be. And I'll do my very best to be a good wife to you."

"You could start by giving me a kiss," Erik teased, waggling a blond eyebrow at her.

Aundy smiled and kissed his cheek, grateful that Erik seemed to have a fun, playful side. "You'll have the town gossiping about me and I haven't even been here two hours."

"Everyone knows I came into Pendleton to marry you today and I can't see a thing wrong with a husband kissing his lovely new bride."

Blushing, Aundy accepted Erik's help into the wagon and sat down, pleased at his words.

Heading out of town, Aundy relaxed as the noise and activity of Pendleton fell behind them and the rolling fields opened up before them. Releasing a sigh, she gazed up at the sky and breathed in the fresh air.

"Anything you want to know? Any questions?" Erik asked, watching Aundy as she seemed to settle into the seat.

"I don't think you ever told me how old you are," Aundy said, studying Erik's profile.

"I'll be thirty-nine next month," he said, turning to look at Aundy.

"And you've never been married?"

"Never. I got so busy building the farm after my parents died, I kept putting off finding someone to court. I woke up one day and realized if I wanted to have a wife and a family, I better do something about it. So I placed the ad and you know the rest of the story."

"I guess I do," Aundy said, looking with interest at the fluffy clouds drifting across the azure sky overhead and the fields that surrounded both sides of the road. If the land had been flat, she was sure she could have seen for miles. Instead, the gently rolling hills provided their own unique perspective to the landscape. Unfamiliar with open ground and such clean air, Aundy breathed as deeply as she dared and soaked up the sunshine.

"And you're how old?" Erik asked, breaking into her thoughts.

"Twenty-one, although people often mistake me for someone older," Aundy said, then let out a soft laugh at a memory. "Someone once asked if Ilsa, my sister, was my daughter. I didn't know whether to be insulted or pleased."

Erik chuckled. "Pleased, I would think. It must be the way you carry yourself, with such confidence and strength. That's a good thing."

"It is?" Aundy asked, thinking she liked the sound of Erik's laugh. Although she'd only just met the man, it wasn't hard for her to imagine spending her lifetime with him. From what she'd seen and experienced since they met, he was gentle and mannerly. He might not be handsome or young, he might not make her heart pound or butterflies take flight in her stomach, but she thought he would treat her with respect and care. If they were fortunate, they might even come to love one another someday.

"Certainly, it is. I wouldn't want some flighty young thing, so wrapped up in herself that she wouldn't take proper care of a home or her husband. It's easy to see that you'll be a good wife, Aundy. You're a sensible girl and I appreciate that," Erik said, turning to look at his new bride with a teasing smile. "I also appreciate your fine figure, beautiful eyes, and that sweet smile."

As her cheeks turned pink and grew hot at Erik's words, Aundy turned her face to gaze across the fields, dotted with a few skiffs of snow.

She heard Erik chuckle before she felt his fingers on her chin. He gently, but firmly, turned her so she was facing him.

"I didn't mean to embarrass you, but I wanted you to know I think this marriage is going to work out just fine," Erik said, leaning over and pressing another quick kiss to her lips.

Aundy closed her eyes and waited to feel something, anything. Instead, Erik pulled back and she opened her eyes to see him studying the road ahead.

"Do you think... if it isn't... what I..." Aundy stuttered, trying to figure out a way to ask if she could take a bath when they reached his farm.

"What is it? Go ahead, Aundy. Don't be afraid to ask me anything."

"May I please have a bath? I feel like I'm wearing dust from way back in Wyoming and half a train car of soot."

"Yes, you may," Erik said, turning his gaze back to Aundy with an indulgent smile. "You can do that while I take care of the evening chores. How does that sound?"

"Wonderful," Aundy said, excited at the prospect of being clean. "As soon as I'm finished, I can fix supper."

"No need. One of the neighbors said she'd have a basket waiting on the table for a cold supper so you wouldn't have to cook on your wedding day."

"How thoughtful," Aundy said, thinking Erik must have some good neighbors. "I'll have to thank her later for her kindness."

"It's Mrs. Nash. She and her husband and son live on the farm to the east of us. They're good folk. Ol' Marvin Tooley lives on the farm to south but he's cantankerous on a good day, so stay away from him if you can."

Aundy nodded her head, wondering what made Mr. Tooley crotchety.

Passing a lane that turned off the road, Erik inclined his head that direction as the horses continued onward. "That's the Nash place. Been here for many years. Raise mostly cattle and wheat. Good folks and good friends as well as our closest neighbors."

Aundy again nodded her head and gazed up the lane, catching a view of the top of the barn over a rise in the road. Pole fences ran along a pasture down to the road and she could see dozens of cattle grazing lazily in the sun.

"Are those..." Aundy's question was cut off when a sharp crack resonated around them and the horses spooked, lunging forward as they began flying down the muddy road.

"Whoa, boys! Whoa!" Erik called, pulling back on the reins, frantic to get the team under control.

Aundy clung to the edge of the wagon and back of the seat, praying for the runaway horses to stop.

"Get down, Aundy," Erik yelled, motioning for her to climb beneath the wagon's seat. She followed his orders, wedging herself into the cramped space, as she listened to the thundering of the horse's hooves and Erik's shouts for them to stop.

The wagon veered sideways then slid back before hitting the side of the ditch bank and flipping over, sliding in the mud.

Aundy's screams mingled with Erik's shouts before everything went black...

ABOUT THE AUTHOR

SHANNA HATFIELD spent 10 years as a newspaper journalist before moving into the field of marketing and public relations. She has a lifelong love of writing, reading and creativity. She and her husband, lovingly referred to as Captain Cavedweller, reside in the Pacific Northwest with their neurotic cat along with a menagerie of wandering wildlife and neighborhood pets.

Shanna loves to hear from readers.
Connect with her online:

Blog: shannahatfield.com

Facebook: Shanna Hatfield's Page

Pinterest: Shanna Hatfield

Email: shanna@shannahatfield.com

20515111R00188

Made in the USA
San Bernardino, CA
13 April 2015